The Flight Of The Osprey

Krissy Lanier

Author's Note

Dear Readers,

Firstly, thank you…for everything. Many of you have been here since my first post where I announced that I was writing a book, where I admitted that even though I didn't know what I was doing, I was going to get it published. And here we are…my third novel is in your hands! Your unwavering support has helped me keep going on those days when I wasn't sure there was a point, when I felt like I wasn't reaching enough people.

Because that's what I crave as a writer—for my words to reach those who need it and for my stories to make readers feel something. That is how my writing started for me as a child. I would write to process my emotions, to say things that I couldn't comprehend enough to speak out loud but was somehow able to paint vividly with a pen.

And that brings me to this story. If you have read and loved my other books, I'm positive you will adore this one even more, but you will also find that my writing has changed. While writing this manuscript, I gave myself permission to go back to my roots as a writer. I didn't hold back. I didn't try to recreate. I dug deep and put it all on the page—ink on the paper mixed with scribbles and tear stains. This story is special to me for many reasons and I hope you can feel that as you read. I ask that you read every word…look for the little bits of heart that are hidden in the lines. Please take your time and savor this one; the experience will be worth it. And when you're done—when you close the book at the end—please take time to process the characters and their journey.

Now, cozy up and get ready to meet Nina and Brett. They're waiting for you.

With love,

Krissy Lanier

For those with recklessly nostalgic hearts who once sat around watching TRL.

Chapter 1

Nina 2016

"They mate for life. Isn't that beautiful?"

Nina glanced at her mother; a pensive expression spread across her tired face. "Those birds?" she questioned, not believing Jane's words. Black specks clouded her vision as she squinted into the sunlight. Attempting to block the sun with the palm of her hand, she gazed up at the large empty nest resting on top of the street pole.

"Mhmm." Jane's response was flippant, nonchalant.

Mate for life?

The concept seemed entirely too unbelievable to Nina, who couldn't figure out how to mate for even two weeks…let alone for life. With a sigh, she picked up her pace to keep up with her mother.

They turned right at the end of the busy road and continued—at a good clip—down the street, parallel to the ocean. Vineyard Sound laid out in front of them to their left, and the sun glistened over the dark green water.

Nina huffed, unsure about her emotions bubbling under the surface. How the smell of salt and seaweed, warm sand, and fried clams lingered in the air—a combination so familiar, it activated memories too vividly.

The pictures in her mind from the past danced erratically—flashing in and out and back again.

Nina shook her head, desperate to release the wave of regret building inside her. How could a beautiful childhood feel equally painful to recall?

They continued to walk swiftly down the street, and her mother's deep, rhythmic breaths lulled Nina into an easy flow, and she allowed her thoughts to wander.

Nina Jackson had arrived back on Cape Cod—in her hometown—only a few days ago. But her despair and self-loathing had hindered her from venturing too far from her childhood home since she had returned…until today.

She felt like a failure.

The dreams she had weaved for herself, dreams of being a business owner in New York City and living an independent life in the East Village, had crumbled so quickly, it seemed—within only three years. And with her tail between her legs, she came running back to her parents.

To her childhood home.

To the life she had once left in a cloud of dust behind her old Honda Civic.

Leaving dependence in the rearview mirror with freedom sprawled out on the horizon, she headed to college all those years ago, a weariness spreading through her bones. Twelve years ago, to be exact. She hadn't been excited back then, not like all the other kids in her class. It had been just the opposite, in fact.

Has it really been that long? Nina shook her head at the realization that so much of her young adult life had disappeared without warning. And what did she have to show for it? She wasn't sure, and coming to terms with that was proving to be quite difficult.

"Felicia is looking forward to meeting with you tomorrow." Her mother's voice abruptly brought Nina back to the stretch of road they were on. Jane stopped and stretched her hamstring, looking out at the water.

"Yeah! Me too," Nina replied, trying to sound enthusiastic, but she was aware that her voice sounded dead, falling flat at the end.

Felicia ran the yoga studio at the rec center in town, where Nina was hoping to teach some classes if they had any openings. It wasn't her own studio, that was for sure. It wasn't her own sweet space that she had built from scratch with her own hands and exorbitant loans that proved impossible to pay back. It wasn't *N Bar*. And it certainly wasn't New York City. But it was potentially some sort of income to hold her over while she figured out what was next. And something to get her out of the house and on with her life.

"Shall we head back, hunny?" Nina's mother asked, smiling at her daughter. "I have to get dinner started before your father gets back. Oh, and I need to let the Warner's dog out. Did I tell you that Brett is coming back? Laura went to pick him up at Logan this morning, and I told her I would let that old dog out a few times. Poor thing can barely see these days." She shook her head in sympathy.

Nina wasn't the least bit interested in the comings and goings of the Warner's dog.

But Brett?

Brett was coming home?

Nina jerked her head toward her mother, and there was a splinter of pain in her chest, a longing that she couldn't quite grapple with. A longing to return to a simpler time when the weight of the world didn't seem to be sitting on her shoulders, pressing her to the ground. Regret for time lost and relationships abandoned.

Looking at her mother, she sighed but tried to cover up the pain on her face and in her tone. "No, you didn't tell me that," she said, her voice shaking a bit.

Brett Warner was once Nina's friend. Her best friend. And now, all that was left was an ache in her chest and an absence where Brett once resided.

Over the years, she had tried not to think about it, though, justifying the lost relationship as the muddied waters of childhood that naturally flow off into the abyss. No sense in harping over something that everyone faces at some point: meaningful people who slip in and out of one another's lives—there for only a flicker of time. But there was more between the lines of their story. A reason much worse than growing pains that drove a wedge between them, a wedge so deep, it was a canyon with no way to cross.

Brett wasn't like other souls that had touched Nina's life and moved on. He wasn't just the boy who sat at her little table in kindergarten and shared his crayons. He wasn't just her neighbor. He wasn't just the boy who sat behind her in AP biology or shared his sandwich with her when she forgot her lunch.

No. Brett wasn't just those things. But Nina wasn't exactly sure what he was to her. And at thirty years old, all she could think to describe him now was estranged at best. The passage of time had made it nearly impossible to pinpoint why they had allowed their bond to crumble to nothingness, causing infinite space—an ocean—to form between them.

Brett was simply gone, and the ache was unbearable. Almost as unbearable as the knowledge she had now…he was coming back.

Chapter 2

Nina 1995

NINA ADJUSTED THE BLUE helmet on her head as she blew the most gigantic bubble she could muster with her bright pink wad of gum. It splattered all over her face, and she used her tongue to pull it all back into her mouth, smacking the wad around her teeth, lacking any manners her poor parents had desperately tried to instill in her. There was no hope that little nine-year-old Nina would turn out ladylike. Not when they chose a neighborhood that was crawling with boys. A whole lot of them. She had to keep up. She had to prove herself. Being a girl wasn't going to hinder her from doing what she wanted in the neighborhood; that was certain.

Nina slammed the wooden hockey stick on the ground. "Let's go!" she yelled, pushing her sweaty hair out of her eyes and away from her filthy forehead. She adjusted her body in front of the little makeshift goal the kids had made and squatted slightly, steadying herself on her rollerblades as the street hockey commenced out at the bottom of the dead end of Carver Road.

The score was tied, and the losing team had to buy the winners ice cream from the truck that came down the street every afternoon at exactly

3:13 p.m. Nina was determined, arguably more than the rest of the neighborhood kids out playing. Their team wasn't going to lose—not on her watch.

Timmy Baker was heading right toward her, swift as anything, faking her out at the end, sliding the little red ball right into the scraggly net behind her. He couldn't stop himself in time and barreled hard into Nina, slamming her to the ground, his shoulder jamming her nose. "Timmy! You asshole!" she yelled, her little voice breaking at the end as she desperately tried to get a grip on her dignity.

"Calm down, Nina," Timmy said, picking himself up off the ground. "Don't be such a sore loser," he smirked. Timmy's team was cheering, gathering around him, hugging each other in a big heap, and celebrating.

Nina rolled her eyes, resting her elbows on her knees as she watched a drop of blood from her nose make contact with her Mighty Ducks T-shirt, the spot widening into the cotton. She made a dramatic noise, her eyebrows wrinkling in anger as some of her teammates came over to her.

"It's ok, Nina," said Ricky Jives. "We'll get 'em next time."

She didn't say anything, not with her words at least, but her face said it all. Being the girl responsible for a loss was something she despised. The team skated away to cruise up and down the street, as if losing was no big thing. Nina didn't understand their complete indifference.

Defeated, she sat there as Brett Warner came and sat next to her, handing her a rag and an ice pack. "I got this from my freezer," he said. "When my brother got punched in the nose once, his whole face blew up like a balloon. Didn't think you would like that very much."

The smile she sent him was weak. "Thanks, B."

Little Nina was comforted by her friend's presence—Brett in his dirty Chicago Bulls T-shirt and baggy, hunter green Bugle Boy shorts, his rumpled sandy brown hair messy from child's play.

"It's just a game." He said the words softly, as if not to ruffle her.

Nina huffed, unable to mask her emotions. "I just like to win," she mumbled, barely opening her mouth when she spoke—too ashamed about the loss or her reaction to it, she wasn't sure which.

The winning team began to sing "*We are the Champions,*" causing Nina to roll her eyes again as she unbuckled her rollerblades.

"I'm going to have zero allowance left after buying their ice cream," Brett said as they got up from the concrete.

"I got enough. You don't have to pitch in," Nina replied. "I did extra chores last night, and my mom gave me a whole five-dollar bill." She wiggled her eyebrows.

"Five dollars?!" Brett was surprised.

Nina giggled. "Yeah, she wanted to give me a dollar, but she only had a five."

"Cool!" Brett said, beaming.

The distant sounds of the ice cream truck cut through the thick summer air as the kids from Carver Road began to gather on the side of the street in front of Nina's house. Brett and Nina headed over in that direction—Nina with her ice pack and rag in one hand, her rollerblades in the other. She tiptoed on the scorched asphalt, her little feet burning with each step until she arrived on the squishy green grass, her soles seeming to thank her as the blades squished in between her toes.

The truck pulled to the side, and the kids swarmed it like mosquitos to a puddle, thrilled for a cool treat. Nina's team dug out the change from their pockets and pulled out warm, wrinkled dollar bills.

Ginny Blake handed out the treats from the truck with a smile that exposed a few missing teeth on the sides of her mouth. Her cheeks were crimson from the humidity, and sweat slicked her hairline but never dripped down any further. The banana clip that held up her strawberry blonde hair seemed to be failing, pieces beginning to frizz on the sides, sliding out from the clip's teeth. She wiped her forehead with the back of her hand. "And you, what do you want?" she asked Gary Stunner. The kids' voices piled over one another, giving Ginny a run for her money.

By the time Ginny was pulling away from the side of the street, the kids of Carver Road were beginning to gather under the shade of the elm tree that hung over the street at the very end of the road. It had only been a few minutes, but already the angst and rivalry between the teams had worn off as they sat catching melted ice cream with eager tongues before it dribbled down their arms. Even Nina had softened. Childish conflicts don't seem to linger among youthful minds.

Minds that still clung to imagination.

Minds that still found joy in the minuscule.

Minds that still believed in things that lurked in the dark.

The worst thing in the world one moment was simply forgotten the next.

"Thanks for the ice," Nina said to Brett, handing the sweating blue block back to him.

"You're welcome," he said, taking it from her hands. "There's blood on your nose."

Nina reached up to her injury, feeling the crusted blood. She scrunched her face. "Gross," she mumbled without much care and shrugged her shoulders. "I'll go wash my face. I have to leave anyway. Mom wanted me back a few minutes ago. We have to go to Bradlee's."

"Ok. Do you want to play cards in the treehouse later?" Brett asked, hopeful.

"Yeah, I'll be over after supper." Nina gathered her rollerblades and scurried toward her front door.

Nina Jackson didn't know then that her time spent with the neighborhood kids on Carver Road were moments that were shaping her to become someone with grit. She couldn't know that, though. Not then. Not yet.

The way the street felt under her bare feet. How the air smelt of brine. The way the gulls' songs became a comforting lullaby for afternoon naps on a torn hammock. The way her heart thundered in her chest when she stood up for herself to the boys. How the freedom of a safe street allowed for her childhood to weave and mold her into a person capable of hard things. And hard things were coming. She couldn't know at nine years old that her soul was stretching—learning who it was to become, and Carver Road was just the beginning of her story.

A story where Brett Warner had always been the main character, since they were five years old. Brett, who held her hand in the haunted house that was scary beyond belief. Brett, who distracted the kids in Johnny Cooper's basement when Nina started crying at the end of *Homeward Bound* (and hugged her later, telling her he thought it was kind of sad, too). Brett, who never made Nina feel like "just a girl."

And it wasn't just Brett who was there for her; she was there for him, too. When the shadows lurked and swarmed behind the doors of Brett's house, Nina was his safety. Nina—fierce and ferocious, loving and loyal. Brett was lucky to have her.

And she was lucky to have him. She had always known that…without a shadow of a doubt. And isn't it true that, sometimes, the things that mean the most to us can be the very entities that tear us apart?

Chapter 3
Nina 2016

Nina and her mother turned off the busy street that led away from the ocean and made their way back to the house from the top of Carver Road. Nina looked up at the trees to see a huge bird sitting in one of the gigantic nests. "Oh, look, Mom."

Jane glanced up. "Yes! That's one of them. The osprey!" Nina stopped for a moment to look at it, perched above them, looking cautiously around the treetops and beyond. "They leave for the whole winter," Jane started. "And when they leave, they separate. The males go to one place, and the females go somewhere else."

Nina crinkled her brows, curiosity piqued. "They don't stay together?" she asked. "But I thought they mated for life."

"That's what makes them so special, hunny," her mother said through a smile. "They always make their way back to their nests here in the spring. The same nests every year. Right back to their mates."

The details only puzzled Nina more as she struggled to fathom the intricacies of certain animals like these birds. Animals with instincts that could lead them across lands and seas but then bring them back time and time again to the same place…without a GPS? Never failing their beloved?

Nina shook her head in wonderment, marveling at the simplicity of the life of these birds resting above the trees. Raise and protect their young, fly with the wind beneath their wings, live with unabashed loyalty to their mates. There was no working hard to climb the ladder only to fall back down. No building up relationships only to have them be destroyed by things beyond your control. Not having to worry about trying and failing at everything seemed like a luxury she longed for—but one she had been denied. She longed to just live up to the expectations with ease.

Nina and Jane continued down the street toward their house at the end of the road. They had moved into the house in 1987 when Nina was a year old, and Jane and Paul had no plans to ever leave it…it was their nest so to speak.

Jane grew up right here on the Cape in a town called Brewster, and she had always been popular and outgoing. Jane and Paul met in college at the University of New Hampshire. Paul, like Jane, was an outgoing guy—easy on the eyes and a sense of humor that tickled Jane. She loved to laugh, and the good-natured way in which he faced life was certainly what attracted Jane to him most. Jane's shiny dark hair and bright white smile had captured Paul in a sort of enchanted aura, and he wasn't even a little mad about any of it.

Paul studied business, with a focus on sales and advertising, and Jane studied business administration. They had a few classes together, where Paul would bring her steaming coffees, just the way she liked, and Jane would slip love notes into the pages of his composition notebooks. Paul was originally from Minnesota but had moved to Maine to live with his grandparents when he was a teenager. It wasn't a problem at all for Paul Jackson to follow Jane home and settle down. He would have gone to Mars with her if she had asked.

And so, Cape bound they were after college, building their lives one twig at a time. A life built around small gestures, little pleasures, and infinite love, a love that only grew as they got older and their family expanded by one. It was a shining example for their daughter.

As Nina and her mother turned into the shell driveway, they faced the family home and Nina smiled. A classic Cape Cod structure with cedar shingles and dormer windows on the second floor, it was weathered and gray from all the years of exposure to the salt air. Stark white flower boxes built by Paul were filled with purple and yellow flowers. Hydrangea bushes lined the front of the house, and an American flag hung next to the front door, billowing in the soft late spring breeze. Nina had always loved her childhood home.

"Here's the key," Jane said, handing it over to Nina. "Head on in while I let the Warner's dog out."

Nina took the key from her mother and watched her walk across the street to the Warner's house. Tenting her eyes from the sun, she scanned the familiar house, and a chill traveled the length of her body—a sensation of nostalgia that caused a deep ache in Nina's bones. The Warner house looked well maintained, like the rest of the homes on the street, but not much seemed to have been changed or updated since they were kids. Nina could see a portion of the old treehouse in the back by the woods that blanketed the end of the street. A smile tugged on Nina's lips, causing her mouth to curve slightly, but with the gesture, a tremble took hold, her lips quivering.

Her childhood was idyllic, yes, a wholesome vision. But the darkness of her adolescence—the secrets—tainted the beauty of it. What they did all those years ago—what *she* did—had eaten away at her, causing a hole inside. A void that never seemed to fill, no matter what she did to pretend it wasn't there.

Nina sucked in a breath and let it out slowly, unsteadily. She had finally done it. She had allowed herself to glance over and actually look at the house across the street.

The act rattled her, though it didn't surprise her much. She loved her family, loved the smell of her coastal town and the comfort of the familiar, but she rarely came home. Jane and Paul blamed it on her lack of a car in New York City and her impossible schedule from owning her own business—and working seven days a week. But truth be told, Nina couldn't face the memories. Not if she didn't have to. Not the memories from that night all those years ago.

College had distracted her some, dulling the hollowness that had settled into her gut during the summer of 2004…the one after senior year. But the trauma was repressed in the confines of her subconscious—never fully forgotten. On nights at UMass when she would have one too many drinks, a flashback to that night would scare her so badly that she feared she would crumble.

In New York, she would click down the streets of Manhattan in spiked stilettos and skirts so tight they looked like skin. On the outside, she looked carefree…and possibly, a lot of the time, she was. When she could successfully forget what had happened. But that wasn't always the case. Not when the images of that Sunday night in June 2004 would creep up uninvited into her mind like the unruly vines of ivy, inching up and around, overtaking everything she was trying to become.

Thoroughly shaken, Nina turned back toward her house and walked through her parents' garage and into the kitchen, placing the keys in the dish by the door. A breeze came through the open windows and the white curtains danced in its wake. Nina filled a cup of water before heading up to her room. She needed some time to try to mentally prepare for her trip to the rec center tomorrow morning.

Her bedroom was the same room as it had been when she was growing up, but her mother's redecoration since she moved out made it feel quite foreign. Nina was glad about that, though. She wasn't sure she would be able to handle the ghosts of her past if the room still looked like it once did. The nostalgia would have taken its toll. The longing to go back and be a carefree kid was already all-consuming. She didn't need tangible reminders to make her longing worse.

The light gray walls were not the floral wallpapered ones she remembered. The queen bed that now filled the space was not her twin bed with the dinged posts and white, frilly bedspread. Her dresser, once filled with makeup dust and Bath and Body Works products, was replaced with a modern set of drawers. Her desk, always piled with Baby-Sitter Club books and crumbled papers, was gone, and in its place, a large reading chair rested in the dormer, catching sunbeams coming in through the plantation shutters.

There were no NSYNC posters or holes on the walls from where the thumb tacks had once held them up. It had all been patched up, the beauty of childhood and adolescence plastered over, as it often does when kids leave the nest. The ending of one stage and the beginning of the next. Nina slid her thumb over a divot on her closet door and a smirk escaped her.

Ok, not all the evidence of a time long gone was lost.

Nina pulled the thin curtain to the side and looked out the dormer window. She could swear it was only yesterday when she was just eleven years old. Back when she would watch the Warner's house—Brett's window specifically—and wait for movement. She would call him on their walkie-talkies, and they would plan their meetings at the treehouse or their bike rides to the beach and corner store. For too many years she avoided spending too much time here, opting for her parents to visit her on most holidays instead. But now, it was inevitable. For the time being, Carver Road was her home again. Nina had to accept that. She needed to come to terms with the fact that all of her plans had fallen to shit.

From the window on the second floor, she noticed that she had a less obscured view of the treehouse than she did from the driveway. Her heart thundered, realizing the truth in her mother's words. The words that she couldn't seem to fathom an hour ago.

Brett was coming home.

Chapter 4

Brett 1995

THE flashlights propped up along the wall of the treehouse cast a yellow glow across the little space. Brett lay on his belly, looking at one of his Wolverine comic books, his hands still a bit sticky from the treats off the ice cream truck. It was just after eight o'clock, and dusk was spreading across the end of Carver Road like a sheet. The crickets sang their summer song—a sound so familiar that Brett barely registered it.

He heard feet creaking up the rickety steps, and he sat up, crossing his legs into a pretzel.

"Hey!" Nina said, out of breath, as she climbed into their little sanctuary.

Brett eyed Nina's shirt, the one she was wearing earlier. The gesture caused her to look down. "Yeah, I didn't have any time to change." She shrugged her shoulders. "Is the blood bothering you or something? Why do you look like your dog died, B?"

"Oh, um, no." Brett stammered. "The shirt just makes it look worse than it was."

Nina moved closer to Brett, the light from the flashlights brightening her face. "Well, check out these black eyes!" she said, letting him get a good look at the tinged skin beneath her eyes.

Brett's own eyes widened. "Whoa," he whispered.

"Oh well. I raided our snack drawer," she said, dumping out her backpack on the middle of the treehouse floor. "Check this out!"

Brett sifted through the loot and laughed. "We'll be good for days!"

The pair dug through the pile, looking for the perfect snack to start with. Nina opened a container of Dunkaroos and crossed her legs, tucking her dirty feet under her. "Let's tell ghost stories," she pleaded.

Brett grabbed a package of Shark Bite fruit snacks and gave Nina a devious smile. Of the two of them, Brett was a better storyteller. Nina would always beg him to tell her spooky stories, and he could never say no. Not to his Nina.

So, he told her stories, and Nina listened with interest to every word. When Brett was tired of talking, and both of their bellies were aching, they lay down on their backs and spoke softly in the language of children—telling secrets and knock-knock jokes that neither of them could remember the punchline to.

Eventually, it grew silent, and Brett could sense Nina wanted to say something. He felt it in the sound of her breathing. In her huffs. In the way her arms couldn't stay still.

"Brett?"

"Yeah?

"Was it your dad?"

"What do you mean?"

Nina lowered her voice, the two of them still staring at the jagged wood of the treehouse ceiling. "Your brother. When he got punched and needed an ice pack—was it your dad who did it?" Nina's voice squeaked at the end, and the fear in her tone worried Brett.

He didn't look at her, and he didn't answer right away, either. Nina didn't push, though. She gave him a moment.

Brett whispered a reply. "Yes." He felt a lump in his throat, but he swallowed hard, pushing down the pain and fear that was emerging there. He waited with bated breath for Nina to say something in her usual way.

He waited for her to get angry, to swear, to threaten. All in the name of protecting him.

But she didn't.

Her pinky brushed against Brett's, and she curled her little finger around his. She didn't have to say anything else; Brett knew what she was saying even though she didn't speak. Their fingers stayed intertwined for what felt like an eternity to Brett, who lay there, never wanting to leave.

Nina was there. Always. Her presence would never falter; their friendship was unbreakable. Her gesture was telling him that, even though he had known it for years. Nina didn't judge him. She would never leave him. She was the light in his world. With her by his side, he could face anything, the shadows dimmed by her light.

"You know what we should do?" Nina asked, sitting up.

Brett followed her lead, sitting up and looking at her intently, eager to hear what crazy idea was going to come out of her mouth.

"We should become blood brothers." She nodded her head confidently, and Brett twisted his face in confusion.

"Blood brothers? But you're a girl."

Nina rolled her eyes. "It's just what you say after the ceremony, B." He looked unsure, the thought of blood making him a bit squeamish.

Nina glanced around the treehouse before getting up and walking to the tiny table filled with art supplies. She pulled a pair of scissors from a cup. Brett's eyes widened, hoping she wasn't being serious.

"Why do you want to do this?" he asked her.

She stared at him for a moment before sighing. "Because Brett." Her eyes darted around his face, and he watched her without blinking. "It's me and you against the world." Her words were kind of sad, and he couldn't fathom why. He longed to be part of Nina's family. The love. The routine. Her home, where his father never stepped foot. It was all so captivatingly beautiful. Why was she so sad right now?

Brett's eyebrows wrinkled, and he got up quickly from the floor, joining Nina by the art table. "But what's the point?" He really didn't see how the gesture was necessary in any way. But Nina had that way about her—making you believe something that you had no business having any opinion about. Whether it was schoolyard politics or the news on TV, Nina had something to say about everything, and it was very easy for Brett to agree with her.

"The point is that we need each other, and we can't ever let ourselves forget it." Her eyes bore into his. Was she about to cry? Brett squinted, stepping closer.

"Why are you crying?" he whispered.

Nina straightened her spine and adjusted her face. "I'm not crying."

But she was lying, and he knew it. He knew that she loved him like a brother. Behind her tomboy tough exterior, Nina was soft and kind, a child who felt with her whole being and struggled to reign it in. He knew she was worried about him—worried about what went on behind the closed doors of 3 Carver Road, and he didn't want to let her down.

"Ok," Brett whispered.

Nina's face brightened. It was as if she truly believed that mixing their blood would have a dramatic effect on their lives, that it would bind them together, and that nothing could ever tear them apart. He didn't have the heart to tell her that it wouldn't do those things, and if anything, it was entirely unsanitary. But when you're nine, truths like that aren't as pressing as they are when you're older.

Nina poured water on the silver blades of the scissors and wiped them on her shirt. Brett wondered if she thought they were clean now, but he didn't dare tell her that they weren't. Taking the scissors from her hand, he inspected them for rust. He wasn't sure why that was important, but he knew it was because of the time his mother stepped on a rusty nail while pulling the kayak off the shed. It was a big ordeal, and it scared him. But his concern, if anything, kept them from needing a tetanus shot. He handed the pair of scissors back to her, and Nina swiped them from his hand.

"Ready?"

Brett nodded.

Nina slowly sliced a tiny cut on her pointer finger, and a moment later, bright red blood oozed out through her skin. She quickly handed the scissors to Brett, and before he could talk himself out of it, he repeated the gesture. They held their fingers up. Nina beamed at him as she moved her finger to his, pressing their pointer fingers together, and both of them let out a laugh.

Brett looked directly into Nina's eyes, which were almost glowing, her smile wide. To Brett, it seemed like the act *had* done something magical to her. Nina licked the excess blood off her finger, causing Brett to furrow his brow, wiping his finger on his shirt.

"Now what?" he asked, unsure about how he was supposed to react.

Nina sat back on the floor, curling her feet under her. "Now we are bound for life."

Brett wasn't sure how that could be true, but Nina seemed to believe it, and he wanted to as well. To be bound to Nina forever meant he would never be alone; he would always be good enough in someone's eyes—someone other than his mother's. He smiled at her as the sound of the foghorn echoed in the distance—a boat warning those around it of its presence coming into the harbor.

Right after came the sound of Mrs. Jackson's distinct whistle calling Nina home.

Brett hated that sound, dreading it the moment that Nina climbed up the treehouse stairs on balmy summer nights. Dreaded the time that always came too quickly when they had to retreat back to their real houses. And each night brought them closer and closer to fall…to school…to hectic schedules that didn't allow for late, lazy summer nights wasted in the trees.

"Gotta go, B," Nina said reluctantly.

They got up from the floor, gathering what they needed. Brett turned off the flashlights—all but one, the one they used to guide them down the warped stairs.

Darkness was all-encompassing now, and when their feet were on solid ground again, they embraced in a quick hug.

"I'll see you tomorrow," Nina said as she turned and hurried off toward her house.

Brett watched her slip further into the darkness, watching her until she signaled to him that she was safely inside by flicking the porch light a few times. He smiled and turned on his heel, heading to his back porch. With a deep breath, he slid the door open and stepped over the threshold. The hum of the television in the other room echoed through the house, and he imagined his father asleep on the recliner, his mother most likely reading in bed. Tiptoeing passed the living room, he only glanced over with his eyes—not turning his head. His dad, Danny Warner, was asleep on the chair, mouth agape and snores billowing in a gentle rhythm. Brett exhaled slowly and made his way to the staircase, where he tiptoed ever so softly up to his room, careful to avoid the stairs that creaked.

Exhausted, Brett crawled under his covers and sighed, letting his body succumb to the sleep calling him. He fell into his dreams to the sounds of the crickets and a throbbing in his pointer finger that mirrored the thumping of his heart.

Chapter 5

Brett 2016

Brett watched the sun inching up over the buildings that seemed to scrape the sky outside his apartment window. After standing there for quite a while, it hit him that it was his last Texas sunrise. He took a sip from his travel mug, the liquid inside burning his tongue. Wincing at the pain, he unscrewed the cap and gently blew on his black coffee in an attempt to cool it down. Running a hand through his sandy blond hair, he pulled air into his lungs, holding it there for a moment before placing his mug on the only remaining piece of furniture in the apartment, an end table. He scanned the large open room as he linked his hands behind his head and turned from the window. It was really time to say goodbye to this place.

Memories of his time here flashed through his mind like old home videos. Stepping away from the window, he headed toward the kitchen island, sliding his hand over the smooth marble, a smirk playing on his lips. It had been somewhat of a bachelor pad over the last few years, even if Brett never thought of himself as a bachelor, although finding someone to settle down with hadn't been on his mind either.

The parties here had been ragers, lingering so far into the night that day would begin to resurface, and bodies would be passed out everywhere. Brett would wake up with a dry mouth and headache from too much beer pong and not enough water or sustenance.

But things had calmed down some in the last year—the way they sometimes do when one turns thirty. Brett was ok with that, too. All the partying was a distraction from reality. He was aware enough to be able to admit that to himself. But in turn, the slowing of the chaos brought quieter moments, which had the tendency to allow emotions and thoughts to break through, feelings that weren't particularly welcome. They would slip in through the silence when he wasn't distracted enough.

But Brett had a good life—he did. He left Massachusetts for Lubbock, Texas, in 2004 and did all the college rites of passage—dorm rooms, skipping morning classes that were too early, fake I.Ds. When the four years ended, he found a job in IT in Austin—a corporate nine-to-five that paid the bills and then some. He had moved quickly from entry-level to a director role. It wasn't a dream job, but he didn't care. Luckily, he'd be able to do his position remotely from Massachusetts, a perk he was grateful for. One less thing to worry about as he transitioned back home to Harborview. Texas and all the experiences he had there—college and the beginning of adulthood—did what he needed them to do…helped him forget the things he'd left in his past.

But can one ever truly forget? Or do things just get locked away for a while behind a door that we wish would stay closed?

Brett's phone buzzed from its spot on the island, sounding entirely too loud, amplified by the stark emptiness of the space. He picked it up, noticing a text from his friend, Dean.

So is it real? Is my best friend really heading back East? Or did you finally change your mind?

Brett chuckled in spite of himself. As quickly as the smile emerged, it faded—a sad sort of frown taking its place. If it had been up to him, Brett would have never made this decision to go back. He would have stayed as far away from Cape Cod as he could—even going further west to get as far away as possible.

But his mother needed him. Or rather, his brother did. Coming home from war hadn't been kind to Seamus Warner, or his psyche. And Brett's mom was losing her grip on him, so it seemed.

Brett worried about what he was going home to: a brother with war injuries—both seen and unseen—and a mother who had a heart that had broken long ago and had never been repaired.

Brett: It's not forever.

Brett thought the response didn't sound like something he'd say. But he couldn't be himself—or rather, the Brett Dean knew. He couldn't make a joke. He couldn't laugh about it. Not yet.

But that was his hope. And if he put the wish into tangible words, maybe it would come true. Maybe he would return to Austin when the time was right, after he saw that his brother was going to be ok. And maybe after he put back the pieces of himself that had broken all those years ago. But he couldn't unravel these thoughts in his mind, and maybe something he wasn't even ready to address right now. But it was there, just under the surface.

Brett rubbed his thumb against the pointer finger on his left hand—feeling the scar that had been there for years. His heart thundered in his chest as the reality set in. He was going home after all these years and after all that had happened.

And the rumor had spread—by way of his mother—that Nina had returned, too. Back to the very end of Carver Road.

Chapter 6

Nina 2016

NINA HAD ALWAYS TAKEN her coffee the same way—black with a splash of cream—ever since she was in high school. It started the way a lot of things do when you're young, learning from watching someone a bit more experienced. She didn't always like coffee, but when she was fifteen, impressing people was a priority that took precedence. The choking down of the bitter liquid eventually turned into a caffeine addiction, and now, like most adults, her days started with a cup of joe.

Her mug sat on the counter as she pulled her hair into a sleek ponytail and wiped sleep from her eyes. She was tired; rest had eluded her last night.

When darkness had covered the end of Carver Road, Nina had lain awake until the headlights of Laura Warner's car shone through the shutters in her room. She hadn't realized that she had sucked in a breath and was holding it, as if her life depended on the stillness of her chest. She couldn't bring herself to get up and look out the window…to get a glimpse of Brett from her room, though she had imagined herself climbing out of bed and looking into his bedroom window like they did when they were kids. Instead, she lay there frozen, her eyes unblinking.

After the faint noise of the car doors slamming shut and the muffled voices dissipating, Nina struggled to fall into a restful space, working hard to slow her heart rate and calm her nervous system. But it hadn't worked, and she slept restlessly for the rest of the night.

She took a sip of her coffee, the taste awakening her a bit. Walking over to the window, she peered out the curtain to see what was going on across the street. All was quiet at the Warner's house. The only difference between last night when she went to bed and this morning was the presence of the car in the driveway. Nina felt her heart quicken with the reminder—Brett was there, just across the way. She began to recall, much to her dismay, the last time she had seen him, the memory saddening her. There had been a pain in both of their expressions, an uneasiness that had begun to grow earlier that summer. She longed to go back to that day and do something—anything—differently. Something that would have saved their friendship and kept it from crumbling to dust.

But secrets can be like cancer, rotting away the source until it's gone.

Nina knew that there would be a day—soon—that she would be face to face with Brett. She wasn't sure if it was dread or excitement that had settled into her gut. Maybe it was both.

She stepped away from the window and went to the kitchen to pour her remaining coffee into a travel mug, topping it off with what was left in the pot. It was time for her meeting at the rec center.

Nina had to admit that there was a quaintness that surrounded her small hometown of Harborview, Massachusetts, and it had always been that way. The town had an air of fiction about it, as if the village wasn't quite real. The storefronts were a mix of pastels and weathered gray shingles, and the way they sprawled the main street made them look almost miniature from afar. It was as if they were plucked from a display window and arranged perfectly.

The year-rounders who actually lived there made the town what it was; they were the heart that beat in the soil and the sand—keeping the town alive during its quiet, cold months, waiting for the summer people to arrive in their Range Rovers and Wagoneers. Summer people appreciated Harborview only for what it was at its best, all sunshine and beach and vacation, causing the locals to roll their eyes while also appreciating the business they brought. The year-rounders had sort of a love-hate relationship with summer people. But they were dependent on them because summer people's wealth was what kept Harborview afloat all year long.

As Nina drove along the main street to the rec center, she noticed the spring weather was inviting the hydrangeas to bloom, and alongside them, colorful wildflowers sprinkled the fronts of the buildings. The main street was lined with small gift shops, most of which sold touristy trinkets and homemade candies. Among the businesses were also a few unique home decor shops, a bookstore, an organic grocery store, and other independent establishments with decorated windows to entice pedestrians off the street and into their little spaces.

Thankfully, the restaurants weren't of the chain variety. Eating out was always a fun event in Harborview, even if the variety wasn't quite as big as New York City. There was a cable car diner, an Italian wine bar, and other places with food from a wide variety of countries; and no cuisine was ever duplicated. It had always made choosing a dinner spot easy. If you wanted Mexican, you went to Jalapeno Bar. If you wanted Greek, you went to Zorbas. If you wanted a classic burger and fries, you went to Fat Willie's. And if you wanted a whole lobster that you needed to wear a bib for and use tools to crack open the shell and pull out the luscious meat, you went to Blue Seafood, which overlooked the harbor.

Set back from the road was a lush area of grass where a gigantic white gazebo sat. A place where Nina had posed countless times for photos for so many high school dances. She smiled as she thought back to those memories: She and her friends rolling their eyes while their moms took "just one more picture." Behind the park was the rec center—a large building that had been remodeled while Nina had been away. It was home to nearly all extracurricular activities for the town: swimming, exercising, spas, summer camps, before and after school care, art classes, racquetball, and much more. Behind the building was a track, two soccer fields, a basketball court, a tennis court, a putting green, and a new flag football field.

Nina turned her mom's car off the main street and followed the little side road that led to the rec center parking lot and found a spot near the front door. She pulled down the visor, revealing the tiny mirror. She pulled at her skin for a moment, trying to bring color to her cheeks. She checked her teeth and quickly applied some lip gloss. Nina flattened out her hair that was still in a ponytail and got out of the car. Felicia had told her to dress comfortably, so she wore her favorite yoga pants, the ones she once sold at the front desk of N Bar. Thinking about that caused an ache in her chest. Nina took a deep breath, hoping that she was mentally prepared to show off her abilities and prove that she could teach classes here. *Easily,* she thought. *After all, I owned a studio,* she told herself, trying to build up her confidence. But then she realized that the smug attitude had to go, and she tried to shake it off. There was no place for her ego. Not when she had lost everything and was begrudgingly starting from scratch. Taking another deep breath, she made her way to the entrance of the rec center.

The mixed aroma of fresh mulch and chlorine reminded Nina of her days of being dropped here for preschool when she was young. Though it looked much different then, the smell was unmistakenly familiar. As she walked up the smooth stone steps to the doors, Nina pictured herself skipping clumsily to the entrance with her yellow backpack that was bigger than her, her jelly shoes slapping against the pavement. A smile tugged on Nina's lips, the memory warming her.

As she took her first few steps into the rec center, Nina glanced around, taking in her surroundings, noting the changes that had happened since she was young. An information desk was straight ahead and to the right were floor-to-ceiling windows that looked down to the pool one floor below. Along the windows there were couches where people lounged in athletic attire, some looking at their phones, others chatting quietly. To the left, she saw the door to the children's wing and two hallways that sprawled to the back on either side of the information desk.

"Hi," Nina said to the young man behind the counter. "I'm here to meet Felicia Harris." Though it felt forced, Nina smiled. She could admit it felt good to be out of the house, but she couldn't shake the feeling that she was taking steps backward, starting back over again at the bottom of the ladder.

"I'll have her paged," the teen said, smiling while stapling a stack of papers.

Nina stepped to the side, her hands clasped in front of her, and waited for Felicia.

She zoned out for a few minutes while she waited and was stirred from her thoughts. "Nina?" Felicia's voice was commanding but calm. Her dirty blond hair was pulled into a thick, frizzy ponytail that sat high on her head. She looked to be in her early 40s. Her makeup was light, and she wore a matching workout set that accentuated her athletic figure.

"Yes, that's me," Nina said, extending her hand in greeting. "It's wonderful to meet you."

Felicia flashed a bright smile, showing her perfectly straight white teeth. "Likewise. Do you want to follow me to my office, where we can chat?"

"Yes, that would be perfect," Nina said, smiling through her turmoil. Her heart thumped in anticipation as discomfort settled in her gut. The act she was putting on was exhausting her.

They walked down the hallway to the right of the information desk and arrived shortly after at Felicia's office—a quaint space filled with hanging plants and smelling of patchouli and oranges.

"Have a seat wherever you're comfortable," Felicia said, gesturing to the arrangement of plush chairs surrounding a light wood coffee table.

Nina took a seat on a seafoam-colored chair, adjusting herself while Felicia took a seat across from her. Nina's mind was spinning as she desperately tried to get control of her racing thoughts. By nature, she was a leader—confident and headstrong—but failure had taken its toll on her over the last six months and seemingly knocked her down a peg…or six. She couldn't help but feel subpar—ill-equipped to market herself for this new position even though she was—if anything—overqualified. She took a steadying breath in an attempt to slow her racing heart.

"So, Nina, what are your goals—professionally? What brought you to apply for the instructor position?"

If it hadn't been for her mother, Nina wouldn't have even known about the job. Most likely, she would have come home from New York and spiraled into despair and self-pity. But here she was.

"Well, I had my own yoga studio in New York City," Nina started. "It was my dream come true. I lived and breathed it—truly." Nina felt the euphoric expression spreading across her face, the memories of breaking her back to make something of herself and seeing it happen. It was who she was—driven and motivated—one who never took no for an answer. But even that strong person that Nina finally believed she was couldn't stop what inevitably happened. She held onto N Bar as long as she could—maybe a bit too long if the bank had an opinion on the matter. She couldn't bear to give up. Letting it slip through her fingers broke her heart, tainting the image she had of herself, someone who doesn't lose or give up.

Felicia smiled at Nina without showing her teeth. "That's quite impressive."

Nina shrugged. "Well, it was, at one point. But I, unfortunately, couldn't keep it running, not financially, at least." She hated how weak her voice sounded at the admission.

Felicia's expression was sympathetic, and the kindness caused Nina to relax her shoulders. "Falling isn't failing, necessarily," Felicia pointed out kindly. Nina looked down at her hands and nodded. She felt emotions bubbling beneath the surface. It was all still so fresh and new—the loss of her business and returning home. Maybe she should have been sitting on a therapist's couch rather than a rec center one, attempting to land a job. Maybe it was too soon. "It isn't the end of your career," Felicia added when

Nina hadn't responded. "It's time for you to reevaluate, maybe. Figure out what's next."

Nina took a breath and swallowed her pride. "Yes. I guess that's true." A nervous sort of laugh escaped.

"Look, I have a lead instructor out on maternity leave. I would like to give you a trial class this week. We can see how you like it here, and we can discuss you filling in for Leah while she is home with her new baby. How does that sound?"

"It sounds great." Nina smiled, and she meant it. She knew she had to take this next stage in little steps. There was no other way.

"Great. Let me show you our studio. A class is starting in a few minutes, and if you want to stay and participate or watch, you are more than welcome."

"I'd like that, thank you," Nina said gratefully, getting up from the chair.

They left the room and headed to the yoga studio at the end of the hall. It was dimly lit with shining wood floors and an entire wall of mirrors. The wall opposite the mirrors had shelves with all the necessities organized to perfection: towels, cleaning sprays, mats, exercise balls, yoga straps, blocks, and bands. Class participants slowly filed in and set up their stations, stretching and hydrating.

Nina entered the room and felt her whole body relax. It was like she was home. It wasn't her own business, no, but it felt familiar, and familiar felt safe.

"Is it ok if I take part in the class?" Nina asked Felicia.

"Yes, of course. I will be watching, though," Felicia said with a wink. "To see your skills."

Nina laughed. "I understand."

She tightened her ponytail, headed over for a mat and towel, and set herself up in the back of the room. She sat in a butterfly position, stretching her legs. Closing her eyes, she rolled her neck gently from side to side. *One day at a time, Nina,* she thought to herself.

The class was taught by a perky woman named Sammy, and as it started, Nina felt herself drift into a peaceful state as she moved through the poses as if they were second nature because they were. It had been a few weeks since Nina had exercised, and she hated letting too much time pass without moving her body. Why hadn't she used yoga in these last few weeks to help her process her emotions? She had always relied on the movements to heal her. The movement kept her sane, kept her feeling alive. Helped her flush out the emotions from her body. And Nina hadn't always had a positive body image, but with a lot of effort, she had gotten there in spite of the hurdles she'd faced throughout her life. Yoga had saved her. There was no denying that.

In the class, she had no trouble finding her groove. By the time it was over, Nina felt like it had only just started. She felt alive and rejuvenated and vowed to keep getting on her mat to process her feelings and care for her body. She cleaned up her things and snuck out into the hall where Felicia was standing with her arms crossed over her chest and a smile spread over her face.

"You are quite talented, Nina." Nina shrugged. "Would you like to come in tomorrow and fill in for Leah's class? And we can discuss what's next at the end of the session."

"Yes. I would like that. Thank you," she replied with a soft smile, relief flooding her. She was determined to do what she did best, and she appreciated the opportunity.

Nina headed outside the rec center and into the crisp spring air. Behind the pastel buildings in the distance, she could see boats coming and going in and out of the harbor. The screech of gulls overhead triggered her to look up at the blue sky. *Nothing like this in New York City*, she thought to herself as she walked past her car and headed to her favorite bakery—Sweet Marie's. It had been on a corner lot in downtown Harborview for as long as Nina could remember. As she opened the door and the bell chimed overhead, she realized that some things never change.

The aroma inside Sweet Marie's was luscious sugar and freshly ground coffee beans. Nina didn't recognize the employees behind the counter, but that didn't surprise her. She hadn't stepped through these doors in eleven years. At one time, in another life, she knew the employees by name—a common occurrence in small towns such as Harborview. She ordered a latte and a pistachio muffin and walked over to the benches across the street that faced the harbor. Pulling the muffin out of the bag, she took an exaggerated bite, moaning quietly, appreciating the sweet treat as she relaxed against the back of the bench.

The late morning sun glistened off the water that lapped softly against the docks. As she took in the scenery that surrounded her, she contemplated that she had, in fact, missed it here—truly—and it pained her someplace deep inside. A place so buried that she couldn't quite pinpoint where the aching hole was. Nina resented the things that had kept her away from the place that built her. It was the little things that she longed for the most. Like sweet bakery treats and sitting and listening to the natural sounds of the ocean. Things that almost seemed make-believe when she was in New York, where the traffic noise and chaos were all she could hear and see.

Nina sat on the bench and relished in the simplicity, hoping that the mundane routine she was about to establish would keep her from slipping into anxiety and panic that would make it hard to function. She looked up and watched the clouds slide across the sky, changing shape as they went. With the observation, she couldn't help it—Brett slid into her mind, and a lump formed in her throat.

Chapter 7

Nina 1996

L ITTLE NINA TENDED TO romanticize the small things. Blanket forts where she would read for hours with a flashlight. Dipping tiny marshmallows into her warm hot chocolate while watching *The Santa Clause* in front of the fireplace. The abandoned wooden canoe at the edge of the private boat landing behind Brett's house. She insisted that the canoe once belonged to pirates, and they needed to use it as their personal play place. Everything was an adventure in Nina's eyes, and though Brett's eyes didn't sparkle with the same wonder that Nina's did, he didn't make her feel like a nuisance. He played along—often swept away into her whimsical aura. He couldn't help it. She had that effect on him.

"Let's lay down on the boat floor and watch the clouds," Nina said to Brett as she climbed over the rickety edge of the canoe.

Brett fell in step behind her, instinctively checking the boat for rust before climbing in. With their hands behind their heads, they gazed up at the clouds, wispy ones mixed with thick, pillowy ones that pulled and stretched before their eyes.

"Look at that castle!" Nina exclaimed, pointing at the sky.

"And the bird!" he added, laughing.

As they gazed at the clouds, a huge bird—a real one—cast a shadow over them, causing the pair to look up, shielding their eyes from the sun, watching it fly up toward the treetops just ahead. "Was that an eagle?" Nina asked in awe.

Brett furrowed his brow, watching the bird. "No, not an eagle," he responded. "I think it's one of those birds that has made a comeback. That's what my mom said, at least."

"A comeback? What do you mean?" Nina wasn't paying much attention, too busy finding treasures in the clouds.

"They were almost extinct or something. Now they are coming back."

"Oh, cool."

"They are called offspring or something."

"Offspring? Like the band?" Nina asked, laughing.

Brett laughed, too. "Ok, no. Not offspring. I don't know. Whatever."

Nina looked at the bird perched in the tree. It seemed to be looking at them, its head jerking slightly from side to side.

Nina's sigh indicated her boredom and indifference toward the winged creature. "What do you want to do now?" she asked Brett, rising to her feet, the old wood of the boat creaking beneath her worn-in sandals.

"I dunno," Brett shrugged, squinting into the summer sun.

Nina sighed again, aggravated with her companion's lack of enthusiasm. She longed for adventure; she craved mischief. "Come on, B." She grabbed his hand and tugged him over the ledge of the boat and down the stretch of beach, their shoes making prints in the damp sand.

That year, the summer days seemed to stretch on for eons—there were copious amounts of boredom intertwined with moments that seemed to be the most amazing snippets of their lives to the kids on Carver Road.

Wiffle ball tournaments they took entirely too seriously.

Water balloon wars that soaked them to the bone and cooled their skin—until the air turned cooler with the setting sun.

Evenings filled with flashlight tag and chasing fireflies.

Days that seemed to stretch endlessly on and would lead to Nina climbing into her bed at night with leaves and sticks in the knots of her hair and dirt caked under her fingernails. Sleep would envelop her, carrying her into her dreams exhausted and spent from hours of child's play.

———

One morning in early July, just before the holiday, Nina was startled awake by the sound of a car door slamming outside her window. Her eyes fluttered open, trying to adjust to the rising sun. She wondered as she came to what the commotion was outside her open window.

Rising from her bed, she padded on bare feet to look, her white nightgown billowing around her knees. As she moved the curtain, she saw Mrs. Warner's car pulling out of the driveway, and as it sped off, she glimpsed Seamus and Brett in the back seat. Brett was looking up at her window, his hair still tousled from the night and a sad expression on his face that unsettled Nina. Something was terribly wrong—she could feel it.

She watched until the car was out of sight, and even after it was gone, her breath was suspended in her lungs until she couldn't stand it any longer and slowly let it out. She noted a Jello-y feeling in her limbs—brought on by her fear. *Where was Brett going? Why was he so sad?*

Nina's loyalty was a positive attribute. But she couldn't know then that the way she absorbed the trauma of those she loved, like Brett, would eat at her until she lost control.

———

Nina used the back of her hand to wipe the sweat from her forehead as she let out a labored breath. The Independence Day Bike Parade was mere hours away, and she wouldn't allow herself to come in second place for the third year in a row.

"Here," her dad said, handing her some sparkly streamers. "Wrap these around your handlebars, and I'll tape them for you."

"Thanks, Dad," she replied, wrapping the festive decor around her Huffy with precision, her tongue poking through her lips in concentration. "I want it to look like there are fireworks coming out of it somehow." Nina stood back to study it and put her hands on her hips, her brows furrowed, wondering how to make it just perfect.

And so it went, for another hour, until it was time to load the bike into the family station wagon and head into town for the festivities. "This is your year, squirt," Paul said as he shut the trunk of the car, securing the bike in. Nina smiled, but the nerves tugged at her as her stomach wretched, her competitive nature bubbling to the surface.

"Are we ready?" Nina's mom asked with a smile, approaching the car wearing her jean shorts and American flag shirt, pulling her sunglasses down from her head.

"We're off like a dirty shirt," Paul said with a laugh as they piled into the car and headed into town.

Harborview was a buzz with people decked out in red, white, and blue. Nina pushed her decorated bike through the crowd as the Jacksons made their way past different vendors selling knickknacks, homemade candies, and snacks that commemorated the occasion. On their way to the parade, they stopped for cotton candy and snow cones, saying hello to friends along the way.

"Happy Fourth, Chris," Paul announced to a fellow Carver Road resident. "Are you coming to the block party this afternoon?"

"Of course," Chris Jenkins replied, his voice thick with smoke. He flicked the excess ash off the end of his cigarette, blowing the smoke up and away from Nina. "Sharon made her famous potato salad."

"Oh, that stuff is delicious!" exclaimed Jane. "You should stop by our house beforehand for a cocktail on the back deck."

"I'm sure that would be fine," Chris said, taking another drag.

"Great, the Warners and my brother-in-law will be there, too," added Paul, smiling.

"We will see you later, then." Chris gave them a wave before heading further into town.

As the sun inched its way up in the sky, the air growing hotter, the Jacksons headed down toward the harbor where the bike parade contest was being held.

Jane knew her daughter well and suspected there was a pit growing in her gut. "It's just for fun. Remember that, Nina." Her words were soft, accompanied by a wink. Nina nodded once, but the sentiment didn't settle her. It couldn't for a kid like her, the only girl on Carver Road. When she wanted something, failure wasn't an option.

The main street had been closed to traffic since the early morning hours, allowing the citizens of Harborview the opportunity to mosey down the street at their leisure, window shopping and stopping along the way for hot dogs and snacks. American flags hung from each flagpole, billowing in the thick, humid ocean breeze coming off the harbor, leaving the scent of the tides in its wake.

The Jacksons passed an elevated stage on their way to where a crowd gathered with their bikes. Nina recognized a few kids from school on the stage. They were singing Yankee Doodle in a sweet melody that warmed her, though she didn't know why—not then. But the combination of the sights, sounds, and smells was creating the type of memory that keeps, never fading, no matter the circumstance.

"Hi, Nina!" a girl called from the bike parade crowd, her sing-songy voice scraping through Nina's ear canal, causing her to flinch.

"Hey, Emma!" Nina smiled at her, eyeing the girl's bike, her competition.

Emma's hair was in two tight French braids and a white visor with fireworks donned her head, shielding her eyes. Neat and tidy, that was Emma Swanson. Nina approached her and stood beside her, and the difference between the two was like night and day. Nina couldn't care any less that her knees were still filthy from kneeling in the dirt to decorate her bike, her lopsided side ponytail coming loose and sagging. She didn't feel inferior to the other ten-year-old girls in Harborview. If anything, in Nina's mind, she was better. Tough and strong-minded. Kind and loyal. The one to sit at the lunch table with girls like Shiloh Porter while others scoffed with their noses turned up. Others like Emma Swanson.

Nina blew a piece of hair out of her line of vision. "Well, I better go get in line. I have a contest to win." She didn't mean to sound cocky. But…Nina *was* cocky. And Emma flinched at the brazen way she declared victory before the actual event had even started. Emma pursed her lips, forcing a smile, as Nina sauntered away with her bike, none the wiser, on her way to claim her prize.

***

Nina wore her medal like a badge of honor for the remainder of the afternoon—allowing it to swing between her two hands, the ring where the medallion hung squeaking as it swung, the ribbon rubbing red lines on the back of her neck.

"You finally won!" Brett congratulated her with genuine enthusiasm, turning the gold medal in his hand.

They beamed at each other before lying back on the grass under the shade of the large elm tree at the end of Carver Road. It had been a big morning for Nina, and she was excited to share it with her best friend; she had wished that he had been there with her all morning.

"Where were you?" Nina asked, immediately regretting it as the words slipped out and she watched Brett's face fall, if only for a moment.

"Dad was pissed about something before we left," he replied, and Nina could tell he was avoiding showing his true feelings. He shrugged his shoulders, turning his gaze down the street. "So, we just stayed back."

Nina narrowed her eyes, contemplating if she should ask more questions before making the decision to leave it for now. She offered Brett a soft smile, one that he returned. From the corner of her eye, Nina saw

Brett's brother, Seamus, heading up the street with his hands in his pockets, head down. Brett followed her gaze to watch his brother hurry down Carver Road and out of sight.

"Where's Seamus going?" she asked.

Brett didn't answer right away. Eventually, he breathed out slowly and responded. "I don't know." His words came out in a whisper. "I'm sure he'll make himself invisible for the whole day."

"Today? The most fun day of the year?" Nina was flabbergasted but immediately regretted her words…again. She knew there was no explaining Seamus and his actions. He was more aloof than any other kid in the neighborhood, always choosing to hang out with kids from the other side of town. But she was also learning that something was behind the shadows of that house that affected Seamus more than she had previously realized. Though it was a humid day—nearly sweltering—a chill scaled her spine.

They could hear the loud voices of the adults gathering in the back of Nina's house—robust laughter and bellowing voices—conversations they couldn't make out, the sounds pulling them from their thoughts. Neighbors from up and down the street had begun to gather near the elm, setting up tables and backyard games for the annual block party. Music began to rumble from open windows as the kids from Carver Road began to shuffle and skip down the street.

Timmy carried a cooler filled with water balloons, and John Cooper ran over to Nina and Brett, handing them each a teeny drink.

"Here, guys!" he said, out of breath. "These didn't fit in the cooler, so they aren't cold, but who cares."

Nina smiled, peeling off the aluminum wrapper, red juice spilling onto her hand. "Thanks, Johnny."

"Yesss, I love these!" Brett sucked the entire barrel down in three gulps, the green juice staining the edges of his mouth.

"I heard my parents talking about a hot dog eating contest," Johnny said, chuckling.

Nina scrunched her nose. "Gross." She shook her head at the thought. "I'd rather do it with pie!" The boys chuckled, agreeing.

The atmosphere on Carver Road was whimsical—always—but the summertime invited a different sort of magic. The kind that took hold of every heart there, especially the children. Traditions they'd started long ago had become a part of them. It was as if their childhoods were etched in a storybook; the illustrations sprinkled with stars and fireflies, skinned knees, and ice cream dripping from chins.

The way the trees lined and hung over Carver Road formed a secret land, protected by the canopy of leaves, shielding those beneath it from the things that could frighten you.

But the Warner's house was different. The last one on the street, it was set close to the edge of the saltwater pond in the back. The only tree in their yard held the nails and pressure-treated wood that made up the kids' treehouse. The house was more exposed to the elements, and even at a young age, Nina could sense the irony of this. The lack of security. The feeling of unsettledness that never went away.

And the only thing that settled the unease for little Nina Jackson was protecting Brett the only way she knew how—by being his rock. By being an observer, never missing a beat.

"Ready to roll?" Nina asked, picking up her rollerblades that were resting beside her on the grass.

"Yeah, let's cruise," Brett replied.

Nina watched Brett as he buckled his rollerblades, scanning him for anything amiss, anything wounded in his soul. She noted, as she buckled her own skates, that although he was smiling and laughing with Johnny Cooper, there was a distance in his eyes that she didn't like. She knew, without a shadow of a doubt, that she had to keep him close today, to be there if things hit the fan, as they often did lately.

"Let's go in the back and get snacks before we blade," Nina suggested, getting up from the grass.

The three kids walked awkwardly on the lawn and across the shell-covered path toward the backyard, their arms outstretched to help them keep their balance.

Nina led the kids up the steps of the deck, careful not to slip on her wheels. She glided to the table where her mother had put out snacks, Johnny and Brett close at her heels.

"Nina Marie, what did I tell you about rollerblading on the deck?" Paul scolded.

Nina felt Brett tense beside her.

"Sorry, Dad," she giggled, swiping a handful of Cool Ranch Doritos.

"You're gonna strip off the stain I just put on." Paul shook his head, but he wasn't really angry with her; he never was.

"Oh, please, Paul," Jane's brother, Nina's Uncle Rider, said. "You know you did a shitty job staining this thing, and I'll be helping you fix it in the fall anyway." Paul and Rider laughed loudly, their banter setting the tone for the adults on the deck.

Nina giggled another apology while her uncle ruffled her hair, and then she rolled away, back toward the stairs, and the boys followed her, unable to control their giggles. The kids made it to the bottom of the stairs before they burst out laughing. As Nina began making her way to the front yard, Mr. and Mrs. Warner caught her eye. They were standing near the hammock, away from the group, Mrs. Warner's arm in Mr. Warner's hand, her skin splaying out through his fingers. She couldn't, for the life of her, hear the words that Mr. Warner spewed, but she knew they were vile. Her head whipped toward Brett, hoping he hadn't seen, but her hope was extinguished when she saw his face. Nina looked into Brett's eyes, and it was as if he wasn't there; his gaze was distant and clouded over.

Johnny was none the wiser, of course. "Let's race to the stop sign!" he announced, wobbling on the grass toward the street.

Nina's eyes darted from Johnny and back to Brett. Brett knew what Nina was saying, even if it was only with her eyes. She was telling him *I'm here, B.* Her eyes bore into him, seemingly saying, *what do you need?* Brett nodded his head before turning in Johnny's direction. The breath in Nina's chest came out in a burst as she followed behind him without hesitation, only looking over her shoulder briefly to see Mr. Warner running his hands through his hair, his cheeks blazing red. Mrs. Warner's shoulders slumped, her head down as if she was attempting to shrink into herself, to become unseen.

Distraction took over the afternoon, and Nina was able to put what she had witnessed with the Warners in the back of her mind. Her thoughts slid out of defense mode and into the peacefulness of childhood. Simple and carefree. Somehow, without even realizing it, Nina helped Brett do the same. And as dusk settled over Carver Road, the anticipation built in the hearts of the kids. They longed for darkness to come—to sit on the hill that overlooked the saltwater pond on the Warner's side of the street and watch the fireworks.

At nearly eight o'clock, Nina went to the freezer in her garage and pulled out the loot she had begged Jane to get for her and the kids. She clumsily pulled the Rocket Pops from the freezer and carried them out to the lawn, passing them out to all the kids who were standing in her vicinity. Exhaustion had begun to settle into her muscles, and her body thanked her for sitting to rest. The afternoon had worn them out, and Nina's stomach ached from too many sweets and excess MSG and not enough of anything satiating. She took a swig of her orange soda as her popsicle dripped onto her hand.

The sounds around her were comforting: The boys teasing one another, lots of laughter, and music off in the distance. The thump of the horseshoes being tossed in the sand pit at the end of the road. And her most favorite sound—the hissing of a fresh can being opened. Nina never wanted nights like these to end. She dreaded the quiet, when everyone would disperse into their own homes—when the adventure and excitement came to an end. But the sound of a Coors Light can being opened meant that the adults were nowhere near ready for that yet. And, in turn, that meant Nina's night was far from ending, too. Adventure still awaited her.

"Sparklers!"

The kids from Carver Road ignited as the word echoed through the atmosphere as Neil Shoemaker summoned them, boxes of sparklers held under his arm. Like moths to a flame, the kids gathered around, talking over one another, all trying to be the first ones to grab a sparkler from the box.

When each little hand had one, the adults began assisting in the lighting. "Now, don't burn each other," Neil said, laughing.

Fifteen sparklers illuminated the darkness as the kids made designs in the air. The sparklers burned to the end of the stick too fast, causing a wave of groans from the kids—a good thing extinguished much too quickly.

The kids caught on fast that, somehow, Timmy Baker had acquired another sparkler. "Why did you get another one, Tim?" Ricky whined. "That's so unfair." The other kids joined in on the grievance, too.

Timmy shrugged, smirking, as the final sparkler spit out the flames, and he spelled out swear words with the smoke and fire.

"Oh, Timmy, knock it off," his mother said, taking a sip of her wine cooler.

The crowd moved behind the Warner's and Jives's homes in preparation for the fireworks show. Blankets and chairs splayed out on the lawn facing the water that was as still as ice, the moon reflecting off the surface.

Neil, who was half in the bag, began belting out the national anthem, sounding like a cat stuck in a bathtub. Everyone, feeling quite patriotic, joined in on the singalong until arms were linked around one another and bodies swayed to the slow beat. And so, it went until the first boom erupted in the skies, followed by the hoots and hollers from everyone as they took a seat wherever they were standing.

Nina plopped down on the grass in between Brett and Johnny, leaning back on her hands. She glanced over at Brett, and for a moment, she watched the colors dancing in his eyes. She loved the fireworks, adored them, but the look on Brett's face needed her attention more. His eyes darted—to and fro—at the explosions of light and sound. She could tell by his expression that although he was looking at the show, he certainly wasn't *seeing* it.

As the aroma from the fireworks wafted under her nose and the smoke built around the edge of the pond, Nina glanced around, looking for Mr. and Mrs. Warner. They weren't in the general vicinity; however, darkness made it difficult to make out the faces of those gathered on the lawn. She glanced up at the window of the Warner's second story just as Danny whipped the drapes shut, blocking out inquisitive eyes from below from witnessing whatever might happen up there. Light peeked out from the sides of the window, and their movements behind the curtains caused shadows to be cast on the wall. Nina watched until the light turned off, causing her breath to hitch and Brett to turn to see where she was looking. He looked at her with his eyes wide, his expression begging her to let it go, to just turn around and forget what she saw.

But Nina didn't forget anything.

They were children, Nina and Brett. Too young to understand the severity of the situation festering behind the doors at the Warner's house. But, also, they were too naive to see it for what it was. Instead of a black-and-white image—as clear as day—the children' twisted the scenarios into nightmares that kept them up at night. Nina, always constructing make-believe stories about the things Brett left hovering between the lines. And Brett, wondering when bad would, inevitably, turn worse. And what would worse even look like?

At ten years old, Nina couldn't pinpoint why even just the thought of Mr. Warner made her stomach sour; she was too young to understand. All she knew was that Brett needed her. Needed her to protect him. And she would always be there for him.

The fireworks finale boomed throughout the neighborhood as the onlookers cheered and clapped. In the commotion, Brett got up from the grass and swiftly headed toward the treehouse. Nina realized he was gone seconds later, and her gaze followed him intensely until she lost him behind the worn walls of their fortress.

"Brett," she whispered to herself, getting up off the ground. She walked swiftly toward the rickety old ladder and made her way up to the landing, skipping every other step. When she reached the doorway, she saw him sitting in the corner, hugging his knees to his chest, his shoulders shaking, unable to mask his emotion.

"What happened, B?" Her voice sounded distant in her ears, as if it was someone else uttering the words. She hated how weak she sounded. She wanted to be strong for him, but seeing him broken was breaking her, too.

"Mom wants to leave Harborview." Brett didn't look at her when he spoke, his words coming out dull and withdrawn. Nina pursed her lips, her breaths coming in short bursts through her little nostrils. Brett stretched out his legs and looked up at the ceiling. A bulging tear was building at the corner of his eye, growing and growing until it spilled out and ran down his cheek in a crooked path.

Nina's head shook ever so slightly. "No," she whispered.

"You know when we left for a few days last week?" he asked. Nina nodded. How could she forget? The days he was gone were agony for her. "We went up to Kennebunk—where my Auntie Ann lives." Brett took his gaze up to meet Nina's. They stared at each other, and Nina couldn't find any words. It was as if her brain was frozen, her muscles unable to move. "She wants to move there…into my aunt's house. Away from my dad." His voice hitched at the end, and Nina's heart crumbled like weathered rocks tumbling off a cliff. She got to her knees and crawled up next to Brett. Her best friend. She rested her heavy head on his shoulder and swallowed the lump building in her throat, unable to fathom this reality. But she knew that being sad about it was selfish because she also knew that his house was not a home. But rather a hell she couldn't imagine.

"So, you're leaving?" she asked, searching for understanding.

Brett didn't answer right away. They sat unmoving, shoulders touching, listening to the faraway sounds of the party beneath them. Fireworks from further down the pond echoed into the night, and drunken laughs and kids squealing went on below, as if nothing was amiss on Carver Road.

But something was amiss.

"I don't know how we would ever be able to leave."

Nina looked at Brett, eyebrows furrowed. He said it like he wanted to go, too. Like he understood his mother's desire to up and leave—to pack a bag and say goodbye to the friends and the street that built him up until now…just to get away from the madness that was his father.

"What do you mean?" Nina asked.

"My dad would never allow that to happen. He'd kill her before he would ever let her leave."

Nina gasped, her hand covering her mouth—a desperate attempt to stave off the emotion.

Kill her.

The harsh words came from Brett's mouth through gritted teeth, a tone that frightened Nina to her core. Her arms and legs began to feel like mush—like Jello.

She couldn't imagine living on Carver Road without Brett, but at the very moment, she wanted him to run away and never come back. She wanted him to disappear and save himself, save his mom. Save his brother. She hated the feelings bubbling inside. The feelings that always bubbled up but never boiled over because she never truly understood what it was really like. But the pot was spilling over now.

Abruptly, she arose from the treehouse floor and grabbed the scissors from the table by the wall. The same scissors they had used last year to slice their skin and form a bond that couldn't be broken. She opened the scissors and started carving into the wall.

"What are you doing?" asked Brett with little to no enthusiasm, the energy wiped from his soul.

"I'm carving our initials in the walls. No matter where you are, no matter where I am, we will always be here somehow. We will always have each other."

Brett's shoulders sank with dread. He loved Nina for so many reasons. One of them being that she was loyal beyond comprehension. But he knew she was delusional, too, because Nina couldn't romanticize this.

It was too big.

Too heartbreaking.

Nina rubbed her finger over the N and B, the jagged wood poking her finger. She bit her bottom lip, looking into Brett's face, her expression unwavering. She was doing it again, attempting, though feebly, to make it all ok by proving to the universe that they were unbreakable—first with blood and now etched into the wall of their favorite spot. So, if he left this house in the dust, a piece of them would still remain.

But Brett didn't leave Carver Road that summer. Maybe if he had—left in the back of his mom's car heading to Kennebunk—their lives would have turned down much less wretched paths. But hindsight is always a bit sharper than the here and now, isn't it?

Chapter 8

Brett 2016

BRETT STOOD AT THE bottom of the old tree with his hands on his hips, looking out toward the pond. He couldn't, for the life of him, understand why bringing himself to look up at their fortress was proving to be next to impossible.

But truly, he couldn't do it.

He had been home for only twelve hours, and half of those hours were spent in his old bedroom, in the dead of night, not sleeping of course. How could he? He was back in his hometown, though it didn't feel like coming home. It seemed like just the opposite—he felt like a tourist abroad in a foreign country.

His mom had been upbeat as he walked out the doors of Logan Airport into the air that felt much crisper than the Texas air he had left behind. Brett was uplifted by seeing his mother dressed in a smile because he hadn't seen one on her in years. And the melancholy tone that came through when he spoke to her had become who she was, and he didn't expect anything different when he called her on Sunday evenings. She had hugged him tightly there on the curb and struggled to let him go, breathing him in, stifling the meekest of sobs. He could tell she was hurting but trying to mask it. Though it made him sad, it didn't shock him much.

For all his life, that was the way of Laura Warner. Painting a face to hide the pain that was always there.

They had pulled into the driveway late at night, and as the car crunched over broken seashells, Brett's breathing had become shallow. He had gotten out of the car, slinging his backpack over his shoulder before slamming the door. He kept his head level, refusing to take in his surroundings. As he grabbed his suitcases out of the trunk, he didn't glance around into the darkness that covered the end of Carver Road; he didn't want to see the ghosts of his past.

The elm tree at the end of the road.

The skid marks he had made with his mom's car during driver's ed.

The treehouse.

Nina Jackson's window, where—unbeknownst to him—she lay wide awake, listening to the Warner's car pull up.

He didn't look. He couldn't.

How could he when could barely breathe?

Stepping into the house, it felt eerie, a scene left over, unchanged for decades. Clean but exactly the same.

Seamus was sitting at the kitchen table when they entered. The same kitchen table that they bought when Brett was five. The light wood was faded and chipped in places—dinged in others. The oblong shape and spindly legs brought memories flooding back that Brett was uninterested in letting in.

Seamus got up from the table, approaching Brett. Brett eyed his brother, checking for broken pieces, the way Nina unknowingly taught him to do all those years ago.

His hair was cut short, buzzed to his head, the military way. His body moved stiffly, and he didn't smile as he put out his hand to shake his brother's. Brett took Seamus's hand in his, and though Seamus didn't initiate, Brett pulled him in for a hug—this was half of the reason he had agreed to come home after all. Leave his happy life in Texas and return to the despair he had left behind. He did it for Seamus. And he did it for Laura. But he also did it for himself, even if he didn't realize it at the time. Because, maybe, if he could start over somewhere else and grow happiness in his heart, he would be able to spread it to the people he loved most. The ones he loved but couldn't bear to even look at anymore because what he saw in them were just reminders of everything that had, at one point in time, broken him.

"How was the flight?" Seamus asked, monotone.

"Easy," Brett shrugged. "How are you?" He winced inwardly, chastising himself for asking the question, knowing very well how Seamus was.

Seamus scanned Brett's face before nodding once. "Good." Brett gave a soft smile and nodded back. "But I'm tired."

"Yes, of course," Brett said. "Thank you for waiting up. We can catch up tomorrow."

"Ok." With that final word, Seamus turned on his heel and headed toward the front of the house and up the stairs.

Brett turned back to his mother, who was busying herself in the cupboards, pulling out two glass tumblers. She pulled a bottle of whiskey from the back of the counter and carefully poured two fingers worth in each glass. She carried them both to the kitchen table and sat down, motioning for Brett to join her. And so, he did.

"Is this ok with your medication, Mom?"

She eyed him, her stare growing glossy with fresh tears. "Yes, Brett. I'm fine." She took a sip, holding it in her mouth a moment before swallowing it. "I'm not your father." Her voice held disgust, startling Brett. *Why would she say that?*

"Um. I know." Brett took a long swig from his own tumbler, barely flinching at the bitter taste. "I just—"

"Listen, Brett. You haven't been here. You don't know what it's been like with him." Laura motioned her head toward the stairs, taking another sip from her glass. Brett listened intently, hoping she would go on. And she did. "The PTSD is taking over. His anxiety is worse than it's ever been." She shook her head sadly.

Brett hung on her words. He wasn't so sure where Seamus's PTSD had come from—the war or his childhood—and it made the sadness in Brett burrow deeper. Because maybe it was both, and that truth was a heavy burden.

"Well, I'm here now. I can help." Brett said the words, and he meant them, wholeheartedly. However, he wasn't sure how he was going to do it. But the commitment was made, and he was a man of his word, even if he would rather be anywhere but Harborview.

It was guilt that had pulled him back. Guilt and something else he hadn't yet been able to label. Leaving Austin was the last thing he had wanted to do; he had thought that being in Texas was the answer to all his problems. Being home for mere minutes was already proving to feel like a disastrous mistake.

Man of his word? Maybe. But that didn't mean he had all the answers.

"He drinks a lot. I worry about him—the way he tries to cover up his pain with *stuff*." Laura gestured to her glass, rolling her eyes. Brett stared at her, memories of his dad's wreckless drinking clouding his vision. Anger began to fester. "I worry I'll lose him to the bottle. Like I lost your father." She choked out the last words, as if losing Danny was an actual *loss*.

Brett got up from his chair with aggression, his chair knocking to the floor. He stalked to the counter and unscrewed the cap of the whiskey before tipping it over and emptying it into the sink. As it glugged down the drain, he looked over his shoulder at his mother, whose mouth was agape.

"Brett. What are you doing?" Her voice was soft but not angry. More defeated than anything.

Through gritted teeth, Brett spoke. "If you are worried about him being like Dad, then why do you have this stuff just laying around?"

"He is a grown man, Brett. I can't stop him from going to the liquor store. If I don't have it in the house, he is just going to get it himself, like he does. You'll see in his room tomorrow." Brett stared at her, leaning back on the counter. "He needs more than an unceremonious emptying of the liquor bottles." She downed the last of her drink. "Much more."

Brett had looked down at his feet then, wishing he was back in his bachelor pad in Austin, pretending that his mom and brother were just fine in Massachusetts without him. He took a deep breath, looking at his mother through narrowed eyes, seeing his reality staring right back at him in his mother's gaze.

"Thank you for picking me up at the airport. I should turn in." Brett put his glass in the dishwasher and took his mother's from the table, doing the same.

"Brett…," Laura didn't have anything to say after that.

"We can talk in the morning, Mom," Brett replied, picking up his bags and heading for the stairs.

The door creaked open as he reached into the room, feeling around for the light switch. He flicked it on, and everything was cast in a dull light—the room mostly as he had left it. The walls were bare, unlike when he'd left. Gone were the Blink 182 posters and the dartboard and the flags from his varsity baseball team. But the bed was the same, as was the bedspread. The rest of the furniture hadn't changed either.

Brett placed his belongings down by the desk he had used as a teenager and pulled his jeans off, slipping into some shorts before walking past the window to his bed. He couldn't look out the window, though. Hadn't even glanced over. It hurt too much.

Just as it ached to look up into the treehouse now.

But he had to go up. The decrepit structure was calling him, or so it seemed—as if it had secrets to share. So, he put one foot on the bottom rung and took the first step up the rickety ladder. It took a moment to get his bearings. Though he was in shape, he was no longer a scrawny, light kid who could fly up the ladder with reckless abandon. His biceps steadied him as he made his way up to the landing.

Once at the top, Brett anchored himself up on the warped and waterlogged slab of wood that was the floor of the treehouse. It didn't feel entirely safe, but Brett trusted that he wouldn't crash to the ground. This treehouse had always been his safety, and he assumed it still could be. Stepping through the entryway, Brett felt like a giant entering a human home. His shoulders hunched forward as he ducked under the uneven hole where the door hung on its hinges, creaking loudly as it opened.

Brett bent down to his knees and took a moment to get his bearings. A sort of dizziness had taken over as he—unknowingly—held his breath in his lungs. It was obvious at that point why it had been so difficult to get himself up that ladder. The past lived on in this space, so much so that he was losing touch with reality. And so, he just let it all in. A jingling of Nina's laughter tickled his ears. The smell of waterlogged cedar and wet leaves brought memories that he welcomed to the surface.

A time when he felt free.

A time when he had Nina.

Moments from *before*.

And as fast as those soft memories trickled in, they were wiped clean with a shutter that moved through Brett's body. A realization that nothing was the same as when he spent his summer nights in this special place.

Brett looked around. The table and chairs sat against the wall, looking aged but the same. He made his way over and pulled out a chair, studying it. Was he ever truly small enough to sit on it? He couldn't fathom this passage of time. He picked up a cup that sat on the table, pulling out a pair of scissors and smirking softly. The same scissors he'd used to slice his finger alongside Nina. To carve an N and a B into the wall. The same scissors used to ensure that he and Nina would always be together.

Brett ran his thumb over the scar on his pointer finger, the way he always did, a habit hard to break. A motion he used to soothe the unease of life.

The initials etched into the wall were, of course, still there, and as they caught Brett's eye, he moved closer to them. He reached up, his thumb gliding over the dented wood.

N & B, carved over and over into the panels.

Closing his eyes tightly, he attempted to fight off the emotion that was erupting in his chest. Memories of Nina were ever present, the background of every thought he ever had. However, the habit of thinking of her became something he ignored. Giving into those thoughts and admitting the truth that he missed her beyond measure wasn't an option. But try as he might to forget her, the treehouse was making it nearly impossible to keep the memories neatly tucked away in his mind.

Twelve years had passed. They were adults—who he was at his core now wasn't who he was back then. Too much had happened. He surmised that the same must be true for Nina as well. He had believed that for their own good, it was better to leave their friendship where it was the strongest—in the past.

Brett squeezed his eyes shut, pinching the bridge of his nose. As time had ticked on, the years passing swiftly the way they tend to do, Brett had decided that the ocean that had formed between them was uncrossable. Too much pain was embedded in the waves, and so, it felt that there was no point in trying to cross it. And although this was true, if there was one thing he wished he could be wrong about, it was his assumption that a life with Nina in it was a never thing.

The minutes ticked on as Brett leaned against the wall of the treehouse. He didn't want to climb down and leave the safety and protection he felt up there. It felt too good. Memories of the time from before, more sweet than bitter.

He didn't know how much time had passed when he heard the familiar sound of wheels on seashells, but not from his mom's driveway. He scrambled up from the ground and peeked out the door to see a car pulling into the Jackson's driveway. It idled there for a moment before turning off and out stepped a woman with long dark hair. Brett knew before she even turned around that it was her. Of course, it was. The way she walked, the way her ponytail swayed on her back, the energy he always channeled with her—it was all Nina.

The desire to yell her name out the treehouse door and have her come running up the stairs with dirty elbows and leaves in her hair was so overpowering that Brett wasn't sure he could control it. But he forced himself to. He breathed in and out with ragged breaths, desperate not to follow the impulse to get his friend back.

To tell her all the things that have gone on during the last twelve years.

To go back to the way it was.

To say sorry.

To apologize for abandoning her when she most likely needed him the most. When they needed each other.

Brett watched as Nina gracefully walked into the house, through the garage, and out of sight. He let out a breath, relaxing his tense shoulders, but aware enough to know that, eventually—come hell or high water—he would have to come face to face with her.

Gilligan dropped the leash by Brett's feet when he entered the kitchen. At thirteen, the old yellow lab was slowing down some, but his tail still wagged at the thrill of the outdoors. Brett smiled at him, rubbing his soft ears.

"Wanna take a walk, buddy?"

Gilligan began to wiggle and shake, his geriatric breathing more audible than it once was. Brett smiled at him while attaching the leash to his worn navy collar, the anchors on it more gray than white now.

Brett stepped back out into the spring air, and he and Gilligan headed up Carver Road in the direction of East Beach. He walked swiftly down Pontiac Street, the main road leading to the shore. The end of Pontiac led right into the ocean. New fluorescent signs with arrows pointing right had recently been put in, in an effort to avoid cars speeding down Pontiac. Speeding cars that more than once ended up flying into the ocean late at night. Brett shuddered at a memory of such an accident back in high school. He wondered if the new signs were actually helpful or just unfortunate eye sores.

As he got closer to the shore, the wind whipped past his face, ruffling his hair. He glanced down at Gilligan, who seemed to be keeping pace with him, not tiring yet, and so, they kept going. Before he knew it, Brett was in town, wondering how he had made the two-mile walk without even realizing where he was going, surprised that Gilligan was still hanging on. But he looked tired, and Brett knew the dog needed a good rest if he was ever going to make the walk back home. Brett tied the leash to a little cafe table outside Sweet Marie's and went in to get himself a coffee.

"Welcome!" a perky voice rang through the little place.

"Hi," Brett smiled at the older woman behind the counter.

"What can I get ya?"

Brett squinted at the chalk-drawn menu, just wanting a black coffee, nothing fancy. "Just a medium coffee, please. And this dog treat," he said, grabbing a bone from a little glass bowl.

"Oh, those are on the house," the woman winked.

Brett offered a soft smile, placing the bone in the front pocket of his hoodie before handing his credit card over to the nice woman.

Taking the cap off the coffee, Brett blew on it gently to cool it down. "Thanks," he smiled.

"Have a great day!"

Brett sat at the table outside in the sunshine with Gilligan's head on his lap. He rubbed his head, placing the bone near his snout. Gilligan sniffed at it before gently taking it from his hand and lying out in the shade under the table. Just then, Brett's phone vibrated in his pocket. Pulling it out, he glanced down to see a text from Jenny, a woman from Austin with whom he had somewhat of a history.

Are you going to Dean's tonight?

Brett sighed. He *wished* he was going to Dean's.

It was Friday, and Fridays at Dean's were commonplace for Brett's friend group in Texas. They would all gather after work for ping pong, cards, and pizza while watching whatever sports were on TV. People would come and go—sometimes, they would head downtown for drinks at Sullivan's or go line dancing at The Headless Horseman—other times, they would just stay and hang out at the apartment.

Brett longed for the freedom and simplicity of the life he left behind just yesterday. A life that he hoped would be his again sooner rather than later.

Brett: Nah. I'm in Massachusetts.

Jenny: Oh. Yeah. I heard someone talking about that. That you were leaving. So sad!!

Brett didn't feel like responding. Jenny wasn't sad. Not really. Not the way that Brett was sad, and so her text nauseated him.

Brett: I'll be back soon. Which was, most likely, a lie, but saying it made him feel slightly better.

Jenny: And then we can pick up where we left off…maybe? ;)

Brett smiled to himself while looking down at his phone. Jenny was fun—low-key and always down for a good time. He'd known her since college and knew she was a good kisser, with a full mouth and thick hair that was good to hold on to. She had the kind of laugh that sounded like a song, and Brett liked that about her. He also liked the ease with which she lived her life, never taking anything too seriously. The Jenny chapter of Brett's story had been a good one, but it had come to an end, fizzling out. But apparently, Jenny was open to rekindling it. Or so it seemed. But the wait time would be longer than she expected, Brett knew that for certain. So, he let any hope of that fizzle out, too, right there on the sidewalk outside of Sweet Marie's.

"No shit." A voice pulled Brett from his thoughts and onto the sidewalk. "Brett Warner? Can't be." The voice was jolly and filled with a smile.

Brett turned slightly toward the street and smiled back at the man standing there. "Mr. Cooper! Hi! Long time no see." Brett pulled his friend's dad in for a hug.

"It sure has been a while. But please, we're both grown-ups. Call me Pat. Look at you! What are you doing back here?"

"First time back since I was eighteen, actually," Brett said. "I'm back to help my mom a bit."

"I saw Laura a few days ago. Didn't mention you'd be back," Pat said this lightly with a smile, but it struck Brett as odd.

"How's Johnny? He still around here?" Brett asked, putting his hands in his pockets.

"Oh, sure. He's a physical therapist. Has his own practice right over there by the rec center." Pat gestured behind the cafe toward the green lawn. "All those injuries he acquired out there on the street with you kids gave him an interest." Pat winked. Brett chuckled, shaking his head knowingly—thinking of all the ice packs the kids used over the years and the x-rays they racked up, giving their parents a run for their money. "What about you? What have you been up to?"

"I stayed in Texas after graduating college. I've been working for a tech company based there, and I'm working remotely for them while I'm in Harborview."

"How long are you in town? I'm sure Johnny would love to catch up with you."

"Uh, yeah, for sure." Brett's voice sounded strange as he thought about how long he would be home—the thought unknowing and daunting. "I'll have plenty of time to catch up with him." Brett felt around for his wallet, pulling it out of his back pocket. Opening it, he pulled out his business card, handing it over to Pat. "My cell is on there. Let him know I'm around."

Pat took the card from him. "Will do!" He put the card in his pocket. "I'll see you around, big guy." They shook hands again and said their goodbyes.

As he walked away, Brett found himself thinking back and smiling. He and Johnny had been inseparable as kids. They were awkward, gangly things in junior high and grew into themselves alongside one another in high school, the way boys tend to do.

But just like the rest of his old life here, Brett had left him in a cloud of dust that summer—any hope of a lifelong friendship lost to the tides of Vineyard Sound. Brett found himself wondering what Johnny was like, the kind of man he'd turned into, guilt settling into his gut. Guilt from realizing that he should know these things. But he didn't because he ran away without ever looking back.

As Brett untied Gilligan from the table leg, he vowed to open up a door to the past, just a little, to see how Johnny was fairing. It was the least he could do after all the Facebook messages and AIM messages he had ignored from Johnny over the years. It wasn't Johnny's fault that Brett had dismissed him. It was just a side effect of what happens when you try and forget.

And forgetting was the only thing on Brett's agenda back then. A goal he worked at with all his might.

On the way home, Brett walked a bit slower than he had on the way into town, taking time to observe all the familiar things he passed by. He tried to shake the uneasy feeling that was settling in his bones, like he was walking through the past. A past that was weighing his shoulders down.

Brett sighed as he walked back into the garage of his house, hanging up the leash by the entrance as Gilligan waddled inside, plopping down on his dog bed by the couch in the living room.

"Hey." Seamus' voice cut through the silence of the house, startling Brett some.

"Oh, hey," he stuttered, caught off guard. "Just got back from taking Gillie for a walk."

Seamus gave a single nod, and the two of them settled into a moment of painful silence. Brett didn't know how to talk to Seamus. He never really had. Seamus was always the punching bag for Danny Warner's anger—at least at first—and being three years younger, Brett didn't know what to do about it when they were kids. Instead of standing up for him, Brett tended to cower and hide. And Seamus didn't seek refuge in Brett—not even a little bit.

There wasn't any negative energy between them. More of a nothing-ness that almost felt worse to Brett. Growing up, he assumed that Seamus just didn't like him, that he was just his annoying kid brother. There was no other way back then to describe the emptiness—the void—between them.

But it was a little bit clearer now. Brett could see it written between the lines, like a secret message scribbled in pencil and then erased. Seamus was mentally unwell, to no fault of his own. It was Danny's fault. Their father caused a switch to flip in Seamus's head that never seemed to right itself. And war is no place for a mind like that—a mind that had already been through its own set of battles time and time again.

Brett couldn't even imagine what the deployments had been like for Seamus. He had gone overseas three separate times during his service in the Army, and from the way things seemed to be going, each time he returned, more pieces of his psyche had been maimed.

So Seamus had begun to wither away, beat down by the past, present, and future to a point that Laura needed help.

Brett followed Seamus into the kitchen, where he began to pour himself a drink. "Want one?"

Brett's eyebrows pulled in, shaking his head no. "It's eleven o'clock in the morning, Seamus."

"Ok, Brett. You can go fuck right off with your pretentious attitude. Coming home for the first time in twelve years like you're the prodigal son, so high and mighty."

"What the fuck, dude?" Brett was ticked off at his brother's words. "What did I ever do to you? Nothing."

Seamus glared at him from his spot at the kitchen table. "A thanks would have been nice." His voice was husky and sounded tired.

"Thanks? For what?" Brett didn't mean to sound like an asshole, but he didn't know how to be thankful to someone he barely knew.

"For keeping his hands off you as long as I could." Time seemed to stop right then, blood rushing through Brett's ears, the sound dizzying him. "I know you don't want to hear it, but Danny didn't target me because he hated me more." They had stopped referring to him as 'dad' long ago. "I was the punching bag because I didn't ever let him get to you."

Brett felt as if he would never breathe normally again, and there was an ache somewhere inside that nagged at him, a place deep that was hard to pinpoint.

"What? Got nothin' to say now?" Seamus leaned back in the wooden chair, his hand clasped around the glass, a semi-permanent fixture.

Brett couldn't find any words. He couldn't, for the life of him, articulate what was racing through his mind. "I...I—"

"Don't even bother." Seamus seemed spent, and again, silence settled between them like fog.

He knew it was true that Seamus (and Laura) took the brunt of the abuse. But by the time Seamus was gone and on his way to Fort Knox, it wasn't long before the attention shifted directly to Brett.

At sixteen, he had started to trump Danny in height and strength, but his gentleness was no match for his father. It didn't matter how perfectly clean he kept the house or how often he took out the trash or mowed the lawn. It was never good enough. And strikeouts in the batter's box brought emotional abuse after the game that ripped him apart, making him feel worthless and stupid.

"He was coming for you once." Seamus took another swig from his drink, shaking his head slowly in disgust. "I think you were eleven, maybe twelve; I can't remember exactly." Brett could feel his pulse pumping at his temples and emotion bubbling that he kept tampered down. "You and Nina had tracked so much mud into the basement, and he was livid." Seamus got up from the table, the chair scraping against the tile, and he approached Brett slowly. "I knew it wasn't going to be good." A laugh escaped him, but Brett could tell it wasn't because he thought it was particularly funny. "It would have wrecked you, right here." Seamus put his finger on Brett's chest, right where his heart was beating out of control.

Brett was perturbed by Seamus's intuitive knowledge of the inner workings of his soul, how he seemed to know that Brett, at eleven, wouldn't have survived that. But Seamus hadn't survived either. His insides—his heart and mind—had been ravaged living under this roof. Brett didn't know what was worse: that Seamus had sacrificed himself or that Brett hadn't noticed.

Brett collapsed into a chair, his head falling into his hands as Seamus walked out of the kitchen and up to his room. He sat there for a long time contemplating this truth that he just learned—that a little bit of dirt traipsed through his home could have been his undoing.

But it hadn't been. Something else had been the culprit of that.

Something much worse.

Chapter 9

Brett 1997-1998

THEY KNEW WHEN SUMMER was officially over by the way the crickets' song seemed to simply cease—there one day, gone the next. It was in the air, too, of course. Mornings no longer sticky with humidity but rather clear and crisp, the smell of dried leaves in the atmosphere.

In late September, all the tourists had left Harborview and wouldn't be back for months, leaving in their wake a stillness that frightened Brett. He despised the change from summer to fall. It was a response his body had without him even realizing it. A fear of the hibernating months that were approaching. The months when he'd have to spend too much time behind the closed doors of 3 Carver Road and not enough time in the open air at the end of the street with the neighborhood kids.

Brett hung on to the mild days of fall with white knuckles of desperation. He became the game planner, the peacekeeper—never wanting strife to cause everyone to stomp off to their houses and the fun to be over. He tried to drag it out as long as he could.

It was an overcast Saturday just before October, and the kids were spent from two hours of playing wiffle ball in the street. Brett and Johnny began shooting hoops at the bottom of the Cooper's driveway. Ricky

Jives and Timmy Baker climbed the elm, the low branches sagging under their weight. A whole lot of the boys were racing their bikes down the street, and in between races, they cruised slow, popping wheelies. After cartwheeling—alone—on the grass in front of her house, Nina sat under the tree in her yard reading a book, sprawled out on her belly, her feet swaying in the air.

Brett had noticed her starting to pull away from the group sometimes to be alone. Not always, but occasionally—as if she needed a break from the boys. She once was in everyone's business all the time, but sixth grade had shifted something in her that only Brett had noticed.

As the sky grew darker, looking like rain, the group gathered in Nina's yard.

"*Sweet Valley High, Jessica Goes for Gold*?" Timmy taunted Nina, swiping the book from her hand. "So girlyyy." He laughed, dragging out the word that Brett knew Nina hated. "You know you aren't going to be in the Olympics, Nina, right?" he scoffed.

The girls around town had become quite infatuated with gymnastics over the last year, idolizing Kerri Strug and fantasizing about goals that were never actually within their reach. However, they couldn't deny the way they had felt watching Kerri land that vault to win the gold, even through a painful injury.

Brett watched Nina's face carefully as she glared at Timmy. "Well, what do you think I am?" she countered Timmy, and he scoffed. "I AM a girl, you asshole."

"Coulda fooled me," Timmy replied, causing a ripple of noise to emerge from the group.

Nina's eyes narrowed.

Brett cringed.

He knew what was coming. Nina stepped toward Timmy, almost methodically, tipping her head to the side, a sinister smile tugging at her mouth. As if she was about to say something to Timmy, her lips parted, but then she closed them. Before anyone could see it coming, she wound up and punched him square in the jaw. She winced, shaking out her hand. "Was that too girly for you, Timmy?"

"Are you serious, Nina!?" Timmy squealed, holding his face in his hands.

Brett smirked, shaking his head as the gaggle of kids worked themselves into a tizzy, laughing at Timmy. No one could get a word in as they all talked over one another, and Timmy sulked off in the direction of his house. Brett took Nina's hand in his, examining it for something out of line. It was red but fine otherwise.

"You should see the other guy," she said, and they both laughed.

"He deserved it," Johnny offered. Nina smiled at him, appreciating his support.

"Um. Duh." Nina rolled her eyes just as the skies opened up, drenching them.

The kids of Carver Road scattered, yelling and laughing into the storm.

"Wanna come play air hockey in the basement?" Brett yelled over the rain.

"Sure!" Nina responded.

They trudged through the wet puddles and mud to the back of the Warner's house. Brett heaved the bulkhead open, and it creaked before producing a loud thud as it fell to the side. The kids entered the dark stairway and descended down into the basement.

There was a hint of mustiness that filled their nostrils as they made their way into the rec room. The wood paneled walls and concrete flooring made the room feel somewhat eerie. The kids of Carver Road joked that the basement was haunted by the Ghost of the Pond—a spirit who would glide in off the water and burrow in between the panels, ready to pounce when the mood struck. Stories that most likely came from watching too much *Are You Afraid of the Dark* on Saturday nights. With their giggles and energy, the space seemed to brighten some.

But there *was* a hauntingness there, though; Brett knew that for sure. He felt it every day of his life. And he ignored it, too. Because what could he do about the nightmare? A solution to their problem never came to mind. He became an expert in walking on eggshells—his only defense against Danny and his shadows.

Eggshells and Nina. Those were the things that saved him.

Nina and Brett played air hockey for a while before rumbling stomachs pulled them up the stairs. In the kitchen, Brett pulled a chair from the table and leaned it against the counter before climbing up onto the counter to get two glasses from the cabinet. Handing Nina a cup with Sylvester the Cat on it, he climbed down off the chair, holding his cup with Tom and Jerry. He opened the fridge and pulled out the brown pitcher of Tang as Nina grabbed cheese balls from the pantry.

"Wanna come over later and watch SNICK at my house?" Nina asked, taking the pitcher from Brett's hands and pouring the orange liquid into both of their cups.

Brett beamed at her, thrilled for the invitation. "Yeah! I'll ask my mom."

"Cool beans."

They sat and drank from their cups. "Knock, knock."

Brett smiled at Nina. "Who's there?"

"Little old lady."

"Little old lady who?"

"Brett, I had no idea you could yodel!"

He opened his mouth to laugh, spilling orange Tang down his chin. Nina pointed at him, cackling loudly, and soon they both were keeled over in hysterics—the way eleven-year-olds tend to do, finding laughter in the mundane.

The laughing led to sighs in order to catch their breaths, their stomachs aching with joy.

"Can we go see the turtle?" Nina asked, her eyes pleading.

Brett shrugged. "Sure."

In Brett's room, Nina went right to the tank on top of his low-standing bureau. She gently tapped on the glass. "Oh, Donatello," she sang, attempting to lure the amphibian from his hiding spot. She clucked her tongue, as if it would listen.

"He's not a dog, Nina," Brett laughed. "He doesn't come when he's called."

"Maybe we should train him," she replied, not taking her eyes off the tank. Brett rolled his eyes playfully. "Oh, look! Here he comes."

They watched as little Donatello swam through the shallow water toward the front side of the tank. Nina gave Brett a proud sort of look. "See, he listens to me."

A loud bang sounded from downstairs, like a door slamming shut, startling the kids. Brett's shoulders tensed, and he sucked in a breath and held the air in his lungs. He could hear his dad's mangled voice yelling something about mud and then came more banging. He let out his breath and stared, wide-eyed at Nina. A calmness took over her face, and for that, he was dumbfounded since his insides rattled like an earthquake. She nodded once at him and took his hand in hers as his breath became panicked. Though he wanted to run and hide, he found himself unable to move, Nina his only source of strength.

"The mud," Brett sputtered. "We tracked mud into the basement. He's pissed." He wanted to cry but held it back. He was too proud, but he should have known that Nina wouldn't judge him for that.

Nina walked to the door, placing her ear up against it, listening intently to what was going on on the other side of the door and down the stairs. "I hear talking," she whispered. "But I can't tell what's being said."

Brett mustered the strength to walk up to the door, and he put his ear up it, too, and listened intently. His thoughts turned to prayers, begging God to quiet the banging, to calm the anger.

"I don't hear anything now," Nina said, turning to face Brett.

Brett nodded his head, agreeing, but no words could leave his lips. But when they could, he said the last thing he wanted to, "I think you should go home."

Nina's eyes darted all over Brett's face, scanning him before she nodded once. "Ok," she whispered. "But you're still coming over tonight, right? I'll make popcorn." Brett noted that there was desperation in her voice.

He knew that she wished he could walk out his door right that minute and be protected under her roof by her parents, who loved her.

"Yeah," he said unconvincingly.

She gave him a closed-mouth smile before pulling him in for a hug. "I'll see you later, B." And with that, she quietly opened the door, and Brett listened as her feet thumped down the stairs and right out the front door. He ran to his window and watched her run across the street and into the safety of her house, and then he breathed a sigh of relief.

An hour later, Laura called Brett down for supper. "Where's Seamus and Dad?" he asked her after sitting down at his usual seat.

Sadness spread across her face, and Brett picked up on it quickly before she forced a smile to try and mask it. "Oh, um, Seamus isn't feeling well, hunny. He turned in early." There was a perkiness in her tone that sounded off. "And your father...he had to run to the hardware store." Laura scooped mashed potatoes onto her fork and took a bite.

Brett was an intuitive kid, and over the last year, he had learned that the *hardware store* was just a code word for the bars his dad frequented. There was a part of Brett that wanted to stay home and keep his mom company, but a bigger part wanted to leave the house and disassociate across the street with Nina and watch *All That.*

Moving his peas around his plate, he asked his mom if he could go over there when he was done. Laura's eyes glossed over, but she smiled at him. "Finish your plate and clean up and you can go over."

Brett beamed. "Thanks, Mom." He shoveled his food into his mouth and cleaned up his plate. He cleaned the dishes in the sink, too, because *saying* thank you was one thing, but Brett had become a child that felt the need to show it, too.

"Can I go now?" Brett asked.

Laura looked around at the sparkling kitchen. She got up and walked to him, ruffling his hair. "You are a good boy, Brett." He smiled, still waiting for her permission. "You can go," she whispered, kissing the top of his head. "Tell Mrs. Jackson to call me when you are heading back so I can watch for you."

"Ok, Mom, adios!"

Without another beat, Brett was running out the front door to the Jackson's, relief flooding him once again.

Winter was bleak that year, sending whipping winds and more snowfall than the Cape had seen in a long while. Locals took advantage of the weather pattern.

Ice fishing on Granite Pond, a small body of water just inland of Carver Road.

Exchanging rollerblades for ice skates on the same pond.

Sledding down the hills of the golf course.

The kids spent hours transforming the end of Carver Road into a snowy fortress with igloos and paths and snowmen. They would all meet in their bulky snow gear and wouldn't retreat back to their warm houses until just before dinner, only unzipping their snowsuits for emergency bathroom breaks.

Mrs. Jackson was keen on delivering mugs of hot cocoa to the kids, while Mrs. Cooper would come out in her slippers, hollering from her porch that there was a fresh batch of cookies, still warm, on the plate in her hand.

After significant snowfalls, the treehouse would be hidden under the branches heavy with snow, with inches of accumulation blown in through the sagging door. But Brett and Nina paid it no mind, acting as if it wasn't even there. They were too distracted by the newness their imaginations glowed with—brand-new adventures in the snow.

One morning in February, the kids sat on the stone wall behind the elementary school, waiting for the bell to ring, talking about all the things sixth graders deemed important.

"I can't believe it. Did you watch it? I gasped! My mom ran in from the kitchen!" Nina's hyper energy got the rest of the girls in the group worked up as the boys looked on in wonderment.

Brett had watched the episode of *Boy Meets World* with Nina at her house on Friday night—his eyes growing wide when Corey kissed Lauren in the ski lodge. But his reaction wasn't anywhere near what Nina's was. *How could he do that to Topanga? What the hell? Do you think this is a dream and not really happening?* Nina's hands had been glued to her cheeks, to her mouth, to the top of her head. She was unable to control her emotions. And Brett had watched her, taking in her reaction like it was something to be studied.

And he did need to study her because he couldn't shake the feeling that with each week that passed, he saw a different version of his best friend—as if she was morphing into someone else entirely right before his eyes.

Well, maybe not entirely.

Nina was still fierce.

Nina still held her own.

Nina still didn't take shit from Timmy Baker, or anyone else for that matter.

But Brett saw more of an outward softening in her that he couldn't quite read. He had always known her heart was soft but the way she put that side of her out into the world was not unnoticed by Brett. And as he watched her going on and on about the betrayal of Corey Mathews and all the girls crowded around her, he realized for the first time ever that Nina was not, in fact, just *one of the boys.* She was now *popular*, fitting in with the boys in the neighborhood and leading the girls in the schoolyard, too.

It didn't worry Brett, though. He didn't even think to be concerned, actually. Because somewhere in the back of his mind, he never thought of imagining a reality where Nina would pull away from him.

Their souls were too entangled—patches sewn together like mismatched quilt squares, unmatching but put together with care.

And it had been like that for as long as he could remember.

When they were in kindergarten, back when the school seemed to engulf the street, swallowing their little bodies up as they entered the doors on that very first day, hearts pounding, Nina was pouting because she forgot her snack. She didn't cry about it like other five-year-olds may have. She furrowed her brows and crossed her arms like the world had wronged her, like she was plotting who to make pay for it.

"You can have some of my snack," Little Brett had said from across the tiny rectangular table. His voice was quiet; he was a bit frightened of her.

Nina's face seemed to relax as she leaned forward a bit. "Fank you!" she smiled a toothless grin.

Brett broke a piece of his Twinkie off and pushed it across the table. Nina reached for it before shoving the whole piece into her mouth.

"I'm Nina. What's your name?" she asked him, her mouth full—a sight that would have made her mother cringe.

"Brett."

"Hi, Bwett! I wiv on Cawvah Road."

"I live on Carver Road!" he beamed. "I just moved there."

Nina gasped. "Across the street fwum me?! New people wiv there now. Is it you?" Nina didn't give Brett even a moment to respond. "You can be my new best fwend."

Brett was thrilled with this new development.

"Knock, knock," Nina said.

"Who's there?"

"Cow says,"

"Cow says who?"

"No, cow says moooo!"

The pair giggled until their teacher told them to clean up their crumbs and head to circle time where they sat beside one another—how they stayed for all the school years that followed.

As the girls gossiped near the wall, Brett bounced the basketball over to Ben Grandsby, and they lollied it back and forth mindlessly. The girls continued to hammer on and on about the comings and goings of *Boy Meets World* before moving on to the other shenanigans from the TGIF lineup over the weekend. Brett pulled his hands into his jacket sleeves, a feeble attempt to warm them from the bitter cold morning wind.

When the bell rang, the classes all gathered in their lines, from kindergarten all the way up to Brett and Nina and their sixth-grade companions. The kids who were no longer swallowed by the building, but more like took it over in their own right. The boys' voices had started to change. Girls were budding into the early stages of puberty. Emotions swirled without a way to wrangle them.

They were outgrowing their school, that was certain. And in a few short months, they would say goodbye to the school that had prepared them for what was coming next. As much as it could, at least. The sixth graders of Harborview Grammar School would soon go from being the queens and kings of the halls to the inexperienced junior high schoolers.

But for now, they felt on top of the world, and the world was their oyster.

Chapter 10

Nina 2016

CONVERSATIONS BETWEEN STRANGERS filled the air as Nina entered the rec center, her workout bag slung over her shoulder. She had pulled her dark hair into a high ponytail, smoothing out the flyaways for a polished look, and was wearing her most favorite athletic attire from her friend Lucy's clothing line. A line Nina carried back at N Bar.

Before leaving her bedroom, she had snapped a selfie in the pants and cropped tank and sent it to Lucy with the words, **With you in spirit! Miss you.**

Lucy most likely wouldn't answer for another day. New York City loved Lucy, and Lucy loved it right back. She'd stay out all hours of the night and wake up with the sun to take in all it had to offer her. And during the little time she was in her apartment, she would inevitably lose her phone between the couch cushions or under her bed.

Nina met Lucy at a yoga conference in Hoboken back in 2009. Nina was working at Stretch, the studio she had started at before venturing out on her own. Lucy was magnetic, and Nina was attracted to her aura right from the start. Lucy was pitching her clothing line to anyone and everyone in the industry, trying to get it to take off. The two had hit it off instantly, their feverish dreams quickly catapulting them into bestie status.

Nina and Lucy were both in their early-twenties then, ready to take life by the horns, as they say. And so, their bond strengthened as they helped each other walk the difficult balance beam of finding themselves while also attempting to prove to the sharks that they, too, had bite.

Not feeling quite as fierce today as she did back when her career was just beginning, Nina straightened her spine to feel more competent in her new role at the rec center. Although her ego had taken a hit recently, Nina knew that, deep down, she was still made of fire and grit. She always had been. And no matter what, that couldn't be undone. She had learned that once before. Learned that she could fall into a pit of darkness, but light could—and *would*—reappear eventually.

Having arrived a bit early, Nina had a few minutes to kill before she needed to head down to the studio, so she stood and eyed the bulletin board near the front desk. Her eyes bobbed over the fliers and business cards, scanning for anything interesting.

Guitar lessons.

Reduced-priced tickets for the high-speed boat for Daffodil Weekend on Nantucket. Nina checked the date, noticing that the weekend had just passed.

And then a flier caught her eye, tugging on her heart a bit, too. *The Osprey Foundation, Volunteers Needed.*

She squinted, trying to get a better look. She pulled off the contact information from the cut tabs at the bottom of the flier and slid it into the pocket on the side of her yoga pants just as Felicia rounded the corner.

"Good morning, Nina! Find anything interesting over there?"

Nina smiled in greeting. "Sort of," she replied. "My mom has been telling me about these ospreys that live around here. I saw this notice on the board." She pointed at the Osprey Foundation notice, and Felicia glanced at it. "Do you know anything about this volunteer stuff?" Nina inquired.

Felicia smiled. "Oh, it's a big deal around here." Nina tipped her head to the side, interested and listening intently. "The birds have been making their huge nests on the telephone poles for years now. Kind of a safety issue because of the fire risk. It's actually happened quite a few times—the nests just catch fire up there." She shook her head.

Nina's brow furrowed. "So, what are the volunteers doing?"

"They're moving the nests off the poles to a safer place. Relocating them if you can believe it." Felicia shook her head, somewhat in awe.

"Wow, that's amazing that people care enough to do that." Nina's voice grew soft as she spoke, eyeing the sign again.

"Like I said, it's a big deal around here. Those birds were almost endangered once, but then they just—"

"Made a comeback." Nina finished Felicia's sentence, recalling a fact that she had long forgotten, stored away with other memories of Brett.

And right then and there—in the hallway of the rec center—she traveled somewhere else entirely. To an abandoned boat she had once turned into her playground, where the salt water lapped poetically against the shore—music to her ears. Where her best friend had told her about these birds being saved as one cast a shadow over them, so large, it blocked their cloud gazing. She instantly went back to a memory she had once folded up neatly and tucked it into the attic of her mind, where it was left abandoned all this time. Never taken out and unfolded. Never visited. Never thought about again.

Nina catapulted back to the present and looked at Felicia, smiling, but all she was really thinking about was: why had she allowed all that sweetness of childhood to turn sour?

"Oh, so you know a little bit about the ospreys, huh?" Felicia mused.

Nina smiled, mostly to herself. "Yeah," she replied. "Like I said, my mom was telling me a little about them the other day. About how they mate for life or something." Nina smiled.

"Yes, they are amazing birds," Felicia added.

As they walked toward the yoga studio, Felicia gabbed about the happenings in town, but Nina only half listened. Because, for the millionth time in the last two days, her thoughts were overcome with Brett.

Her stomach had been flipping in a way it hadn't in a while. The kind of dropping sensation one gets when they're in a dream, about to do a cartwheel off of a tall building, but then they're jerked awake just in time. Imagining how the inevitable encounter with Brett was going to go made Nina feel like she might cry…and Nina didn't cry.

Sometimes, she yelled.

Sometimes, she got angry and didn't hold back.

A lot of times, she felt things so deeply that she assumed the ache was real.

But still, Nina didn't cry.

She hadn't cried since that summer of 2004. She had always assumed that she had used up her lifetime supply of tears back then. Since the events of that summer, nothing had elicited the emotions that could bring about tears.

Not when she graduated college.

Not when she couldn't bring herself to come home to visit.

Not when she had to close down her business.

No. Her tears were all gone. They had all dried up after she killed Danny Warner.

There was only one other person who knew Nina's secret, the secret that had weighed her down since that night like an anchor heavy on the ocean floor.

Brett.

Brett was the keeper of her secret. The only other soul who was there that night, unless you count the fictional Ghost of the Pond. Nina wished there had been an actual ghost so she could blame something else, someone else. Something haunted. Because that is how her life had felt since then, the sun cast out by the shadows that followed her every day—haunted by the ghosts.

For weeks after the horrific event, she had clung to Brett like he was the buoy keeping her afloat. That summer, Nina had only seemed able to breathe while sucking from the tiny bits of Brett's strength. It all crumbled at the end of that summer, and looking back, she tried to put a pin on where exactly their bond had begun to fray, but she wasn't able to see what had severed them for eternity. She couldn't fathom her life without Brett. And when Nina left for UMass, she had never imagined there was no going back. But there she was at college doing just that, barely breathing without the other half of her soul.

All she had wanted on that terrible night was to save Brett but protecting him had cost her. For a long while, this made her regret settle deep inside.

But as the years went on, she chose to accept and forget. Because if it had not been Danny who took his last breath that night, it would have been Brett.

"You alright?"

Felicia's voice summoned Nina back from her thoughts as they stopped at the door to the studio. Nina was unsettled by these flashbacks, remembering why she had chosen not to come back to Harborview for all those years. To relive it was a curse.

"Oh, yeah, I'm good." Nina smiled, attempting to level her breaths, which were either coming in short bursts or not at all, dizzying her.

"Anyways, back to the Osprey Foundation. Are you interested in volunteering? They have meetings over at Town Hall once a month," Felicia informed her.

Nina pondered the thought, brows furrowed, a *yes* escaping her mouth before she even had a chance to realize it. These birds were tugging at her heart for some reason, and she had very little to fill up her time these days.

"I grabbed the information from the flier out front," Nina told Felicia.

Felicia smiled at her. "Great. But I think you will want to talk to Mary Harlow. Her number isn't on that flier. She does a lot for the foundation, but she also works with other animals that you might be interested in. When you're done teaching, stop by my office."

"That would be great, thanks."

Felicia waved to Nina as she walked away. "Good luck, and have fun on your first day!"

Nina chuckled a bit. "Thanks, I'll do that."

And then she took a deep breath and stepped over the threshold of the studio. The dimmed lights calmed her, and the diffuser gave off a hint of orange that helped her relax. It wasn't her own spot, but she was determined to make it home, at least for the time being. And making that happen began with having a positive mindset. Ultimately, she was aware of this truth and knew she had to work to make it a reality.

Placing her bag down at the front corner of the studio, she rested her hands on her hips and took a look around. She wanted to make this introductory level class something special, something unique, a small gesture that would help her feel like she belonged. She looked around, making mental notes of things she wanted to bring into the studio: her water fountain for a soothing ambience, her own essential oils, some large plants, warm, moist towels for sore muscles, and cool towels to use after class. All the things that had been commonplace at N Bar.

When the class attendees began shuffling into the room, bringing an energy that uplifted Nina, she turned on her own energy and greeted people at the door. It wasn't long before she felt comfortable, settling into something that felt natural. For quite some time, yoga had been her saving grace…her gift to a body she had once despised.

One step at a time, Nina.

As class ended, she was excited about how well it had gone. Her body felt fluid and loose, even after not having consistently practiced yoga in a few weeks. She stood at the door, her hands behind her back and a smile on her face, wishing everyone a good day as they left. And to her surprise, she was thrilled when some initiated conversations with her. Nina learned that Juliann insisted on being called Jules and would live in a yoga studio if she could. But of course, she couldn't because she was a mom to a rambunctious toddler. "It's a miracle I even make it here for this class, you know what I mean?" Jules said to Nina, who smiled in agreement, even though she didn't actually know what she meant—Nina being childless with zero responsibilities and all.

"Welcome to Harborview!" said a woman with a straight blonde bob that had become slicked with sweat during the class as she made her way to the door. "You'll love it here!" Her name was Amber, and Nina couldn't bring herself to tell her that she was actually from Harborview, that the better part of her was etched into the air here, and how this little coastal town was part of her and how much she missed it for what it had been *before*.

Nina wasn't what the locals called a "washashore," someone who wasn't 100 percent Cape Codder, born and raised. She was a local who, much to her dismay, had drifted out to sea like wood broken off from an old boat, left to bob in the abyss. As they talked, she learned that Amber was a washashore, though. She was from Virginia and moved to Harborview with her husband, Tim, after they graduated college. At the sound of his name, Nina's ears perked, thinking of Timmy Baker from Carver Road. But she held her tongue. It wasn't the time to ask any questions.

"You have to try Blue over on the harbor. Best swordfish I've ever had!" Amber said.

Nina beamed. "Oh, I've been there! Great lobster mac and cheese, too."

"You're fast! Not wasting any time trying out the hot spots." Amber winked.

The truth was, Nina hadn't been to Blue in the two weeks since she'd been back. However, her mom had ordered take-out from there on one of the first nights she was home—Nina having been in no mood to be out and about.

But Nina knew Blue. She remembered how the navy shutters looked against the worn shingles and how the water looked through the slats of the wood on the dock where she and her parents would sit feeding the seagulls while waiting for a table. She knew the shape of the glass dish at the hostess station that held the after-dinner mints —and what the little mints tasted like when she was walking out after eating a delicious seafood dinner there.

And she even knew the way the gutter hung a tad low on the right side of the roof. She learned this when she stared at the building while slouched in the front seat of the car that belonged to a guy she shouldn't have been dating in high school. Slouched so she wouldn't be seen while he went in to pick up take-out that they ate sitting in his car parked in the lot at East Beach, sharing clam strips and fried scallops dripping with tartar sauce.

"I'll have to try the swordfish next time," Nina offered, smiling.

"You won't regret it," Amber said, shifting her rolled-up yoga mat under her arm. "See you Thursday!" she said as she headed out of the studio and down the hall toward the entrance of the rec center, Nina following behind her and veering toward Felicia's office.

When she reached Felicia's door, she knocked gently, noticing her sitting at her desk on the phone. Felicia gestured for her to come in, holding up her index finger, indicating *one minute*. Nina took a seat on the edge of the chair and waited. When the call ended, Felicia got up and went to sit with Nina.

"Here's the card I was telling you about," she said, handing Nina a simple business card with Mary Harlow's email and number listed in plain black font. And a little logo containing a nest and a bird, she assumed was representative of the osprey. "She is extremely passionate about this cause, that Mary," Felicia said, leaning back against the couch.

"I'm not sure what's drawing me to these birds, but whatever it is, it's strong." Nina let out a laugh louder than she had intended.

"I'm sure Mary will be thrilled to hear from you. She does more than just work with the ospreys, and she appreciates any and all assistance she can get."

"So, you said she works with other animals?" Nina pondered, intrigued.

"Yes. Whales, seals, abused farm animals, you name it, she's got her hands in it."

Nina glanced out the window, a wistful look spreading over her face. "Well, thank you for this," she said as she held up the card. "I'm going to reach out later today and see if there's anything I can do for the organizations she works with."

"That's wonderful." Felicia smiled at her warmly. "How was your first class?"

"It was really smooth," said Nina. "It felt good to get back into what I love. A routine will be good for me, too."

"Perfect. I'm thinking of adding a Saturday morning class to the rotation. Earlier than we usually do, but the demand is there right now, and I think it would be a good addition. It would be a more intermediate-level class. Would that be something you would be interested in?"

Nina's eyes widened, a smile breaking out on her face. "Absolutely! Thank you." She relaxed her shoulders, settling into a comfort that hadn't been there since she'd left New York. "Would it be ok if I brought in some things that were from my studio? I could leave them in the closet and only bring them out for my classes so it's not in anyone else's way." Nina sounded hopeful.

"Of course, and I'm sure you won't need to move them. Bring your things in, and we can see how it works out. I want you to feel comfortable here, Nina."

"I know. And thank you." Nina got up from the chair. "I'm going to head out. See you Thursday!"

"See you then!" Felicia beamed.

Outside the air was warm, and May was starting off as it typically does in Harborview. Warm days that felt chilly when a breeze whipped through the buildings. The kind of weather that usually meant the first sunburns of the season for the locals. Forgetting sunscreen was common on those first few warm days of the season—and skin exposed for the first time all winter seemed to burn quickly.

Instead of heading straight home, Nina decided to stroll down the main street, heading nowhere in particular, when her phone buzzed in her pocket. Pulling it out, she was surprised to see a text from Lucy. Nina laughed to herself at the spew of texts Lucy sent all at once.

Lucy: in spirit isn't good enough, Neen.

Lucy: honestly. How could you just leave me?

Lucy: you should have just let me pay your part of the rent. UGH. I can't do this here without you.

Nina: wow, that was a quick response! I didn't expect to hear from you for at least 24 more hours. Haha

Lucy: come back. Please!!

Nina: I wish. You know that. :(

Lucy: eye friggin roll. Maybe i'll come to the cape this summer to see you

Nina: :) yes please!

Lucy: make friends, nina. Don't stay in a slump.

Lucy: but not better friends than me, of course. HAHA

Nina smiled, in spite of herself.

Nina: promise. Call me sometime this week and we can catch up.

Lucy: <3

Make friends. Could she make that promise? Nina wasn't sure anymore. A skill she had once been quite good at had become a weakness over the years. Personable Little Nina Jackson used to have clout in the neighborhood. She had to or else that little girl wouldn't have survived that lot of boys. Her personality was molded as a direct result of spending so much time with them.

Junior high brought a gaggle of friends, too. Girls, boys, everyone loved Nina.

Everyone.

Even people who maybe shouldn't have.

But, of course, life had taken a turn for Nina, inevitably changing her personality and the way she interacted with others. Guys. Girls. She struggled to connect, unlike she did before the shadows emerged.

There were a few good friends in college, mostly guys, but the connections there were lost almost immediately after graduation. Holding onto people just hadn't seemed important to Nina. What was the point? Her inability to keep a relationship was a direct result of having lost everything once before. Everything that mattered, at least.

It was impossible for her to determine what was still holding her back after all this time. Was it that Brett had slipped away from her? Or was it that she had taken a life, and the guilt made it so she didn't know how to live her own? One thing was certain—nothing felt right.

When she moved to New York City, Nina had it in her mind that it was her new beginning. Determined to start a fresh new life rich with experience, she held onto the word *connect*. It was always at the forefront of her mind, knowing that if she wanted any sort of happiness going forward, she needed to connect with people, to let go of the old Nina—at least the part of her that was covered in shadows. The old Nina, who had learned, from necessity, to shut the world out completely.

And then there had been an inevitable pull away from her parents. And even though it was a must, it didn't make it easier. Nina called frequently and forced her voice to sound normal, like there wasn't sadness hidden there. Their relationship had been dulled out of necessity because Nina wasn't the daughter they thought she was, and that guilt had eaten away at her for the last twelve years.

The way people would see her if they knew the truth…it was a thought Nina simply couldn't bear.

Because Brett knew.

And Brett had left, abandoned her.

She was beginning to think that after what she did, he had realized she wasn't the same person he once thought he loved.

But Lucy didn't know what Nina had done. She didn't know the Nina from *before*.

Lucy was kind and fun and hardworking, so Nina clung to her in desperation.

In order to connect with someone.

In order to not lose herself to the past forever.

A bridge to the future, not to the past.

Though the friendship started off in desperation, Lucy quickly became Nina's best friend. And the relationship was real and deep. But Nina's secrets remained locked behind a door that would never budge because she reasoned that some secrets weren't meant to be shared with anyone. Ever. Even Lucy. So, it stayed buried, the horrible truth. Buried so Nina could pretend it hadn't ruined her and she could try and move on. And this made leaving and going back to Massachusetts utterly gut wrenching for both of them. The idea of being without one another was a reality neither of them wanted to face. As Nina walked aimlessly through downtown Harborview, she contemplated needing to find connection again.

Amber seems nice, she thought to herself. *And maybe Jules would be fun to hang out with.*

These thoughts felt entirely too forced, as if they were what she should have felt but didn't really. Letting people in was just too hard a task—something that was unnatural to her now.

She heaved a sigh, and as she breathed out completely, she heard a voice calling her name.

"Nina! My mom told me you were back!"

Nina turned to see Emma Swanson jogging over to her from the crosswalk, pushing a sleek baby stroller. "Hi, Emma," Nina greeted, trying to suffocate the discomfort taking over.

Emma stood in front of her, beaming a smile of stark white teeth, her light blonde hair pulled into a low bun, her face dewy, cheeks slightly pink as if they were recently pinched. She wore athleisure wear, by way of looking like she worked out but most likely didn't. Nina mentally noted that she looked just as she had back in high school. Poised. Effortlessly put together. Moving as if she was floating down the sidewalk rather than walking. Emma had always been a bit shallow and into her appearance.

And as Emma approached her on the sidewalk, scenes from their adolescence danced in Nina's head—enemies to friends, to frenemies, and back to friends again—until they were simply nothing, which Nina blamed herself for, of course. And now, here they were, reuniting as Nina desperately tried to steady her thoughts and her beating heart.

Another piece of her past coming to greet her.

"It's great to see you! How are you doing?" Emma's perkiness instantly drained Nina. But she smiled back at her.

"I'm good. It's great to be back. Just settling in."

"Oh, I'm sure it's a trip to be back after all this time! Everything is almost exactly the same, huh? Does it feel like you traveled back in a time machine?" Her laugh was loud, startling Nina.

Nina nodded her head. "Uh, yeah. It brings back a lot of memories."

"And what are you doing while you're back here? My mom mentioned you were a yoga instructor or something?"

It was masked in pleasant curiosity, but Nina heard the pretentiousness clear as the cloudless Harborview sky—like being a yoga instructor was so far beneath Emma.

Nina took a deep breath. "Yeah, I had my own studio in New York. I'm teaching a few classes over at the rec center for the time being," she said nonchalantly and shrugged her shoulders, hoping the conversation was just about over. "And what have you been up to?" Nina smiled down at the sleeping baby in the stroller.

"Oh, I'm home with this little one right now," she answered, beaming. "This is my daughter Marley; she's ten months old."

"She's adorable," Nina said.

"She is—keeps me on my toes, that's for sure!"

Nina couldn't help but notice the forcedness in Emma's tone. "Ok, well—" she was ready to end this conversation.

"We should grab a drink soon! How about tonight? Landon—that's my husband—will be home early from work!" Emma sounded manic, her voice rising.

Nina's eyes widened as she panicked, desperate to come up with an excuse, but, unfortunately, words were elusive to her. "Uh. Um. Sure!" She regretted it as soon as the words came out of her mouth.

"Great!" Emma glanced around the street before pointing to a door, its outline painted a pale purple. "Let's go there. They have great strawberry basil martinis."

Nina looked at the purple door and then up at the sign that said Lilac Bouquet. "Sounds like a floral shop," was what came out of her mouth.

Emma laughed again. "I know. But it's not. It's a tiny little bar; you'll like it."

Nina couldn't help but agree. *Tiny little bars* reminded her—immensely—of all the joints she and Lucy had found throughout the years. Bars where they would slip in and pretend to be different people, oftentimes with fake, botched accents, ordering cosmopolitans and giggling into their first sips. The flashes of memories seemed so foreign to Nina. *Was that real? Was that really me?* Because New York had done what she needed it to do. It gave her a new identity. It helped her forget her past. And she couldn't help but think that it was another lifetime.

"Ok. Sure." Nina knew that she didn't have anything on her calendar for this evening and warmed up to the idea. She agreed to meet Emma right here on the sidewalk at seven. They waved goodbye, and she headed back toward her mother's car at the rec center. Downtown Harborview had provided her with enough excitement for the afternoon and going home to recharge seemed like the best use of her time.

A night on the town was the last thing Nina pictured herself doing today, but she thought she better start somewhere.

Back at 2 Carver Road, Nina decided to do something she knew she needed—a reset. She sat in the oversized chair in her bedroom, her feet up on the ottoman, and cracked open an old paperback she found lodged on the bookshelf in her parent's living room.

Summer Sisters by Judy Blume.

It wasn't long before she fell asleep right there on the chair. She was entirely unbothered by the sun coming through the slats of the blinds, shining directly on her face. Sleep came over her in a wave, and she let it, allowing herself to sink into oblivion.

When she awoke, she felt refreshed in a way she hadn't since she'd been home. The morning and early afternoon had given her some hope.

Another class was added to her schedule.

The idea that she was the tiniest bit interested in getting out of the house for something other than work.

And the possibility of volunteering with animals—something she was very interested in.

She got up from the chair and stretched her arms over her head, thinking about the card Felicia had given her. Pulling it out of her purse, she examined it for a second time before sitting down at the desk in the room.

She opened her laptop and tapped the keys without pressing them, thinking of what to say. Settling on a few simple sentences, Nina sent the email to Mary.

Hi Mary!

My name's Nina, and I work over at the rec center. I saw the flier for the Osprey Foundation, and I'm interested in learning more about the work you do. Felicia gave me your card. Look forward to hearing back from you!

Sincerely,

Nina Jackson

Nina parked her mom's car at the lot on the north side of town. Stepping out of the vehicle, she smoothed down her shirt and pulled her jeans up around her hips before she began walking. *It feels good to dress up a bit,* Nina had thought as she pulled a white shirt out of her closet, one that had frills on the sleeves and an open back.

She arrived in town a bit early, giving herself plenty of time to walk that end of the street, something she had yet to do since she'd arrived back in

Harborview. There was Dicky's Hardware store on the corner lot of the main street. Nina noted the trim color was the same as it was way back when, a soft blue, some chips nicked into the paint. Nina could almost still smell the inside, having been there so many times with her dad for quick trips to get nails or fishing wire, buckets and rakes. It had always smelled of mower gasoline and soil, a smell she could recall so vividly, even out here on the sidewalk all these years later. She smiled to herself, the sweet memory delighting her.

Nina continued up the road in the direction of the rec center and Lilac Bouquet, passing a toy shop called The Secret Garden, which had been there since before the Jacksons moved to town in the 80s. A wooden *Closed* sign hung in the window, so Nina shielded the sides of her face and peered into the dark room, prickles pulling at her skin.

From what she could see, it was still the same as she remembered. The floors looked like planks from a pirate ship. The back was covered in a blanket of darkness, but right at the entrance was a tower with a variety of bins containing different toys. She couldn't see them from the door, but the image brought a memory of the toys that used to be there: plastic fish of all different colors that could squirt water, pinwheels, boxes of Whipper Snappers, bubble gum. The sweetness of these memories from *before* was causing a warmth to bloom in her chest, something she had not expected.

Because so much she had forgotten.

When a memory isn't triggered often and it isn't revisited, it gets buried deep in the subconscious mind. And new memories take their place, the not-so-great ones, in Nina's case. The goodness of her childhood had been snuffed out by the darkness that came after those precious, happy years. But there was a softness lingering over her now with the sweet memories being activated. And Nina was realizing that if you're lucky, the good moments can come back.

Nina walked along, looking down at her feet, remembering a time when she and Brett had turned left out of The Secret Garden, heading in this same direction. They looked down at their feet as they threw Whipper

Snappers at the ground with reckless abandon—each pop eliciting a laugh from both of them.

Carefree laughter.

The laughs of childhood.

Brett.

Sooner or later, she would have to see him. Every time her thoughts wandered in an attempt to devise a plan to try and talk to him, her mind would simply freeze. For so long, talking to Brett had seemed like something that she'd never do again. And the fact that they were living right across the street from one another didn't seem like a reality Nina could trust. It seemed entirely too good to be true. Too perfect, the strings of fate plucked in just the right fashion. So, she didn't let herself trust it. Instead, her mind took her to other places when all she wanted to do was crawl up into the treehouse with a flashlight and for Brett to be waiting there to tell her a ghost story. Like nothing had ever happened and everything was still the same between them. How she had missed him over all these years. Her heart broke for their friendship and the way things once were and the way things had turned out instead.

Nina looked up at the sky, a feeling of sadness beginning to take over, a feeling she needed to suffocate if she was going to make it through these martinis with Emma.

Upon entering Lilac Bouquet, Nina glanced around. The little bar hadn't always been there, at least not that she remembered. The room was rather dark, with dim light sweeping through the space, looking like it was aglow with candlelight. Miniscule twinkle lights hung around the bar like tiny fireflies. The bar was a light-colored wood with a glossy sheen that glistened under the dull lights.

A few booths lined the wall, and some high-top tables were sprinkled through the area. The upholstery was a light purple, of course, and simple chandeliers hung from the ceiling. It didn't look like Harborview inside that little bar, Nina noted with a quizzical expression. There was absolutely nothing nautical about it. No anchors, no pictures of ships at sea, no buoys.

It was posh, and to Nina, it almost felt like she was in New York City again, a feeling she welcomed.

"Nina! Over here!"

Nina looked over to the end of the bar to see Emma waving her down, a half-drunk martini resting in front of her. She was wearing dark-washed skinny jeans and a flowy black blouse, her wavy hair cascading down her shoulders.

Nina pulled out the plush bar stool, smiling at Emma, before hopping up on the seat. "Hi."

"Hi! I'm so glad you could make it. I'm sorry, I already ordered one; I got here a little early. When I get a night out alone, I gotta take advantage." Emma laughed at her own joke.

"No problem," Nina responded, catching eyes with the bartender—a young man with flowy bangs and a pointed nose.

"I'm Russ. Welcome to Lilac Bouquet; here's a drink menu. Let me know if you have any questions," Russ said, sliding a cocktail napkin in front of Nina.

"Thanks, but I think I'll just have what she's having," Nina said, motioning to Emma's martini glass. "It looks good."

"Oh, you won't regret that choice, right, Russ," Emma said, smiling at the bartender.

"Best martini on the Cape," he said with a wink as he pulled out the materials he needed to make the concoction. "Muddled strawberries and fresh basil? Can't go wrong there."

Nina lifted her brows. She couldn't disagree and looked forward to tasting it.

"So, Landon, your husband, he's home tonight? Does he work a lot?" Nina asked, glancing at the side of the menu that listed a variety of small plates. She remembered that earlier Emma had been ecstatic at the prospect of leaving the house for the evening.

Emma took a sip from her glass, rolling her eyes over the top. "Yes, he commutes to Boston three to four days a week, and on the days he works from our home office, he considers the time he's saving on the commute as extra work hours." She shook her head, displeased. "Rather than extra family hours." Another sip, accompanied by a nervous sort of laugh.

Nina felt like she should sympathize and say sorry or something of the sort, but she had only exchanged a handful of words with this woman in the last twelve years, and she didn't want things to get heavy. But she couldn't think of any other response. "Oh, I'm sor—"

Emma cut Nina off with a flick of her wrist, a universal sign that it was no big deal. "Enough about me! How are things with you since you just up and vanished, leaving us all to the dust!" Another laugh. "Did you travel the world? See some cool, exotic things?" Emma wiggled her eyebrows.

Another sip.

Nina made a questioning face. "What? Uh, no." She dragged out the word. *What gossip has the town been spreading?* Nina wondered. Jet setting? Exotic? Her time since leaving Harborview was far from that. She looked at Emma, who seemed desperate for something interesting, anything to distract her from the mundane life she had settled into.

Nina took a breath as Russ placed her drink in front of her. "Enjoy," he said with a charming smile.

"Thank you." Nina pulled the dainty glass closer to herself and brought it up to her lips, taking a sip. It was slightly frothy, with fresh pieces of strawberry and basil floating through the light pink liquid. She closed her eyes in enjoyment. "Mmmm."

"So good, right?" Emma said.

Nina took another sip. "Amazing." With that, she leaned against the back of the bar stool and relaxed her shoulders. "So, anyway, I'm sorry to disappoint you, but I don't really have anything interesting to share about the last decade or so."

Emma's face turned into a playful pout. "Nina, please." Her eyes were filled with doubt, not believing Nina. "Tell me what you've been up to! Even if it's boring to you. I went to school at URI and then came back here practically married at twenty-two. Now THAT'S boring." She giggled at her own expense, and Nina began to wonder how many martinis Emma had actually had before she'd arrived.

"Ok. Let's see, short story short: I went to UMass, moved to New York City, and lived on ramen and cereal for years in a space barely bigger than a bathtub, which, I know, is completely cliche. I worked at a yoga studio called Stretch for three and a half years while I worked to open my own place. In 2013, I opened N Bar, which I ran for about three years." Nina's shoulders slumped, her mouth tipping into a frown. She looked up from her drink to see Emma leaning close, hanging on her every word. "And then I lost it." The last sentences came through her mouth so softly that Emma barely heard. "And now, I'm back here, having yet to determine what's next for me." Nina took a long sip from her glass, leaving only a bit left at the bottom. She held up her glass, motioning Russ for another. An Uber home was certainly in her future.

"Oh, me too, Russ," Emma said. "You're so brave." As Emma said this, her eyes glistened with tears. Nina's brows furrowed in confusion. Brave? She felt anything but. "Don't make that face." Emma shook her head. "You did something scary, not knowing what would happen. It's more than we can say for most of the people in this town. So many of us all came back or never flew away, even for a little bit. You and Brett. You are the only two I can think of who actually ventured away from this corner of the planet."

Russ placed the two new martinis in front of them on top of fresh cocktail napkins.

"Well, thanks, I guess," Nina finally responded.

"In my opinion, what you did is infinitely better than what I did," Emma said, taking a sip from her drink. She put her hands to her mouth, ready to tell a secret. "Ya know? Settling," she whispered. Nina didn't respond right away, and so Emma continued. "Everyone thinks I have the perfect life. I live in a beautiful house close to the water and I get to stay home with my daughter—who I love more than anything, don't get me wrong—but I feel like a shell of the person I could have been."

Nina hadn't expected the conversation to be going in this direction. It all felt like too much, too fast, and she wasn't sure how she felt about it. She hadn't talked to Emma at all in the last twelve years and didn't know her anymore. She didn't feel like she cared, either. But looking at Emma's face, into her eyes, made Nina feel a bit sad for her.

At Harborview Grammar School, Emma was Nina's nemesis. Nina despised her and her upturned nose and her snide remarks. In junior high, Emma softened a tad, much to Nina's surprise. Her mother had warned her that those years took place in the trenches, and she needed to buckle up. And she had needed a seat belt…and a helmet…but not because of Emma. Then, in high school, they were friends; the animosity about bike parades and other childish nuances was so far in the rearview mirror, it was like they hadn't even happened. They played on the same lacrosse team and got along fine, forgetting their childhood feuds and building a friendship.

And then Nina left, as many of them did after that summer, off to college. But when everyone trickled back into town after graduation, after having tasted a bit of the air outside Harborview, Nina (and Brett) was nowhere in sight.

Apparently, according to Emma, Nina was out being brave, and Nina pondered this with another sip of her martini. They say the grass isn't always greener, and Emma was proving that right now, her expressions and tears showing Nina that her seemingly perfect life was more of an illusion than anything.

"I'm sorry," Nina muttered, unsure of what to say.

Emma wiped away a stubborn tear that was making its way down her cheek. "It's ok," she replied, though it didn't sound like the truth. "I never thought I would be a trophy wife," she laughed through a sob, and Nina cringed. "My husband likes me on his arm, but that's about it." Her voice turned away from the lightness that she was attempting to portray to one riddled with sadness. And the tears came down in a steadier stream.

Nina leaned over the bar to grab a dry napkin and handed it to Emma. "Here," she said sympathetically.

"Thanks," Emma mustered.

Emma and Nina exchanged looks for a moment, Nina offering a soft smile as a sort of mutual understanding settled over them. An understanding that they had traveled different paths and ended up experiencing different things. Neither of them was better nor worse off than the other.

"Can we hang out more?" Emma asked, hopeful.

"Sure," Nina nodded. "I'd like that." And she thought her words might be true, a realization that felt promising. Flashes of their high school friendship skimmed across her brain, reminding her of what Emma once was to her.

"Landon and I hang out with Tim and his wife, Amber, once in a while…when we can get a sitter. Do you remember Tim?"

Nina laughed loudly, the martini going to her head. "Yeah, I remember Timmy. And the many times I roughed him up as a kid!" Emma laughed at that. "And I actually just met Amber. She was in my yoga class today. She mentioned her husband's name, and I wondered if it was the same Tim."

"Sure is," Emma said. "He owns a few restaurants across the Cape now. He and Landon get along really well, and Amber's nice. Can't believe he got a ring on a girl that great." Nina and Emma both laughed at that.

Nina guessed that Emma's comment meant Tim hadn't changed much since high school; once a meathead, always a meathead.

"What about Brett? Do you still talk to him?" Emma asked.

Nina stared at Emma blankly for a beat. "Um—"

Her attempt to respond was cut off by Emma, "We all thought the two of you were destined to end up together for all eternity." Her tone was light and jovial.

"Are you hungry?" Nina asked, picking up the menu again in complete avoidance. "Some of these small plates sound good."

"So, that's a no, I take it," Emma said, smirking.

"Yes. And a hard one at that. Russ, excuse me," Nina said, her finger in the air, summoning him over. "Can I have, um, one more of these and an order of the Buffalo wontons?"

"Coming right up."

Nina turned back to Emma sheepishly, hoping she was drunk enough to have moved on from the question at hand.

But much to Nina's dismay, she hadn't. She was sitting there waiting, eyes wide with inquisitiveness. "So, what's the story there?"

Chapter 11

Brett 2016

Dusk was settling over Harborview as Brett made his way toward Chapel, a formerly well-known dive bar recently renovated by some new owners. Tucked behind a coffee shop on the far end of the main street, Chapel was a bit inconspicuous.

Brett had never been, having left when he was only eighteen, but he remembered all the times in high school he had walked by it while dilly-dallying with his friends, playing Truth or Dare, or simply loitering, the way kids do. He could recall the smokey smell that billowed out of the place and the cast of characters who would enter, or stumble out, too.

When Johnny suggested they meet there, Brett was surprised. *Chapel? That dingy place?* he had wondered to himself. However, he was pleasantly surprised as he approached the modern door where two sconces glowed on either side, giving off a golden hue, like candles in a breeze. Brett immediately knew that Chapel had changed.

Pulling open the door brought a loud hum of music and conversation to Brett's ears as he stepped over the threshold, scanning the place for Johnny. It didn't take long before he spotted him in the middle of the bar area, the last remaining empty seat beside him.

Brett headed that way. "Johnny Cooper, look at you!" he exclaimed boisterously over the loud hum of the bar.

Johnny turned, beaming. "Brett Warner! My long-lost mate!"

They embraced lovingly, like they meant it. As if their friendship had simply paused for a moment, not missing a beat. Brett noted the twelve years of aging in Johnny—broader, taller, with a beard that trimmed his face with precision.

A ring on his left hand.

"Look at you, Mr. Big Shot Texan," Johnny joked. "Looking good," he added, grabbing Brett's shoulders.

Brett did look good; that was true. Light sandy brown hair, tall, with an athletic build. Light green eyes that the girls in Texas called "cowboy eyes," which always caused Brett to blush.

Brett let out a husky laugh. "Good to see you, man. It's been way too long." They took seats at the bar and began the process of catching up.

"First round is on me," Johnny said, slamming his hand on the bar in celebration. "We're ordering, and then I need to hear all about what you've been up to, man." He shook his head, almost in awe, like he couldn't believe that his old friend was sitting beside him.

Brett didn't know that down the road, just past The Secret Garden, sat Nina with Emma Swanson—doing the same thing, catching up after being away far too long.

With thoughts of each other not far from their minds.

"Hey, there, John," the bartender said. "What can I get you, gentlemen?"

"Blue Moon for me," Johnny replied, turning to look at Brett.

"What's good on tap?" he asked, looking behind the bar. Before anyone could give him a suggestion, he said, "Actually, I'll have the Cape Cod IPA back there."

"Great beer," Johnny said, swiveling the bar stool to face Brett.

"I'll be right back with those."

"Thanks, Terri," Johnny said. "Hey, how's your mom?"

"Oh, she's ok," Terri answered. "Thanks for asking, doll. You're sweet." Terri's Boston accent was thick, and it sounded a bit familiar to Brett, but, for the life of him, he couldn't place her. She walked away to fill their orders.

"You remember Terri?" Johnny asked softly.

Brett shook his head. "She seems familiar, but I can't figure out how I know her."

"She worked in the cafeteria when we were in high school, her mom—"

"Ginny Blake," Brett said, finishing Johnny's sentence.

"Yup." Johnny nodded. "Our ice cream queen." He let out an endearing laugh.

"Is something wrong with her mom? Is Ginny ok?" Brett asked quietly, glancing around the bar to make sure Terri wasn't within earshot.

Johnny gave a tight, sympathetic smile before responding. "She had a few strokes last year. She struggles to walk and talk." He stopped and shook his head. "Terri takes care of her. Brings her into my office for physical therapy."

A frown pulled at Brett's mouth, sadness settling inside of him. "Oh, no. That's really sad," he offered, looking up at Terri, who was laughing with someone sitting at the other end of the bar while she filled a glass with his IPA.

"It is," Johnny said. "But the two of them have always looked on the bright side. Ginny was still driving that ice cream truck up until the first stroke hit her." He laughed at this. "Can you believe that?"

Honestly, Brett couldn't. A beacon of his childhood that he had assumed was no longer had just gone on while he was away, like nothing had changed. Moments of a time long gone played on a reel in his mind for a moment, as if he was transported back to those hot summer days right from the bar.

The clinking of the music from the truck.

The smell of the sweet treats.

The taste of the delicious ice cream, the perfect cold treat on a hot day.

The feeling of safety among friends on the street.

"Here you go, boys," Terri said, placing the drinks in front of them.

"Thanks," Johnny and Brett said in unison.

"Terri, this is Brett; we grew up together. He remembers your mom pretty fondly," Johnny said with a smile, taking a sip of his beer. "Ginny was our savior every summer afternoon."

Terri smiled, appreciating the sentiment. "I thought I recognized you," she said, pointing at Brett. "But you're quite grown up since your years of getting mashed slop in the lunch line." A hardy laugh escaped her.

Brett laughed, too. "Yup, I'm an old man now." He took a sip of his beer.

Terri rolled her eyes in jest. "It's a privilege, is what it is," she said with a wink. "Ya know? Getting old."

"That's for sure!" Johnny said.

"I'll be in with Mom tomorrow afternoon, John. Her appointment is at two-thirty."

"Yeah! I'm looking forward to seeing her progress since last week."

Terri gave Johnny a warm sort of smile. "Well, you two enjoy those cold ones. I'll be around if you need anything."

"Thanks so much," Brett said.

And then the two settled into a comfortable sort of conversation. The kind that flows with someone who truly knows you. Well, most of you. Because Johnny didn't know everything, and Brett planned to make sure that he, and everyone else for that matter, never did know.

Not the secrets.

Definitely not the dark ones. The ones hidden beneath the shadows that haunted him.

Brett filled Johnny in on what he'd been doing, giving him the CliffsNotes version—the fun parts, the bachelor stories, a brief synopsis of his job. He said it all with a happy sort of wistfulness. Because Brett's life truly made him happy. Recalling memories from Texas was reminding him that he had a home to return to when Harborview inevitably sucked him dry. Because he knew it would. It was only a matter of time. He could already feel it…the completely unsettled feeling in his chest and the inability to think clearly or take a full breath.

Johnny went on to tell Brett about UConn. He told him how he met his wife, Erica, who started out as a good friend—their friendship blooming into something more while they shared an aisle on the airplane flying to the Florida Panhandle for spring break their last year with twenty-five of their friends. Friends who were pretending they wouldn't be leaving college in a few short months, hanging on to the last bits of the freedom they so relished.

Johnny's parents still lived on Carver Road, and he and his wife owned a condo on Granite Pond.

"We live the good life," Johnny said, sipping his beer. "We do. Nothing like pulling the kayaks into the pond on a Sunday morning before the last of the morning fog lifts."

"That's deep, man," Brett joked, causing Johnny to laugh.

"Shut up, dude!" Johnny shook his head in good fun. "But yeah, you're right. I have turned into a simpleton." More laughs erupted from both of them. "We aren't really sure yet if we want kids," a shrug accompanied his words as he looked around the bar. "So, right now, we enjoy just doing whatever we want, whenever we want."

"That's great for you. I think more people should follow their own paths. Not the one they think they are supposed to follow."

"Now who's deep?"

Brett smiled into his beer mug, lines forming at the corners of his cowboy eyes.

The evening continued, two long-lost friends rekindling a bond with an ease that surprised both of them. When they left for the night, they shook hands that ended in a hug, each of them holding on for an extra beat.

"Don't be a stranger," Johnny said. "Let me talk to Erica, and we'll pick a day to have you over for steamers on the deck."

"That sounds perfect," Brett replied before strolling down the main street in the opposite direction of his car. He looked in familiar windows, smiling to himself at the images that flashed in his mind. He looked in unfamiliar windows, too, finding new gift shops, a used bookstore, and a surf shop, where skimboards hung ornamentally in the windows beside mannequins in bright Billabong swimsuits.

As he thought about the evening, he found himself pleasantly surprised at the ease with which Johnny and him had reconnected, as if no time had passed. It comforted him some. One positive of leaving his Texas life behind and coming back home.

When Brett had originally moved to Texas for school, he had worried about making friends. He wondered if he even knew *how* to make friends. Carver Road friendships had just become part of who he was over the years. He didn't even remember meeting the kids from the block; they were just a given due to location and proximity. And it was as if their bonds had just organically solidified into a cohesive group. Those friends had made junior high and high school easier for him, too. But college? He headed there alone. No Johnny or Ricky. No Timmy Baker.

No Nina.

And that had been the hardest loss for him to grapple with. He had blamed Nina at first, though he knew deep down that none of it was her fault. But he also blamed himself back then, and still, to this day, he was riddled with guilt. In truth, there was no one to blame but himself for losing Nina. But, although he knew it was his fault for the rift in their relationship, he didn't know why he'd allowed it to be eternal. It was as if, through the passage of time, an invisible door had sealed shut between them. Truthfully, he felt like a coward now when he thought about it; he knew he had run away without looking back. It had been selfish; he knew that now.

The worst part about the whole thing was that Brett knew Nina to her core. And so, he knew—deep down—that she had spent the last twelve years doing anything but blaming him. She blamed herself; of this, Brett was sure. And he resented himself for allowing that to happen.

In Texas, Brett had used this loss as motivation to desperately try and fill the void. New friends meant distractions that he really needed. And making new friends came surprisingly easy to him. But all the while, he had one thought in the back of his mind…

Nina will be there when I'm ready to go back.

But that thought became flawed and less believable as time passed. Because he never looked back to see what he had left in his wake. After a while, he stopped believing in the safety of Nina. How could he rely on her to be there when he wasn't there for her? As the years passed, the possibility of fixing everything seemed nearly impossible.

Until now.

Now, Nina was so close. This was a fact he knew but also one he felt. He felt her…

In the breeze coming off the harbor.

In the flap of the gulls' wings overhead.

He saw her…

In the treehouse every time he looked out his window.

In the shapes the clouds made as they moved across the sky.

In the scar on his finger.

Walking out of the bar on the other side of the main street.

Wait, what was that? he thought. Was he really seeing her, or was he just imagining it? Brett abruptly stopped as he realized it was her. And then he stood there, frozen. He watched Nina as she smiled and hugged Emma Swanson on the sidewalk. He watched her as she stood there, looking at her phone, until a car came and picked her up.

It was only when the Uber was out of sight that Brett finally took a breath, running his hands through his hair, frustrated. When he finally snapped out of the trance he was in, he reasoned that here on the side of the main street was, in fact, not the right spot for their reunion. After shoving his hands in his pockets, he turned on his heel and swiftly headed toward his car. He knew he should just get back to Carver Road and knock on the Jackson's door.

As he walked, daydreams flooded Brett's mind. In his mind, he knocked on their door and Nina came, opening it, and they embraced. He imagined her falling into his arms, into the spaces she fit best, and hugging her until it was all ok. That it would be as if no time had passed between them and all was water under the bridge.

But he shook his head, knowing he wouldn't do that. That steel door between them was too heavy a burden to budge.

As Brett entered the house through the garage, he half expected to find his father asleep in the recliner like he always did back in the day and Laura and Seamus off hiding behind closed doors upstairs, anything to not be seen.

But no, Danny Warner was long gone. And Brett knew that all too well.

"Who's there?" He heard Seamus's voice barreling through the house, his footsteps coming in heavy toward the kitchen.

"It's just me," Brett announced as Seamus entered the kitchen, a bat held up, ready to swing.

"Dude, it's ok. It's just me. Everything's fine." Brett's voice was meant to be soothing, but it didn't seem to calm Seamus down much. His shoulders relaxed, though, if only slightly; the scowl on his face remained as he lowered the bat slowly.

And Brett's heart crumbled a bit at the sight of his brother. His wounded brother with his PTSD on full display. There it was, staring right back at him, another reason that Brett was riddled with guilt.

Another person he'd abandoned.

A person he'd abandoned who had only tried to protect him.

It settled in the marrow of Brett's bones right then and there—shame. That was the feeling he had been unable to identify recently. The heaviness that he was carrying around maiming his psyche. In the process of running away from his nightmares all those years ago, he'd left the people who needed him the most in the shadows.

Shame.

It was an ugly feeling. And looking into Seamus' pitiful eyes made it all the more sufferable. He needed to make it right. But how?

"Watching anything good in there?" Brett asked softly, the olive branch hanging desperately between them.

Seamus narrowed his eyes. "Sox game just ended," he said. "I turned it off."

Brett nodded. "Want to sit in there and hang for a bit?"

Seamus's eyes scanned the kitchen, darting to the bottles of whiskey and wine. Brett's gaze looked to where Seamus was looking, and he attempted to steer his brother back to the living room without a tumbler of alcohol, stepping toward the living room, hoping Seamus would just follow him.

"I need a smoke. Want to sit on the deck?" Seamus's voice was hollow, with no life behind it at all.

Brett pursed his lips, turning toward the sliding glass door and stepping over the threshold.

The night air was balmy, smelling of sea salt and Brett pulled a deep breath through his nose as he approached the patio table. The deck furniture had changed while Brett had been away. The white vinyl table and chairs set that had been splattered with black mold and dirt had been replaced with a heavy, dark, wrought iron set. The patterned cushions that had long faded by his senior year were now replaced with plush cushions with navy and white stripes. Brett noted that it seemed like no one had sat on them before as he pulled a chair out from the table. A thought that saddened him, though he wasn't sure why.

"Is it everything you imagined it would be?" Seamus asked, not looking at Brett as he lit his cigarette and pulled a long drag into his lungs.

"What?" Brett asked.

"Coming back to this shithole?" Seamus blew smoke into the air, and the smell made Brett feel like he was going to vomit up his IPA onto the deck.

Was it what he imagined? He guessed it kind of was. The way he had been unsettled since arriving on this side of the Bourne Bridge, straight down to his bones. The way that he hadn't felt like he had come home at all; there wasn't any comfort or ease in his return. Things had changed just enough to feel a bit foreign while also changing so little that it was almost eerie.

Which is exactly what he was expecting.

Nothing soothing.

Nothing welcoming.

"Actually, yeah," Brett said with a smirk, knitting his hands behind his head and leaning back, relaxing into the chair. Seamus offered a closed-mouth smile, a sign to Brett that he was letting his guard down, even if just a little. "But I wouldn't call Harborview a shithole, man."

Seamus turned his gaze toward Brett, narrowing his eyes while sucking on his cigarette, and Brett eyed him, waiting for a response.

"Sometimes the prettiest things are actually the ugliest."

"Is Harborview worse than war, Seamus?" Brett's tone was soft but probing a bit. "Especially a Harborview without Danny?"

They held each other's gazes for longer than what could be deemed comfortable until Seamus shifted in his seat, leaning over the table toward Brett. "Harborview. Massachusetts. The country in general. It's all ugly."

Brett started to realize that the PTSD was talking, and he wanted to be there for his brother. "What do you mean?" he asked.

"You're lucky you don't know what I'm talking about." Another drag. "People here think their problems are actual problems. That the signs they put up at the end of Pontiac Street are the worst things to happen to this town. That the paving of the beach road around the corner is blasphemy. Enough so that they picket outside of town hall." Seamus shook his head in disgust. "Can you believe that?" He pointed a finger at Brett. "And those signs were put there to protect people. It's entitlement, is what it is."

"Sounds kinda pointless to me," Brett replied. His response was honest, but he cared more about his brother feeling connected to him. A common grievance shared.

"Pointless, yes. Because who cares?" Seamus turned and looked out onto the surface of the pond. "If these people had seen even a day's worth of what I saw over there." He shook his head in disbelief like he was trying to shake away the images. He turned back to Brett and looked him straight in the eyes. "If they had to carry their friend across land mines…a friend who was bleeding out. If they had stumbled and were unable to make it back in time to save them, or if they had to see innocent women and children dying, then maybe they would fucking have something to complain about." The last words came through clenched teeth, choked out over a gargling throat.

Brett tried to settle his breathing despite his brother's admission.

The horror.

The pain.

He couldn't imagine it.

"Fuck, Seamus. I can't even imagine what that was like." Tears pricked the side of Brett's eyes. He hated himself for turning away from Seamus all this time and being unable to be there for him now.

"Well, this will make you feel better," Seamus said in a matter-of-fact tone. "I'd take war over Danny Warner any day. What does that tell you?"

Brett sucked in a breath. "What?" The word was whispered, mostly to himself.

"Yup." Seamus nodded, sure of himself and his statement. "Rather fight against a known enemy than fight against the one person who is supposed to love you most. That shit fucks you up."

Brett didn't have any words. Because he knew that the war had tangled Seamus's mind and wrapped it into a knot that was proving difficult to untangle. And Brett knew the truth in Seamus's words. Because Danny Warner had ruined him, too.

"And you know what? The people of Harborview turned their eyes away from us, man. Couldn't be bothered to help us, the kids maimed right in front of their faces." Brett slowly nodded his head as if realizing the truth right at that moment. "See? Harborview…it's ugly."

And with that, it wasn't the nicotine that was nauseating Brett any longer. It was the realization of the hard truth after all this time. That no one had cared enough to look a little deeper into what was going on with the Warner's. No one except Nina.

Chapter 12

Brett 1998-1999

WALKING THE HALLS OF Seaview Regional Junior High School was a trip for the seventh graders; they were awestruck—their eyes wide with wonder. It's like they were all back in kindergarten—the nervousness and unease, the walls seeming to swallow them up once again. Brett wondered how a school with only two grades could feel so vast, but it did, and it unsettled him some.

But his heart also swelled with the excitement that the change brought. A change he hadn't realized he needed.

"Are you going to do a sport this year?" Johnny asked Brett one chilly October afternoon. The kids were waiting on the bus, which was running late.

Brett shrugged, pondering the question. Little League had been fun—for the most part—and he had always imagined playing in high school. "Probably baseball in the spring. You?" He kicked a rogue stone off the sidewalk and into the road.

"Yeah, I'll try out with you in the spring. But I think I want to try basketball. Want to go with me? Tryouts are next week." Johnny sounded hopeful, his eyes wide, as he attempted to convince his best friend to try out with him.

Brett smiled at Johnny. "Ok, cool."

When the bus dropped them off, the kids of Carver Road would shuffle off and congregate, their hangout location entirely dependent on the weather and their moods. This afternoon, the air had grown cold quickly, and the kids gathered in Johnny's driveway before heading straight for the basement—a room entirely designed for preteens. Johnny Cooper's house was a warm and inviting place to Brett, way better than dropping his backpack off at his own house, if he was being honest.

All the things kids loved in one location.

A ping pong table.

A vintage Pac-Man arcade game.

A bar stocked with sodas and snacks where the kids could sit on swivel bar stools, sipping Mountain Dew and orange soda through leftover McDonald's straws. The couch, though threadbare, wasn't unsightly. It had been placed down there after the Coopers had updated their living room furniture. The sectional curved around the room, facing the large but clunky television, where all the kids would drape their awkward and changing bodies. They would complain about their homework assignments or joke about the way Mrs. Heinman had Expo marker remnants on her forehead all through English class—all while watching Carson Daly countdown the top ten music videos of the day on TRL.

"Oh my God. All the girls in my math class were singing this today," Timmy said, stuffing a handful of popcorn in his mouth as "Don't Wanna Miss a Thing" from the *Armageddon* soundtrack began playing in the number seven spot. "They think the words are like written for them or something."

Brett laughed, but as all the boys agreed, he watched Nina roll her eyes. Though a change had started to take its hold on her, Nina hadn't changed completely—to what Brett thought of as the dark side. He dreaded Nina pulling away from the crew of boys, and so he treasured the little eye roll, her tomboyish nature showing itself.

"Lame," she said, indifferent, her body lazily draped on the end of the couch. An expression showed on her face that Brett couldn't quite place, although he categorized it as *off* in some sort of way.

Brett had friends. Everyone loved him. Because he was a good sport, it made him a desired teammate in their neighborhood games. His kindness never came off as a weakness to the group of boys. In fact, it was just the opposite; he was a role model and had been since the beginning. He was the peacekeeper, and it was a valuable position with so many different personalities. They needed him.

But Brett needed Nina most. He couldn't explain it. Neither of them could. They had always gravitated to one another. But lately, the shift in Nina had caused a dreadful feeling, one Brett didn't have words for. It was a shift in the tectonic plates of their lives, the foundation they had been standing on for years.

And he had noticed her body was changing well before Timmy started commenting on it, attempting to poke the bear as he always did with her. Brett's observations weren't crude, but more intrigue; his best friend was going through some strange metamorphosis that confused him and scared him, too. It alarmed him that there was more than one reason for him to hang out with Nina. He didn't comprehend it, but all the confusion made him more protective of her and their friendship.

Because of all the instability at home, Brett had become a master at watching for changes in the behavior of the people he loved most. It was how he kept himself safe, using those changes to gauge his own movements. Therefore, any change in Nina felt like a threat.

"Seriously? NSYNC is number one again?" Gary laughed, his voice cracking, an orange ring around his mouth from the soda, a boy teetering on the line between boyhood and manhood. They all began singing "Tearin' Up My Heart" in a mocking tone, attempting to show that they, in fact, did not find it catchy but failing miserably.

Nina sat up from her slumped position on the couch. "NSYNC will always trump Backstreet Boys. It's just a fact. Get over it."

Johnny threw a piece of popcorn over at Nina. Laughing, she got up and threw a handful back at him.

"Food fight!" Timmy yelled as all the kids scrambled to join in on the chaos.

But they'd barely made a dent in the popcorn bowl before Mrs. Cooper was banging on the basement door. "I don't think so, kids!"

"Sorry, Mrs. Cooper," they yelled in unison, Johnny shaking his head while picking up the mess.

Hours later, the kids mosied out of Johnny's house in time to head home for dinner. Nina and Brett shuffled their feet on the way down the street, in no rush: Brett because entering his home brought a darkness over him, and Nina because she simply wanted to hang out with her friends a little longer, especially Brett.

"You're quiet, B." Nina cocked her head to the side, facing him as they walked, her voice a tad concerned. "What's wrong?"

"Oh, what?" Brett looked at Nina, eyes narrowed. "Uh, no, nothing. I'm fine." He smiled, attempting to ease her worry.

She stopped on the street, reaching to grab Brett's arm and stop him, and he turned to face her, sighing. She scanned his face the way she had done since they were miniature people, her eyebrows furrowed into one another. "I don't believe you, B." She shook her head. "But I know you'll tell me what's on your mind eventually." They began walking again, and a moment of silence spread between them. "Right, B?"

Brett smiled at Nina as sincerely as he could. "Of course, Neen," he said. "I don't know what's going on with me." His voice was light but honest.

She looked up at the sky, which was nearly dark, the gray clouds heavy overhead. "Yeah, growing up sucks." Brett nodded slowly in agreement but didn't say anything. "We changed schools, and it's like all of a sudden, I have no idea what's going on up here." She pointed to her head, a smile on her lips. But their personal changes weren't the same, and Brett felt weird talking about it, even with Nina.

She linked arms with him as their speed picked up a bit toward the end of the road by their houses. "See ya in the morning," Nina said, slinging her backpack further up on her shoulder. They put out their hands and began their secret handshake they had made up last summer. The handshake they had made as an oath to each other, a promise to head into junior high together, never apart, no matter what.

"See ya," Brett said when they finished, smiling and watching her go.

As he headed to the sliding glass doors on the deck, Brett noticed his brother standing down by the edge of the pond, his hands on his hips, looking out. With his fingers on the door handle, ready to slide it open, Brett halted, letting go of the knob. He dropped his backpack by the door, and his steps took him down toward the pond's edge.

The water appeared like glass out in the middle with little ripples at the edge; the sound of the tiny waves was a sort of comfort as the unease of standing next to his brother settled over him.

"Hey," Brett said. "What are you doing out here?"

At first, Seamus didn't acknowledge Brett's presence, but that wasn't entirely unusual. Brett took his gaze out to the water, shoving his hands into the pockets of his jeans. The pull he had to connect with Seamus was dulling as he got older. A pointless venture, really, because Seamus never did budge. Never smiled or let his guard down. Never let Brett in.

But Brett wished he did, even just a little. Because the loneliness Brett felt inside his home was suffocating. He knew the two of them had a connection, an equal amount of hatred for their father, and he wished Seamus would confide in him rather than making him feel like he was the problem.

Seamus turned his head toward Brett, and the movement caused him to quickly face his brother. And Brett immediately grimaced. Seamus's face had a new bruise surrounding his left eye. When Brett scanned the rest of him, he noticed his knuckles were red and battered.

Brett sucked in a breath.

Seamus had fought back.

"Danny's in a mood." The warning came out ragged, and his voice sounded entirely too haggard and old for Seamus's fifteen-year-old self.

Brett's breaths began coming out labored and quick. The swirl of emotion made it impossible for him to find the words to respond. He stuttered, much to his dismay, before Seamus simply turned and headed up the small sandy embankment toward the house.

Brett could hear his breathing in his ears, and he almost wished that the Ghost of the Pond would rise up from the glass water and pull him under. But he knew that wouldn't happen.

Of course not.

He attempted to settle his breathing before fumbling up the sand on shaky legs toward the deck, into the unknown on the other side of the door. *Why is he like this?* The *he* being his father. The question hung in the salty air, one Brett often asked himself, never able to come up with an answer that made any sort of sense. It always just led to more questions that were never answered. *Isn't Dad supposed to love us? What does he think we did to him to deserve this?*

Brett couldn't pinpoint when Danny Warner had begun treating them poorly. The indifference toward Brett and aggression toward Seamus and Laura. It seemed to just have always been that way for as long as he could remember.

Danny Warner, a project manager for Tides Construction, spent his working hours traveling up and down the Cape and venturing to the islands by ferry to oversee construction jobs. A functioning alcoholic, he never allowed the bottle to interfere with his job. The position paid him a sizable salary, allowing the Warners to live comfortably with Laura as a stay-at-home mother while the boys were small until just last year, during Brett's final year at the grammar school, when she was hired as the school's secretary. It had been good for her to feel needed as her boys—her lifelines—were inevitably growing up and pulling away.

Laura and Danny had met in 1979 at a small coffee house outside Charleston, South Carolina. Laura was barely 20, and Danny had recently turned 25. And he was handsome, his green eyes captivating her right from the beginning.

And deceiving her right from the start.

Danny swept Laura off her feet. He projected his dreams on her, painting whimsical adventures in her mind of boats and waves, hammocks and Zen. Comfort and ease. Having everything she ever needed and more. His dreams became hers, and in the blink of her parent's eyes, Laura was swept up in Daniel Warner's orbit, and there was no pulling her out. Danny had been offered a job managing a construction company in coastal Massachusetts, and if he was leaving, well, so was Laura.

Danny had nothing holding him to the South anymore. His parents had passed a few years prior. His mother went first, and his father's heart broke shortly thereafter, catapulting his own illness into high gear. Danny wanted a change of scenery, and the job offer was his chance. Charleston had taken enough from him. It was time he made the rules for his life, a stickler for being in control.

Laura was too young for it, too young and inexperienced for such a life-altering change. Her older sister, Ann, tried to talk her out of it. Tried to convince her to take it slow, spending some time visiting him and getting to know him before uprooting her whole life for someone she'd just met.

Danny could sense the hesitation that had come over Laura, the influence of the sister she loved dearly. Danny needed to win the battle; he needed to be in control. So, he enticed Laura with a fairytale, a promise…a proposal.

And the ring was too beautiful for Laura to resist. A single diamond bigger than she had ever imagined, and the *yes* came without question. Any doubt that lingered was washed away with the excited tears of the proposal.

And so, Laura and Danny left for the Cape as "the Warners," unfortunately for Laura's family.

Their nest on Carver Road was built in 1980, although they weren't the first to move in there. Danny managed the construction of both Number 3 and Number 2 across the road from each other at the same time.

Built one twig at a time.

Foundations and roofs, windows, and doors.

As they watched them rise up from nothing, Danny told Laura that one day, they would move into one of those houses. Laura had smiled at the daydream. They had been living in a small condo near the center of town since arriving there. Money had been tighter than Laura had expected, but Danny was working tirelessly to land a higher-paying promotion at the company. She watched him, day after day, tormented by his own lack, which wasn't actually lacking. Laura could see that they were already living a beautiful dream.

But she never could convince him that what they had was enough. That *she* was enough. That he was enough. And try as she might—the effort taking its toll on her—his demons were stronger than her.

And stronger than their kids.

And so, the bottle became a lifeline to Danny Warner—until it became the end of him.

Brett pushed the sliding door open and entered the kitchen to a scene that should have comforted him but instead only unsettled his nerves.

The aroma of roasting chicken, rosemary, and thyme.

The image of his mother in an apron, stirring a pot at the stove, looking like a real-life Betty Crocker. She turned to him, a shaky smile on her lips, and greeted him. "Hi, Brett!" Her voice was enthusiastic but soft as if she was afraid to make too much noise. "How was school, honey?"

"Good, Mom." Brett hung his backpack on its hook and slid off his fall jacket. "How was your day?" He heaved a heavy breath, knowing that whatever his mom was going to say would be a lie. A lie to protect him because she thought she could still do that.

"It was good." Laura turned back to the stove, adjusting the temperature on a pot of pilaf. "Mrs. Larsen says hello!"

"Oh, cool. Tell her I said hi," Brett replied, thinking of his former principal. "Is dinner almost ready?" His eyes darted around the kitchen, looking for signs of Danny or Seamus.

"About five minutes," Laura said without turning her gaze from the stove.

"Ok. Where's Dad?" Brett asked out of fear, not interest.

Laura turned abruptly toward Brett. "He's in the living room, baby. He's tired from work. It was a long day traveling back from Nantucket, so we are going to just let him be. He can eat dinner later, ok?"

It was nothing to Brett; in fact, it was better that way. A dinner in peace. "And Seamus?" he asked, actually interested, truly caring. He had walked into the house only a few steps ahead of Brett but now was nowhere in sight.

"Oh, he went upstairs, I think," Laura said, unsure.

Brett imagined Seamus walking in through the slider and upstairs without even a thought of their mother. And it pained him more than he could fathom, really.

It was true that Brett overcompensated for his brother's lack of interest, trying his best to treat their mother with love and respect for both of them. To always be helpful and kind. And not because he felt like he had to. He truly did love his mother. His heart hurt for her, too, though, which caused him to try and protect her heart from crumbling any more than it already had.

Seamus, Brett, and Laura ate at the table with the dulled sounds of television in the living room. Their forks scraping against the brown and tan dinner plates was the background noise that filled the otherwise awkward silence throughout much of the meal. Brett noted that Laura didn't say anything to Seamus about his face, and this irked Brett. The secrets. The pain. The unknowing all of the time. *What happened to Seamus? And why? Why is Dad like this?* There were never any answers to the questions that constantly swarmed.

"How did that interview go, Seamus?" Laura asked in between bites of carrots and pilaf.

Seamus glared a moment, looking up at her from his plate. "Good," he said, his mouth full. "I'll be working there five days a week."

"Five days?" Laura sounded concerned. "That's a lot for a kid your age. What about your studies?"

Seamus leaned back in his chair, unconcerned about his mother's opinion. "I'll be fine, Mom. It's a seafood shop. It's not rocket science."

"Those fishermen work really hard, Seamus." Laura seemed weirdly offended by Seamus' comment.

"Mom, I know. But I'm not a fisherman. I'm just ringing people up. I won't fail out of school. I promise." Seamus smirked then, shoving a huge bite of food into his mouth.

Brett's eyes darted back and forth between Seamus and his mother, following their conversation.

Laura sighed. "Ok, well, we will see how it goes. But your grades can't suffer, Seamus. I mean it."

Seamus rolled his eyes, getting up from the table to clear his plate. "Yes, mommy dearest."

Brett cringed at the comment, knowing it left a bitter taste in his mother's mouth. She didn't reply, and Brett held his breath until Seamus's footsteps were clunking up the stairs. "Are you ok, Mom?" he asked, chastising himself for sounding like a little boy.

Laura smiled at her youngest child, a thin-lipped smile through growing tears. "Yes, baby. I'm fine." She batted her hand at him. "You know how Seamus is." She whispered the words lightly, attempting to make the heaviness dissolve, but that wasn't a game worth playing. Brett knew that.

"Ok. I'll clean up the kitchen," he said, getting up from his chair.

"Thank you, Brett. You are such a good boy."

And he wanted to be a good boy for his mother and help her feel loved and appreciated for all she did. But he also wanted to be a good boy in his father's eyes, and that was an uphill battle with no peak in sight. But he would never stop trying.

When he was at bat and hit an RBI, he looked at his dad and saw him standing there with his arms hanging over the fence. Was he smiling? Was he proud? He had to be because when Brett struck out, his father called him a useless teammate on their drive home. When he caught a ball in the outfield on a slide, and the team cheered for him because he got the game-winning out, he would look to Danny for his approval. But his dad never clapped. He never smiled. And when Brett asked him in the car if he saw the awesome catch, Danny would tell him that outfielders don't get scholarships.

Brett was special because he knew he was a good person despite what his father thought of him. Yes, he wanted his approval, like any young boy wants, but even with the lack of love from his father, Brett still felt love in his heart. No, not from his father. But from his mother, from his own soul, and mostly from Nina. Deep in his chest, where his heart beat, he felt it and knew it. He was good.

———

"Two to three. Are you there? Over." Nina's staticky voice came through mangled from Brett's nightstand drawer.

Nina was two; Brett was three, on account of their house numbers. That was the way it had been since they got those walkie-talkies when they were seven years old. Neither of them ever thought about just simply calling their names over the speakers to get each other's attention. Where was the fun in that?

Brett hopped up from his desk chair and made his way to the drawer, pulling it open quickly and grabbing his walkie-talkie.

"Three to two. I'm here. Over."

A lightness settled over him then, and he sprawled out on his bed. A comfort that soothed the unease he felt after dinner with his family. A comfort he only found in Nina.

"Oh, good. I thought you went to sleep already. Over."

Brett looked at his clock. It was only eight-thirty.

"Uh, it's kinda early, Neen. Over," he laughed.

Nina laughed through the janky speakers. "Yeah, I guess you're right." There was a pause for a moment, static still coming through. "I have a question. Do you have a crush on someone, B? Over."

Brett's eyes widened, wondering why she was asking that. "Uh, no, not really. Do you? Over." Thirty seconds passed without a response from

Nina. "Actually, Avril Lavigne. Over," Brett added jokingly while looking at the poster of her on his wall.

Nina's laugh came through the speaker, followed by a sigh. "Hey, B. Knock, knock. Over."

Chapter 13

Nina 2016

"That one there? He was sick when I got him," Mary Harlow said as Nina crouched down, petting a small pink and brown pig that was gnawing on an apple. "He's doing great now, though, aren't you, George?"

Nina smiled at the pig. "His name's George?" She found that to be adorable.

"Sure is!" Mary responded. "I named him after my husband, who died a few years back." A sad look came over her face, followed by a sweet smile. "Now, he was no pig, mind you," she chuckled at that, and so did Nina. "He was sweet and gentle, just like this little guy."

"That's so cute." Nina couldn't think of anything appropriate to say. "I'm sorry for your loss."

Mary flicked her wrist at Nina. "Part of life, my dear," she responded nonchalantly. "I was lucky to know him and have him as long as I did."

Nina pondered the sweetness of Mary's words. She had received a response from Mary to her email when she arrived home after drinks with Emma, and they settled on meeting in the morning. Nina was thankful for the quick response, giving her something else to focus her energy on.

Mary's farm was small, located a mile inland from the ocean line, a bike ride away from Carver Road. Nina had pedaled her old bike, the one her parents had kept in the shed all this time, down a dirt road lined with wildflowers until she came to Mary's midsized, shingled cape that was surrounded by a small plot of land with a manmade duck pond right out front.

Beside the house, Nina saw a barn that appeared bigger than the house, and behind that were pens that housed a variety of animals—pigs, goats, sheep, one miniature pony, and two wily peacocks that Mary later told her were constantly in need of a time out, which made Nina chuckle.

Mary had greeted Nina on her porch, her long gray hair in a plait down her back, her dirty overalls rolled up at the bottom—cuffed over red galoshes. "Nina, is it?" she had asked, smiling.

"That's me! Nice to meet you, Mary."

Mary showed Nina around the little farm, starting with the barn, which held a tiny store where Mary sold handmade soaps and jams. The animal enclosures were the last part of the tour, and Nina met the animals that were sick and needed care, some that had been abandoned, and others that had been rescued from neglect and abuse.

She instantly fell in love with them all because that was Nina. A protector of the wounded. A trait that was ingrained in her DNA.

From the get-go, George was her favorite. "How does it work? Do you keep them until they are old and pass away? Or do you rehabilitate them to bigger farms?" Nina asked, petting George behind his scraggly ears.

Mary laughed. "It can be complicated, dear, but I mostly just love them. No animal has the same journey. Sometimes they get better and move on to other places; sometimes they don't get well enough to leave." Nina looked up at Mary, the sun in her eyes. "Technically, I'm known as the rehab place, but no one checks up on me, and I'm just fine with that. I love these animals. So, if I keep them forever, I keep them forever."

Nina wondered how she could afford this. The upkeep of this farm and the food and shelter of these animals. But she didn't want to sound crass, so she kept her questions to herself.

"I can't pay you, dear," Mary said, almost reading Nina's mind. "I hate to say it, but if you want to help me, it will have to be on a volunteer basis." She sounded apologetic, and Nina was quick to ease Mary's worry.

"Oh, no, no, Mary. I have a job. But helping you would give me a purpose that I think I truly need right now." Nina's shoulders slumped. "I just moved back from New York City." She shook her head. "It's a long, drawn-out story that I'm sure you don't want to hear, but I'm back now, and I guess you could say I'm sort of looking for myself. I have been a bit lost, I guess." Nina smiled sheepishly. And Mary smiled back. "I have been really interested in learning about the ospreys, too, which is what brought me to email you in the first place."

"Dear, why don't I go put on some tea for us? You can tell me about New York, and I'll tell you about the ospreys."

Nina relaxed the muscles she hadn't even realized were tense. "Ok," she said. "I'd like that."

Mary and Nina walked across the dried grass outside the pig enclosure and down the dirt drive to the front steps of the house, entering through the heavy, red, wooden door. Nina glanced around at the quaint living room, a cozy space for sure. Mary's kitchen was seaside meets farmhouse, and Nina relished in the homeyness of the space. A large painting of a mermaid hung over the farm table, and she took a seat under it on a worn wooden bench. Daisies sat in an antique vase in the center of the table. Nina watched Mary fill the teapot with water from the deep porcelain sink. As it filled, Mary stared out the window that looked out over the animal enclosures and beyond, where above the treeline, Nina could make out the edge of the Atlantic Ocean.

And then, over steaming mugs of chamomile tea, Nina told Mary about how she arrived back here, Cape side.

"Sounds like New York is your home now, and you miss it," Mary said after Nina had gone on and on about it for nearly thirty minutes. Tears pricked the sides of Nina's eyes but never released, and emotion built in her throat. She nodded once, missing Lucy desperately in that moment. "Will you go back, do ya think?"

Nina pondered her question, squinting her eyes while looking out the window, searching for a response that she couldn't find. She took a sip of her tea, which had grown quite cold. "I'm not sure, Mary," she whispered. "I'm actually not quite sure where *home* is at the moment." Mary nodded, rheumy eyes glistening. Nina sighed and said, "Limbo is what my new boss called it in my interview. I'm trying to embrace it, hoping I find my place eventually."

"Oh, you will, dear. Take it from an old lady like me; home will find you, if you let it."

Nina let out a soft laugh, allowing the words to swim through her mind and take hold.

It had been nearly three weeks since she hopped on the train at Grand Central, heading to North Station in Boston. Three weeks? That was it? It felt like much longer. Being on the Cape for the last three weeks felt like a lifetime while Nina turned in circles, trying to find her equilibrium.

"Remember, you always have a home under whatever roof I'm perched on," Lucy had said in her best Australian accent the night before Nina left. They had been sitting on swanky bar stools in a newer Middle Eastern bar that had just popped up in the village. They were pretending to be nannies from down under. The room was dark, mustard and mauve curtains draped from the ceilings, and crystal chandeliers hung throughout. Hookah smoke billowed through the room as they sipped botanical-infused Old Fashioneds.

They laughed loudly, as they tended to do when they were together, until, eventually, the laughter turned to sadness. Through their whiskey buzz, they mourned the ending of the season they were in, neither of them wanting to admit that it was over. That Nina was leaving.

Lucy took Nina's hand on the walk back to their apartment. Their final walk back felt entirely too painful, as if their hearts were being shattered right on the greasy sidewalk.

"I've never had a friend like you, Nina," Lucy had said as they sat down on the steps outside their minuscule apartment. "And I never will again."

Lucy's mascara had formed tracks down her face, and if Nina had the ability to cry, her face would have been a mirror image. Nina's long hair had been curled before heading out and was now being pulled into a messy ponytail as she gathered her thoughts. It had been a long time since she had felt like she had a good friend. Lucy had been the best one she could have imagined, everything she needed.

The years between leaving Harborside and finding Lucy were confusing at best. Growing up, the always reliable Nina had solid friendships and knew what it was like to be depended on, but she had slipped into a gray area—when her huge mistake had seemingly cost her everything.

Making her believe that she was anything *but* good. But Lucy had changed all of that.

Nina looked into Lucy's eyes before pulling her into her embrace. "I love you, Lucy."

"I love you more, Ethel."

Nina tapped on Mary's table as she longingly thought of the life she had walked away from.

"Come on. Let me show you a nest," Mary said, getting up from the table. Nina and Mary walked out of the house and down the porch steps, heading toward the dirt road that Nina had biked up earlier. "These birds are magnificent. I started the project to try and help them many years back. Their nests were catching on fire, and I just couldn't stomach the idea of it anymore. Something had to be done." She placed her shaky hands on her hips. "My friend, Roger, and I started making plans about twelve years back, I'd say."

"You're doing amazing things here, Mary," Nina said, and she meant it.

When they got closer to the main road, Mary stopped and tented her eyes as she looked up at the trees. Nina followed her lead, mimicking the gesture. And there they were. Two huge ospreys were looking down at them from their nest.

"Oh, I haven't seen a pair of them yet," Nina said, not able to take her eyes off the beautiful birds.

"Yup. They are just now returning," Mary said, "from their winter adventures around the world." She chuckled at that. She told Nina how they separate for the winter, confirming what her mother had told her, making it a bit more believable than Nina had originally thought, though still amazing, nonetheless.

"These two are quite cheeky," Mary said.

"What do you mean?"

"That female up there, I call her Bonnie. She is protective of that male, who I refer to as Clyde." Mary winked at Nina.

"Why?"

"Oh, I think he returned a bit injured. His wing looked mangled, and so did his leg, from what I could see." Mary looked at Nina. "They don't have many predators, those birds. But they'll kill to protect each other." Nina sucked in a breath at hearing this. "I watched it happen. A bald eagle saw him struggling on the ground a few weeks back and went after him. A bald eagle. Can you believe that?" Nina couldn't answer; she was hanging on Mary's every word, holding her breath. "Anyway, Bonnie up there came squawking down. Killed that eagle. It was a gruesome fight. She shouldn't have survived a bald eagle encounter." Mary shook her head again, looking back up at the pair endearingly. "But she did. She'd do anything for that Clyde. I reckon she'd do it again if she had to."

"Oh my God," was all Nina could mutter, her heart beating out of her chest.

Mary, none the wiser, went on about the birds. "Now, I didn't tell Bonnie that killing the nation's signature bird was illegal." She laughed at her own joke. "I just scooped up the big guy and put him in the duck pond. It was as heavy as sin—I've never seen anything like it. Didn't want it to rot there, though. The pond seemed like a proper burial for the thing." She shrugged then, feeling like Nina might have thought she was rambling on and on.

But Nina had drifted somewhere else entirely. The rushing in her ears was blocking out all her senses. And all she could imagine at that moment was Brett.

Her Brett.

The Brett she had killed for to protect.

———

Nina was unprepared for what Mary's story would do to her. For several days after her visit to the farm, she felt as if she was untethered from the earth. But the unsettled and unnatural pattern of her heartbeat really shouldn't have surprised her.

Coming back to Carver Road meant visiting her repressed shadows. The Ghost of the Pond seemed to have a face, one that eerily resembled Danny Warner. She imagined it while teaching yoga at the rec center and was haunted by it in her dreams—the familiar scowl riddled with algae and sea foam, the wide eyes and gurgle of his mouth, hands reaching out to get her, jostling her from sleep each night and sending her catapulting awake with heavy sweat and exasperated breathing.

Way down deep inside, where Nina hid her secret, she felt (and knew) that she could never recover from this. She needed to accept that for as long as she was alive, Nina Jackson, murderer, would be the only way she would be able to see herself.

———

One Saturday morning, a month after arriving back, Nina awoke with a start, sucking air into her lungs and sitting up swiftly. She wiped the sweat from her brow line and attempted to settle her breathing. The nightmare was there in the back of her mind but fading as the minutes ticked by. Nina slid out of her bed, her body being pulled to the window, seemingly on its own volition.

Glancing out the window, she wondered how it could be possible that after two weeks of Brett being home, she had yet to bump into him. As soon as her mother had spilled the news that he was coming home, she had imagined that she would have talked to him by now. But they had avoided each other for weeks, and that fact tugged at her soul, solidifying the idea that recovering from this reality was impossible.

Nina's once pure and loving heart had turned black, and Brett hated her for it.

Or so she thought.

She watched out the window for longer than necessary until a large tow truck drove to the end of the road carrying a four-door black pickup truck. As she looked closer, Nina could see Texas license plates and immediately knew it was Brett's car. Her fingers moved the slits of the plantation shutters for a better view, and she watched as the truck reversed into the driveway.

And then she saw him—Brett Warner—walking out of the garage of 3 Carver Road. A bit taller than she remembered and much broader. His hair, the color of the sand at East Beach, was cut close on the sides, a tiny bit hanging over his forehead. Nina watched him greet the tow truck driver before placing his hands in his pocket and kicking his head back in easy laughter.

A noise arose from inside of Nina, a longing that needed to make itself known. And the sound hurt her physically, an ache building behind her empty heart. A longing to erase time and go back to do it over again. To pick up her walkie-talkie and get Brett's attention the way she once did.

She wondered what someone else would do if they were in her shoes. What would they do to right this incredible wrong that was gnawing away at her insides? But the sad truth was that her shoes weren't a pair that anyone else could wriggle on. She'd known that for a long time.

With shaky legs, Nina made her way to her bathroom and opened the medicine cabinet, taking out her SSRI and swallowing it down with water from the sink. She looked at herself in the mirror and tried to smile, an attempt to perk herself up.

Think of the positive, she thought to herself. *A new job, possibly rekindling a friendship with Emma, new friendships with the women from the rec center, Mary, finding your purpose.*

Nina sucked in a deep, slow breath and nodded at herself before placing the orange prescription bottle back on the shelf. *And Citalopram,* she thought, too, mildly joking with herself.

But it was true; her medication had been helping her for years. It had taken a lot of convincing by her team of doctors that she might need a little help calming her mind. She was a junior in college when she started taking medication. She had told her therapist that she felt silly. "I'm from a nice family. I had a great childhood. Why am I depressed?" (Though she actually did know, but those were secrets she wouldn't share.)

Her therapist, Jasmine, had smiled softly at her, explaining that it didn't work that way. "We've talked about this," she had said gently. "Sometimes, little things happen in our lives that add up to big things that impact our stress levels, our anxiety levels, and how we perceive the world. And sometimes, it's chemical. It can all impact how we function."

Nina nodded at her. "I guess."

"And Nina, the things you have told me about high school? Those things are traumatic. You know that."

Nina nodded, taking in a breath, fighting back the tears. She had told Jasmine about things that had shaped her adolescence. Things that would shock anyone. Things that had probably impacted her just as much as her darkest secret. She hoped Jasmine thought the threat of her tears was due to the overwhelming relief she felt now that she'd made a decision to try medication. Because she wasn't going to say that they were actually caused by—the undeniable pressure she felt from harboring her shadows.

"You don't have to take medication, Nina," Jasmine said at the end of one session. "But if you want to, you shouldn't feel ashamed either."

"I want to try." Those four words were the beginning of Nina's journey, and now, nine years later, she wasn't sure what would happen if she stopped taking them. Some days, she wondered that now that she was home, did she maybe need a higher dose?

Chapter 14

Nina 1999

IF YOU'VE EVER BEEN there, then you know that the hallways of any junior high aren't for the faint of heart. And Nina Jackson's heart was not the least bit faint. However, there were times at the beginning of her journey through those halls that made her believe they weren't for *her* either, fierce heart and all.

Puberty tugged at Nina's chest like the brazen bitch that it was, tormenting her until she didn't recognize the face that stared back at her in the dingy girl's bathroom mirror. Nina leaned on the sink, which was the color of Pepto Bismol and matched the wall tiles. One hand on the porcelain, the other picking at the new crater that had formed on her chin, seemingly out of nowhere, in between third and fourth periods.

Along with the changes that were visible—the pimples and the molehills growing on her chest—there were also the unseen horrors, which Nina disliked even more. The things she couldn't label. The thoughts that didn't seem like her own.

The confusion.

The sudden lack of self-confidence that irked her to her core.

Why is that girl looking at me like that? Does she hate me? Is there something in my teeth? Is that eighth grader looking at my boobs? I better cross my arms just in case.

Most of the kids from Harborview Grammar School had come over to the regional junior high. But the familiarity of the faces walking the halls did little to soothe the unease she felt. Then there were the strangers. The kids who came from Seaview Elementary seemed more mature, and the kids who came from Hedgewood Grammar School looked like they were already in high school. Nina wondered how this could be—how her cohort of friends seemed to have been locked in a machine keeping them young and wild forever.

These new seventh graders certainly didn't play Red Rover at the end of their street, and it showed.

One afternoon in late March, Brett and Nina sat together on the bus ride home. Nina played Rock Paper Scissors with Addison Marks across the aisle while Brett leaned over to the seat in front of them, playing with Johnny Cooper.

"Want to get off at my stop?" Addison asked Nina. "I just got some new *Tiger Beat* magazines we could read."

Nina made a face of longing, wishing she could, but she knew her mom wouldn't be pleased if she just got off at another stop. Not wanting to sound uncool, she made up an excuse. "Oh. Um, I can't. My mom has aerobics at the rec center, and I'm going with her to swim."

Addison smiled, shrugging her shoulders. "Ok," she replied, indifferent, then her eyes widened in wonderment. "Do you ever do aerobics with your mom?"

Nina scrunched her face, "Uh, definitely not. My mom just says she needs to tone up her pudge. Whatever that means," Nina said, sticking out her hand in paper to cover Addison's rock.

Addison laughed, reaching over and pinching Nina's stomach. "It's this," she squealed, laughing and making a joke of it.

Nina stiffened, pushing Addison's hand away. "Stop," she said hotly, pulling down her shirt that had ridden up, exposing the pale skin on her side. She turned to face forward, placing her backpack on her lap with purpose, to hide what she now assumed was a massive stomach. She breathed out, blowing a piece of hair out of her face. From the corner of one eye, she could see Brett staring at her, concerned. And with the other eye, she could see that Addison's face had turned white, her eyes wide.

"Shit, Nina. I'm sorry. I was just joking," she said kindly.

Nina didn't respond immediately, but when she did, her voice didn't sound like her own. Something she was beginning to get used to. She smiled, though it wasn't genuine. "Oh, yeah. Whatever, it's fine!"

But it wasn't fine.

Until then, she didn't know that being self-conscious could be physically felt, but Addison's comment festered, starting in Nina's ears and then inching its way to her cheeks, burning them red. The words settled in her core then—in her gut and her chest, where her heart beat rapidly. And for Nina, it was true that when something inched its way into her heart, good or bad, well, it never really left.

Nina and Brett walked slowly down Carver Road from the bus stop and the rest of the neighborhood kids ran up ahead. Brett held back with Nina, knowing she needed to mosey. They were silent for a beat, Nina's brows furrowed.

"Neen…you know…um…you're not—" Brett stuttered, uncomfortable, and Nina stopped abruptly facing him. "You're not—" Brett grimaced. "Pudgy." He said it softly, like it was a sin to utter the word aloud. They stared at each other for a few beats. Nina bit her bottom lip, desperate to get a hold of herself, to ease the ugly emotion that was about to erupt. She mustered a laugh. Anything to stave off the tears. She was stronger than that. Wasn't she? She guessed she wasn't so sure anymore.

"Now, Jeckles?" Brett said matter-of-factly. "He's pudgy."

Nina laughed for real then. And the laugh felt like medicine. Jeckles was Timmy Baker's cat. A cat who had grown so fat, his orange belly rubbed the ground when he walked. But mostly, he lay sprawled in the sun on the front porch or smushed against the screen in the front window of their house.

"Jeckles is more than pudgy," Nina said, shaking her head.

"Yeah, you're right. He's obese." The pair laughed loudly, throwing their heads back, faces upturned toward the crisp blue sky that poked through the bare branches of late winter. Brett opened his arms, inviting his best friend in for a hug.

"Since when do you let words get to you like this?" Brett's voice was hushed into Nina's hair, his chin resting gently on her head.

Nina sighed, hugging him tighter. "Since when do you tower over me, B?" The swiftness in which she changed the subject was a hint to Brett, a hint to let it go. So, he did.

And for that, Nina was grateful. Because she didn't have an answer to Brett's question. Who was she? Where was the girl she knew so well? The girl who could stand her ground better than anyone. The girl who built herself up and empathetically did the same for others. Why did her skin feel like it belonged on someone else's bones?

"Maybe I'll feel better if I just go give Timmy a quick punch in the nose," Nina said. When Brett didn't respond right away, she recovered quickly. "Kidding, B. I'm just kidding."

Then Brett shrugged, indifferent. "You could say that's what you get for overfeeding your cat or something." He laughed at his own joke. And Nina was grateful that he wasn't judging her for her bereft comment. "But for real, I think I have something that will cheer you up."

"What?!"

"I know it's much earlier than we usually do it, but whatta ya say we go into the treehouse for the first time this season?" Brett's eyes were wide.

Nina beamed a response that elicited not one single word. But Brett could easily read her expression. And with that, they were off running toward the end of Carver Road, toward their beloved house in the sky.

It wasn't on their radar that afternoon that their days and nights of loving that treehouse were numbered. The years where they'd savored the nights in there were numerous. But the days they had left were minuscule in comparison. And they couldn't know that afternoon that their adult versions of themselves would long to go back to that afternoon, even for a second. To remember the excitement of the first visit to the treehouse in 1999.

The last *first* that was unchanged.

Nina climbed up the rickety stairs, looking up as Brett reached the top, ducking his head to fit through the door. His height had alarmed her when he embraced her on the street, and it alarmed her now as she watched him avoid bumping his head on the janky archway. *What is happening to us?* she wondered to herself. She still felt so much like a kid, and she wasn't sure she was ready for all the confusion that was happening inside.

Other girls seemed to embrace it and even welcome it. Everyone was seemingly owning their new bodies and the idea of having a crush on someone and it actually meaning something. Notes in lockers, group dates to the movie theater on the main street, landline phone calls where barely a word was exchanged.

But Nina didn't understand any of it. All she wanted to do was hunker away in the treehouse and tell ghost stories with Brett.

They sat on their knees inside the little room, looking around. "Why does it feel so much smaller?" Brett asked. Nina didn't answer, and she silently scolded herself for the lump growing in her throat. She tried swallowing it down. She knew why it felt smaller, but she didn't want to admit it. She didn't want it to be true. "I guess it's because we are growing," Brett said, answering his own question with a shrug.

Nina wanted to go on pretending life wasn't changing right in front of her eyes. To distract herself from the pain, she yelled, "Come on, let's carve our initials!"

The tradition they'd started a few years ago when Nina was desperate to convince Brett that they would never be apart had become a yearly tradition. The first trip up the stairs every year wasn't complete until they put their N and B into the wood.

Brett got the old scissors out of the cup, and although they were dull and required a bit of elbow grease to open and shut, they did the job.

When they finished carving, they sat beside each other against the waterlogged wall and looked around. "Brett, you gotta promise me something."

"Ok. What's up? You called me Brett…it must be serious." He tried to be light, but the seriousness in Nina's voice unsettled him.

"Even when we're too old to do this, you have to pinky promise me, right now, B, that we will still come up here and carve our initials."

"Of course, Ni—"

"Promise me," Nina said through gritted teeth as she held back her tears.

"I promise," Brett whispered. "Neen, why are you crying?"

Nina, at thirteen years old, didn't have the words to explain to him what she was feeling or why she was crying. She couldn't even explain it to herself.

Brett stuck out his pinky, waiting for Nina to grasp it. And when she did, the air felt lighter around her, their promise easing her a bit.

As winter turned to spring and the temperature increased, the kids started riding their bikes for so long on the weekends that it seemed like they were out from morning to night. As they grew older and independence stretched out in front of them, their speeds increased, and they pushed the limits on how far they could go outside the neighborhood. Their usual childish games—Red Rover and Red Light, Green Light—had advanced to short bike rides to sit on the beach in their sweatshirts, throwing shells into the water, or longer rides into town to sit on benches with fruit smoothies, joking around and wasting time, the way kids do.

Almost everyone in the group had turned thirteen by April that year, all but Timmy, who didn't officially transfer into his teen years until summer. Nina couldn't let it go, either, always finding moments to poke him about it, all in good fun—or so she said.

On a chilly Sunday in early May, Nina, Brett, Johnny, Gary, and Tyler cruised all the way down Carver Road to the opposite end. They cut through a small, wooded area that led to a dirt road that followed the saltwater pond and brought them out right to the beach. On the way, they passed all the houses that belonged to the summer people. Houses with signs displaying the names of the houses they loved but only adored in the summertime.

Summer Song
Windswept
Sea Breeze Inn
Sunset Cottage

The houses were still closed up for the winter, but the rose bushes and spring flowers were beginning to bud. The summer home dwellers would soon come back to flowers in bloom, late sunsets, and balmy summer nights filled with crickets and lightning bugs—completely unaware of what the Cape had looked like during the long and often harsh fall and winter months.

But the year-rounders knew what life was like during the cold months, which made them appreciate the first signs of summer that pulled them to the beach, even in the cold with their hoodies on.

As they rode, Johnny serenaded the group the whole way to the beach with a variety of songs from Nickelback to Limp Bizkit to Eminem. And everyone expected it, his dramatics making them laugh. But that was Johnny. They skidded at the end of the street, checking to see who made the longest mark in the sand before hopping off their bikes and walking them across the street to the worn-out bike rack along the parking lot of East Beach.

"I brought a football," Tyler informed the group, taking his backpack off his shoulder and unzipping it to pull out the ball as they all formed a single file line through the dunes down to the beach.

Other groups of kids were also there, playing catch and horseshoes, frisbee, and paddle ball. Further down, specks of people were soaring kites, the cool wind just perfect for the activity.

Nina wasn't interested in playing football, so she slipped out of her sneakers and stood on one leg to slide off her socks, leaving them in the sand by the dunes. Then she headed straight for the shore, stepping on spiky shells and large chunks of seaweed along the way. She smiled as she stepped into the waves, the foamy water crashing up over her bare feet, wetting the edges of her bellbottoms. She inhaled deeply, feeling the serenity of the ocean deep in her heart.

"Hi, Nina!" Emma Swanson's voice came through the wind, pulling Nina from her reverie.

She turned toward Emma and backed out of the water, her feet cold. "Hey, Emma. What's up?" She bent down to roll up her pants a bit, the sloppy and soggy denim making her uncomfortable. "I probably should have done this before stepping in the water," Nina laughed.

Emma laughed, too. "Isn't it freezing!?"

Nina shrugged. "Nah. It's fine. I love it." The two began heading back to the group of boys. "Did you ride your bike here, too?"

"Oh, no. I just jogged over from my grandmother's house," Emma replied.

"Cool."

Nina and Emma had grown a bit closer since starting junior high. Emma had mellowed out a bit, and Nina had grown closer to the girls in their grade. Emma was still high maintenance and more self-indulgent than Nina liked, but she was accepting of her. Nina assumed that deep down, she must just be insecure, so she had no problem letting her in—at least a little bit. And Nina was a role model, too. Her empathy and kindness had started to rub off on Emma a bit, which was much better than the other way around. The Harborview kids tended to band together a bit with the merging of schools. Emma was no match for the mean girls from the other districts.

The girls joined the circle of boys, who had dumped out an array of snacks onto Johnny's old Bugs Bunny towel. Doritos, Bugles, Cheetos, and a box of Twinkies. It was a junk food lover's dream.

"Geez, guys, what are you trying to do? Have an early heart attack?" Emma said, half joking, half judging.

"What? You don't want any?" Gary asked. "Well good, more for the boys. And Nina, of course!"

Nina. Always just one of the boys. She giggled awkwardly, feeling Emma's eyes on her. She bent down and grabbed a handful of Cheetos, her favorite, and stuffed some in her mouth. Emma smiled uncomfortably. "What?" Nina asked, her mouth full.

Emma shook her head. "Oh, nothing. I can't eat junk like that. It makes me so pudgy."

Nina swallowed, her shoulders sinking. There was that word again. *Pudgy.* A five-letter word that sent Nina reeling, but she didn't really understand why.

Up until now, she never even thought about her body. She never thought about what she ate. It had never occurred to her before junior high that she could be fat or pudgy. She didn't think about the other girls' bodies in that way, either. But she was starting to realize that the other girls *did* do those things and think those ways. And she couldn't control what this was doing to her own self-image.

Nina felt Brett's eyes on her, and her own eyes fluttered to him. He looked the way Brett always looked at her. Like he cared more about her than anything else in the whole world. She sighed and smiled at him before grabbing another handful and cramming it in her mouth, smiling at Emma.

"I'm jealous," Emma said under her breath before sitting down on the sand next to Gary. "So, who wants to play truth or dare?"

By the start of eighth grade, the full-length mirror in Nina's room knew every angle of her body. It was all the mirror ever saw: Nina turning herself and lifting her shirt to poke and pinch. Though she was eating, she approached food with indignation. She didn't want to starve herself thin; it never did reach that point. However, the tangled way she viewed her body scared her. But she just couldn't help herself.

She knew she wasn't *pudgy,* yet this obsession was becoming difficult for her to manage.

Nina pulled away from the mirror and threw herself on top of her bed, staring off into her room. *Stop it,* she told herself. She did that a lot—talked to herself, gave herself pep talks. She loathed this new part of her, a part she simply didn't recognize, didn't understand.

She sighed, annoyed and not wanting to give this obsession any more airtime than it was already sucking from her. Heaving herself over the top of her bed, she grabbed her walkie-talkie out of the drawer. "Two to three, over."

Laying against her pillow, Nina waited, staring up at the ceiling, until the familiar sound of the crackly signal told her Brett was home and available.

"Hey, Neen. Over." Brett said.

"Too cool now for house number codes? Over." Nina chuckled at this.

"You know it." His tone was playful, and it lifted Nina's heart. "Are you getting ready for tonight yet? Over."

"Not yet," Nina said, glancing toward her closet where her dress hung. "I should probably start getting ready soon, though. Over."

"It will take me ten minutes to get ready. I'm glad I'm not a girl," Brett laughed. "Over."

Nina was starting to wish she wasn't a girl either, honestly. *Just one of the boys* had been her identity for so long, and it made sense to her; it felt right. She had been comfortable in her skin with the boys. Until now. Until her body had started turning against her and her mind seemed like a mystery she couldn't unravel.

The kids were heading to their first semi-formal dance this evening, The Snow Ball. Though Chet Robbins had asked her to go with him, Nina decided she was going as a friend group. The eighth graders from the street were heading to her house to take pictures, and Addison, Emma, and a girl named Allie were joining them for the pre-ball festivities on Carver Road, too.

As tradition had it, the eighth graders were invited to the Snow Ball as an introduction to the high school they would soon be attending. It was just eighth graders and freshmen at the dance, and the kids had looked forward to this event since they were in sixth grade. The freshmen were in charge of the theme and the decorating. It was chaperoned by some high school teachers and a few daring parents.

"Yeah, I know; you don't have to do your hair or your makeup. You just have to put pants on and button a shirt. It's entirely unfair. Over." Nina drew pictures in the air with her idle hand while waiting for Brett to respond, putting off getting ready even though she was quite excited about the event.

"Do you want me to put makeup on, Neen? Over." Brett's voice sounded serious, which made Nina laugh so hard that she choked on her own spit. Getting up from the bed, she took a few steps toward the window and looked out, searching Brett's window for signs of him. She knew he was there, of course, but she wanted to see him.

"Go to the window. Over." A moment later, Brett was waving from his window. Nina smiled at him, laughing out loud at the funny faces he was making. Although she was enjoying this time of feeling like a kid, she realized it was time to get ready. "Actually, not over. I'm gonna go, though. I'll see you in a few hours. You better look dapper. Over…for real."

"Oh, don't you worry. I will. Over and out."

As Nina slid the walkie-talkie into its charger, her mom knocked gently on her door.

"Come in!" Nina hollered, walking over to her closet.

"Hi, honey. Are you getting excited for the evening?" Jane asked, stepping into Nina's room—eyeing the mess but trying, desperately, to hold her tongue and keep any disgust from casting shadows across her face.

"Yeah, but I don't know what to do with my hair," Nina said, a slight whine in her tone. "All the girls at school were talking about getting their hair done at a salon. Can you even believe that?"

Nina couldn't for the life of her comprehend the desire to spend that much effort on her hair for a school dance. However, she was equally concerned that she wouldn't look as pretty as the other girls, and she didn't enjoy the way that feeling crept deep inside her.

Her mother gave her a soft, sweet smile, which calmed Nina a bit. "What do you envision for your hair? Tell me, and we will make it happen."

Jane had a way of calming Nina with just a few words. It was the way she said it, the soft and gentle way she spoke to her daughter, that always allowed Nina to succumb to her mother's spell. She relaxed her shoulders and walked up to her mother, allowing Jane to pull her into her embrace.

"Everyone said they are wearing their hair up somehow," Nina said, her voice muffled into her mother's shoulder. "But when I picture my hair up like the pictures they showed me, I feel like I'll look like a swan or something."

"A swan?!" Jane let out a laugh.

"Ok, maybe not a swan. But a clown, for sure." Nina huffed out an exaggerated breath.

"Why don't we leave it down then—or dress up your usual ponytail?" Jane offered, giving Nina options she couldn't visualize on her own.

Nina nodded, feeling a bit better. "Oh, that's a good idea…I think I want to wear it down," she said.

"Ok, why don't I go get everything we need, and I'll meet you in the kitchen. We'll have more space down there. I'll do your makeup, too. Then you can come back up and put your dress on. How does that sound?"

"You'll do my makeup?" Nina asked, a little surprised. She hadn't been wearing much makeup—nothing like the other girls. But she had played around a bit but lost interest in it quickly. She hadn't planned on wearing any tonight because she wasn't sure how to do it.

"If you want me to, honey," Jane said.

"Yes, please." Her voice was quiet and unsure. All this dressing up business was overwhelming her, and her mom could see it, She tried to ease her jitters with another hug.

Jane had always been a girly girl.

When Nina was born, Jane was delighted. *A girl?!* She had shrieked and cried in the delivery room when the little bundle of mucus came screaming into existence. A girl to spoil. She dreamed about a future with tea parties and bows, shopping dates, and teaching her little lady about style and makeup.

But as it turns out, Nina wasn't that type of girl. Little Nina had no such interest in being the way her mother had imagined. She wasn't concerned about dresses and bows, but more like jeans and tennis shoes, skinned knees, and crooked ponytails. Nina was unique and special. She was caring and loyal, competitive, and a fighter for all the things she held dear.

And Jane loved her for it.

She simply accepted Nina for all of who she was.

A few minutes later, Nina sat at the kitchen table, ready for her hair styling. "Ok, Nina, I'm going to get started. You just relax." Jane checked the temperature on the curling iron before getting started on the first chunk of Nina's long, thick, dark hair, hair that had never once felt heat on it. "Your hair reminds me so much of mine when I was younger."

Nina smiled at the comment, the girlie part deep inside of her awakening just a bit.

"Jane? Who is that sitting at our table?" Paul joked as he entered the kitchen from the other side of the house.

"It's me, Dad," Nina laughed.

"I know, honey, but you look different. I just didn't recognize my little bean." He placed a soft kiss on the top of her head.

"Dad! Don't mess up all of Mom's hard work," Nina squealed but not at all mad.

"Sorry, ladies, I'll be out of your HAIR now," Paul joked. "See what I did there?"

Jane rolled her eyes in jest. "Yes, honey, we get it. Now go! You can see Nina when she's all ready."

Paul winked at his girls before heading to the living room to watch something on TV.

Jane finished up Nina's hair, a full head of classic curls. She brushed through them lightly, stretching them some. She pinned the top half loosely near the crown of Nina's head, using more bobby pins than Nina had ever seen. Then, she gave it a light spray.

"Ok, it's all done. Do you want to see it? Or do you want to wait until your makeup is done and get a big reveal?"

Nina noted the ecstasy in her mother's voice, catching on that her mother was fully enjoying getting her daughter all dolled up. She was actually enjoying this, too. "Um. Let's wait," Nina replied, shrugging her shoulders. She was excited to see the transformation all at once.

"Great!" Jane said, clapping her hands together and then grabbing some makeup off the table.

Thankfully, her mother went light on the makeup, which made Nina happy. Light foundation, a bit of blush, a sparkly golden shadow over her eyes, mascara, and a light pink gloss on her lips.

When she was done, Jane handed Nina a mirror. She turned it toward her and took it all in. She held the air in her lungs a moment longer than she had expected, literally losing her breath. She looked like a shinier version of herself, but she still felt like Nina. She couldn't believe the transformation a little bit of makeup, bobby pins, and hairspray made.

"Wow, Mom." She couldn't find any other words to utter.

Jane gently touched her daughter's cheek. "You are beautiful, Nina," she said softly. "I hope you never forget that."

Nina smiled genuinely and got up from the chair to hug her mom. "Thank you so much," Nina said as he reached for her mom, and they embraced for a moment. "I should go get dressed!" The hair and makeup transformation had ignited something in Nina that would be hard to extinguish now.

How simple it was to transform.

Up in her room, Nina pulled her dress out of the closet: a strapless navy satin gown with a white block of color across the chest and a navy satin shawl to wear around her shoulders. She slipped awkwardly into the sheer nylons her mother had purchased for the occasion, against Nina's protests. *Oh lord, Nina,* her mother had said. *It's winter!* She pulled them up past her belly button and, feeling like an elephant with wrinkly legs, she adjusted all the lines from her toes to her hips. It made her short of breath. Then she pulled up the dress and zipped it as high as she could before calling her mom to help with the last inch.

"Where are your shoes?" Jane asked.

"In the closet," Nina replied while looking at herself in the full-length mirror, her voice sounding distant.

Jane got the new shoes out of the closet, a pair of chunky heeled Mary Janes. "What's the matter, honey?" she asked Nina while bending down to help her slide into the shoes.

"Nothing's wrong," Nina whispered, still not taking her eyes off her reflection.

"Are you sure?" Jane questioned. Nina nodded. "Then why do I sense tears coming?" Jane asked caringly. "We don't want to mess up this makeup," she said with a wink, causing Nina to laugh a little.

"I don't know what's going on," Nina said, starting to panic slightly. "The dress and the whole makeover make me not look like *me*. I saw myself standing there, and it scared me because I didn't recognize my reflection, and I…and I…"

"Shhh, honey, it's ok." Jane pulled Nina into her and rocked her in her arms. The comfort of her mom's embrace made Nina want to let out all the emotions she had inside. But she took a breath instead and let it out shakily. "You're growing up, and growing up is a hard job to do. Everyone does it, and there are tricky parts for all of us. Your tricky years may be different from your friends' tricky years. But you aren't alone, do you understand that?"

Nina nodded again, though she wasn't so sure she understood. Nothing seemed to make much sense these days. But in that moment, she felt connected to her mom, and the connection made her feel solid instead of as if she was floating away haphazardly.

"Everyone will be here in a few minutes. Are you ready or do you need some time?"

"Can I just sit here for a minute? Once I hear people coming, I'll come down," Nina said as she sat down on her bed, feeling the nylons push into the skin on her waist.

"Of course, sweetheart," Jane said before leaving and closing the door behind her.

Nina took another breath before standing up and looking once again into the mirror. She smiled at herself, willing her heart to accept the changes that were happening, knowing that she most likely would wake up tomorrow and feel different. But for right now, she felt beautiful, and an excitement hung in the air that she most certainly couldn't ignore. She walked to the window and peeked out to see two cars pulling into their shell driveway, Allie's and Addison's. Glancing over at the Warner's, she saw Brett and his parents heading out of their house and toward hers.

She squinted to get a better look at her best friend. From what she could see, he looked handsome, his tall, somewhat lanky frame looked much older in a suit. A sight she couldn't even imagine until she saw it with her own eyes. His floppy hair was swept away from his face a bit. *Did he use gel?* Nina smiled, a giddiness erupting inside her.

She watched the girls exiting their cars, their dresses similar to hers but their hair, most certainly not. Huge curls pinned in piles on their heads, with curls flowing down the sides of their faces. She couldn't see from the window, but Nina would bet a million dollars that they had on blue eyeshadow, a trend she just couldn't comprehend.

Nina pulled herself from the window as the muffled sounds of the doorbell rang through the house. It was time to go downstairs. Grabbing her shawl and the tiny purse her mother had lent her, Nina headed out to greet everyone. She stood at the top of the stairs for a moment, feeling silly all of a sudden, wearing fancy clothes that she had never worn before, and walking in shoes that were difficult to balance on made her feel like a fawn trying to walk after it's just been born.

But she knew everyone would look and feel similar, and so she reasoned, while turning the corner around the newel post, that no one would be looking at her funny. She took a breath and looked down at everyone gathered in the entryway. The parents were talking to each other, and her friends were inching their way into the living room where the Christmas tree was set up and lit, ready for pictures.

As Nina took the first step, she noted that her palms were sweaty. And then she saw him: Brett looking up at her from the door. His green eyes shone, and a shy smile pulled at his lips. Her eyes widened as she took him in with a closer look than she had from her window. Just like she felt about herself, Brett looked different, too.

Brett looked down at his feet sheepishly, his hands in his pockets. But it was only a few heartbeats before he lifted his head again and met Nina's gaze. On shaky legs, she stepped slowly down the stairs, desperate not to fall on her face.

"Wow, Nina!" Addison's voice broke through the hum of conversations, reminding Nina that it wasn't only her and Brett in the room. She shook away her wayward thoughts about him and turned to smile at Addison and Allie. The girls squealed over each other's hair, makeup, and dresses, commenting on their makeover routines, barely able to get a word in over one another. Nina looked over her shoulder to see Brett talking to Gary and Tyler, but he turned and smiled at her, feeling her gaze on him.

The two of them, always in sync.

Once Emma and the rest of the Carver Road crew had arrived, the kids took group pictures in front of the tree, posing formally and then in silly poses until the kids whined with boredom to leave and get the show on the road. They piled into the cars, and the adults drove them to the high school for the Ball.

"You guys have fun, now," Paul said, as they pulled up to the sprawling high school building. "But not too much fun," he said, winking at them in the rearview mirror.

"Bye, Dad," Nina said, opening the passenger door as Johnny, Brett, and Emma piled out of the back of the car. It took her a moment to gain her footing with her heeled shoes, and as she made her way to the front of the building, Brett was waiting for her on the curb.

"You ok?" he asked, smiling.

"Yeah, I'm good," Nina laughed nervously, feeling awkward but trying to brush off the feelings.

The kids all walked into the high school in awe, looking around at everything. Banners, trophy cases, a nurse's office that looked like a hospital, the main office that felt like the size of their cafeteria. They had only been at their new school for a year and a half and now they were getting ready to have to adjust again. It felt thrilling, if not a bit frightening, too.

They followed the crowd to the gym, their heads on swivels. The lights were turned down low, "Bailamos" by Enrique Iglesias played from the elevated DJ station in the back. There were white Christmas trees throughout and handmade snowflakes hanging from the metal rafters. Tables with snacks and punch bowls lined the walls, and the bleachers were pulled out on one side to rest tired feet.

"Oh my God," Emma hissed, causing Nina to turn abruptly toward her.

"What?" Addison asked.

Emma grabbed Nina's arm. "That's Mr. Gomes. Over there, but don't look." Her face became poised and elegant as she attempted to be cool. The girls huddled in a circle and stared at each other before attempting to inconspicuously get a peek.

"Wow. He's majorly fine," Allie said, fanning her face.

Nina scanned the room in that direction until she found the famous Mr. Gomes standing with a cup in his hand, talking to another teacher, a woman with dull brown hair and wearing a sensible skirt. Her cheeks reddened at the sight of him, finding him more attractive than she had imagined. Rumors of the gorgeous Mr. Gomes had been swimming through the hallways of their junior high school since the middle of seventh grade. After the eighth graders went to the Snow Ball last year, that's all they talked about, sending the seventh graders into a tizzy, too.

And the rumors, apparently, were true. With a strong jawline and glossy dark hair that most likely stayed perfectly in place with the help of a whole bottle of gel, he was dreamy. The girls were instantly smitten. Nina was uncomfortable to say the least. He was a grown-up. Like her parents. She wasn't even interested in boys yet. Not in the same way that the other girls were, at least.

"Ok, can we stop drooling and go have some fun on the dance floor?" Nina asked, desperate to get this night going in another direction.

"What, you don't think he's hot, Nina?" Emma asked, not believing it.

Nina shrugged. "I don't know. He's old," she replied honestly.

"I dare you to go ask him where the bathroom is," Allie said, barking out a laugh.

They all joined in on the laughter, including Nina. "Fine," she said. She was not about to leave a dare unanswered. She gathered her courage and started walking toward Mr. Gomes. Behind her, she heard the giggles and gasps of the girls as she walked away, noticing how her heels were getting a bit easier to walk in.

"Excuse me," Nina said sweetly, being dramatic, even though the other girls were too far away to hear.

"Hello, young lady. I don't recognize you," Mr. Gomes said, smiling. "You must be from the junior high." Nina noted that he was quite friendly.

"Um, yes, hi, I'm Nina. And my friends over there dared me to come over and ask you where the bathroom is." Nina smiled, showing her teeth and pointing at the group. Mr. Gomes kicked his head back and laughed as the other teacher expressed her annoyance through her body language, her arms stiffening in front of her, eyebrows raised.

"Well, Nina, it's right out the gym doors, first door on your right."

"Thank you, I will go and tell them." Mr. Gomes smiled, holding her gaze, and the gesture caused Nina's heart to quicken, unsettling her a bit.

"Ok, then bye," she added as she turned on her heel and walked back to the girls, who all but screeched as she reached them.

"You are SO brave!" Emma said, straightening out her dress and tucking her hair behind her ears before glancing over at Mr. Gomes, who was already in conversation with a male chaperone and of course completely uninterested in the girls.

Nina shrugged. "Whatever. Now can we dance?"

The evening was more fun than the eighth graders ever could have imagined. Here they were, on the precipice of this next journey, desperate for it to come and equally trying to make these moments last forever. Nina's long, curly hair bounced all down her back the whole night as she danced to every song, never leaving the dance floor.

The kids put their arms around each other, singing "God Must Have Spent a Little More Time on You" by NSYNC, and even the boys joined in. By the last song, Nina was moist with sweat and desperate to put her hair in a ponytail but relented, having seen in the bathroom mirror that although it was sweaty, it still looked good.

"Ok, everyone, we are going to slow this down for the last time," the DJ announced. Everyone groaned, not wanting the night to end. "I know, I know, but all good things must come to an end," he joked in response to their complaints.

"Kiss Me" by Sixpence None the Richer began playing, and Nina sniffed a laugh to herself, looking down at her dress and pulling a curl between her fingers. In a way, she felt a bit like Laney Boggs from the movie *She's All That*, the movie she and Addison had watched on repeat over the last few months. The song fit the bill, and at that moment, a core memory began to form in her mind. An image that she would later recall anytime she heard this song, causing her to conjure up the memories of the smell of the sweaty gym, the sound of their shoes squeaking against the shiny panels of the shellacked wood, and the feeling of Brett's presence.

"Hey, wanna dance with me?" Brett asked as he turned toward her. "You know, as best friends?" he added with a wink.

Nina smiled, linking arms with him. "Sure, B."

They walked to the dance floor where kids were coupled off, swaying awkwardly, too embarrassed to even look at one another. But not Brett and Nina. They swayed, looking into each other's eyes and smiling, their closeness not awkward in the slightest. "You look really beautiful, Neen." He said the words in such a way that made her truly believe it.

She smiled, looking down. "Thanks," she whispered because she feared if she didn't, she would cry. She took a breath. "B, it won't be long before we are all here, doing high school together."

Brett nodded. "I know." He looked around the gym. "Are you going to make me promise you that it's me and you, always?" he asked with a smile, sensing her unease.

Nina looked right into his green eyes. "Yup."

Brett leaned his head down. "You'll always have me," he whispered in her ear. "Promise."

"Good," she said, trying to push down the emotion that was coming out of nowhere. "All girlfriends have to be screened through me," Nina joked, trying to lighten the mood.

A seriousness spread over Brett's expression, and though it was brief, Nina saw it and wondered what it meant. He nodded once. "Ok, Neen."

They kept their eyes locked on one another for a long moment; Nina's pulse activated as she silently swore hateful words at her raging hormones.

When the song ended, Brett pulled her in for a hug, and she let him, laying her head on his shoulders and breathing in the comfort he always gave her.

Chapter 15

Brett 2016

B RETT JAUNTED UP THE three steps in front of Johnny and Erica's townhouse, carrying in his arm a six-pack of the Summer Shandy that Johnny had mentioned his wife enjoyed. While giving a knuckle rap on the navy door, Brett whistled, looking around at the property. The birds' song caused him to look up into the trees, hoping to see a winged singer; the sounds comforted him more than he expected. Their front lawn stretched out to a wide side yard that led back to Granite Pond. Under two tall elm trees close to the water, a large kayak rack rested—the rack holding a red kayak and a yellow one.

Brett smiled to himself, remembering how Johnny had referred to himself and Erica as simpletons, but he could already tell that the home they had built here was quite lovely.

The door opened, and Johnny and Erica greeted him with smiles, welcoming him into their home. Johnny outstretched his hand for a friendly shake before pulling Brett in for a hug.

"Brett, this is my wife, Erica. Erica, Brett." Johnny was beaming, thrilled to have his childhood friend meeting his wife.

"It's so nice to meet you, Brett," Erica said, smiling. "I have heard many legends about that Carver Road crew." She winked at him. "It's great to put a face to your name. Johnny says you were his best friend back then."

The three moved toward the back of the house, into the kitchen that overlooked the pond. "Yeah, we certainly were close back then," Brett replied, beaming a smile while they all gathered around the kitchen island. "Sorry that we have drifted a bit over the years."

Johnny shook his head at Brett. "Ah, that's life, isn't it? Nothing to harp on, now."

"No, I guess not," Brett said with a laugh. He did feel bad for the distance, but he was grateful that Johnny didn't hold any hard feelings. Their estrangement had been 100 percent Brett's doing—in spite of all Johnny's outreach that he had dismissed or ignored. It had been too hard to stay connected while he was away—out of sight, out of mind, as they say. Brett had used the distance as a crutch in his journey toward forgetting.

"Can I get you something to drink?" Johnny asked. "We have a variety of choices. What are you in the mood for?"

"Oh, um, I'll just have a beer; thanks, man," Brett said. "Oh, and I grabbed these. Johnny said you were a fan, Erica."

"Thanks, Brett!" she replied. "I'll put them in the cooler outside. How about we go sit on the deck?"

"Let's do it," said Johnny, grabbing some glasses and a bottle opener before heading to the sliding door while Erica went to the fridge for provisions.

"Can I help you with anything?" Brett asked her.

She smiled at him, thankful for the offer. "Oh, sure! Can you grab this tray of veggies and dip, and I'll be right out?"

"Sure thing." Brett grabbed the tray from Erica's hands and headed out the door where Johnny was laying out placemats and winding up the fan.

"Wow, what a view," Brett voiced, looking out over Granite Pond, where the water lapped in gentle waves and the sun reflected blindly off the surface—the sky so blue that Brett wondered how it could be real.

"Yeah, it's like back home on Carver Road, sort of," Johnny said while gazing out at the water. "I guess that's why I felt so connected to it when we looked at this place. It was winter when we checked it out with our real estate agent. I looked out at the frozen water, and all I could think about was how it reminded me a bit of our view out the window on Carver. And, of course, when we'd skate out here in the winters."

The nostalgia pulled at Brett's heart—the memories of his childhood that were warm and worth recalling. The times with his friends. "We did have fun out there, didn't we," Brett said.

Johnny nodded once, smiling, looking like he might get emotional. "I've missed you, man."

Brett's shoulders sank, the guilt building once again. "Same, Johnny. Same."

"Well, we should continue making up for lost time, right?" Johnny said, opening up the cooler, pulling out two IPAs, and bringing them to the table. They sat down as Erica came out of the house with some napkins and two bowls of chips. They took seats around the weathered wooden table, relaxing into the back of their chairs with sighs of relaxation.

Brett smiled at the couple. "So, tell me how you guys met."

The three of them spent the afternoon enjoying the slow, calm feeling of being in each other's presence. Erica laughed while telling Brett how she and Johnny made their relationship official while nursing their buzzes that they had earned drinking lukewarm cans of Bud Light on a Panama City Beach on spring break back in 2008.

He marveled at them, the glimmers in their eyes, the love they shared, Johnny's hand lovingly on Erica's knee while they talked in the late afternoon sun.

"Texas must have been a trip, Brett," Erica said. "Totally different from coastal Massachusetts, I'd say."

They all chuckled, and Brett nodded, shifting in his seat. "It sure is different," he said, pulling his IPA to his lips, images of Austin flashing in his mind. He wasn't sure what parts to delve into and what points were most important to share. Texas had been his entire life over the past twelve years, and he never imagined he would leave there.

How could he put into words how Texas had become his saving grace? How the slow and steady days in Texas were exactly what he had needed when he left.

"Texas is amazing, man," he said. "I love it there so much. Great people, it never snows, so many fun and interesting things to do."

Brett shared, if only a little bit, some of his adventures over the previous decade, allowing Johnny and Erica a peek into the scenes from the Southwest. Times that now seemed like a lifetime ago, not mere weeks. Harborview was a time warp, Brett knew this to be true—the town sucking him back in time.

"Hey, there's great people here, too, bro," Johnny joked. "I mean, I can't change the snow, but we have fun." He laughed loudly at that.

Brett smiled at his old friend. "You're right," he said. There was no use harping on the things he couldn't change, at least for the time being. "And it was important that I came home, at least for now."

"Yeah, what's going on with the family?" Erica asked. "Johnny told me you were home helping your mom?"

Brett cleared his throat, suddenly feeling completely exposed. "Yeah," he began. "My brother, Seamus, has been struggling with some PTSD. He was in the Army for a long time and did a few active-duty tours. It kind of messed him up." *That and my dad.* "My mom has been struggling to help him, and so I came home to see if I can be of any assistance." Deep breath. "I'm not sure what I can do, but I'll try." Brett gave a weak smile, not wanting to talk anymore about the inner secrets of his family.

"Has he looked into getting a service dog?" Erica asked, taking a chip from the bowl and dipping it in the salsa before bringing it to her mouth. "My cousin was overseas for some time as well. His dog really helps him."

Brett contemplated that. A service dog. He had to admit, he hadn't ever thought about the prospect. He hadn't really given Seamus much thought at all, regrettably. "I'm not sure if he has looked into that, actually. I'm going to have to ask him. Might be good for him."

Brett made a mental note to bring it up to Seamus soon. Or actually look into it on his own before mentioning it to Seamus because he assumed he would brush off Brett, and any of his ideas.

Brett changed the subject. "Nina's back. Have you talked to her?"

Johnny cocked an eyebrow. "No, I didn't know she was back," he replied. "Have you?"

Brett shook his head slowly. "Nope."

"I wonder when she got back. Or what she's doing. I haven't talked to her since we graduated and left. Same as you."

"Same," Brett said quietly.

"Are you serious?" Johnny asked, not believing what Brett said.

Brett swigged another sip. "Dead serious."

"Man, you guys were like two peas in a pod," he said. "Hard to believe you got disconnected." Johnny turned toward Erica. "Nina lived on Carver Road, too. Right across from Brett. The two of them were so in sync it was actually kind of frightening." He laughed at his own comment. Brett did, too, though it was more forced than he would have liked it to be. But talking about Nina just made him sad now, and he knew he had to make it right. He just wasn't sure how.

Brett offered a thin-lipped smile, hoping to change the subject. "Yeah, we were close," he said, spinning the final sip of his beer in the bottle. "Anyways…" Brett dragged out the word, and Johnny sent him a look that seemed to say, *We can talk about something else,* an invitation accepted greatly by Brett.

"Well, it's great to have you back, man," Johnny said as Brett's shoulders relaxed. "I think we should make an effort not to be strangers."

"I agree," Brett said through a genuine smile. "I should be heading out, though. I have an early meeting in the morning."

They all rose from the table and headed in through the sliding door, back into the kitchen.

"It was so nice to meet you," Erica said gleefully. "The Carver Road stories seem a little more real now," she added, and they all chuckled.

"It was great to meet you, too," Brett said, opening his arms for a friendly hug before reaching out his hand to Johnny. Johnny took it, pulling him into his embrace.

As Brett climbed into his truck, the smell of citronella embedded into his nostrils and seeping into the fabric of his sweatshirt, he drove away and spent the five-minute car ride back to Carver Road reliving the afternoon, which led into evening. He thought about the conversations they'd had, the memories they'd recalled, and the question that had come to his mind. He stayed later than he had intended—until the sun had slipped behind the pond and they heard the sounds of the evening insects making themselves known.

Brett had experienced the sights and sounds of Harborview back there on Johnny's deck, and he wasn't sure how he felt about it. The bird's song led effortlessly into the choir of insects as dusk fell. The color of the sky as it turned, the sun rolling beneath the line of the trees. The water lapped gently against the pond's edge. It was the sights and songs of his childhood, one that was quite tarnished. But today, he was reminded of the beauty of the world outside of his house, where his friends were, and where Nina was.

The afternoon had warmed something that had frozen inside of him long ago.

It had felt safe.

Reconnecting with Johnny had allowed a contentment to settle in Brett's bones. Hearing about how his life had been over the years while they were apart made Brett's guilt subside a bit.

And talking about Texas reminded him that he had made something of himself, despite what Harborview had done to him. Both the good and the bad things, really. Because even though there were good memories that made him yearn for the simplicity of being a kid again and playing in the street, there were things that had happened here that had ruined him.

And now he even had some new idea of how he could try to help his brother.

When Brett pulled his truck into the driveway, his wheels crunching on the white seashells underneath it, he saw his mom in the shadows of the front porch, gliding on the hanging swing, bugs swirling around the light overhead.

As he got out of the truck and walked up to the door, the crickets sang as loud as anything.

Laura smiled at him, a tumbler in her hand. "Hi, honey."

"Hey, Mom. Just came from Johnny's."

"Oh, how's he doing? Just saw his dad the other week." Laura swung methodically, one foot tucked underneath her, the other pushing off the ground, giving her momentum.

"He's good," Brett replied. "Real good. His wife is nice. They met in college." He took a seat in the wooden Adirondack chair next to the swing, his back to the house, his eyes cast out, looking toward the Jackson's. He couldn't help but long for Nina at that moment. His insides felt hollow. It was like he was a soul with unfinished business—roaming Carver Road like the Ghost of the Pond. It was almost as if part of him had died twelve years ago, and even though he thought he had found happiness far, far away, his soul could never find peace with all the words he'd left unsaid.

"Something on your mind, Brett?" Laura asked, taking a sip from her drink, the ice long melted. He knew she had been watching him eye the house across the way. Whatever he was feeling inside and trying to keep buried was pushing its way out, making it obvious to his mother that something was brewing under his surface. He didn't respond to his mother's question—he didn't know how to. Laura took in a long breath and let it out slowly. "I always thought it was your father's death that pulled you away from here. From me." Emotion sounded in her throat. "But the more time that's passed and the more I have had to sit and reflect on all that happened back then, the more I finally realized that it was more than that."

Brett finally turned his head away from 2 Carver Road and looked straight at his mother through narrowed eyes.

"Say somethin', honey." Laura sounded tired and desperate, unleashing something inside Brett that he didn't like.

"You're right," he said. "It was so much more than Danny. You always gave him too much credit." He shook his head slowly, leaning back on the sloped chair, and placed his hands behind his head.

She stared at him, upset. "When are you going to forgive me?" Laura asked, sounding equally agitated as she was sad.

"I forgave you a long time ago, Mom," Brett said. "So, tell me, when are you going to forgive yourself?" He watched a tear descend from each eye. He hadn't meant to make her cry. "Do you ever regret it…do you regret him?"

"Oh, God, Brett." Laura put her empty glass on the ground and her elbows on her knees. Laura allowed her head to fall into her hands. "I can't regret your father. Because if I didn't have him, I wouldn't have you two."

"That's a cop-out, Mom," Brett said, trying to keep the disgust from his voice.

"How is it a cop-out?" she hissed. "You and Seamus were the only things that kept me afloat during those dark days, Brett."

"And you just let him ruin us, too, Mom." It was Brett's turn to sound desperate—all the words that had been left unsaid for years and years just spilled out onto the porch of his childhood home. "We should have left. We could have gone to Auntie Ann's when she moved to Maine. Sometimes, I think she just moved closer to us to try and save us, and you wouldn't let her."

"You would have hated me—you told me so, that you would run away if I took you away from Nina."

Well, I lost her anyway, Brett thought, and it broke his heart a little bit. "I was ten years old, Mom. You were the parent. Me threatening to run away sounds better to me than what we all went through for the next eight years."

Laura seemed lost for words, lost in her thoughts, swimming in the heaviest of guilt. Guilt that had rattled her nerves for all this time.

"Well, I can't go back now, can I?" It sounded like she was talking to herself, uninterested in facing the past.

"No one can, Mom." He kept all the other things that began swarming his mind inside, primarily the state of his older brother. Brett wasn't sure his mother could handle him bringing up the fact that Seamus was fighting inner demons that grew inside him long before he went overseas.

The crickets filled the silence that seemed to stretch on entirely too long. Brett sat there contemplating more than he had planned to tonight. Mostly, he thought of Seamus and all that his brother had done for him over the years. Things he had never even realized.

"Anyways," Brett said, breaking the silence. "Has Seamus ever considered reaching out to an organization that gives service members service dogs?"

Laura looked exasperated at the mention of Seamus. Brett could see on her face how caring for him had done more than take a toll. It had sent Laura right over the edge. Brett felt bad, but then he remembered that this was the reason he was home. He had been given a chance to redeem himself, and he was going to take it.

"I take your silence as a no."

Laura leaned back on the swing. "No, I don't think he has ever thought about that."

"Well, I'm going to look into it," Brett said as he got up from his chair and headed for the front door. But Laura stopped him before he could cross the threshold.

"I don't know what happened to you two, but don't you think whatever it was is just water under the bridge now?" Brett knew they were no longer talking about Seamus, his eyes darting across the street. When he didn't respond, Laura pressed on. "You've been home for two weeks,

Brett. Maybe just go over there tomorrow and say hi? You aren't kids anymore, honey. I think you—"

"Yeah, I know," Brett said, cutting his mother off. "I'm going to. God willing," he said under his breath as he walked into the house and up the stairs to his old bedroom.

With his hands behind his head, Brett lay looking at the ceiling, finding himself desperate for the staticky sound of a walkie-talkie.

Chapter 16

Nina 1999-2001

T HE TURN OF THE century brought an excitement that hummed throughout the junior high. Rumors spread through the hallways that come midnight on January 1, 2000, the world was just going to cease to exist. Nina chuckled at her locker as Timmy tried to convince the crowd that had gathered there that it was true. He knew it for certain, he said.

"You just wait. The grid is just going to combust or something," he rattled on. "Computers, electricity, it's all going to just go off, and it's going to be chaos."

Nina didn't know what *the grid* was, but she was almost certain that Timmy was full of shit—her opinion of him hadn't changed much in the last five years. "Well then, I guess we'll need to have as much fun as humanly possible in the next six weeks, won't we," she said, a condescending smile reaching her ears.

He scoffed but didn't have much of a retort, causing Brett to laugh and shake his head. "I'll make sure I'm as far away from you as I can get on New Year's, Tim-man," he said jokingly. "I wouldn't want your face to be the last one I see before I die."

Everyone laughed, including Timmy, just as the bell rang, causing the group to break apart and run to get to their first period classes.

"See you at lunch," Nina said to Brett, slinging her light pink JanSport backpack onto her shoulder and heading toward the stairs with Emma Swanson and Allie Jones.

"I just got the new Mary Kate and Ashley movie yesterday! You guys have to come over and watch it this weekend," Allie said, her voice growing with excitement.

"*Passport to Paris*?" Emma said, her eyes widening.

"Yup!"

"Oh, I am there!" Emma said. "What about you, Nina?"

Nina had loved Mary Kate and Ashley since the time she believed they were just one person playing Michelle Tanner on *Full House*—her favorite show as a little tyke. Her mom and dad would not only measure time in the number of sleeps but also in the length of a *Full House* episode.

One more sleep until Disney World, Nina!

Two more Full Houses, *Nina. Then it's time to go.*

One more Full House, *and then the park gates are closing, Nina.*

"Yeah, definitely!" she replied. "But you should bring it to my house. We can have a sleepover in the basement with tons of snacks." She wiggled her eyebrows, assuming this would entice the girls. Instead, they exchanged glances with tight-lipped expressions. "What?" Nina asked, eyeing them both as they all walked into room 212 for their physical science class.

"Let's just do it at my house," Allie said, her voice sounding more serious than Nina thought necessary. In her biased opinion, sleepovers were the most fun at her house. The basement was all hers, and her mom always had the best snacks.

"No, come on!" Nina said, trying to up the energy that was fizzling between the three of them. They took their seats, and she noticed Emma's eyes darting nervously around the room, trying to avoid the awkwardness that was setting in. For what? Nina didn't understand.

"You're so bossy, Nina," Allie blurted out, pulling the comment out of thin air, the words sounding utterly shocking to Nina's ears.

Bossy?

No one had ever called her bossy before. Timmy, of course, didn't always have the nicest things to say to her, but she always figured he just picked on her simply because she was the only girl on Carver Road, an easy target. And she always had a sassy retort for him, without fail.

But this was different. This time, she did not have a smart comeback.

And maybe she was bossy *because* she was the only girl on Carver Road, always needing to hold her own with the boys for all those years.

She felt her face getting flushed, and she hated herself for it. For her complete lack of confidence to say anything back. But she was a bit shocked, and it felt like this was coming from left field. Her eyes grew wide, her body's desperate attempt to curb the tears threatening to fall.

Emma attempted to ease the discomfort. "It's just that we always go to your house, Nina," she said lightly. "We thought we could switch it up a little, that's all."

"But also," Allie added, less kindly, "we always have to do what you want to do. It has to be your idea, or it doesn't fly. Someone had to say it." She shook her head, proud to have gotten this off her chest.

And there Nina sat, dumbfounded for the first time in her life. She swallowed the rock in her throat, utterly embarrassed, her breaths coming in short, quiet bursts through her nose.

In the broad scheme of things, this blip should not have had as profound an impact on Nina as it did. She had always known how to stand up for herself and to speak her mind, for all it was worth.

Sticks and stones had broken her on more than one occasion, but, as the saying goes, the words never hurt her. If anything, up until now, they had built her into the strong person that she was.

So why now? she wondered. Maybe it was wrecking her because, deep down, she knew it must be true. Was it really that big of a deal to be known as bossy? She wasn't sure, but at that moment, she wanted to crawl under her desk and disappear until the grid shut down, and she, along with the rest of humanity, no longer existed.

———

Of course, Y2K didn't turn out to be the storm that Timmy had predicted. In fact, 1999 turned into 2000 the same as all the years before it had, complete with a countdown, loads of junk food, and singing "Auld Lang Syne." The families of Carver Road had partied at the Cooper's—dressing up in fancy attire and sending the kids off to the basement with copious amounts of snacks and zero supervision. While eating cold lo mein, the kids gathered around the TV to watch Dick Clark prepare for the ball to drop.

"Nina, do you want to play Twister, or should we have an air hockey tournament?" Johnny asked her.

"Oh, I don't care," she replied. "Whatever everybody else wants."

Brett plopped down next to her on the Cooper's sectional. "Do you have a fever?" he asked her, smiling, his dimple showing, his bangs slicked straight up with gel.

"What do you mean?" she asked, looking down at her hands.

"You always want to be the one to pick the games."

She lifted her head quickly, her brows furrowing at Brett's comment. "Is that because I'm bossy or something?" Her words weren't accusatory, more sad than anything.

"What? Where did you get that from what I said?" Brett asked, concerned.

Nina slumped back against the couch cushion, sighing. "Allie and Emma informed me a few weeks ago that I'm bossy." The words came out weak.

"Neen." He said her name like it was a full sentence, knowing she would be able to hear what he was saying just by his tone. But when he looked into her eyes, he was alarmed to see that there wasn't a knowingness in them. She looked the exact opposite of the Nina he knew and loved. She looked pained and sad. "You aren't bossy," he said softly, looking into her eyes.

"Then what is it that I am, B?" she asked breathlessly.

He furrowed his brows as she spoke, and he took a leveled breath before responding. "I think what you are struggling to remember is *who* you are amongst that gaggle of girls at school." He took a sip from his Sprite can, acting as if he had just made the most profound statement that's ever been said.

Nina nodded slowly, looking right into his eyes. "Maybe," she whispered, comforted by Brett's words and presence, even if deep down, she wasn't actually sure he was right.

Brett opened up his arm, inviting her into his embrace, and she took the invitation, leaning against his shoulder as if her life depended on it. And maybe it did. "Thanks, B."

He put his chin on the top of her head, the gesture that said everything and nothing at the same time.

At 11:32 p.m., as Billy Joel sang "We Didn't Start the Fire," a pit began to grow in Nina's stomach that she couldn't quite calm. She knew the lights would stay on, but the anticipation of the God-forsaken grid going out was sending her into a tizzy as he sang his heart out without a care.

The remaining minutes of the twentieth century ticked on by, and the world slid into the next century without a hitch as far as the kids on Carver Road were concerned. They all yelled "Happy New Year" at the top of their lungs, blowing their air horns and popping their bottle of pretend champagne that, of course, was pretty anticlimactic.

Nothing out of the ordinary happened, so Nina never did find out what the hell the grid was.

"Nina, you have to kiss all of us. It's the New Year's rule," Timmy said, laughing obnoxiously.

"Yeah, ok, Tim. Everyone gets a kiss but you. The idiot who said the world would go dark tonight."

The group joined in on a collective and dramatic, *ohhhhhhhh.*

But there were no kisses for Nina, Timmy's joke dying off with the laughter from Nina's retort.

———

The kids graduated from junior high a few months later, and the summer of 2000 stretched out in front of them, the anticipation of starting high school in the fall growing deep inside them.

One morning in early July, Nina sat glancing out her bedroom window, a pang of longing tugging at her as she looked over at the Warner's yard, the treehouse looming there in her line of sight. Her shoulders slumped. She and Brett hadn't been up there once yet that summer, and their first trips up usually took place in April.

What happened? she wondered. Did they forget? Did they outgrow it? Did Brett just not want to go up there anymore?

Nina stood there at the window, as she had a million times before, but instead of a thrill building in her gut, it was a sort of dread. Swiftly, she made her way to her bedside table, pulling out her walkie-talkie that was buried under body sprays and tubes of lip gloss. Desperate to call Brett, she pressed the power button—over and over—but to no avail. Her shoulders slumped.

Of course, it wasn't charged.

She couldn't even recall the last time she and Brett had used them.

Sitting down on her unmade bed, she picked up her phone, wrapped the cord around her finger, and dialed up the Warner's phone number, listening to the ring.

"Hello?" She heard Mrs. Warner's soft voice on the other end of the line.

"Hi, Mrs. Warner. It's Nina. Is Brett home?"

"Hi, Nina. Yes, let me get him for you. Just a minute."

Nina waited patiently to hear Brett's voice on the other end.

"Hey," he said, finally, sounding breathless. "Sorry, I was playing Nintendo in the basement."

"Meet me at the treehouse," she said before abruptly hanging up and hurrying out the door and across the street to the base of the elm. She looked up the ladder, familiarity welcoming her up the steps. She placed one foot in front of the other until she reached the rickety door at the top. She crawled in and waited for Brett.

It was only a few moments of waiting before he crawled in through the door. He laughed lightly, "Wow. It's been a while since we've been up here, huh?" he said, looking around at the familiar walls.

"Yeah," Nina replied. "I was looking out my window and saw the treehouse and realized we hadn't come yet this season. It felt wrong, kinda. Don't you think so?" She eyed their initials from years past.

"Very wrong." Brett nodded in agreement. "Shall we?" he asked, grabbing the scissors that still sat in the cup on the table.

Nina smiled genuinely at her best friend, a rightness settling in her, a sense of calmness, if only slightly.

They kneeled, taking turns carving N and B into the wood, and when it was done, they leaned against the wall, a comfortable silence settling over them.

Brett took Nina's hand in his. "Are you ok, Neen?"

She noted how, over the last year, Brett had asked that of her quite a few times. It made her feel all jumbled up inside, knowing that he could sense what she was trying to keep hidden made her want to cry right then and there.

Was she fine? She wasn't sure. All she knew was that puberty was continuing to confuse her more and more each day. She thought—no, she knew—there would be growing pains. She knew there would be changes, but she wasn't prepared for the unexplained feelings blooming inside her. A sort of sadness that loomed, sometimes right over her head like a cloud, other times just out of reach but a threat, nonetheless.

"What do you mean?"

Brett shrugged. "I'm just checking on you. You seem different, that's all."

Nina sighed, not really sure how to respond. She kind of felt like a jerk, really, being sad and vulnerable around Brett when she didn't really feel like she had a reason to be. Especially when her best friend surely did have a reason—with what went on behind his front door and all.

She pushed the confusing emotions down, bringing her smile back to her face. She knew the real Nina was there, somewhere inside, buried under whatever had taken over her mind since she turned thirteen. "I think I'm fine. Just girl stuff," she laughed.

Brett chuckled. "Well, I'm not a girl, obviously, but you know I'm always here if you need me."

"I know, B," she whispered. "I know."

When Josie Fable got her period at the end of sixth grade and made sure the whole school knew about it, like it was some sort of badge of blood honor, Nina was intrigued. The whole process of menstruation was an elusive figment of womanhood that seemed to be just another sign that growing up was a tradition she, quite frankly, was not interested in participating in.

Nina wondered how on earth all the women before her had managed this transition when it seemed to her that she was failing miserably.

Where Josie Fable got her first period in the dead of night, in the comfort of her own home, Nina got hers at the end of third period, noticing only from the spot she left on her chair in her ninth-grade history class once the bell rang. She gasped and sat back down, eyes wide, hands shaking, the sweat in her armpits beginning to drip down the sides of her torso.

"Come on, Nina, let's go," her new friend Maggie said, turning back from the door. "What are you doing?"

"Oh, I just need to write down the homework; I forgot." Her sheepish grin gave her away, and Maggie contorted her face in confusion.

Shakily, Nina fumbled with her stuff, trying to figure out what she was going to do. She grabbed her Aeropostale sweatshirt out of her backpack, and with a deep breath, she slid her bottom across the seat, hoping that she didn't leave a mark. She tied the sweatshirt around her waist and scurried to where Maggie stood befuddled.

Maggie seemed concerned, too. "Seriously, are you ok?"

Wide-eyed, Nina shook her head. "Bathroom. Now." She stormed out of the room.

Maggie fell in line behind her. "We don't have time to go to the bathroom before fourth period, Nina. Tell me what is going—" She stopped dead in the hallway, grabbing Nina's arm gently. "Did Aunt Flow come to town?" she asked in a whisper.

A scowl fell across Nina's face. She hated that reference—couldn't fathom the point of it. How was it hiding the truth if everyone knew what it meant?

It's so dumb, she had said to Brett one day in the treehouse after a seventh-grade health class discussion, and he looked at her without comprehension but agreed still.

Nina nodded once at Maggie as her friend pulled her swiftly into the girls' bathroom.

"Here," Maggie said, unzipping the front of her backpack. "I always have pads in my backpack in case of emergencies like this." She handed Nina a white package that felt entirely too thick for her to wear in her underwear, almost like a diaper, really.

"But it's on my pants, Mags," Nina whimpered, nearly in tears.

Maggie looked down, gauging the damage. "With the sweatshirt wrapped around your waist, you can't even see it."

Nina stood on her tiptoes in front of the mirror, confirming what Maggie had said was true. Taking the pad from her friend, she turned into a stall and pulled in the deepest breath she could muster. Her arms felt jiggly and light as the adrenaline began to leave her body, and her panic dissipated.

When she was all set, she waddled out of the stall and looked begrudgingly at Maggie. "This is so uncomfortable."

Maggie gave her a closed-lipped smile. "But you're a woman now!" she said, clapping her hands.

Nina could tell she was just trying to make her feel better, and she appreciated the sentiment, but she only felt more like a child than she did an hour ago. An unprepared, awkward child.

As a kid, Nina never did go through a boys-have-cooties phase. In fact, her eyes would roll when girls at school would say it. Because she knew, without a shadow of a doubt, that she was one of them. It was just the way it had always been. However, she wasn't entirely sure about Timmy Baker. But he was a one-off in her mind. An annoying amoeba in the crowd that she just had to tolerate.

But the rest of them? The remainder of the boys from Carver Road?

They were hers.

They made her laugh, and she made them laugh. She held her own in competitive games, none of them ever letting her off easy. And they always had her back, as she had theirs.

As a little girl with dirty fingernails and twigs in her hair, Nina never imagined anything other than friendship with them. As girls at school started talking about kissing boys at the end of grammar school, Nina had always scrunched her nose. Not in disgust. No, it wasn't that. It was more of an indifference; it was neither disgusting nor fathomable. Nina was a little bit of a late bloomer, as they say.

So, it came as quite a surprise to her when she was stricken one day when she watched Brett walking into the cafeteria from afar. She sat at their table, waiting for the rest of their group. She couldn't hear him, but she could see him laughing, his head back, white teeth displayed, and sandy hair spiked straight up with gel. Her eyes widened as she watched him approach her.

Why is my heart beating so fast?

Why aren't I breathing?

"What's the matter, Neen?" he asked, taking a seat beside her on the bench.

Nina could feel her eyebrows touching her hairline. Was she sweating? What the hell was going on?

"What?" she asked, her voice coming out as a squeak.

Brett placed the back of his hand on her forehead in jest. "You look unwell," he said, his smile reaching his ears.

Nina tucked a non-existent piece of hair behind her ear, fiddling and desperate to snap herself back into reality. The reality where Brett was only the best friend she ever had. The yin to her yang. The missing piece to her soul.

But what does that mean? My soul? *So, is he my* soulmate?

Do I love him?

"Earth to Ninaaaa," Brett said, waving his hand in front of her face.

"Oh, um—" Nina blinked her eyes. "I just realized I forgot to do my English homework." A wayward laugh escaped.

Brett's humorous expression changed to one of concern. "We didn't have English homework last night, Neen."

Nina's shoulders slumped as she let out a dramatic sigh. "Oh! Right!" she said. "I feel better. Thanks for reminding me." Her shaky smile did little to ease the look on Brett's face, but he let it go, and the remainder of their lunch continued uneventfully.

For the weeks that followed, Nina couldn't shake the butterflies that came in swarms whenever she was with Brett, which was—of course—nearly always. At least whenever their sports didn't interfere.

Basketball and baseball for Brett. Field hockey and lacrosse for Nina.

It scared her, really, the strange feelings brewing inside her. Especially since the feelings were directed toward Brett. She wasn't about to ruin what they had always had between them, so she channeled her newly discovered attraction to boys to someone else. That did the trick, for the time being, and distracted her from the problem building roots inside her chest.

"I have a crush," Nina said one afternoon as she and the girls from lacrosse sat snacking in the basement, *Bring It On* playing in the background. "And I'm asking him to the Spring Dance."

Four other sets of eyes turned to her, unblinking, waiting for her to go on.

"Who is it?" Emma squealed. "Is it Brett?"

"What?" Nina gasped, alarmed at the inquisition. "No, it's not Brett." She didn't mean to come off so defensive, but she couldn't help that.

Emma shrugged, none the wiser.

"Then who is it?" Maggie asked.

"Ryan Jenkins." Nina said the name with a coolness that she had to work to control, ripping a piece of Twizzlers off the vine with her teeth.

The girls all looked at her, dumbfounded. "R.J.?" Jillian Morrows asked. "The junior?"

"Mmmhmm." Nina didn't look over to meet the sets of eyes staring at her. She just smirked, her lips turning up slightly as she stared at the TV while Torrence carried on and on about a problem with her cheerleading team.

"He's the most popular guy in the school, Nina," Sharon Wallace said, flipping her red hair over her shoulder.

Nina turned her head toward Sharon. "Yeah. So?"

The girls all exchanged glances. Emma's face brightened. "Well, he's so hot, Nina. What's your plan?"

The girls all stared at her, and Nina shrugged. "I'm going to ask him to the dance tomorrow after school. I always see him heading to the lax fields. I'm just going to do it."

It was a tradition at Seaview Regional High School that the girls were the askers for the spring dance. But a freshman asking a junior? That wasn't a common occurrence, but the act made her feel like she was coming back into the Nina she had always known.

The confident one.

The girl who knew who she was.

The girl who wasn't bossy but rather just a girl who knew what she wanted and wasn't afraid to go for it. She knew there was a difference between being bossy and being a leader.

Nina had been fighting the ghosts of her mind for some time.

The thoughts that swarmed through her head, egging her on to pinch the skin on her belly—the term *pudgy* swimming through her thoughts, no matter how much she pushed it away.

The image of Brett as someone more than her best friend, which was all she ever wanted him to be.

The emotions that had been tormenting her for years, causing lumps to form in her throat that had been more difficult to swallow than she had cared to admit. She was sick of it; truly, she was.

She was determined to take back control of her body and mind.

R.J. was her next conquest. An attempt, albeit a desperate one, to pull back the reins on the chaos. To quiet those ghosts that had haunted her for way too long.

The girls responded to this news with squeals of excitement, causing Nina to laugh while also attempting to play it cool.

———

The following day, on the way to the fields, Nina saw R.J. and some other kids from the boys' varsity team, and she jogged up ahead of her friends. She bit back the nerves she was feeling about what she was getting ready to do.

It's no big deal.

At least that's what she had told herself as she had lain awake the night before, staring at the ceiling.

"Hey, R.J., wait up," Nina said as she approached him from behind. His initials felt strange on her tongue as she said them, his nickname feeling like it was made for only those closest to him. Momentarily, she felt like an imposter, and as he turned around toward her, she sucked in a breath. "Ryan…hey." Her smile felt weird as she awkwardly tucked a stray hair behind her ear, a nervous habit she had recently acquired.

R.J. smiled as he looked around, his eyes landing back on Nina. She smiled back at him, her cheeks growing red with embarrassment. He seemed so much older standing right there in front of her. His floppy brown hair tucked into his backward baseball hat, his dark eyes burning. "Hey…" His voice trailed off.

"Nina," she hurried to respond. "I'm Nina; I play on J.V." She held up her lacrosse stick as an explanation.

"Oh, cool," he replied, shifting his gear. "What's up, Nina?"

She noted how cool he sounded. How suave he looked. So much more than the guys in her grade. It made her light-headed, but she refused to back down from her plan.

Nina looked down at her feet before reprimanding herself and forcing her eyes back to Ryan's. "Um. I was curious…uh, if you wanted to go to the spring dance with me. I'm sure someone already asked you, but I was just thinking maybe—" She was rambling. But he saved her from further embarrassment by cutting her off.

R.J. flashed her a sideways smile. "Sure," he said, his voice smooth as butter. "I'll go to the dance with you. Two lax players? Sounds great to me." He winked at her, and her heart felt like it fell to the gravel at her feet.

"Oh, really?" She heard her voice and hated how eager it sounded, how surprised. "I mean, awesome," she added, trying to play it cool.

"Why don't you give me your address, and I'll pick you up at around six."

"Oh, ok, yeah," Nina said, reaching into her bag for a piece of paper and a pen. "My friends are meeting at the gazebo at five-thirty though, for pictures and stuff. So, if you want to meet me there or pick me up earlier?

I don't care. Whatever you want to do." *Chill out, you idiot*, she chastised herself.

R.J. laughed softly. "I'll pick you up at five-fifteen. How does that sound?"

"Oh. Good. Yeah. Great, thanks." Nina handed over the ripped piece of paper with her name and address sketched onto the little blue lines. "Oh, let me put my number on there, too," she said, taking the paper back from his hands and scribbling it on there.

She handed it back to him, a sheepish expression on her face.

"Thanks," he said coolly. "See ya."

Three short words ended the conversation, but the look on his face lingered for a brief moment but felt like a lifetime to Nina. Not having anything left to say, she simply smiled and watched him turn and walk away, up toward the upper field, just as her friends approached her.

"Oh my God, Nina!" Daisy said, grabbing her arm.

"Shh," Nina said through a laugh, looking to make sure R.J. was far enough away. "He said yes," she hissed, her smile reaching her ears.

"I can't believe you did that!" Emma said, looking over Nina's shoulder and watching R.J. ascend further up the hill to the field. "I mean, you're a catch, girl, but I could never have the balls to do that. No way."

Nina laughed, shaking her head. "Let's get to practice, guys."

The girls carried their gear up to their field, and as they did, Nina felt as if she was floating, like nothing in the world could touch her.

It should have alarmed her some—how she could go from down in the dumps to high as a kite so quickly. She, like all girls her age, hadn't yet learned that the faster you fly, the harder you fall.

Unlike the eighth-grade dance where Jane did Nina's hair at home, the spring dance on Ryan Jenkins's arm was reason enough to go all out. Nina and Maggie spent nearly two hours at the salon getting their hair curled and pinned robustly on top of their heads, with little pieces curled and hanging down the sides of their heads. Then they went to Nina's house, where Sharon, a self-proclaimed makeup artist, did her makeup.

"What do you think?" Sharon asked her when she was done, turning Nina to face the mirror to check out her work.

"Wow, Sharon," Nina marveled. "It looks amazing. Thank you."

"R.J. will melt to a puddle at your feet," Sharon laughed.

Nina rolled her eyes playfully. "Ok, I'm going to get dressed. Thanks again." She pulled Sharon in for a hug.

"Ok, I'm going home to get ready. I'll meet you at the gazebo at five-thirty."

"See you then!"

As Sharon left her room, Nina walked to her closet to pull her dress out—a pale yellow halter dress with a satin finish. The dress slinked over her growing curves and fell just above her knees. She zipped up the side of the dress and looked at herself in her mirror, a small smile spreading across her face.

Over the last few months, Nina had been getting a bit more comfortable with her changing body and less inclined to hide her growing chest, which at one point she had despised. It had taken her quite some time to accept the girly things that were always pushed on her by her friends, her tomboyish nature still lingering there, taunting her. Nina had begun to reason that maybe she actually wasn't a tomboy at all. That it had just been a label put on her out of necessity because of the neighbor kids. Well, she was done fighting it. If she wanted to look pretty and done up, she was going to do it. Pulling in a deep breath, she fiddled with her hair, touched her face, and smoothed out her dress before grabbing her shoes and going downstairs.

"Wow, Nina!" Jane said as Nina entered the kitchen. "Sharon has quite a talent."

"I know, she should be a makeup artist," Nina replied, as she slid her foot into the strappy heel she chose for the occasion.

"Smile!" Jane said, holding up her camera. Nina giggled, rolling her eyes but still managing to send a smile toward her mom. "So, what's the plan?"

"Well, R.J. will be here in a few minutes, and then we are going to the gazebo for pictures. You and Dad can meet us there, and then we will head to the dance from town." Nina clipped the strap of her second shoe into place and stood up, glancing out the front window to the street, feeling her hands begin to shake.

She and R.J. had talked a few times since she'd asked him to go with her. They smiled and waved in the hallways, and one time, after dinner, when the phone rang, she was utterly surprised to hear him on the other end of the line, claiming he was calling to ask what color her dress was.

"Sounds like a plan," Jane said, zipping her purse. "Dad will meet us over there. He's heading there straight from his work meeting."

"He's here," Nina said, her voice shaking, just like her hands. Watching his black Chevy Cavalier pull into the driveway, she wiped her sweaty hands on the sides of her dress and wobbled slightly on her heels as she went to pick up her tiny purse from the stairs. "Will you get him at the door, Mom?" she asked.

"Of course, hunny. Don't be nervous!"

Easier said than done, Nina thought to herself as she wondered how she had gotten here. To be going to the spring dance with one of the most popular boys at school. The nagging feeling in her belly was the kind you get when you think that, just maybe, something might be too good to be true.

As R.J. shut his door and headed toward the house, she watched him. His dark hair was spiked all over and his suit made him look entirely different than the athlete he was at school. And there it was, a yellow tie that matched her dress nearly perfectly. And in his hand, a bouquet of white daisies.

Her nerves mellowed a bit at the sight of him walking to the door, and she scurried into the kitchen, away from the windows, to wait. She listened to him knock and to her mother opening the door to greet him.

Her breath suspended, she heard her mom introducing herself and the muffled but pleasant response of her date.

And then she entered the living room. "Hi, R.J.," she said, pulling her confidence up from deep within her, though she was still nervous. Clasping her hands in front of her, she cringed at their clamminess.

"Hi, Nina," he said. "You look nice."

"Thanks, so do you." Nina walked closer toward him.

"Here, I brought these." R.J. held out the flowers, and Nina took them from his hands.

"Thanks, I love daisies," she said.

"I'll put them in water," Jane said, taking them from Nina's hand. "That was sweet of you, Ryan."

"No big thing," he replied, rolling back on his heels, his hands shoved into his pants pockets.

"So, want to head out?" Nina asked.

"Sure, let's go."

"Wait, wait, wait," Jane said. "Let me just take some pictures outside before we head over to town."

"Mom," Nina said, warningly, embarrassed and just wanting to get in R.J.'s car.

"It's fine," R.J. smiled. "Let's do it."

And so, they posed in front of the house, and Nina couldn't fathom the reality of R.J.'s arm around her waist, his body so close to hers, his Axe Body Spray sending her into a tailspin.

"You two look adorable!" Jane said, causing Nina to groan as she took R.J.'s elbow and pulled him toward his car.

"See you in town, Mom."

R.J. held open the passenger side door as Nina awkwardly lowered herself in and he shut the door, walking swiftly to the driver side. Nina had never been in a car driven by a boy before. In fact, she only ever had been in a car driven by adults, except the one time Jane allowed a girl from the varsity lacrosse team to drive her home after practice. Even though Jane was not at all thrilled about it, it was a necessity that day.

She felt like a grown up.

As the car backed up toward the trees at the end of the road and reversed direction, Nina glanced out the window to see Brett getting into his brother's car, looking handsome in his suit. She waved eagerly as Brett gave her a wave back.

"Who's that?" R.J. asked.

"That's Brett."

"Your neighbor?" he asked.

"Yeah, and my best friend."

For a brief moment, Nina longed to be climbing into Seamus's car, heading to the gazebo, and dancing with Brett. But as quick as the thought entered her mind, she dismissed it, uninterested in letting the confusing emotions she'd been wrestling lately dampen her evening. It was time to start accepting the changes and rolling with them, as best she could.

An hour later, Nina's cheeks ached from the smiles she had been pulling for all of the pictures, and her eyes still glowed from the camera flashes. R.J. took Nina's hand as they entered the high school, into the decorated gymnasium where the floors thumped from the D.J.'s table. Dream's "Loves U Not" was playing so loudly it was a shock to Nina's system.

She wondered if her hand was sweating, and if it was, she wondered even more if R.J. noticed.

"Hey, I'm going to find some of my boys," R.J. said. "I'll meet up with you in a bit. Do you see any of your friends?"

Nina felt R.J.'s hand loosen around hers, telling her he was trying to let go. She released the hold she had on him even though she didn't want to. She had imagined being tethered to him for the evening, not him dropping her the second they got there. She hated the feeling of disappointment that bubbled inside. *Foolish girl*, she thought. *Pull yourself together.*

"Oh, yeah. Ok," she fumbled with her words, glancing around for her friends but not seeing any of them. "See ya later."

"Save me a dance," he said to her, his signature smile on full display.

Nina was confused. Weren't they supposed to dance together the whole time? Isn't that what it means when you go to a dance together?

"Ok." She started to say something else, but R.J. had already headed off in another direction, and Nina was left standing there alone. She scanned the gym again for a familiar face, but her eyes were becoming cloudy with tears of embarrassment.

Turning on her heel to head for the bathroom, she rammed right into the person coming up behind her.

Brett.

"Oh, hi, B," she said, overcome with relief to have a friend by her side.

"Has anyone told you that you look beautiful tonight?" he asked casually—friendly but honest. Nina giggled, looking down at her shoes and shaking her head. Brett lifted her chin with his finger, and when their eyes met, she felt her insides settle. "I'm serious," he said.

"I know. I know I look good," she replied, and they both laughed.

The dance wasn't at all what Nina had expected. She and R.J. danced for a total of one song, Brandy's "Have You Ever," and didn't speak otherwise. She danced with her friends, and in spite of feeling let down by R.J., she was able to shake it off and enjoy the night.

Toward the end of the evening, Nina's skin felt moist with perspiration. The air in the gym was thick with the heat of hundreds of kids dancing. As one of the last songs of the evening played, she sat in the darkness on the bleachers to catch her breath, watching kids pairing off for a slow dance. She wasn't eavesdropping, but by chance, she overheard the upper-class girls talking behind her.

"Can you believe R.J. came here with a freshman," one of them scoffed.

"Oh my God, I know," said the other. "I asked him if he wanted to go, and he told me he wished he could, but some freshman had asked him, and he felt bad for her, so he said yes." Both girls laughed, and Nina froze, unable to breathe. "But he danced with me basically the whole time, so whatever."

"Yeah, it's not like she's his type at all."

The first girl laughed. "Um, obviously! Brown hair? Frumpy? I don't think so."

"When are you two just going to make it official?" the first girl asked.

"Oh, I think tonight! He's dropping off the girl and then coming to my house," the second girl said.

The ringing in Nina's ears was dizzying, to say the least, and she sat there, her back to the girls. She said a silent prayer, thanking God for the darkness that surrounded her. But the insatiable need to exit the gym took over, and she got up swiftly and walked toward the door as she heard the girls' embarrassed giggles at her back. She knew they saw her yellow dress and realized what they had done, but Nina also knew that they weren't at all concerned about her hurt feelings.

She found Brett and Johnny Cooper out at the vending machines getting sodas. "Hi, B, can Seamus bring me home with you?"

Brett looked at her, confused. "Yeah, of course. You ok?"

Nina painted a smile. "Yeah. Absolutely."

Though she knew she wasn't ok. She knew she would cry herself to sleep when she got home—her previously high-floating feeling popped instantly like a balloon.

Nina started her sophomore year feeling like an imposter. She didn't know who she was or what she wanted. When the summer was winding down, the kids in the neighborhood were getting antsy, and they all looked forward to starting fall sports and seeing what the school year would bring, Nina held on to summer with a grip so tight it pained her.

She had spent the entire summer swimming, riding her bike, running, and begging her mom to take her to aerobics classes at the rec center. She'd be damned if she was going to show up back at school this year a frumpy, pudgy mess. Her body was tanned and toned at the start of school, her reflection in the mirror looking like someone else's. She was proud of her body. Of the effort she had put into changing it.

But as she walked into the school on the first day, she was reminded of what she had left there in the spring. Her ego busted and her self-image was a direct reflection of what other people said about her. Her low-rise jeans that exposed her midriff, ever so slightly, made her feel like she had something to prove.

Look, see, everyone, I'm not frumpy.

"Are you taking AP History this year, Maggie?" Nina asked as the crowd gathered around the welcome table to get their schedules for the semester.

"No, are you?"

"Yeah," Nina said, looking at her schedule. "Looks like I have Mr. Gomes."

"Shut up!" said Maggie. "You are so lucky. He's so hot."

Nina rolled her eyes. The girls at Seaview Regional High School had yet to let up on that teacher. Nina hadn't understood it before—before the time she began blooming, as they say. But she understood now. She had run into Mr. Gomes in town over the summer quite a few times in Sweet Marie's while he was getting coffee.

He had a way about him that intrigued Nina. And he looked at her like she wasn't just some dumb kid. As Nina worked herself to the bone to fix her body over the summer, she marveled at his looks and rubbed away goosebumps on her arms whenever he spoke to her. She found herself wondering if he noticed how she had changed. How she had grown up a bit during her time away from school.

With her iced green tea, she would sit and watch him order his coffee the same every time—adding just a splash of cream.

One day in August, just before school started back, Nina strolled into Sweet Marie's.

"Iced green tea for ya?" the owner asked with a smile.

"I'd like an iced coffee, actually, Judy, just black."

"Coffee, honey? The caffeine's going to stunt your growth," Judy said with a boisterous laugh. "And you're already so petite as it is!"

Nina straightened her spine in an effort to appear taller—fed up with the comments people always made about her appearance, her body. She shrugged her shoulders. "Whatever."

She paid for her drink and took it from Judy, walking over to the table of accouterments. She took the plastic cap off, the straw dripping some coffee onto the counter. Nina picked up the silver carafe and splashed a bit of cream into her cup. She watched the white liquid slowly cascade throughout the dark coffee as she snapped the lid back in place.

Nina walked out of Sweet Marie's, the bell ringing overhead, and into the humid air outside.

With her coffee…and one splash of cream.

Chapter 17

Nina 2001-2002

I**F YOU ASKED N**INA now, having hindsight and all, she would tell you
that she had been a victim of Mr. Gomes.

Of Glen.

Being on a first-name basis came quickly and from there, the novelty
only grew.

But all the while, in the glow of it, she *had* been a victim; she just
hadn't known it at the time. Glen Gomes was coveted. The girls gossiped
about him, dreamed about him, fantasized about him. And though it was
a secret that she kept locked up so no one found out, Nina was swept up
in something much bigger than herself.

She had been at her lowest. R.J. had dismissed her. The older girls had
called her frumpy, mocking her. And in her own head, being pudgy had
become a false identity she took on without knowing why.

But Nina did what she knew how to do—she took control. Her adoles-
cent mind had become so warped that she was quite desperate for anything
that would make her feel the way she once did—before things had gotten
hard. Back when she was just one of the boys on Carver Road. Shaping

her body to make it acceptable to others was the only way she thought she could do that.

In doing so, she gained a sort of mock confidence that didn't mirror the old Nina, not even a little bit, and somewhere inside, she felt like an imposter, though she ignored these doubts that nagged her. It was a sort of demeanor that attracted the wrong kind of attention. Attention she received from someone willing to prey on her weakness.

She had been wrong—about all of it. But she didn't know that then, and there was certainly no stopping her on the path toward destruction.

On the second Tuesday of September, the air was crisp, and the sky was clear as the kids from Carver Road slumped out of their houses while wiping sleep from their eyes, dragging their feet to the bus stop, where it had been picking them up since they were five years old. Nina drew a circle in the dirt that was scattered on the sidewalk while everyone gathered around. Hearing the cry of a bird louder than a gull, she pulled her gaze up to a large nest that rested on the street pole where there were two large birds taking flight in opposite directions. And it was an afterthought, really, but what she noticed while looking at the sky was the brightness of it. It was unimaginably blue. The air had seemed to turn that morning, crisper than yesterday, reminding Nina that summer was certainly over, and fall was taking hold.

Nina sat in her second period class, American history, the only class where she tended to sit completely upright, eager to hear what Mr. Gomes had to say. She tapped her pen on the pages of her notebook, never taking her eyes off him as he went on about Gettysburg. They had only been back in school for a few weeks, but Mr. Gomes had already winked at her three times.

Nina was keeping count.

At 8:53 a.m., Nina glanced at the clock, silently hoping the class would last forever. The lecture was just getting started as Mr. Gomes got quite animated and excited about the topic when the beige phone on the wall let out an ear-piercing ring.

Mr. Gomes sighed. "Sorry, friends. Just a second." He strode to the wall and picked up the phone as Nina watched his every move. The rest of the class began to mumble and chat, turning to face one another. Nina would have done the same…had it been any other class.

Instead, she watched Mr. Gomes. Watched the concern grow between his eyebrows and watched as he took a labored breath while running his hands through his thick, dark hair. He stepped out into the hall, the spiral cord of the phone bending around the frame of the doorway. She could barely make out anything he was saying, but she swore she heard the strange and offensive word *hijacker*.

It wasn't a word that Nina heard often, if ever, but she knew it wasn't good. Was the school in danger?

Nina began to feel her intuition bubbling in her belly as she usually did when something alarming was happening, and she sat up straight as a rod. Something wasn't right. She could feel it. Mr. Gomes walked back into the room, the same concern still written on his face. She looked around the room. No one was paying any attention. Mr. Gomes put the phone back in its cradle and cleared his throat, causing the rest of the glass to simmer down and face him.

"Um," Mr. Gomes started. Nina noted that he looked nervous, unsure of how to address the class. She held her breath. "Boys and girls, I'm going to turn on the television. An airplane has crashed into one of the World Trade Center Towers in New York. I don't know much else; it only just happened." He turned his back to the class, grabbing the remote from his desk before pointing it to the TV. When it came on, the fuzzy screen showed smoke billowing out of the tower that seemed to touch the New York City sky.

The kids in the class all quieted down immediately, all eyes on the screen as the news broadcasters nervously reported on the disaster, not knowing many details of what had actually happened. While the students whispered to each other, apprehension spun through each word they spoke.

The kids were only fifteen, for the most part, old enough to understand when something dire had happened but too young to comprehend the magnitude of such things and too self-centered, though to no fault of their own. It was just where they were in their stage of growing up. They felt entirely too invincible for their own good. To them, this tragedy they were watching unfold seemed to be too far away to impact them. Though it was frightening, there was no way for them to grasp the severity of it.

And then the unthinkable happened… another plane hit the remaining tower, and the room gasped.

"Holy shit," Timmy said, his voice rising above the murmurs.

Nina's eyes widened, and her heart began to race. *What is happening?*

Mr. Gomes muted the ancient television that was suspended from the wall above the chalkboard. Muted it, yes, but taking away the sound didn't take away the visual that the entire class could still see. Smoke billowing through Manhattan. People running. Fire trucks racing down smoke-filled streets.

Chaos and confusion.

And a sense of unease started to burrow deep inside Nina, in there with the other pieces of her that were already mangled and unsettled. Because that's the way Nina was, and how she had always been, completely and utterly affected by everyone and everything around her. Unable to let anything go. Just like the way her mind would wander and her heart would sink when she saw those shelter commercials with the Sarah McLachlan song playing over it. The unbelievably sad look in the animals' eyes seemed to glare into her soul, ruining her day every time. *Maybe I can give my allowance to the animals. Maybe Mom and Dad will let me get one.* As if she saved them, she would save herself.

"Should we even be watching this?" a girl named Shelly asked from the back row. "Are you even allowed to show us this?" Her voice wasn't the least bit respectful.

Mr. Gomes eyed her compassionately. "This sort of thing isn't in the teacher handbook, actually." He was serious, but his comment caused some kids to chuckle. "You are in history class, Shelly. And right here, on the television, is history, happening right in front of you." He gestured toward the old box on the wall, and his face softened. "If you need to go take a walk, you are more than welcome to take a break."

Abruptly, Shelly rose from her seat and strode out of the classroom, slinging her backpack over her shoulder. She wouldn't be returning. Nina could tell that much. Mr. Gomes hung his head briefly before taking his glance back up to the news, unmuting it.

By the time the bell rang, Nina's legs felt like jelly, and she couldn't bring herself to get up from her seat. As everyone around her clambered up, gathering their belongings, hurrying out to see what everyone else was saying about the current state of the airlines and the skyscrapers around the country, Nina just sat there in the front row, unable to move.

When the classroom cleared out entirely, Nina's ears felt like they were ringing as she brought her eyes up to meet Mr. Gomes, and the look on his face caused her heart to flutter. She was scared, and she wanted to hug someone. Preferably him.

"Are you ok, Ms. Jackson?" She didn't reply. "Nina?" he said, concern in his tone.

Nina got flustered, stuttering her words. "Oh. Um. I don't know," she said, her voice squeaking. "What's happening?"

Mr. Gomes approached the front of his desk and leaned on it, facing Nina. "Tell me what you're thinking," he said softly.

The sound of his voice pricked something in Nina, as if a friend was talking to her, not her teacher. "I don't know," she uttered, a tear slipping down her cheek.

"This will get sorted out, Nina. I know we aren't sure what is going on right now, but nothing is going to happen to you." Even though she knew that there was no way for him to be sure of his words, he said this with such conviction that Nina almost believed him.

Almost.

Because Nina had already felt what she was going to feel with this initial news report. The hollowness had already begun to settle. There was no changing that, at least not for the time being. Her intuitive nature was telling her that something dark was on the horizon. And she was right about that, not just with the fate of the country but her own personal fate as well; it all felt bleak. With sad eyes, she looked at her teacher, who held out his arms. She wasn't sure at first what he was doing, but she quickly realized he was inviting her in for a hug. She got up from her desk, put her backpack on her shoulder, and walked into his embrace, swallowing down the lump in her throat.

She noted that Mr. Gomes smelled different from her guy friends. More grown up. She closed her eyes and allowed him to hug her, even though she knew it felt off. A tad bit forbidden. But she was sad and frightened, and Mr. Gomes was comforting her.

Nina pulled away and wiped her eyes, taking in a deep breath. She smiled weakly at him. "Thanks," she muttered, sounding meek. All she wanted to do was go to the front office and call home to talk to her mom. Knowing how childish that sounded, she kept it to herself as she walked out of the classroom, not before looking over at her shoulder to see Mr. Gomes giving her a look that she couldn't place. But it caused her to smile at him again, staring for an extra beat before she turned toward her next class, which she undoubtedly would be late for.

On her way to geometry, she passed the office and saw a crowd of students waiting in line to use the phones. The vision made her stomach plummet again, a daunting scene—so many kids trying to connect, to get answers to questions that were unclear. *What is going on?* Nina internally wondered. Geometry could wait. Nina walked into the office to wait with the crowd.

By the time it was her turn, geometry was well underway, and the secretary was on a constant string of calls with teachers confirming that students had been in the office. She didn't care if she was going to get in trouble for this today. She dialed her number and waited impatiently, tapping her finger on the countertop in the office, her eyes darting all over the room until her mother finally answered, "Hello?" She sounded breathless.

"Mom?" Nina's voice squeaked on the line.

"Oh, hunny!" Jane huffed into the phone and sounded relieved. "I have been calling the school for thirty minutes! Busy signals! I wanted—"

"Mom," Nina cut her off. "The office is filled with kids trying to call home. It's crazy here." She looked around to see if anyone was looking at her. "What's going on, Mom?" she asked in a hushed whisper.

"We are trying to figure that out, hunny. I'm going to come get you and Brett right now. Can you find him? Mrs. Warner is in hysterics."

"Are we in danger?" Nina asked, looking at the TV that had been turned on in the office. Her eyes narrowed to make out what was happening. "More planes hit?" she whispered, mostly to herself.

Her mom sighed on the other end of the line, worrying for her daughter. "Yes, love."

"Wait, wasn't Mr. Warner..." Nina's voice trailed off.

"Yes, that's why I'm coming to get both of you. I'm leaving right now, Nina."

"Ok, Mom. Bye." After hanging up, Nina gave the phone to the next kid waiting and rushed out of the office, trying to figure out where Brett was, but her mind was racing, and she struggled to remember where he usually was while she was in geometry. She brought her hands to her hair, pushing it out of her face.

"Nina!" She turned her head and saw Brett hurrying toward her, panic on his face.

"B! I was just coming to look for you. Are you ok? Have you talked to your mom yet? My mom is coming to get us. She said—"

"I called her from the athletics' office. She hasn't heard from my dad yet," Brett said, cutting her off.

Danny Warner was scheduled to leave from Logan that morning, heading to Los Angeles for a construction design conference. And according to the Boston news station, that was the exact route of one of the planes that hit a tower.

Nina pulled away from Brett's embrace and looked up at him. His hair was tousled like he had been anxiously messing with it. She knew he had been. She knew everything about him. His green eyes looked red and raw like he hadn't slept in 100 years. She knew that was because of the tortuous and dark thoughts that were running through his mind at that very moment. They were the same thoughts that she was having.

Was this awful and unimaginable thing that was happening to their country going to be the thing that saved the Warner's from their nightmares?

That thought mixed with the agony of the reality they were all facing. The fear of what was happening and what they were thinking. But Nina had those thoughts because she loved Brett. He was her best friend, who was always hurting, no matter the happiness he tried to exude. No matter the positive attitude he always had.

He was always taping back together broken pieces of himself. But because of Nina, he was never alone in it. And as the pair stood there in the hall, Nina knew that she wasn't leaving Brett's side until someone physically forced her to.

Back on Carver Road, many of the neighbors had gathered at the Warner's house. Nina, Brett, Johnny, Gary, and Timmy were hunkered around the coffee table in the living room, no one touching the large bowl of popcorn that Jane had made while Laura sat weeping at the kitchen table. Laura couldn't confirm the flight number because Danny hadn't left that information with her. All the adults were gathered around her trembling body, trying to get her to eat and drink something of substance. The TV brought zero reprieve, but no one could turn it off. They were glued to it with reckless abandon.

Nina sat on the floor beside Brett with her hand on his leg. They locked eyes with one another, and Nina's expression did all the talking. *You ok?*

Brett gave her a single nod. But she put her head on his shoulder because she knew he wasn't fine. How could he be? And just as Nina's emotions started to bubble for the 100th time that day, the sound of the phone ringing brought the whole house to absolute silence.

Laura got up from the chair, knocking it over in the process, and scurried to the phone on the wall. "Hello?" she said urgently into the receiver. Everyone looked on in wonderment. A moment later, Laura Warner's shoulders sank, and her sobs were difficult to read. Was it grief? Was it relief? Nina wondered how and why she couldn't tell. It seemed like something that should be obvious.

A moment later, Laura hung up the phone and turned to the group of neighbors and friends. "He missed his flight."

And it was then that Nina could read Laura Warner's emotions. Relief? Grief? It was undoubtedly both.

During the weeks following 9/11, life for the kids went back to something that mirrored normal. They didn't have the wherewithal yet to feel the burdens of the world following the terrorist attack. They didn't know then that the waves from that fateful day would follow them throughout their whole lives. As they grew and moved along their paths in life, they would continue to hear the words "ever since 9/11" and "had it not been for 9/11…" and the sentences always ended with some sort of a complaint, whether it was a minor nuisance or something catastrophic, like a market crash.

But those things were in the future. For now, sophomore year for Nina and her friends carried on.

Football games on chilly evenings.

Ping pong, movies, and snacks in Johnny Cooper's basement.

The kids sitting in a crowded theater watching *Jeepers Creepers*, Nina covering her eyes through half of it.

Normal teenage things. They were in their own little world for the time being.

But there was something that wasn't normal. And that was Nina's growing desperation to be near Mr. Gomes.

"Glen Gomes, your name sounds like a cartoon character," Nina had joked one afternoon in late November. She had been in his classroom on the accord that she needed extra help, which was far from reality. History was easy for her. In fact, all her subjects were. But there she was, nonetheless, seeking something she had no business looking for in a teacher.

Looking back on it now, she might tell you that it was the way he looked at her after her little joke. The way one side of his mouth turned up and his eyes seemed to sparkle with something dark that taunted her. It was a look that ignited something inside her that would prove difficult to tame.

"It's Mr. Gomes to you, Ms. Jackson." He was reprimanding her in a playful way that made it very obvious that he didn't actually mind her calling him by his first name. Or maybe he liked her calling him *Mr.* Either way, from that moment on, Nina was stuck in a trance that would, inevitably, nearly ruin her.

She placed her hands behind her, leaning on her desk in the front row that was directly in front of his desk, a spot that all the girls had clambered for but the one Nina had claimed for herself on the first day of class. It wasn't long before Nina began catching the little looks and the winks that Mr. Gomes sent her way—when she shared her arguments and opinions on Louis and Clark, her theories with facts to back them up. She knew that the handsome man—her teacher—was proud of her.

That she was accomplishing something.

That the looks he was giving her were due to her quick wit and charm.

But also, because she was attractive and worthy of his attention for other reasons that had nothing to do with her academic achievements.

And so, she indulged in her fantasies.

She relished in the newfound confidence that had resurfaced—however misdirected it was.

One night, while getting ready for bed, Nina began to wonder how she would survive Christmas break without seeing Mr. Gomes. It would be twelve long days without his smiles, his encouragement…his hand on her shoulder, or brushing her hair off of it. Recent gestures that were beginning to feel a bit more immoral. And though she knew it was wrong, that her parents would be mortified, the danger and the thrill of it, and the validation, were too tempting to stop her.

She lay on her bed, facing the door, where a poster of NSYNC seemed to glare at her, her childhood gawking at her. She shifted onto her back, staring at the ceiling, which she knew every groove of because she had been staring at it for years.

What would Brett say?

The thought startled her a bit. For the last two and a half months, Nina hadn't even thought about what anyone would have to say about her dream of Glen Gomes. But as she sat on her childhood bed—the same bed where she used to talk to her best friend across the way with her staticky walkie-talkie—she thought of Brett, and a sinking feeling settled into her gut.

Her best friend, who would do anything to protect her.

Her best friend, who, in spite of his own shit life, saw only the good in everything and everyone around him…would be utterly disappointed in her.

Nina knew this.

And she hated it. Because the voice in her head, the one that tells you right from wrong, was leaning so far away from the angel on one of her shoulders—and too close toward that little devil on the other.

Chapter 18

Nina 2016

NINA WAS SICK WITH it, physically ill from the weight of nostalgia, the memories pushing her into a depressive state, though she didn't know why. She certainly couldn't put words to her feelings, and she was back to struggling to understand how her happy moments were making her feel completely down on her luck. The memories were making her feel frozen and unimaginably sad, and she just wasn't certain how this could be. Because all she wanted to do was go back in time.

She wished her childhood would come back to her. She wished the clocks would reverse and she could relive the moments exactly as they were.

The warmth.

The laughter.

The wholeness.

Why did it feel like her past was all that made her and that nothing in her present mattered even a tiny bit?

As Nina sat on a small dune bathed in the colors of the setting sun, she watched the waves and smelled the smoke from the bonfire just down the beach. A group of people who didn't belong to her sat at the fire's edge doing things that felt so memorable to Nina that it broke her heart. Their laughter floated through the air, pulling at both her ear lobes and her heartstrings.

Taking her back to her childhood years, the years that had made her…the part of herself that she loved the most.

The part of her that felt the purest. The pictures in her mind flickered back to 1993, right there on this very beach—with a burnt hot dog in one hand and green fluorescent Pro Kadima paddle in the other, she played happily. Her cheeks just below her eyes were tinged a light pink from a day on the beach, her bare legs poking out beneath an oversized sweatshirt, her bathing suit damp underneath.

With a childlike glee, she anticipated what was next.

The group gathered around the fire, huddling together on damp towels.

Marshmallows roasted on the ends of sticks the kids found in the yard before they headed to the beach.

Spooky stories told by her Uncle Rider. Her favorite was always the retelling of the man in the woods, moaning for his golden arm. Uncle Rider would yell, "Got it!" while grabbing one of the kid's limbs, causing them all to shriek and laugh.

As Nina watched the group down at the other end of the beach now, she wondered if joy was growing in their hearts just like it had hers all those years ago. She wondered if they, too, had a tradition of yelling "I hate rabbit stew" when smoke got into their eyes and mouths the way Uncle Rider always said to do—to clear the smoky discomfort. *It works every time. Don't ask me why,* he had always said.

Uncle Rider and Auntie Karen had come over for dinner a few nights before, and while they all sat around the Jackson family table, Nina found herself smiling but also on the verge of tears. She looked at her uncle across the table, his face aged in a way that pained her. He sounded the same, though, his voice reminding her of years long gone—another lifetime, it seemed. She hadn't seen them in so long, and she silently reprimanded herself for causing the disconnect between her and her extended family over the years…again, she wished she simply could go back to her child-hood and do it all over again, exactly the same.

But maybe if she could have gone back, she would have chosen to take a few different paths along the way, paths that would have led her away from the darkness that smothered her at the end of her adolescence.

Nina looked down at her phone resting on the sand beside her, surprised that she had been sitting there for more than an hour. Sighing, she got up from the cool patch and brushed the specks of sand off her jeans before heading back toward the parking lot and turning right in the direction of Carver Road.

The fluorescent arrows at the end of the main street—the ones that deterred oncoming cars from catapulting into the ocean—brought Nina to a dead stop, her emotions overcoming her. The sensation in her ears sounded like a wind tunnel, and the dilution caused her to lose her footing. She bent down, resting her hands on her knees a moment before realizing that the stance was making it more difficult to breathe. So, she stood straight up, her face toward the twilight sky and her hands on her hips, and she desperately tried to calm her soul.

But this spot. This memory taking hold was all too consuming.

A sob escaped her trembling mouth, followed by a desperate attempt to bring air into her lungs. Nina turned her head slightly down the road toward where she needed to go and willed herself to move, one foot in front of the other.

One day at a time, Nina, she said to herself. *One day at a time.*

As Nina pulled her mom's car into a spot on Mary Harlow's property, she glanced around the little haven covered in the post-dawn glow. She opened the car door to the sounds of the bird song as they were all waking—communicating with one another. The screech of an osprey sounded in her ears, alerting her eyes to look to the sky. Nina squinted to see the shadow of one heading toward its nest. Bonnie, or possibly Clyde.

Nina's heart warmed, thinking of the pair.

The loyalty and all.

She smiled at the spot where the bird had disappeared.

"Watching my friends, are ya?" Mary's voice cut through the sounds of nature, causing Nina to turn toward the house and see Mary standing on her porch, a steaming mug in her hand.

"I'm drawn to them," Nina replied, smiling sheepishly as she walked toward the steps of the porch.

Mary's rheumy eyes sparkled. "Come in, dear," she said. "I made this for you." She handed Nina the mug, and the aroma of chamomile and honey tickled her nose.

"Thank you, Mary." Nina held the mug carefully as they walked into the house. "What's on the agenda for today?"

For the last week, Nina had been over a few times, helping tend to a sick goat that Mary had in her care. She had done a few errands for her, getting food and buckets from Cape Cod Feed and Seed. She had bought her own pair of galoshes that she was beginning to treasure as an important article of clothing. A meaningful article. She felt like she had a purpose when she was with Mary. She felt like she was doing something important. Something good for her heart, and her soul.

"There's a meeting at town hall this afternoon about the next steps for aiding in the safety of the ospreys," Mary began, taking a sip of her tea. "I think we are going to start moving the two nests that are over on Carver Road."

Nina straightened her spine. "Carver Road? That's where I live," she said.

"Oh, really? Those nests have been there for quite some time, dear." Mary's smile was soft. "Ospreys tend to live seven to ten years, but it's not impossible for them to live much longer. Roger Sims has been studying and watching the birds in this town for decades. He thinks the birds on Carver Road are over twenty years old."

Nina's eyebrows nearly reached her hairline. "Over twenty years old?" She couldn't hide her surprise.

"Yes, dear," Mary said.

Nina pulled a memory from her mind, a memory from her days of living the life she often dreamed about going back to since coming here. Life before the darkness. A memory that has come up more than once since she has been home: The time that she and Brett lay on the bottom of the rickety, abandoned boat looking at the clouds, an osprey casting a shadow over them.

Could that bird be the same one that still lives on Carver Road now?

In the nests that Mary and her team were trying to protect?

"I would like to help with the moving process over there," Nina said, insisting really.

"Sure, dear," Mary replied. "Can you come to the meeting?"

"What time is it at? I'm teaching a class at the rec center at three-thirty."

"Oh, it's at one o'clock; it shouldn't take much more than an hour. If that."

"Ok, I'll head home after I leave here and get ready for work. I can meet you at town hall a little before one."

"Sounds great, thank you, Nina."

Nina smiled, taking the last sip of her tea. "Shall we head out to see Leo?"

Mary had named the sick little goat she had acquired Leo after her late father, and Nina had asked if she had a habit of doing that, of naming the animals after people she had lost in life. To which Mary had smiled at her while tossing her long gray braid over her shoulder. "I do seem to do that, don't I?" she had chuckled.

Mary Harlow had a deep love for family, though they all seemed to be behind the veil now, as far as Nina could tell. Or maybe Mary Harlow just had a deep love in general—for both people and animals. In only a few weeks, Nina had already become quite knowledgeable about Mary's life stories and the people she held dear, especially her George. The stories Mary shared of her and George made Nina daydream about the simple, beautiful life that they had created here on this piece of property—a farm with the ocean just within reach. Mary and George had met when she was sixteen and he was eighteen, heading off to the Navy. They shared Coca-Colas out of glass bottles, sitting on stools at the bar of their local ice cream shop, savoring the sips before he was shipped off. They corresponded for months through handwritten letters that Mary still had in a chest in their bedroom on the first floor of her gray-shingled home.

When he had returned, his physical appearance had changed some—a more defined jaw and a sadness in his eyes that hadn't been there before. But together, they had built a life from the ashes of World War II. A beautiful life in Harborview, Massachusetts.

Listening to Mary's stories was like getting a glimpse into the personal histories of people from the times Nina had learned about in high school.

Civil Rights. JFK's assassination. Riots during the Vietnam War.

The lines on Mary's face even seemed to tell a story. The way her eyes moved told Nina exactly what her emotions were deep down inside and also blatantly on her face. Nina had quickly learned that Mary was special, and their friendship was almost instantaneous—something Nina appreciated.

Leo greeted them at the edge of the gate as they walked up to him, bleating noisily. "Oh, hello there, little Leo," Nina crooned. "How are you this morning?"

Nina and Mary worked together to bottle-feed the babies in the pens, brush the sheep in the barn, and check on the pigs, giving George a few extra scratches behind his scraggly ears.

When it was time to head back home to get ready for the meeting and her classes at the rec center, Nina was filled to the brim, exactly as she needed to be.

Jules was already stretching when Nina arrived in the yoga studio at three o'clock. "You're early," Nina said cheerfully.

"Yeah," Jules replied. "Needed some peace and quiet." She winked, and Nina began to create the ambience in the studio—exactly how she liked it.

Lights dimmed.

Orange essential oil misting from the diffuser.

The sounds of a bubbling brook coming from her stone fountain.

She checked to make sure the towels were ample and the mats were neat and clean. And all the while, she thought of the meeting at town hall. Nina sat with Mary, and they listened to the conversations regarding the money they needed to raise and the need to spread awareness and ask for more volunteers in the community.

A woman that Nina recognized from her past named Terri had said she would use her mother's old ice cream truck to raise some money at the upcoming food truck events and Independence Day festivities—and they could use that money to help get the materials they needed to move all the nests in town.

It came over Nina in a wave, the realization of who Terri was.

Ginny Blake, of course. That was her mother. Ginny Blake, also known as the savior of Carver Road, back in the 90s when the kids—Nina and the boys—were hammering for something cold on a hot summer day.

Nina had overheard the other members of the committee talking about how Ginny was down on her luck, having suffered a few strokes recently. When there was a lull in the conversation, Nina had asked Mary if Ginny was going to be ok, and that she had remembered her from long ago. Mary had assured Nina, in her soft and sweet tone, touching her elbow, that, yes, Ginny was in good hands. John Cooper over at the town PT office was working his magic.

And then Nina had spiraled again into memories of her good friend Johnny and a strange feeling took her over. All these sweet and happy memories swarming into her mind had wilted over time. She had smiled at Mary, glad to know Ginny was on the up and up and pleasantly thrilled that Johnny had a hand in it.

That was the Johnny Cooper she remembered. The kid who carried Logan Branson around school when the power went out and Logan's wheelchair couldn't get in the elevator; the kid who gave all the money in his pockets to homeless people on the street; the kid who gave a voice to people who struggled to use theirs.

The following day, she was going to be walking down Carver Road to meet up with the committee members and get a feel for what they were up against for that particular nest. She couldn't wait to get involved in this effort.

At three-fifteen, Nina stood at the entrance to the studio and welcomed everyone, greeting them with a warm smile. By the time three-thirty rolled around and class was starting, she noted that every space was occupied; it was at full capacity. She smiled to herself, proud of the accomplishment. Easing into the class, she gave herself some time to settle into the motions, to feel the pulls and stretches, allowing her muscles to fully relax.

One day at a time, Nina.

After the class, Felicia was waiting outside the studio to talk to Nina. "Want to come to my office? Just for a quick second," she asked Nina, her tone pleasant and not at all threatening.

Nina smiled. "Sure." And they walked the short walk to Felicia's office where Nina took a seat in the big chair that she'd sat in for her interview not too long ago.

Felicia took a breath and smiled. "Full class today, Nina," she said.

Nina shrugged. "Guess so," she replied happily.

"I think word has spread quickly around here that your classes are quite good." Felicia seemed undeniably impressed. However, she didn't give off that she was surprised. "Your demeanor before, during, and after classes are the difference between you and some other instructors," she continued, and Nina listened intently. Felicia leaned forward on her knees. "These women come for a little release and some peace, and you make them feel like their bodies are enough, that they are capable."

Nina's eyes widened; the praise was more than she expected. Felicia was telling her that she was making women feel the way she had always wanted to feel since she was in middle school…like she was enough. It had been a journey for Nina to finally feel that way, that was certain. But Felicia's words reminded her why she began this career path in the first place…where the ideas for N Bar had come from, the whole reason it existed—to make women strong and comfortable in their skin.

She was good at this. She knew she was and her quick success and the adoration she felt since being back in her hometown proved to be very validating for Nina.

She heaved a heavy, content sigh. "Thank you, Felicia. Thank you so much. That is wonderful feedback, and I'm really enjoying myself."

"Well, that's a relief because I just found out this morning that one of my main instructors, Melissa, is moving to Ohio to help care for her grandmother." She paused, and Nina noted that Felicia was waiting to see how she would react.

"Oh…I see." Nina figured she knew what Felicia was hinting at, but she waited for more information.

"So, I wanted to ask you if you would like more classes," Felicia informed with a smile. "She teaches all ability levels and even some Pilates and barre if—"

"I love barre! And I have some experience with Pilates, too. And, of course, I'm willing to learn anything new." Nina took a breath and smiled, trying to reign in her overexcitement, her complete lack of chill.

To her amusement, Felicia only laughed with her. "I thought that this would be something you would be thrilled about."

"Thanks for trusting in me, Felicia, honestly," Nina said, exhaling swiftly. "I really needed someone to have faith in me as I started picking myself up from the ground." She chuckled a bit in spite of herself.

"Nina, you don't give yourself enough credit."

Nina rolled her eyes in jest. "I know, I'm working on that." And she was, truly. She was working on getting behind the cage that she'd built around her heart, where it was still pure. Where her soul was vibrant. It pained her to think about how these last twelve years she muddled through therapy, pinpointing the love she had for little Nina and how she could have turned out had the clouds not darkened her path, leading her astray. She had had trouble trusting that this part of her was still in there. But being back here in Harborview was stirring something inside that was surprising her.

The terrible memories? Sure, she expected those. But the softness of her childhood and the nostalgia of it all that she thought she'd never retrieve? It was all there, still, too. It was just buried beneath the ash of the fire that had once burned.

"Look at them," Mary said to Nina as they stared up at the large nest on Carver Road. The other committee members were trickling over from their cars, too.

"Do you think we will anger them?" Nina asked, worried about disturbing their home.

Mary shrugged, a caring look on her face. "It's for their own good, dear."

Nina nodded, understanding but still feeling bad that they couldn't communicate with the birds and tell them that they weren't there to harm them.

"Hey, there!" a voice sounded from just beyond the ospreys' tree as a man about Mary's age exited his pickup truck and lumbered over to the group growing on the side of the road.

"Hey, there, Roger," Mary announced into the warm spring air. "Our friends are here. See them up there?"

"Oh, I sure do," he said, reaching out his hand to shake the those standing around. "Are we ready to get these beauties a safer place for their abode?" The group nodded their agreement, and Nina looked up, unsure how this was going to work. Ronnie personally greeted Nina, his watery eyes smiling. "Glad to have a new helper, my friend," he said.

"I'm glad to be here, Roger," Nina replied.

"This pair up here has been through it, I'll tell ya," Roger said, shaking his head and placing his hands on his hips, his eyes cast up to the nest. "Their nest has already caught fire once. When I arrived, they weren't in it, thank God. They must have up and left." He pointed to the tree he was speaking of, and Nina looked up at it, at the tree with just leaves now—no nest resting on its branches, her mouth agape. *It burned?*

"But they were ok, obviously?" Nina asked, wanting more information.

"Apparently!" Roger laughed. "This was back in late 2004. We didn't have a committee back then. It was just me, crazy Roger, and Mary trying to save the birds." Everyone chuckled at that. "They flew off, they did, as they do every fall. But I got up there with my buddies and moved the nests myself with some of my construction gear. Built a huge pole with a landing and placed the nest on it. Sure as shit, they came back in the spring." His smile warmed Nina, and she felt his pride. "I would check on them frequently. I watched as, day by day, they fixed the broken parts of their nests."

And she was astonished by this story. By the fate of it and the miraculous nature, the fact that it just didn't seem possible.

"So, if it was already moved once, and it's not on a wire anymore, what is our plan for the nest now?" Nina asked, curious.

Roger sighed. "The pole I built back then is sagging and leaning in, back toward the wires. For this here nest, it will be about stabilizing the pole so that it's upright and more secure for them." He squinted up to the top of the pole. "See what I mean up there?"

The group all craned their necks to get a feel for what they were dealing with while Roger walked back to his truck and came back with a clipboard. "Now, for this nest, I have everything I need to fix this pole back at the office in the garage. I'll just need three to five volunteers to assist me," he said. "Why don't you all take a look at the projects we have in limbo and sign up to assist on one or more? Does that sound good?" Everyone nodded and murmured their acceptance of the plan as he passed around his clipboard. "Each project will have a construction supervisor and/or a lineman to aid in the safety of the projects."

Nina watched the little eyes of the birds in the nest looking down at her, almost as if they recognized her, as strange as it sounded. She narrowed her eyes. "What do you think?" Mary asked, pulling Nina from her reverie.

"Oh, I'm so into this," she replied with gusto. "Sign me up for all of them." Nina and Mary both laughed.

Chapter 19

Nina 2002

NINA STARED AT HERSELF in the mirror in her bedroom, sighing dramatically as she tugged at her clothing, annoyed with how it fell over her skin. She had become quite skilled at being her own worst critic.

The sweater she wore, a cream-colored V-neck fitted to her frame, was not something she would have bought for herself. It was more grown-up than she'd typically wear, but Glen had purchased it for her as a birthday gift.

Her sweet sixteenth, to be exact.

Which happened to fall on Valentine's Day.

It was a Thursday, and after the last period of the day let out, Nina did what she always did before heading to her after-school practice, she stopped by Glen Gomes's classroom, always shutting the door behind her. He had gotten her a coffee, with just a splash of cream, and handed her a box tied with a bow. She was giddy but suppressed it just enough to not come off as childish. That was her biggest fear, Mr. Gomes coming to the realization that she was just like the other girls in her grade rather than the mature one he treated her as.

Since the school year began, Mr. Gomes had become more like a friend than a teacher. It felt like a natural connection had sparked, the flames growing each day. While Nina's emotions had gone haywire the last few years—nothing seemed to make any sort of sense—Glen Gomes had eased his way into her life, giving Nina some semblance of control and stability. Even though the reality of the situation was anything but normal. Anything but healthy.

Anything but good for Nina Jackson.

He was giving her late passes for her next class when she stayed after in his class a little too long.

Always complimenting her on her participation in class and her ability to debate her opinions with reasoning and skill.

Showing up at her field hockey games. And basketball games.

He had positioned himself just so at his desk, blocking her from the door, as she opened the box, peeling back the tissue paper and pulling out the cream sweater. "For my favorite student on her birthday," he said with a wink, his voice husky, making her blush.

"You didn't have to get me anything," she said, tucking a piece of hair behind her ear and fumbling with the sweater to hide it in her backpack. She folded the box and placed it in the trash can next to Glen's desk.

"I know, but I wanted to."

It was wrong.

So wrong.

But Nina told herself that nothing was really happening. There was nothing physical going on. He didn't touch her, except for the occasional hug or hand on her shoulder. He didn't drive her around in his car.

He didn't do any of those things.

Until he did.

Until, seemingly out of nowhere, or maybe it was a tiny bit each day, things escalated until there was no going back. Not for Nina at least.

The beginning of March had been blisteringly cold on Cape Cod—the month coming in like the jingle says, like a lion, ready to bite. And as Nina stood in front of the mirror in the sweater her teacher had given her, she reminded herself, despite the temporary fog of her body dysmorphia, that her handsome teacher had chosen her.

Of all the other girls. The ones who called her pudgy and frumpy. The ones who said she wasn't good enough for R.J. None of them were good enough for Glen Gomes. And that was enough for Nina.

The validation was taking her further than it should have.

It was around that time that they first started texting one another, the act making Nina sick with apprehension. Her parents had given her a Nokia cell phone for her birthday, having been tired of practices running late or getting out early and not being able to get in touch with their daughter. But the text messages cost ten cents to send and five cents to receive, which didn't seem like a lot at first, but Nina came to find out that it added up.

After sending hundreds of texts to Brett and her girlfriends in February, Jane and Paul sat her down and told her that she had to limit the messages. But now, Glen was texting her, and the risk was worth the reward. If you could have crawled into Nina's head back then, you would have understood that for certain.

She had him saved in her phone as *Allie Cell*. Allie was the only one of her friends who didn't have a cell phone yet, so it was the easiest way to keep him hidden in her phone without her getting confused.

Without sending something suspicious to her friend by accident.

Nina pulled her hair into a ponytail as her phone beeped on her bed. She ran to it to see *1 unread message* on her screen. Her heart began to pound, her hands sweating as she rushed to open it. A message from Glen.

Morning sunshine.

Nina's face reddened, and her body tingled with anticipation. *Worth the five cents*, she thought to herself.

Nina: Morning. :)

Glen: Come to my classroom before homeroom. I have a coffee for you.

Nina smiled as she tucked her phone into her backpack, slid it onto her shoulder, and grabbed her coat before heading to the kitchen to grab something to eat. Her mother was sitting at the table, sipping coffee from a steaming mug.

"Hi, sweety," Jane said through a smile.

Nina gave her a close-lipped smile in return, entirely too aware that her guilt could be written on her face, and if it was, her mother would certainly be able to read it.

Because that was Jane Jackson. Hardworking. A loving wife. But an intuitive mother, above all else.

"Are you ok, Nina?" she asked lightly as Nina pulled a strawberry Pop-Tart from the bottom drawer next to the sink. She froze for a second, her back to her mother, gathering her thoughts. *Don't sweat*, she thought to herself as she calmed the muscles in her jaw and her shoulders.

Nina turned away from the counter with a grin that filled her face. "Yeah!" she replied, feeling the forced nature of it. "I didn't sleep great last night," she added, rolling her eyes. "But I'm great!"

Jane smiled but narrowed her eyes, taking her daughter in.

Yes, Jane was attuned.

But Nina was becoming a master at manipulation, and though the guilt settled somewhere deep inside her, she was learning to ignore it.

"Gotta get to the bus," she said, grateful for an out.

Jane got up from the table and pulled Nina in for a hug, kissing the top of her head. "Have a great day, sweetheart."

Nina closed her eyes, accepting her mother's love. "Thanks, Mom," she whispered, confused at the emotion bubbling in her throat.

Nina pulled away, adjusting her backpack, before heading outside to meet Brett at the bus stop.

She saw him up ahead and jogged to catch up. "B!" she yelled. "Hey!"

Brett looked over his shoulder and smiled. "Hey, Neen."

Nina zipped her coat up to her chin, the March wind entirely too harsh to bear. "I can't wait for spring," she huffed, her eyes beginning to water.

"No kidding," Brett replied, tucking his hands into his pockets.

"How's Jo?" Nina asked.

"She's good," Brett said with a smile.

Jo and Brett had been dating since the fall, around the time of Homecoming. Jo had asked Brett to the dance, and that was the beginning of their relationship. Nina had scoped her out, questioning her, assuring that she was good enough for her best friend.

She was a freshman, quiet and reserved.

Pretty and petite.

Good enough, so it seemed. Especially when Nina was tied up worrying about her own love life—forbidden and all.

"What are we doing this weekend?" he asked as the bus pulled up to the curb and they all trudged onto it.

"We can hang at my house," Johnny said, taking a seat toward the back of the bus. "It's going to be freezing, but we could also cruise into town."

This is what their group always did, and Nina couldn't help but feel, at that moment, that it was getting old.

Overdone.

Seemingly childish.

What she really wanted to do was hang out with Glen.

"Yeah, let's hang in the basement. I'll grab *American Pie 2* from Blockbuster and bring it over," Brett said.

Nina rolled her eyes, if only to herself. Same old thing. Week after week. "I'll be there at some point on Saturday."

"At some point?" Johnny asked, smiling. "Got something better to do, Nina?"

Nina laughed, shaking her head. She could only hope.

The first time Nina was in Mr. Gomes's car, she felt the sweat pooling under her arms, soaking her shirt and making her feel entirely too self-conscious. It was next to impossible to breathe, and the lack of oxygen dizzied her.

"You ok?" he asked, looking over at her.

Nina turned her head to match his gaze. She nodded through a smile, though her lips were pulled tight, her nerves pulsing.

"Are you afraid someone will see us? And you'll get in trouble?" Glen asked nonchalantly as if he was trying to belittle the fear that festered inside her.

"Kind of," she muttered.

Nina studied his face, his expression pondering her response. "Yeah, I understand," he chuckled. "People wouldn't understand, would they?"

"Understand what?"

"What's going on with us," he said, looking over at her briefly before turning back toward the road.

"What *is* going on with us?" Nina asked. She didn't mean to sound desperate and needy, but she was entirely too consumed with thoughts of him that she couldn't distinguish fact from fiction, or her feelings from what was actually happening. Thinking about him was all-consuming, her grades slipping, her friends falling from view.

"You don't feel it?" he asked, sounding concerned. "There's something special here." His smile reached his eyes, and his handsome face seemed to sparkle, making Nina's stomach flip.

"No, I definitely feel it," Nina said, her nerves easing, her shoulders relaxing. "I just wasn't sure if you did."

And then his hand was on her knee, squeezing it gently, and this gave Nina a sort of superpower that she wasn't aware was inside her, a bravery igniting that had long ago been extinguished. She put her hand on top of his.

Darkness was beginning to settle over Harborview when Glen had picked her up in the corner lot of East Beach, and it was pitch black when they pulled up in front of Blue. He turned to her and continued the conversation, "So, because no one will understand, we have to keep this our secret, Nina, ok?"

This made Nina's heart sink, casting a shadow over the lightness she found with him. Somewhere in the back of her mind, she knew that this was wrong. But it didn't matter. She was in too deep now. "Yeah, I know," she said.

"I'm going to go get our food," Glen said, looking all around the main street, presumably for a familiar face. "Can you scoot down from the window? Just in case?" He gave her a sheepish sort of look.

"Yeah," she said, unbuckling her seat belt and wiggling out of view from anyone who may walk by.

"I'll be right back."

Nina watched from beneath the dashboard as Glen walked into Blue's front door, the act cheapening what was brewing inside of her. She studied the building. The weathered shingles. The gutter that was hanging amiss on the edge of the roof; her perspective gave her a deranged view of things that she had once found beautiful.

The backdrop of her childhood looked warped from the angle she found herself in as she hid in her teacher's car.

When Glen came back, the car filled with the aroma of fried fish and tangy slaw, making Nina's stomach rumble.

"Where are we going to eat this?" she asked.

Glen looked pensive. "I would say we could go to the East Beach parking lot. Do you think other people will be in the lot?"

Nina shook her head. "Probably not. Late March isn't a prime time to be at East Beach this late at night."

"Let's go there then," he said, shifting the gear into drive.

Once they were going at a good clip, Nina shimmied back up into her seat and buckled her seat belt, holding the brown paper bag on her lap, the contents warming her legs.

The beach was vacant, just as Nina had predicted, when Glen pulled his Honda Accord into a space at the end of the lot. She opened the bag and began to pull out the food. Nina handed Glen a Styrofoam container that contained his surf and turf meal. Then she pulled out hers, fried clams and French fries.

Dipping a fry into a bit of ketchup, Nina savored the tangy and salty taste as she popped it into her mouth. She was starved, having not eaten since breakfast.

"Hungry?" Glen asked, smirking and making Nina feel self-conscious.

She nodded, wiping her mouth with the stiff restaurant napkin. "I didn't eat much today."

Glen shook his head, disapproving. "That's not good for your metabolism."

What the fuck? She wasn't expecting that retort. Nina's eyes grew wide with shame. "Oh, well, I was busy today," she replied, her voice showing that she was offended.

"Make time to take care of yourself," he said, taking a bite of his shrimp. "You can't not eat all day and then fill your body with that fried stuff." He swallowed his food. "It's not good for your figure."

Nina felt like she had been punched in the gut, and her stomach felt so full that she thought she'd never be able to eat again. She closed the container and placed it back in the brown bag. "I'm full," she muttered.

"Nina." Glen only said her name, as if she was a little child, and she couldn't help but feel that he was patronizing her.

"What?" she replied, the word laced with more venom than she meant to.

"Did I say something wrong?"

Nina noted his apologetic tone and forced a smile. "No, sorry. I'm fine."

He reached up and put his hand on her cheek, and she instinctively leaned into the embrace. "I didn't mean to upset you," he said softly.

And he had upset her, truly he had, hitting a nerve that had already been damaged by the comments of many others over the years. But she wanted to forget it, to pretend he hadn't said anything about her body and her eating habits. She wanted Glen Gomes to do right by her. She wanted, *needed*, to be in his sphere.

With his hand on her cheek, she allowed her shame to melt away.

"Hey, why don't we pick a day each week that's just for us? I can find a spot that's secluded. I can help you with your math homework…and stuff?"

"Ok. I can do Tuesdays," Nina said.

Glen looked deep in thought, then shook his head. "No, I can't do Tuesdays. I have late help, and I coach racquetball at the rec center, remember? Fridays?"

"I can't on Fridays," Nina said. "We do family dinner early after lacrosse, and then I hang out with the kids in my neighborhood." As soon as the words came out, she regretted them. "It would be suspicious if I bailed on it," she added, attempting to justify.

Nina already knew that Mondays were staff meetings, and Glen always went out with other teachers for trivia in town afterward.

"So, that leaves Wednesdays," Glen said, sounding hopeful.

"You know I have lacrosse on Wednesdays and Fridays," Nina said, trying not to sound annoyed.

Glen looked at her, the moon lighting up the lines on his face. "You could always take a break," he offered. "You play a sport every season. What's the harm in taking one season off?" His smile melted her, but his words did the opposite—turning her insides to ice.

Quit lacrosse?

She couldn't.

She wouldn't.

Glen leaned over the center console and took her face in his hands once more. "We don't need to talk about it now, Nina," he whispered, his mouth getting close to hers.

"Ok," she uttered quietly.

He nudged her nose with his and closed his eyes. She followed his lead and closed hers, desperately trying to calm her racing heart.

She was sixteen and hadn't been kissed yet, a fact that had gnawed at her for some time. A reminder of what she'd been missing out on. While her friends would gossip and trade stories of their escapades with boys at school, Nina would listen in, feeling inferior and inexperienced.

Was this going to be her first kiss?

She sucked in a breath, embarrassed by the way the air shook on its way in. Glen tipped his head to the side, pulling away, the look on his face pained. "Are you ok?"

Nina nudged closer to him, suddenly wanting to be comforted. "I'm fine."

Glen leaned in again and placed his lips on hers, softly at first, before turning the kiss into something much more desperate.

Nina was lost then, falling fast into an abyss that she couldn't quite identify. One she would never be able to label—an indescribable void that she would learn to associate as her new normal. Just what her life was. Something she had to accept. All she knew at that moment was that she was on fire inside and the hairs on her arms were standing up straight.

And there Nina went…into the dark unknown that most certainly wasn't where she should have ventured.

***

"Something isn't right with you," Brett said to Nina one Monday afternoon in mid-April as they walked down to the end of Carver Road after school.

Nina didn't answer right away. She knew this was coming. Brett seemed to know when her heart skipped a beat or when her temperature was off. She didn't question his ability to truly see her because she knew him in that same way. In fact, she knew him better than she knew herself.

"Neen, what's going on? You don't smile. You friggin' quit lacrosse? I can't believe you did that." When she still didn't respond, he added, "I'm worried about you."

Nina was also worried. Quitting the team was a mistake, she knew it immediately after she had done it. Sophomore year was a pivotal one, and lacrosse was her favorite out of all of her activities—but she blew it by abandoning the team.

And for what? To hang out with her thirty-year-old teacher? It was ludicrous. She knew that. But she was trapped in a web, and it was impossible to find a way out. She couldn't tell Brett, though, and that hurt her more than anything really. Because Brett was her safe space. He was the one who saved her from herself. So many times, he'd been there for her, and now he couldn't be because she couldn't let him in.

"I was getting overwhelmed, B." She took her gaze to the sky. "That's all."

She knew he didn't believe her.

She also knew that he wouldn't let it go, or, at least, that his eyes and his heart would always be checking on her for signs that the cracks in her soul were deepening. He knew they were already there; she was sure of it. Nina wondered if she was being held up by the rock she had in her best friend. How frightening a thought…that she would most certainly crumble without him.

"You know what I'm thinking?" Nina asked, feigning bliss.

"Treehouse?" Brett asked, smiling, showing his dimple, his green eyes sparkling.

"Please?" Nina didn't know if Brett had outgrown it, or if she had, too. But there was also a part of her that believed she never would, at least not entirely.

"Yeah, let's do it."

They didn't run to the end of the road this time. They walked patiently, their spindly, bruised legs of childhood replaced with the muscle and tone legs of adolescence. They understood that the scraps of cedar would still be there when they finally made it to the end of the road, so what was the rush?

Inside the treehouse was the familiar smell of moist wood and the decay of leaves left over from the fall. Parts of the floorboards were still soaked from where little piles of snow from a late March storm had recently melted. The doors and windows of the little house had become much more warped over the last two years, letting in more water than was considered ideal. Like the kids, the house was aging, and there wasn't much they could do about that. The inside now felt entirely too small for them as they craned their necks. Their growing bodies crawled around the space, their size making it feel cumbersome and quite awkward.

"Maybe we should nail some new wood over some of these molding pieces," Nina said, running her fingers over the waterlogged parts.

"Yeah, we don't want it collapsing," Brett said, eyeing the wear and tear for himself.

Nina and Brett crouched down and lay on their backs as if their bodies were moving on autopilot. With their hands behind their heads, they stared at the ceiling.

Nina inhaled deeply and at that moment felt the incredible divide that separated her from Glen Gomes because she felt like a kid again there in the trees. Being next to Brett in this way, like they used to do in the past, made her utterly desperate to go back. To crawl into the crook of Brett's arm and daydream together. "Hey, B," she said. "Knock, knock."

***

Over the next few weeks, Nina and Brett made makeshift repairs to the treehouse, bringing up an old toolbox from the Jackson's garage that Paul no longer used. They had no idea what they were doing of course, but that was the beauty of their treehouse.

"This hammer is mad rusty," Brett said as he pulled it from the box for inspection.

Nina rolled her eyes through a laugh. "You and the damn rust, B." She shook her head. "You're not licking it…or slamming it into your skin."

Brett laughed, too. "I could accidently!"

"Gimme the damn hammer," Nina said, pulling it from his grip.

"Careful with that," Brett said, winking at her.

And for a moment, Nina's world seemed to stabilize. Her life felt upright, rather than turned upside down, for the first time in a very long time.

But the web was still tangled, and she felt too weak to peel away the pieces that held her in its grasp. She was reminded of this as her phone vibrated in her backpack, letting her know that Glen had sent her a message.

Chapter 20

Brett 2002

The horrific events of 9/11 had ignited something in Seamus Warner, a fire that hadn't been there before. And it burned with a kind of aggression that took hold of his entire being. Brett noticed it right away, as soon as the wheels in Seamus's mind began to spin. The theories Seamus would present to anyone who would listen (or even if they wouldn't) concerned Brett.

It was May—a few months shy of the first anniversary of that treacherous day—and the entire family sat, tense as it could be, around the kitchen table eating the dinner that Laura had made and Danny had criticized. That's when Seamus announced that he had enlisted in the Army.

As he told them the news, Laura sucked in her bottom lip, her eyes brimming with fresh tears. "No, Seamus. Please don't."

Brett studied her face, searching for what she actually was feeling. What he found was the truth written in the lines between her brows and the creases from her frown. She was torn, Brett knew that much. As much as their mother wanted Seamus and Brett to run from their father, to be free—to be safe—an equal part of her yearned for the comfort that her sons' presence gave her.

And Brett reasoned that she must not be relieved that Seamus was getting away from their father only to walk into a different kind of danger. One that brought on a whole new set of horrors. Brett continued to watch his mother as her throat bobbed and tears filled her eyes, flowing down her cheeks. Brett knew she had never been able to protect them. And unfortunately for her, there was nothing she could do to save Seamus from this.

Brett also knew that Seamus wasn't going to change his mind.

"Mom, I already committed." Seamus's words came out tired and annoyed as he leaned back in his chair, crossing his arms across his chest.

Brett glanced at Danny, who was chewing slowly as he picked up his can of Budweiser and took a swig.

"Sounds like you're making a decision that a man would make, son," Danny said. "Hope you're man enough to survive it."

Brett's face warped into a grimace. *What the fuck does that even mean?* he thought to himself.

Seamus glared at his father. "I think you have sort of prepared me, wouldn't ya say, *Pops?*"

"Please, the both of you. Stop it," Laura begged. "What about your job, Seamus?"

"At the mechanics?" Seamus scoffed. "I think they'll be fine. Besides, I already put in a good word for Brett. He can take my place when I leave. He just has to go down and meet with Carl." Seamus's smile was a rictus of spite, his lips pulled tight over his teeth. The image was menacing, really, and it stopped Brett's breath in his chest.

"Got it all figured out, do ya?" Danny said.

"Yup," Seamus clapped back.

To Brett's relief, Danny removed himself from the table and headed toward the television, beer in hand, not without leaving his dishes on the table for his family to take care of.

Brett, Seamus, and Laura eyed one another, and Brett was the first to talk. "I'm proud of you, Seamus," he said. He wasn't sure if that was how he actually felt, but he believed it was the right thing to say. Even though he didn't understand it then, and wouldn't for quite some time, Brett had a sour feeling that the decision wasn't a good one. Not for someone like his brother.

Seamus gave him a single nod of his head but said nothing. "So, Carl said he would give me your job?"

Seamus had worked two jobs since leaving the clam shack. A short stint at Blockbuster, where he claimed the kids that came in there were annoying and lacked any cinematic taste. And then, he became the front-end office manager at the mechanic shop in town. He answered phone calls, scheduled appointments, and checked people out. He had recently begun some training in the garage with the owner, hoping to eventually start fixing engines.

Until his plans changed, and now the Army was in his front view window.

"Yup, he said you can just be my replacement. Easy as that."

Brett nodded, contemplating that this was his first job. It would get him out of the house even more, and that was a reason all on its own. Baseball was time-consuming, but it wasn't enough. And he could save money to pay his own way out of Harborview when the time came. It seemed like an easy decision.

"Ok. Yeah, I'll go talk to him tomorrow."

Laura's shaky voice came next. "When do you leave?"

"Basic training starts in three weeks," Seamus replied.

"Three weeks! That's it?" Laura said, breathless.

"What's the difference if it's three weeks or three years, Mom? Honestly, if I could leave in three days, I would." Laura's face fell, her heart clearly breaking at Seamus's admission. "Mom, don't look at me like that. If anything, you should blame yourself for this turn of events. You and Danny. And we all know that I don't need to say anything more about what I'm talking about. We all know."

He got up from the table and headed upstairs to his room. Brett listened to the thumps of his footsteps on the stairs and waited for the thud of the door closing behind him, and then he got up and hugged his mother. He held on an extra moment before clearing everyone's plates from the table and washing them in the sink.

Because that was Brett.

And Laura? Well, she sat there at the table, staring at the wall, losing herself a little more than she had the day before. And maybe, a little less than she would the days that would follow.

Because that was Laura, her existence in its entirety.

"Which island is your favorite?" Jo asked Brett one balmy May evening as they sat on a waterlogged piece of driftwood that rested on the dunes along East Beach. The sky was turning purple as the sun sank behind their back. Jo pulled the hood of Brett's sweatshirt up onto her head and pulled her knees to her chest.

"Like of all the islands in the world?" Brett asked, finding the question odd.

Jo rolled her eyes playfully. "No, Brett. Of the two islands here." She gestured to Vineyard Sound, where they could see the rounded edges of Martha's Vineyard a few miles out to sea. And miles beyond that, past where their eyes could see, Nantucket emerged from the ocean.

"Oh, yeah, obviously," Brett said, leaning back on his elbows, staring at the Vineyard. "It's hard to pick."

The kids ventured to the Vineyard often as it was only a short ferry ride from Harborview. They took class trips there as kids and went to museums and historic buildings, learning about the island's past. They had a lot of fun memories on that island.

But Nantucket, too, had its perks. It was smaller and a bit more quaint. Brett and his family used to frequent the island for a week in the summer when his mom's family would come to visit. They were happier moments when Danny would put on a show, and everyone had a little reprieve from his anger.

Brett rubbed his thumb over the faded scar on his knee, the one he got on one of those vacations when he jumped onto the soft sand on his knees, not knowing a jagged piece of driftwood was just below the surface. The cut bled steadily for hours and was constantly reopening throughout the vacation, leading to a scar that remained. But he didn't mind it. It was a reminder of his trips over there. Memories filled with skimboarding on Miacomet Beach, driving the rusted-out Jeep they rented onto the beaches near Brant Point, and washing loads of sand off in the outdoor shower once the sun began to dip behind the horizon—the smell of fresh fish cooking on the charcoal grill in the backyard.

"Nantucket," Brett answered finally. "You?"

"See, that's why we were made for each other," Jo said, sounding entirely too serious for Brett's liking. He furrowed his brows at the comment. "Everyone is obsessed with the Vineyard. I think Nantucket is way better."

Brett didn't think that agreeing about an island made them compatible, but he tried not to think too much about the comment or how Nina floated through his mind's eye. "We should go out there soon, get a group together."

"Ok!" Jo beamed.

Brett smiled at her. "Ready to head to Johnny's?"

They got up, brushed the sand from their clothes, and climbed the dunes to the parking lot before crossing the street to the dirt path that led to Carver Road, where Johnny and the crew were waiting for them in the Cooper's basement.

***

"Dude, I'm 'bout to slaughter you in this game," Tim Baker said, biting his lower lip and slapping the ping pong paddle against his palm.

Ricky Jives just rolled his eyes, the usual retort for anything Tim had said since the beginning of time. "Really, Baker? Like how you struck out three times in our last game against Hyannis?"

Gary barked out a laugh from the couch, where he, Johnny, and Tyler sat with the Nintendo controllers in their hands and their eyes fixated on the television.

"Oh! There they are!" Ricky announced as Brett and Jo walked down the stairs, hand in hand. "Love connection!"

"Kiss her, kiss her!" Tim began to chant.

Brett laughed, shaking his head but ignoring the demand, refusing to indulge Tim.

"Oh, he's a bad kisser, isn't he, Jo?" Tim said, laughing.

Jo laughed, her cheeks turning a crimson red. She hadn't quite warmed up to the crew on Carver Road.

"Yup, I sure am, Baker. I'm a sucky kisser," Brett said with humor in his tone. "Sucky as your horrendous batting average, dick head."

A collective *ohhhhh* resounded through the basement, shutting Tim up fast.

"Actually, he is a good kisser," Jo said, her tiny voice shocking the guys, who turned to look at her.

"She speaks!" Tyler said, climbing over the back of the couch and putting his hands on her shoulders. "I wasn't sure you had words in there."

Jo laughed nervously, looking at Brett as he rolled his eyes and gave Tyler a friendly shove.

Tyler laughed. "Jo, do you want to play a round of Mario Kart? Gary's bored, and we need a third."

"Uh. Ok." She sounded entirely uninterested, but Brett could tell she just didn't want to seem lame.

Once Jo was settled on the couch, Brett joined Tim and Ricky at the ping pong table, giving them each a high five.

"Has Nina stopped by?" Brett asked, looking around the room.

"No," Tim said, sending the ball back to Ricky.

"She's definitely been mad shady lately," Ricky said, not taking his eye off the little plastic ball. "My point!" he yelled as Tim sent it back and it hit the net.

Brett's eyes furrowed. "Shady?" he asked. He knew she had been off; of course he did. But shady? That wasn't a word he felt fit to describe Nina. "Why do you think she's acting shady?"

"Come on, Brett, you know you've seen it, too," Johnny said from the couch. "She's so quiet on the bus. She's sneaky when her phone's out. She slips in and out of my house, sometimes without saying hi or bye. She must have a boy toy and doesn't want any of us to know or something."

"Yeah, but Nina's always been a little weird. We all know that," Tim added. "I mean, I love her, I do." He shrugged then, picking the ball off the floor and volleying it over the table. "But something isn't right with her. Ricky's right on about that."

Brett rolled his eyes. "Ok, Tim, you never have anything nice to say *about* Nina or *to* Nina. You're always picking on her."

Johnny glanced over from the couch again. "Probably because he still hasn't gotten over the fact that she punched him in the face when we were ten years old."

The group laughed obnoxiously until the shrillness was broken by footsteps on the stairs. "What's so funny?" Nina asked, coming into view.

"Speak of the devil," Johnny said, walking up to her and pulling her into his embrace.

"Good things, I hope," Nina said, a forced smile on her lips as Brett inspected her face.

"Oh, for sure, Neen," Brett said, putting his arm around her. "We were just reminding Baker how you punched him in the face a few years ago." Brett could feel Nina's muscles relax in his embrace, and he wondered what had her so riled up. He looked her in the eye and spoke with just a look, the language of Neen and B. *What's wrong?*

She shook her head in two short motions, back and forth, telling him to leave it be. And he would do that for her. For now. But he knew he wanted, *needed*, to get her alone tonight, to find out just what was going on.

Some of the older and younger kids from the street began to shuffle in. Instead of walking through the house, they snuck in through the sliding glass door from the backyard and the pond and brought things their parents certainly would not approve of.

Keith Haden, a junior, slipped behind the bar, grabbed an opened package of Solo cups, and untwirled the bag, pulling out the stack of red cups. "Yo, Johnny Boy, where's the soda at? We need mixers!"

Plastic nips of Captain Morgan and large bottles of raspberry Rubinoff were soon poured into cups of lukewarm soda as the lights dimmed and Nelly's *Country Grammar* album played at a reasonable decibel. Johnny's parents weren't home, but the entire clan of kids from Carver Road knew that noise traveled quite easily through the trees, and wherever they were hanging out, it was an unwritten rule that they couldn't draw an exorbitant amount of attention to themselves.

The crowd increased as kids from around town began to come in through the back door, and Brett quickly noticed through his buzz that things in the Cooper's basement were getting out of hand. Apparently, news was spreading like wildfire as kids texted their friends to join them for the action. And tonight, apparently, it was the Cooper's.

Brett scanned the room for Jo, but he couldn't find her. He stepped outside into the night that had turned chilly since he and Jo had left the beach. He glanced around and saw only a few people hanging out on the Cooper's patio, and he was grateful that at least the party hadn't begun to spill out there. Not everyone there knew the rules that the Carver Road kids had decided to live by this last year. Jo wasn't out there either, so Brett turned to head back into the house. Before he could make it to the door, he spotted Nina sitting alone on the bench near the side yard that faced the pond.

"Can I join you?" Brett asked as he approached Nina, who didn't even turn her head to look at him. Her eyes stayed glued to the pond, where the moon cast a glare so bright across the surface that Brett felt it seemed ominous, though he wasn't sure why. "Neen?"

Finally, she turned her eyes toward Brett and blinked, and from the light of the moon, he saw the tears she was trying desperately to curb. "Hi," she muttered.

Brett sat and quickly placed his arm around her shoulder. "What's wrong?" he whispered into her hair. Waiting for a beat, he held his breath, but she didn't respond. "Nina," he said softly as he gently turned her body to face him. "What happened?"

Their eyes met, and Brett watched Nina's lower lip tremble in such a way that made his insides wretch. And then she let go and sobbed; the sound made fear bubble inside of Brett, a fear that scared him more than anything ever had. Something was very wrong; he knew that for certain.

Brett stood and pulled Nina up into his chest and wrapped her in his arms, rocking her steadily, desperate to calm the panic that was rising in her. Brett noted how small and frail she felt in his arms. This wasn't his Nina, but who was she? What was happening to her? Her body looked like it was wasting away. "Ricky guessed that you had a boyfriend or something that you weren't telling us about," Brett prodded. "Is that true?" The question brought her to a full-on breakdown, shaking in his arms. And so, Brett sufficed that the assumption was true. "Did he do something to you?" Nina didn't say anything. "Who is this person? Why haven't you told me about this, Neen?" Brett knew he was beginning to sound untethered, but he couldn't help it. He was close to panicking.

Nina pulled away and lifted her hands to her head, pushing them through her hair, the gesture causing her zip-up to fall down her shoulder, exposing the tops of her arms and the marks that riddled her. When Brett noticed, his eyes widened. "I'm in too deep, B," Nina whimpered.

But Brett had barely heard her; he was seeing too many shades of red. He gently took hold of her arm and pushed the sleeves up, along with the multiple rubber bracelets that donned her forearm. "What is this?" he deadpanned.

The air she sucked into her chest was audible as she pulled her arm away defensively. "B, it's nothing."

Brett narrowed his eyes, his thoughts racing. *How dare she say that?* With all that he had experienced in his life. All he had witnessed and bore; she knew every bit of it. She even took it upon herself to *feel* it. For him. She always had, and he knew that. So, how dare she say it was nothing. He knew what it was. Nina was hurting. And come hell or high water, *no one* was going to hurt his Nina. Not if he had anything to do with it.

"Nothing?!" Brett's voice was elevated as he tried to talk himself off a ledge, not wanting to scare her and make it worse. He knew he needed to remain calm, so that she would let him back in. It was only then that he would be able to help her get out of whatever mess she had found herself in.

Nina inhaled a deep, shaky breath before sitting back down on the bench, sitting on her hands.

Brett bent down to look her in the eye and softly reminded her of what she already knew. "Nina, you've already been down this road with me so many times before. You know that violence in relationships is never ok. And it never gets better."

"B..." Her voice sounded meek and scared like she was lost in a nightmare.

"Neen, you just said to me that you were in too deep, and in the same conversation, you said that the bruises on your arm in the shape of fingers are *nothing*." He tried not to sound angry, but he was. Brett took a breath and forced a softness in his tone. "You need to end this with him, Neen. You know that, right?"

Nina looked up at the inky sky. "Yes, I know that. I just don't know how."

"Who is it?" Brett asked. "Is it someone I know?"

"Yeah. You know him, but I'm not telling you his name."

"Why?!" Brett was getting frustrated, and he was done trying to push it down. "Can you at least tell me how long this has been going on?"

Nina wiped a tear from her cheek and shrugged. "Since the beginning of the school year, kinda."

Brett sighed. "You have been hooking up with someone since the beginning of the school year and you never told me?" He wondered how this was possible, for a secret to have festered between them for so long—nearly an entire school year. But Nina didn't look happy about this either. And there was no way for him to know that the events that led to this moment had taken Nina by complete surprise. There was no way for him to know yet how much of a victim she actually was.

"I'm sorry, B," she said. "I know we tell each other everything. But I don't know…" Her voice trailed off, and Brett waited on bated breath. "I don't know what is happening to me. I don't know how I let it get this far."

Brett looked into her dark and sad eyes, and he couldn't explain the feeling in his chest, but he did know it felt a lot like love. Like he would lay down his life for this girl without question. "What can I do? Tell me what you need, and I'll do it?"

"Just be there for me, B. I need to think this over and figure out what's next."

What's next? Brett couldn't comprehend how a teenage boy could be warping her mind like this, hurting her and not allowing her to think there was anything to do but walk away. But he needed to give her some time to mull it over, and he made a mental note to keep himself a little closer to her in the meantime. To not let her slip through the cracks again.

"There you are!" Jo's loud voice startled Brett as he looked toward the door to the basement. He watched her stumble out of the house and groaned audibly, knowing that she was most certainly under a bit too much influence of the liquid in the Solo cups. He looked back at Nina and realized instantly what he had to do, and fast. Josephine Barr was soon to be his ex-girlfriend.

"I have to walk her home," Brett said to Nina. "Can you stay here for a little longer, and then I'll come back and get you, and we can walk home together?"

Nina nodded. "Thanks, B." She placed her shaking hand on his. He entangled his fingers with hers and squeezed gently for a brief moment, offering her a smile that he could tell warmed her.

Right then, on the shore of the pond, Brett made a vow to himself that his Nina wasn't going to turn into his mother. He was going to save her, come hell or high water.

Much to Brett's dismay, Nina wasn't as pliable as he had hoped. If anything, as the summer approached, she only seemed to be getting worse. Sadder. Smaller, in all the ways that mattered; her fiery heart seemed to be more like ash, no longer a flicker or an ember in sight. Brett wasn't sure what he was up against with her anymore, and he began to feel as if he couldn't help her, and that she wouldn't allow herself to change. Or worse, that she *couldn't* because too much had happened.

Though his eyes were constantly focused on the movement of Nina Jackson, he had yet to determine who the asshole was that was whittling away his best friend.

That summer of 2002, the kids were about to get their drivers' licenses, a new level of independence dangling in front of their noses like forbidden fruit. They dreamed about driving to school and parking at the high school instead of taking the bus next year.

The Fourth of July block party had brought in kids from all over town. Girls in their jean skirts and tube tops, more interested in catching the eyes of the boys than in running around with sparklers and teeny drinks—a natural evolution.

All summer, Brett continued to work at the mechanic's shop. Most of the time, he worked at the front desk, but, as Seamus had done, Brett was beginning to learn the trade in bits and pieces. It was true that he had often wondered if he would be happier working at the beach clam shacks, cleaning boats in the harbor, or selling ice cream in one of the seasonal shops. That's what most of the Harborview kids were doing this summer. But Brett was making more money than all his friends, and saving up gave him a vision of getting out of his house and away from Danny. And that was well worth the smell of gasoline and motor oil all day.

By the time the summer people were shuffling out of Harborview and over the bridge, Tyler, Brett, and Johnny all had their licenses. Even though they weren't allowed to drive anyone but family members, that didn't stop the Warner's and the Jackson's from letting Brett drive Nina to school.

"I mean, we're practically related," Brett had argued as their families sat on the Jackson's deck one evening right before school started. The comment made Brett cringe a little inside, but he was committed to making a point so he and Nina could get their way. He didn't want Nina to have to take the bus until she got her license and her car, which wasn't happening until November. She was getting an old Honda Civic handed down from her Uncle Rider.

And they did get their way. On the first day of their junior year, Nina walked over to the Warner's driveway and waited by Brett's hunter green Oldsmobile he had snagged from the mechanics shop for a fair deal. It was worn and had a lot of miles, but his boss had made sure it was tuned up and safe as can be before handing over the keys to Brett.

One Wednesday afternoon, after the last bell had rung, Brett was waiting outside by his car for Nina. While he waited, he started talking to some of the guys from his baseball team. It was early October, and fall sports were well underway. But today neither one of them had practice, so Brett and Nina were planning on heading to town with the crew for froyo.

Brett was relieved that Nina had decided to play field hockey this season. Her decision to get back into sports after leaving her lacrosse team in the spring was a relief to Brett. It made him feel like, just maybe, she was coming back to life. She had told him that she needed to talk to Mr. Gomes about a project, and she would be out a few minutes after the bell, but there he was, still shooting the shit with the team when he realized it had almost been a half hour.

"I'll be back," he said, shaking hands with Bruce and Keith from the team. "I gotta go get Nina. Are you guys heading into town?"

"Yeah," replied Keith. "We'll meet you down there."

Brett ran up the steps, skipping every other one. He walked in the school and headed toward Mr. Gomes's classroom. When he got there, the door was shut, and he assumed that meant that he had left for the day. Brett sighed as he looked up and down the hallway for signs of Nina.

But then, he heard voices beyond the door, and it made him turn back. He approached it and peeked in through the window, only to find that the blinds were closed. He could barely make out anything on the other side of the door. He craned his neck, desperate to see if he could spot Nina and try to hurry her up.

And it was then that he not only found Nina but he discovered the answers to all the questions that had been lingering for the last few months.

It was Mr. Gomes.

Mr. Gomes had his hand on Nina's cheek. A cheek that cradled a frown, a frown that had been Nina's mask for far too long.

Their teacher was the one who was hurting Nina.

Brett's breaths began to come in and out in short gasps, his heart pounding in his ears. He watched Mr. Gomes slam his hand on his desk and Nina flinch, folding her arms self-consciously over her stomach.

Brett was frozen; he didn't know what to do. If he burst in, he feared he would be putting her at risk somehow. But it was also agony to think about what she would go through if he walked back to his car to wait for her, what she would be exposed to if she was in there for even one minute longer. He moved away from the door and leaned his back against the lockers nearby. A moment later, his phone buzzed in his pocket with a new text message.

A message from Nina: **Sorry you've been waiting. I'll meet you downtown in a bit. I need to do some work on this AP project before I leave.**

And then, Brett no longer felt very protective. He was just angry. At Mr. Gomes. He should know better than to get involved with a student. He definitely shouldn't be violent toward her. And angry at Nina. For the lies she kept telling him and the half-truths that had become second nature for her.

Brett glanced back in through the blinds to see Mr. Gomes gripping her arms…her forearms, certainly leaving fresh marks. And he was back to feeling protective. It wasn't her fault, he decided. He texted her back.

I can see you.

Nina.

You need to get out of there. I'm going to my car, and I'm not leaving without you. Let's go.

Was he really seeing this? *How could I have missed this?* he wondered, as the rage began to bubble under the surface. The previous eight months flashed through his mind's eye as he desperately tried to figure out where things had gone so terribly wrong—completely off the rails.

A rattled and hearty groan escaped his mouth as he momentarily blamed himself for the whole situation. The changes he had seen in Nina—the ones he either denied or missed. The marks on her skin. The distraction he found in Jo, which he had welcomed. Anything to help him deny the simmering and changing feelings for Nina that were reaching a boiling point. And from Danny and all the turmoil under his own roof.

But his ignorance had denied Nina the protection she needed, and he couldn't forgive himself. His mind was a jumbled mess, and he knew he needed to get her out of there.

He ran his hands through his hair, pushing out an exasperated breath. He sped walked to the car and then paced behind it, linking his hands behind his neck until he saw Nina walking down the stairs of the school toward his car, panic written all over her face. Brett let out a sigh of relief, though he feared where their next conversation was going to take them.

"Are you fucking kidding me?" He was aware enough to know that she was a victim in this situation, but he was angry at her, still. Angry for keeping this from him, for not allowing him to help her. And angry at himself, truly. For failing her. She walked by him and got in the car, slamming the door. Brett got in, too, and stared at her. "Nina," he said through bared teeth.

"What?!" she spat, her red eyes glaring into him.

Brett's eyes were wide, unblinking. "What? That's all you have to say is *what*?" He slammed his hand on the steering wheel. "I just watched the most horrific thing I have ever seen, my best friend in the worst situation I could possibly imagine, and you are going to just say *what* to me?!"

He wanted to cry. Brett, who never cried, felt the lump bubbling in his throat.

"My parents aren't home. Come over, and I'll tell you everything," she muttered, all the life drained from her voice.

Nina sat on her bed, and Brett moved her desk chair to face her. He leaned forward, desperate to hear every word she had to say. But it felt like eons before she spoke, and Brett was losing his mind. He rubbed his hands over his face, frustration mounting, his nerves wracked.

He tried to be patient and give her the time she needed to gather her thoughts, but it was next to impossible.

Nina. His Nina looked so helpless and small, sitting there on her bed, surrounded by so many things from her childhood, yet here she was in this entirely too grown-up predicament.

Her room was a mess: clothes and books on the floor, papers strewn across the desk, makeup covering every square inch of her dresser. It was a teenage girl's room. Brett glanced around, waiting, and it seemed like Justin Timberlake was smiling at him, making a mockery of the seriousness of the situation.

And then, she finally opened her mouth. Once Nina started, she had a hard time stopping. Brett assumed it was her feelings of relief that brought her words out in abundance. Relief to finally be able to share this with someone. Relief to be heard. Relief to not be drowning all on her own.

She told him everything. About how Mr. Gomes…Glen…had spun a web, entrapping her. How at first, she felt seen and grown up. She felt like maybe there was a reason for all the commotion going on in her psyche: she was more grown up than the other girls her age. Maybe Glen was what she needed to make her feel right in her skin.

Nina told Brett that she quickly knew she had been wrong. Mr. Gomes would not be the one to make her feel good about herself. She told Brett about how the pain first started with his words and then escalated to being physical toward the end. How, over the summer, he took her out for a late-night bite under the guise of the darkness, and after the first bite of her lobster roll, he told her that it would attach to her insides and never leave, making her fat. She told Brett that he always did that with anything she put to her lips.

And Brett's hearts broke then, thinking of his wild Nina, the first to challenge anyone in the pie-eating contests on the Fourth of July, and the pride she exuded with blueberries all over her face when she won first place, every year. The joy it brought her, the fun she had as she soaked up everything life had to offer her. But his heart was breaking because she was so far from herself, broken beyond belief.

Nina told him how Mr. Gomes grew angry last week when she was unwilling to take things further than he was expecting. And how the guilt she felt almost made her change her mind. Almost, but not quite, thank God.

She told him that inside the history classroom that afternoon, she had threatened to tell someone what he had been doing, and with her threat came a retaliation from Mr. Gomes. He told her that she was at an age of consent now. That she would be judged just as much as he would. Teachers wouldn't be inclined to write her letters of recommendations for colleges. Her friends would look down on her. He grabbed her then and held on tight, trying to manipulate Nina with violence and fear.

And then he had apologized, putting his hand on her cheek and promising to make it right for her. But Nina had shaken her head, saying she was ending it. It was over. And that angered him even more.

"I'm scared, B," she said, beginning to sob. "He has already hurt me in so many ways. And he will keep doing it. What if I'm not strong enough to stay away?" She was crying so hard, and Brett got up to pull her into him, but before he could, she got up from the bed and began pacing. "Why is this happening to me?" she screamed, her hands pulling at her scalp. She picked up a glass bottle of perfume that Glen Gomes had given her and threw it across the room with so much force that it slammed into the wood trim around her closet, nicking a piece of wood right off the frame. Nina took in labored, short breaths and cried into her hands as she fell to the ground.

Brett approached her and kneeled down beside her shaking body and pulled her into him. He held on to her with so much pressure until she eventually relented and cried on his shoulder, grabbing his sweatshirt in her hands and holding on for dear life.

It felt like a million years had passed on the floor of Nina's bedroom, and when he felt it was time, Brett pulled away from her and placed his hands gently on her cheeks. "Look at me," he said softly. Nina's sad eyes lifted up to his. "You are not alone, Neen. I am here now, and I will do whatever it takes to make you feel better."

His words were wiser than a sixteen-year-old should be able to muster, but that was the way it had always been with them, a timeless connection that went beyond anything they could possibly understand.

Her phone buzzed from her desk. "That's him," Nina uttered, visibly disgusted and scared of what was in the message.

And it was then that Brett knew that getting rid of Glen Gomes, getting him out of Nina's life for real, would be harder than he expected.

———

It was a Saturday in mid-November, and Brett had been at work for a few hours doing some filing that Carl had asked him to do. He welcomed the distraction. Nina had been fighting with Mr. Gomes. She was adamant that she was done with the inappropriate relationship, but he wasn't taking it well. Brett wanted to report it, but Nina made him promise that he wouldn't. So, he made sure that his eyes were always open, his senses on high alert.

He was just about to help the mechanics when he saw Mr. Gomes pulling his car into the garage on the side of the building. Brett narrowed his eyes and stayed put, uninterested in interacting. Their muffled voices and laughs carried through the walls, and Brett watched as Mr. Gomes climbed into the front seat of the gym teacher's pickup truck.

Brett immediately began devising a plan to avoid checking out Mr. Gomes when his car was ready because he didn't want to be there when he came back.

Carl entered the office from the garage. "Last minute oil change, Brett. Can you get the account ready, G. Gomes. He should be in the system."

"Yeah, no problem, boss," he said. "Oh, is it ok if I work through lunch and leave an hour early? My mom needs me," Brett lied.

"Really, man? We were going to close for lunch and go down to Charlie's BBQ. You can't join us?"

"Nah, I can't. I'll stay here and get more filing done." Brett smiled, appreciating that he would most likely avoid running into this man that he despised.

When the mechanics left for lunch, Brett called Nina. "What's up?" he asked when she answered. "Are you ok?"

Nina sighed on the other end of the line. "He's losing his mind," she whispered.

"Why? What did he say now?" Brett rubbed his forehead with his hand.

"He *called* me. Not texted. *Called.*"

"And?"

"He said I have to meet him at our spot tonight. Just to talk, that he has something to tell me." It was silent for a moment. "And if I don't, I'll be sorry," she added through tears.

Brett rolled his eyes. "He's bluffing, Neen. Just ignore it. What did you say?"

"I just hung up."

"Good. As soon as I get off work, I'll come right over, ok? We can go to Johnny's."

"Ok," she said, sounding a bit relieved.

When they hung up, Brett pulled as much air into his lungs as he could. He hadn't let on to Nina but there was a pit growing in his stomach about Mr. Gomes. He seemed to have become erratic lately, and Brett wasn't sure what he could possibly do to protect Nina. He slammed his hand on the counter and let out an audible and frustrated yell for no one to hear but himself.

They had to do something. He knew that now. Tell someone or do *something*.

Anything to make it stop.

Chapter 21

Nina 2002-2003

JOHNNY'S BASEMENT WAS ALWAYS a good distraction for Nina. And walking down the street with Brett to the house where endless memories had been made, caused something to click in her brain, reminding Nina of the person she used to be. Though she was afraid of what Glen was capable of, relief had suddenly become her primary emotion, relief that she was no longer harboring a secret. The weight of holding it had been too much to bear.

Brett was quiet on the quick walk to Johnny's, his hands in his pockets, but when Nina looked at him, he glanced over, offering her a warm smile that comforted her.

"Thank you for helping me, B."

Brett stopped in the middle of the street, facing her. "You're welcome," he said quietly.

"What's wrong?" Nina asked, sensing something.

Brett shook his head and hugged her. "Nothing's wrong. Let's go beat Tim in any game and shut him up for a bit."

Nina laughed and noted how good it felt to laugh—and actually mean it.

With the weight noticeably lifted from her shoulders, Nina allowed herself to enjoy the night with her friends. She texted Maggie, Allie, and Emma, inviting them to join in on the *Scream* marathon they were having, and she was content when they showed up. It gave her hope that she hadn't lost them completely. That she could earn their friendship back after the months of abandonment that she'd inflicted.

The night stretched on, gloriously slow, allowing Nina to appreciate it as she remained present and reflected on the turn her life was thankfully taking.

As she filled up her cup with root beer that had grown quite stale, Johnny plopped himself down at the basement bar, smiling at her. "You look good, Nina," he said, and Nina smiled into her cup as she placed a plastic straw in it.

"Thanks, Johnny."

"I mean it," he stressed. "I feel like you were gone for a while…like even when you were down here with us, you weren't really here." He winced then, seeming to regret his words. "Ya know what I mean?"

Nina sighed, leaning her elbows on the shellacked bar. "I know," she whispered, stifling her emotion. "I'm sorry I wasn't *me,* but I think I'm getting back to that. So, thanks for caring."

Johnny walked behind the bar and pulled her in for a friendly hug that she held onto for an extra beat, appreciating his friendship more than she could fathom, really.

This street. These people. They had always been in her corner, and she knew she couldn't take that for granted anymore.

The walk home was drastically chillier than it had been earlier in the evening. When Brett noticed her shivering, he pulled off his sweatshirt and handed it to Nina.

"Thanks," she said, pulling it over her head, relishing in the warmth it gave her. The subtle hint of Brett's Axe Body Spray wafting around her nose as she nuzzled her chin into the neckline.

They stopped dead in their tracks as a swarm of sirens sped down Pontiac Street just on the other side of the tree line on Carver Road. They watched between the leaves as the sounds of the sirens got closer and louder, heading toward the ocean.

"Sounds pretty serious," Brett said, beginning to walk toward the end of the street.

Sirens were few and far between in Harborview, especially once the crowds of tourists left at the end of the summer and things settled down for the off-season. As the sound became a distant echo, Nina couldn't ignore the unsettledness in her gut—the feeling that something wasn't right.

But she ignored it, too elated by the recent changes in her mind, in her soul. The end of Carver Road was utterly dark, lit only by the moon and the dull cast of the porch lights from the Warner's and Jackson's houses. Nina began taking Brett's sweatshirt off.

"Just keep it for now, Neen. You can give it back to me later."

She smiled at him while he took her hands in his, and the flutter in her stomach was undeniable, her breath catching in her throat. When their eyes met, the fire in his flickered above the smile that played on his lips. Nina wondered how she could have denied it for all this time.

This love that she had for this boy.

To her, he wasn't just her best friend, and the truth of it was beginning to show.

"Neen," Brett said, his voice sounding strained.

"Yeah?"

"I see you again," he whispered, and Nina furrowed her brows, hearing Johnny's sentiment repeated by Brett. It made her feel sad that she had done this to them. His hand reached up to her face, his knuckles caressing her cheek. "Over the last few weeks, my best friend has come back. I…" His voice trailed off.

"What?" Nina asked.

"You have been gone for so long, Neen…and I missed you so much…like, the way you used to be." Nina's shame began to bubble up, and her gaze fell to the ground. Brett tipped her chin up with his finger. "Look at me," he said. And with wet eyes, she did. She looked right back into Brett's eyes. "Don't be sad. It's over. He won't hurt you anymore. He was in the wrong. We should get him fired, honestly. I think we—"

Nina cut him off, grabbing his sides. "No, Brett. I just want to forget about it. You need to let it go." She didn't want to tell him that she was still afraid of Glen, petrified of what he was capable of, of what he had already done to damage her. But she could see it in his eyes that he, too, was afraid. She also knew that he would do anything he could to protect her. She knew that with every fiber of her soul. It would be hard to forget about the events of the last year, but she was determined to. "Just be there for me, please."

Brett wrapped his arms around her, resting his chin on her head. "Always."

Pulling her head off his chest, Nina looked back up at Brett. Their eyes were locked, their chests moving in sync until Brett leaned down and placed his lips on hers. It was awkward at first, an unknown territory for the two of them.

No longer were they children scraping their knees from endless play.

No longer were they finding refuge in their treehouse or giggling about inappropriate jokes.

They were growing and molding into two young people capable of a deep and meaningful love story. The kiss, their first one, was gentle, if not a bit juvenile. But Nina felt her bones turn to liquid and her muscles ease into a calmness she had long forgotten.

When they pulled away, Nina found it difficult to catch her breath. "It's always been me and you, hasn't it?" Brett whispered.

"It kinda feels like that's how it always will be," Nina replied.

Brett smiled. "I'll text you in the morning."

Nina grasped Brett around the waist, not wanting the moment to end. "Ok, B. Goodnight."

"Night," he said before placing a kiss on her nose.

Nina lay in her bed, staring up at the glowing stars, refusing to take Brett's sweatshirt off. And she slept the soundest she had in years.

In the morning, Nina skipped down the stairs as if she was weightless, humming her way into the kitchen. She stopped dead in her tracks when she saw her mom at the table, a mug in her hands, sorrow on her face. Paul was standing against the counter, arms crossed over his chest, and a similar look on his face.

Her smile was wiped immediately. "What's wrong?" she asked her parents.

Had they found out her secret? Was it too late to run away from the mess entirely?

Paul and Jane exchanged looks that did little to ease Nina's worry. "Sit down, love," Paul said, pulling out two chairs. He sat down and waited for Nina to join them at the table.

"You're scaring me," Nina said, eyes wide in fear.

"There was an accident last night," Jane said.

Nina immediately thought of Brett, the only person who mattered to her as much as the ones in the room with her right now. "Ok?" she said quietly. She reasoned it couldn't be anything with Brett. She was with him until late, and she assumed he probably was still sleeping.

"Mr. Gomes, your history teacher…" Paul swallowed hard, and Nina straightened her spine, her arms and legs beginning to tingle. "His car went into the ocean at the end of Pontiac Street, just down the road." Nina didn't blink, her eyes growing dry. "He didn't make it, Nina."

Jane put her hand on Nina's, tears in her eyes. There was a ringing in Nina's ears; she felt her labored breathing, but she couldn't hear the breaths coming in and out. She felt like she might be sick.

"We don't have any other information yet, honey," Jane said. "But we know you enjoyed his classes last year and this year, too. I'm sure it's shocking, and whatever you need, we are here for you."

Nina's eyes darted to her mother, then her father, and back again. "Can I go to Brett's?" she asked, feeling like she was on the verge of losing the contents of her stomach.

"Yes, yes, of course," Jane said.

Nina didn't wait another moment; still in her pajamas, she ran out the front door and across the road.

Rumors spread and burned through Harborview following the accident, rumors that Mr. Gomes had been drowned by both alcohol and sea water. Eventually it was confirmed that there *had* been alcohol in his system.

A tragic loss, the community said.

And though she was relieved to not have to live in fear anymore, Nina felt the weight of guilt, heavy on her back.

Because she assumed he had drunk himself into a stupor that night, after she had threatened to report him and then ignored his calls.

She kept her feelings of guilt to herself, not wanting to bring Brett into her web of turmoil more than he already had been. He'd done enough to save her as it was. She didn't want him carrying any more of the weight for her than he had to.

"I can't believe Mr. Gomes died," Allie said a few days later, the comment causing Nina to freeze, her breath suspended in her chest. "Right, Nina?" she added, waiting for a response.

"Oh, um, yeah," Nina muttered through a release of breath. "I can't believe it either."

These comments came up frequently in the days and weeks that followed the terrible accident at the end of Pontiac Street. Nina couldn't get used to the jolt she felt inside anytime someone brought it up. It was as if her heart dropped and was floating around in her gut.

The moments of silence held at school, the celebration of his life, they all brought on tears for Nina—tears that mirrored those of everyone else around her who was mourning, everyone devastated by the loss. But it wasn't heartbreak that was bringing Nina to tears. It was the unrelenting pressure of the guilt she carried…with a little bit of dread for what the entire ordeal would inevitably do to her heart. Because it felt like a part of her would never be the same again. And for that, she mourned.

For the rest of the school year, anytime anyone would bring up the tragedy, Nina did her best to change the subject. Anything to get her mind off of it all. Soon, the incident was all but forgotten by the kids at school as they moved on to the self-indulgent issues that surrounded them.

No one was the least bit surprised to find out about the budding relationship between Nina and Brett.

"How long have I been telling you that you and Brett are BLIND to not go out with each other," Emma said at lunch one day soon after the news had been leached into the hallways of the school.

Nina smiled, looking down at her lunch. A lunch that she was eating without worrying about where it was going to stick to her. "I guess I should have listened to you all along," she said, laughing.

Emma clapped her hands in celebration.

"It's so cool that you live right across the street from each other," Allie said. "You can always have your eyes on him."

Emma batted her hand in Allie's direction. "No, no, no," she said, dismissing her comment. "Nina doesn't need eyes on him. Because his eyes are always on *her*." She wiggled her eyebrows in Nina's direction, and Nina rolled her eyes.

"Ok, guys, we can talk about something else now, yeah?"

And so, as girls tend to do, they moved on to other things, the chatter and hum of the cafeteria enveloping them.

Winter that year brought an abundance of mild days, days that allowed the kids to meander the main street in just sweatshirts—no need for winter coats.

"I'm gonna ask one of the guys that comes out of Chapel if I can have a cigarette," Tim said one mild evening in late February.

Nina wanted to wipe off the smug look that had spread across his face, but rolling her eyes had to suffice. "Who are you trying to impress, Tim?"

He put his arm around her shoulder. "You," he said, wiggling his eyebrows.

Brett pushed him away from Nina. "Dude, come on," he said, annoyed with Tim, an occurrence that had become more and more frequent over the years. "Also, since when do you smoke?"

Tim choked on a laugh. "For like a year." He looked over his shoulder toward the door to the dive bar.

"Dude, you're a shit liar," Gary said, shaking his head.

"I'm not lying!" Tim backed up as he said it before turning and jaunting to the door as two inebriated guys walked out; their robust laughter made it seem as if they were hollowing at the moon.

"I'm confused," Nina said. "Does he think we think he's cool for doing this or something?" She glared down the sidewalk, watching him conversing with the guys.

"Tim's a tool, we all know that," Johnny said. "We love him but also agree that he's a tool."

The group chuckled.

"What's so funny?" Tim asked as he made his way back to the group, a cigarette tucked behind his ear, and one hanging between his lips. He pulled out a lighter he got from God knew where.

Nina choked on her own breath, laughing at his stupidity. "Seriously, Tim? Who do you think you are? Kenickie? Where's your T-Bird jacket?"

The group broke out into hysterics as they started moseying down the street toward the harbor. As they broke out into song, singing "Grease

Lightning," the smell of Tim's cigarette secured a memory in Nina's brain that would be triggered frequently for years to come.

Brett slid his hand into Nina's, and she met his gaze. He motioned his head toward the docks, and she nodded once before they broke off from the rest of the group. They walked down the quaint alley between Blue and the homemade candy shop next door, careful not to trip on the cobblestones that lined the path. When they got to the back of the restaurant, they turned left onto the docks and passed the weathered, white Adirondack chairs splayed out and lowered themselves to sit at the edge of the dock.

Nina and Brett's legs swung absentmindedly, the gentle movement of the ocean lapping underneath their feet. Nina began to shiver, the temperature dropping as the sun went down and the night grew later. Brett wrapped his arm around her, pulling her close, and Nina's head fell gently against his shoulder.

"I'm so happy," Nina whispered, looking out at the inky water. She seemed to feel Brett smile, and she turned her head to see Brett looking at her, eyes glistening above a wide grin.

"Me too, Neen."

Nina pulled her legs up and crossed them into a pretzel, turning to face Brett. He turned, too, toward her, taking both her hands in his. Thoughts swam through her mind in a jumble. She wanted to tell him everything she felt, to allow him into the cavernous space of her mind. But she didn't know how. It was too much.

How could she put into words how this boy had saved her, pulled her straight from the darkness and despair her life had turned into? He had brought her back into the light. But with her immature mind, she couldn't get to a place where she could explain her feelings, her gratitude…her love. He had always known who she was—even when she had forgotten.

So, she just smiled at him.

And he smiled back.

Brett pulled her into him, and she shimmied around to rest her back against his chest. His arms wrapped around her caused her muscle to turn to mush.

And so, they sat, time standing still for their benefit alone, healing the pieces of them that had been broken…Brett humming soft tunes into her hair.

"Neen…" Brett's voice broke her from her reverie.

"Yeah," she said, her voice sounding husky.

"Thank you…"

Nina's eyebrows knitted together as she wondered why he was thanking her when she truly believed that she owed him her life. The words *thank you* couldn't possibly be enough to convey how grateful she was to him. But what had she done for him?

"Why are you thanking me?" she asked.

Brett took a deep, audible breath, kissing the top of her head. "Danny's been getting worse. It's like ever since Seamus left, he's been coming for me more than he used to. It's like he blames me for Seamus leaving or something. Even though he acted like he hated Seamus." Nina turned to face him, her expression grim and sad. "But you…" he said, biting his bottom lip. "You make it easier. You make me want to jump out of bed in the morning and make this life a good one. You have been teaching me that there's something on the other side of this…that the end of being in that house isn't too far away. And there is so much waiting for me…for us."

Nina's lips trembled in sadness. For Brett's pain, for her own, and for the thought of their time on Carver Road slipping from their grasp. But wanting that for him at the same time. She sighed, staving off the tears.

"Brett, I—"

"Neen," he said, cutting her off. "I love you."

Nina let out a sob and fell into his embrace, squeezing him tightly. "I love you, too," she said, meaning it with every ounce of her being.

Brett placed his hands on her cheeks, her favorite thing in the world, and he kissed her—under the moon and beneath the blanket of stars. And they held onto each other until their phones started buzzing with texts from the group wondering where they had drifted off to.

Brett laughed. "We should go."

"Yeah," Nina said, taking his hand as they began heading toward the street. "Hey, B…?"

"What?"

"Knock, knock."

Nina and Brett entered the doors of Seaview Regional High School on the first day of senior year the way it always should have been—hand in hand.

Nina noted the lightness she felt inside, the ache in her cheeks from smiling. They walked up the steps to the senior hallway, Brett humming the beat to "Stacy's Mom," causing Nina to giggle and roll her eyes. Since the song came out at the beginning of the summer, no one had been able to stop singing it, while also commenting on how utterly dumb it was.

Nina looked down at her new schedule before taking Brett's, examining it for similarities. "Oh, sweet," she exclaimed. "We both have A.P. English with Jones second period."

"Sick," Brett said through a smile. "Those essays are going to suck this year, I heard."

Nina didn't acknowledge the tidbit, not caring, as long as she was with Brett. "And I'll see you for lunch and study hall." She stopped in the hallway and looked up at him, a soft and pleasant smile on her face.

Brett took her face in his hands gently and rested his forehead on hers before placing a kiss on the tip of her nose. Though the hallway was buzzing with first-day noise—lockers slamming, kids high-fiving each other, and loud and boisterous seniors ready to rule the school—to Nina, it was as if it was just them there in the hallway. Just her and Brett.

No one else existed.

"Nina!" The muffled sound of her name coming from down the hall eventually brought her back to reality. Nina looked to see Allie approaching, her suntanned face smiling, her hair lightened from excessive amounts of Sun In and freshly squeezed lemon.

"Hey, Allie!" Nina greeted, pulling her friend in for a hug.

"Are you ready to rule the school finally?" Allie asked jokingly.

Nina laughed. "Something like that."

And so began the year that would go down in the books for Nina as the best one of her adolescence. A school year filled with dances, fundraisers, college applications, field hockey tournaments, and a young love that was growing so deep, Nina couldn't explain it. But there was also no need to. Nina and Brett were building something that made them the envy of all their friends, and they knew that what they had was something other people longed for. They had loved one another in so many different ways since they were five, but the journey finally made sense. It had all been leading to where they were now.

And Nina could, without a doubt, see all those times throughout their lives—as children on Carver Road—that her heart had ached with him, rejoiced with him, and eventually yearned for him. And though it was quite confusing at times, when she couldn't read the feelings brewing inside, it had all been worth it. The road she had traveled, though at times rocky, had finally been smoothing out, allowing her the ability to breathe and appreciate all that she had in her life.

Things were looking up.

What could possibly go wrong?

Throughout senior year, she reasoned that absolutely nothing could. And when you float so high up into the blissful space that she found herself in, well, it inevitably makes the fall that much worse.

Doesn't it?

Chapter 22

Nina 2016

Nina rubbed a thumb over the divot in the wood trim of her closet. Though it had been painted over and was barely noticeable, she knew it was there and could feel the dip in the wood. Feel it with her finger and feel it with her soul, an ache that had been there for far too long. A deep, throbbing sort of pain that she had learned to live with long ago. One that turned numb when it was dormant, but coming home to Harborview was triggering her into periods of utter suffocation.

She was proud, though. For finding peace in places that she hadn't known would be possible. In a new yoga studio, in her volunteer work with Mary and the Osprey Foundation, in sitting on the patio with her parents in the evening, surrounded by the scent of citronella.

She wasn't quite sure if she would ever recover from the weight of the guilt that lay on her shoulders—all the deaths on her conscience. But she was beginning to feel uplifted, knowing that maybe she would be able to live with it and function despite the weight of it…eventually.

Don't be mad.

Lucy's text came in, and before Nina could reply, her phone dinged again.

I have a new friend and we went to Glass last night and we pretended we were from Sweden. I know I know. I don't even look remotely Swedish but I went with it.

Nina giggled at her best friend's apology. An apology that absolutely wasn't justified. Of course, Lucy was going to meet new people without Nina. But knowing Lucy was still thinking of her and their silly traditions warmed Nina's heart.

Another text arrived.

I'm sorry, Ethel—Followed by three crying emojis.

Nina sighed, conflicted about how to feel. Lucy was making her laugh, like always, but she also missed her so much it hurt.

Swedish! Huh, we never did that one, Nina texted back. **Probably because, you're right, we both look nothing like Swedes haha**

Nina sat down in the chair tucked into the dormer window and relaxed into the plush fabric. Memories of New York flickered in her mind as she texted back and forth with Lucy. She missed the city.

The noise that distracted her.

The way she could disappear into the crowds on the sidewalk, people minding their own business, people not concerned about the past of Nina Jackson.

The friend she made who was able to convince Nina that she was worthy of a friend at all.

It was true that New York City had numbed Nina, and she was beginning to realize that numbness wasn't a sensation she wanted. It wasn't a feeling she wanted to be stuck in forever, on an endless loop.

With the text from Lucy came a deep yearning to be sitting on the hand-me-down couch they shared in their tiny apartment, their heart-to-hearts healing both of them. Lucy had this uncanny ability to make Nina feel safe. She thought about the many times they had stayed up watching the sun rise over the buildings after they had shared their dreams and goals and things that hurt their hearts. Like Nina, Lucy was an empath, and because of that, Nina felt safe with her. She felt safe because Lucy accepted her brokenness, even if she didn't know the entirety of what had broken her. Lucy knew enough to know that Nina needed a true friend.

Nina looked around her bedroom, and instantly, her mind flashed with images of what it had once looked like in here, the place where she grew and changed. Where she had once been happier than she had ever been. But the walls of her room had also seen her more hollowed out than she could even fathom now.

She rested her head on the back of the chair and felt her breaths becoming ragged. She shook her head, desperate to shake away the thoughts and feelings swarming her.

Mostly thoughts of Brett.

Brett Warner.

The whole reason there was a gaping hole beneath her ribs.

Nina loved how Mary Harlow's farm brought her peace and a sort of serenity that invigorated her.

"Good morning, George," Nina said, crouching down to scratch the misfit pig behind the ears. "You're looking dapper this morning." She smiled at him, an automatic gesture.

"Nina, can you help me dear?" Mary's voice came from behind the barn doors.

"Coming!" Nina hollered, getting up from the ground with George.

Inside, the barn smelled of moist wood and fresh hay, a scent Nina had been growing quite fond of. She saw that Mary had boxes laying by the old cash register.

"I have packaging materials in here, dear," she said. "To put my hand-made soaps in."

Nina picked up a box and put it on the counter. "Do you want me to start packing some of the soaps in these?" she asked, holding up a small plastic bag with a pretty label on the front that said *Mary's Homemade Soaps.*

"Yes, please," she said, taking in a tired breath. "We can work together. I have been selling these faster than I ever thought I could." She chuckled softly.

"People want natural items now, Mary," Nina said, smiling at her. "And you have the best there is, right here in Harborview."

Mary flicked her wrist at her. "Oh, dear. You are too kind."

After hundreds of soaps were packaged, Nina glanced at her phone, checking the time to make sure she wouldn't be late for her class at the rec center. She had plenty of time, but with her phone out, she noticed a text from Emma Swanson.

Hi! Want to go out for dinner at Blue tonight with me and Amber?

Nina took her eyes off her phone and stared off into the abyss momentarily. Did she want to go? Her first thought was no, she didn't. She hadn't felt like socializing much since she had been back for a little over a month. The times that she had been out took every ounce of her energy. But why? Was it really fair to herself to not allow anyone in? To let herself to smile and be happy?

But the thought was countered with another. The guilt. The unexplained pull that her own mind had to remind her of the guilt. "No," she whispered to herself. *Stop doing this to yourself.*

Sure! What time?

"How about some tea and a break, Nina?" Mary asked. "This old lady here needs to rest her weary bones." The chuckle she let out made Nina smile, too. "I know you have to get going soon, too."

"Sure," Nina agreed. "Let's go rest."

Inside Mary's kitchen, Nina took the teapot from the stove and filled it with tap water from the sink, noting how already Mary Harlow's house felt like another home to her. Mary pulled out a chair at the kitchen table, the legs scraping against the linoleum. Nina stared out the window, and she couldn't help the way her mind drifted to Brett. Without warning. Without a trigger. He was just there in her mind. And then she was startled by the water overflowing. Hearing Mary giggle behind her, she glanced over her shoulder, rolling her eyes at herself.

"Wow, I zoned out there for a minute."

"Something's gotten you in a bit of a daze there?"

Nina moved the pot to the stove, turned it on, and joined Mary at the table. "I guess so, Mary."

"Is it a fella?" Mary's sympathetic smile elicited an ache in Nina's heart.

"Partly, yes," Nina admitted. Because wasn't that the truth? Brett was her whole past; he was the reason for everything up until now. She was who she was, in large part, because of him. But it wasn't simply *a fella* that was causing Nina to daydream out the farmhouse window. She knew that but could she to explain the twisted nature of her life to sweet Mary Harlow? "It's kind of complicated, I guess." Mary was quiet for a moment, and Nina was inclined to say, "I know you have experienced loss, Mary, so I don't feel like I have the right to bring this to you. My loss doesn't feel worthy of pain when the person...the fella... isn't really *gone*. You know?"

"George..." Mary began but paused, a whimsical look on her warm, weathered face. "It's true that I lost him here on this earth last year, but when he died, I had already known the emptiness that missing him had caused me throughout our lives together." Nina leaned forward in her chair. "I mean right from the start, we only knew distance, and there were times during the war when us ladies back here were just waiting with bated breath for news. Months would go by without a word." She sighed, but a smile played on her lips.

"Oh, Mary," Nina breathed. "I can't even imagine what that was like. It seems torturous, really." Tears moistened her eyes as the teapot screeched. Nina jumped from her seat, hurriedly getting the mugs ready so that she could sit back down and hear Mary's story. "Let me do this quickly." She stirred in the sugar cube and a bit of milk before taking the mugs back to the table. "I'm sorry you had to experience that," she said while sitting back in her seat.

Mary rested her delicate and lined hand atop Nina's. "Oh, darling, it's nothing that needs apologizing for. It's simply the little details of life. We all have them—little pieces that bring sorrow, but thankfully, the joy is woven in there, too." Nina nodded once, agreeing. "Like when I received correspondence in the mail from George. Those would carry me until the next tidbit. His words scribbled on dirty, wrinkled paper that held his strong voice within those lines—as if I could hear him. And when he returned home to me?" Mary shook her head in disbelief. "Well, there aren't really words to describe it."

"Can you try?" Nina's words came out as just a whisper.

Mary waited a few beats before answering. "Have you ever had something move you so much that you feel it? Physically?"

Nina's eyes widened. Mary had only just begun, but already she felt as if the conversation was awakening something inside her. Something she thought was long gone. "Yes."

Mary nodded. "Well, that's what seeing him after being apart so long was like. The edges of my nerves, the hairs on my skin, the space under my ribs…they all had feelings in them. Like I was electrified, coming alive for the first time. But it wasn't just the overly exciting feeling of being reunited. It was the everyday connection we developed once we were back together physically. The comfort. The friendship that grew deeply."

Nina felt a single tear slide down her right cheek, and she couldn't pinpoint exactly where it was coming from. Was it Mary's emotion? Her own? Or was it both? Taking other people's emotions on as her own was Nina's MO. It always had been. She only wished that she could use her empathetic gift for good, rather than simply allowing it to ravage her from the inside. It had been so long since Nina had actually cried that the sensation was a bit foreign. All she knew was that she felt Mary's heartache, and she understood the joy and connection she had with George. Because there had never been a stronger connection than the one she had with Brett. So, she reasoned that her tears were for Mary and for her. For the feeling she once had with Brett and how she was now without him.

Grief is what it was.

Grief for what was lost.

For what could have been.

"I have an inkling that you know what I'm talking about," Mary uttered quietly.

Nina's mouth quivered as she nodded. "I'm afraid so." She wiped her tears and offered Mary a wayward smile. "But it all seems lost, if I'm being honest. Some terrible things happened, and…I don't know. I think it may have ruined us."

Mary, too, had moist eyes. "Oh, no, sweetheart. There's always time, you know." She reached over again for Nina's hand. "Until there isn't," she whispered sadly.

And Nina knew what she meant. When death took George from Mary, there was no longer time to say things left unsaid. Nina didn't want that. She truly feared that scenario. But she also knew that her and Brett's situation didn't come with a manual, she was sure of that.

"Promise me that you will be bold, Nina," Mary said. "Don't be afraid. Fight for what you want."

And then Nina pictured the birds in the nest at the end of Mary's driveway. And she had a feeling that she knew what she had to do.

Amber Baker wasn't a pushover, Nina noted, and she figured she must be a good match for her old friend, Tim, who had been a tad bit obnoxious as a kid, mixed with his perpetual lack of self-confidence. *Loud and assholish* was how she had once described him. But he was part of the group, and because of that, at the end of the day, she always had his back for all those years.

"So, you knew my Tim way back when?" Amber asked, laughing. Nina, Amber, and Emma were sitting in the back of Blue, resting in the Adirondacks, sipping chilled pinot grigio, the early June heat making the condensation forming on her glass satisfying to Nina's senses. A sign that summer in Harborview was just within reach.

Nina looked out to the boats swaying over small waves and smiled, taking a small sip from her glass. "I sure did."

"I told her how annoying he was back then," Emma laughed.

Amber laughed, too. "Who are we kidding, he's still annoying," she joked. "But I love him."

Nina looked at Amber, a trillion memories swimming in her mind. Pieces of the puzzle that felt scattered and untethered. "I punched him in the face once when we were kids," Nina said, instantly regretting it.

Amber barked out a laugh. "What?!"

Nina met her eyes and then allowed herself to smile, seeing that Amber was going to love this story. So, she shared the details. How Tim had pushed her a bit too far, and she did what she had to do.

Amber shook her head slowly, sipping from her glass. "Maybe he was annoying to you because he liked you or something."

Emma cut in. "Actually, that's probably true."

Nina's face turned into a scowl, pinched in disgust. "Definitely not. It wasn't like that with—"

Emma cut her off. "Well, how could he get anywhere back then? You belonged to Brett and only Brett."

Nina's heart skipped three beats, it seemed, making her lightheaded instantly.

"Who's Brett?" Amber asked.

"He was in our group of friends," Emma informed her, nonchalantly.

But the phrase she used to describe him didn't fit, and Nina knew that. If anything, Emma was barely part of that group. So how could she understand the magnitude of what Brett was? Of who he was to Nina.

He was everything.

As Amber and Emma began talking about the high school days of Seaview Regional High School, Nina drifted, her eyes looking just down the dock to where the memories pulled her.

"I'll be right back," Nina said. "I just need to stretch my legs."

And so, she took her almost empty glass and strolled a bit down the docks. She stopped right where she and Brett had sat one cold February night when they were seventeen. Where he had told her that he loved her, that she was saving him. And where she had told him the same. That she loved him, too, knowing that the actual truth was that he was the one who had saved her.

Nina didn't want to cry. But she felt it coming, building with the force of a tidal wave deep inside. The sadness and emptiness of losing the only person who mattered.

She sat on the edge of the dock, her feet hanging over the side, her sundress billowing in the soft ocean breeze. The gulls flying above pulled her eyes to the sky, and she smiled at the sound of them and the smell of the brine bringing her home again.

She needed to talk to Brett. She had to. She wondered how he felt. If he wanted to see her. If he missed her the way she missed him. Why hadn't he reached out? Why hadn't he just walked across the street?

Maybe he was torn just as much as she was, she reasoned. *I'll do it. I'll be the one to break the tension between us.*

She took a deep breath and stretched her arms above her head, her training reminding her that moving her body was how she could heal it, soften the heart inside her, kill the shadows and darkness with light.

Emma's approaching footsteps pulled her from her thoughts. "Our table's ready," she said softly. Nina turned and smiled at her, her eyes a bit glossy. "Are you ok, Nina?"

She nodded, putting her hand on Emma's arm. "Yeah, I'm good."

"Was it Brett?" she asked, concerned. "Maybe I shouldn't have brought him up. I know you were kind of weird about it when I first asked you about him last time we were out. I'm sorry."

"No, Emma. You didn't do anything wrong," Nina assured her. Because she hadn't. It wasn't Emma's fault that his name was a trigger for her. Nina was aware enough to acknowledge that.

"Ok, let's go eat," Emma said, linking her arm through Nina's as they headed back to where Amber was waiting for them.

The inside of Blue had been updated a bit, but the atmosphere and the view still felt entirely unchanged to Nina. As they took their seats at a table next to the windows against the docks, Nina looked out, admiring the scenery.

"We should all get together soon!" Emma said after they had ordered another round and light appetizers. "Like all of us from high school."

"That would be fun!" Amber said. "I would love to meet the old crew that I haven't met yet. Do you hang out with John?" she asked Emma and Nina.

"Johnny Cooper?" Nina asked, her interest piqued.

"I haven't seen him in ages," Emma said. "I really wasn't close with Johnny. But he was so nice."

"Tim and I get together with him and his wife sometimes. She's so sweet."

"Me and Landon don't double date much," Emma said, rolling her eyes. "Sometimes I feel like I'm single."

The admission settled into a silence between the three women, Nina and Amber feeling a bit sorry for Emma.

Emma laughed uncomfortably, flicking her wrist, diminishing the obvious sadness there. "So yeah, let's plan something!"

And Nina settled into the idea that her past was catching up to her, and she couldn't run. Not anymore.

Chapter 23

Brett 2016

Brett held his breath and pressed the "submit" button on the Veteran Service Dog website he had found while scrolling the internet a few days prior. Knowing Seamus wasn't in any sort of headspace to do it himself, Brett filled out the application with all of Seamus information, except the phone number and email address. For those, he used his own. He needed to be the one to answer the calls and emails; if they went to Seamus, they would surely be ignored.

Brett blew air into his cheeks and placed his intertwined fingers behind his head, staring at the screen that said: *Thanks for submitting your application. Someone will be in touch soon.*

There was no going back now. All he could do was wait, and when the information came in, he would do whatever he could to get Seamus something, anything that could help him. It was the least he could do.

Brett got up from the desk chair, stuffing his phone in his pocket and headed out to meet Johnny at the East Beach bridge—fishing was on their agenda.

The sun looked like a pat of butter, sliding behind Johnny and Brett and slipping beneath the pond on Carver Road. In front of them, out over the

Atlantic, the sky was painted melon and lilac, a mesmerizing watercolor piece of art.

"I'm still really bad at this," Johnny said, casting his line over the bridge.

Brett laughed, the flashbacks of their childhood seeming to be crystal clear in his mind. "Remember that time we all caught fish, and you pulled out a boot and a sandal?"

Johnny laughed, rolling his eyes. "Yeah, that's still my track record," he said. "Last week, Erica and I fished off the shore of Grant Pond. She caught two fish, and I got lumps of lake weeds."

Brett chuckled, shaking his head.

"Hey, I got wind from some patients that they are doing some fundraising for the Osprey Foundation," Johnny said, fiddling with his fishing pole. "Ginny's still not feeling up to driving the ice cream truck, but she wants to sell ice cream for the project and donate proceeds."

"That's awesome," Brett said, casting out.

"I talked to Terri, and I offered to drive it around." He gave Brett a mischievous sort of look. "Want to do it with me? For old time's sake?"

"Oh shit!" Brett said. "I'm definitely in."

"I think we should get Tim and see if anyone else is around, have ourselves a Carver Road reunion," Johnny suggested. "We can park it over at the Food Truck Festival on the Fourth of July, too."

To Brett's surprise, the idea excited him a bit, the memories of his childhood warming him rather than turning his nerves to ice. He relished in this feeling, assuming it would be fleeting. These days, thoughts of Texas were sending him into despair. Did he want to rush back? He wasn't so sure anymore, and thinking about it too much was causing unwanted strife.

"Yeah, that sounds great. I haven't talked to Tim in years," he said. The exact number of years was roughly twelve. Since he had left for college. Just like he had abandoned Johnny, the rest of the group got the same treatment. They got nothing from Brett.

But he knew he had to make it right. No matter how hard it was. Especially with Nina. He had to start there.

Brett had been home one month, and though the conversation with Johnny on the bridge gave him hope, Texas was still calling him in a way he wished it wouldn't. He'd hoped that he would get back to Harborview and be ready to take on the challenges with acceptance and a little bit of grace, at least after a few weeks.

But Brett was restless and longing for his Texas life, longing for a night out with friends at Sullivan's where he could kick back and listen to some live music on the dueling pianos, a tumbler of whiskey in his hand.

He would kill for a barbeque smash burger from Slaw on South First Street; he could almost smell the way the aromas drifted out onto the street, making his stomach rumble with the memory. One night last fall, Brett, Dean, and a few other friends from college had stumbled in there after a night out, and the burger he got, dripping with sauce, was the best he had ever had. And he made it a point to say it over and over again, making Dean laugh at his drunkenness.

And with his mind clouded from the alcohol, he watched a woman of Nina's stature with long dark hair walk by him. He chased after her until he caught up and grabbed her shoulder, turning her around. "Neen," he said, breathless.

"Yo, dude, what are you doing?" the man beside her said, his voice rising.

Brett's shoulders slumped. It wasn't Nina. Of course, it wasn't. "Sorry," he muttered. "I thought you were someone else."

He turned around to see Dean looking concerned. "Dude, what happened?"

"Oh, uh, nothing," he stuttered, looking again at the woman walking away. The woman who wasn't Nina. "I thought I knew that person," he added, his voice sounding distant and strange.

And he almost told him. Brett, with his whiskey brain, almost told Dean about Nina and his deep dark secrets. He was drunk enough that he found it difficult to control the torment he had suffered in silence for over a decade.

But like the steel trap his shadows had been locked behind for a long time, he was able to keep the doors locked that night, somehow. He never did tell Dean, or anyone in Texas, about Nina and how he lost the love of his life, how the hole inside was a cave that would never be filled.

With his sober mind, he reasoned that their love wasn't as sacred and strong as he had once thought, that they had only been molded together through a shared trauma. But this reasoning never stuck because the truth was that the trauma was what had actually torn them apart.

Brett ran his hands through his hair. He was doing it. He was going to go across the street right now and face her, finally, and say the things that had been left unsaid for all these years. He hurried down the stairs and out the door before he could change his mind. When he got to the end of the driveway, he finally looked up from his hurried feet to see Nina walking slowly off of her driveway and into the street, right toward him.

The ringing in Brett's ears was deafening, truly. It was as if time was both stopping and speeding up, all at once. He was being swallowed up by memories from long ago, tricking his mind into thinking he was seeing Nina as a teenager, or a feral child.

Brett tried desperately to settle his rapid breathing as he put one foot in front of the other until she was right there in front of him, close enough for him to reach out and touch her.

And then he heard it. The sound that once filled his dreams. The voice that haunted him on drunk nights in Austin when he swore she was there. The voice that had once saved him and crushed him. But now, it sounded like a melody, putting his soul back together.

"Hey, B."

Chapter 24

Nina 2004

NINA TRIED TO SWALLOW down the lump in her throat and blink back the tears threatening to break through, but she wasn't emotionally capable of handling the impending doom that was approaching come summer's end.

She felt Brett's gaze shift to her from the driver's seat, and she tried to save him the trouble of having to pick up the pieces of her crumbling heart. But looking out the window wasn't enough; he still saw her shoulders shaking, still heard the squeak of emotion slip from the lips that she tried to mold shut.

"Neen." Her name on his lips was her undoing. "What's the matter?"

She shook her head, unable to answer. Brett pulled into his driveway and hurried out of the car to her side, opening the door and pulling her into his embrace. She softly cried into his chest, her tears leaving wet spots on his Texas Tech T-shirt.

"Treehouse?" he asked, his words muffled into her hair.

Nina nodded sadly as they trudged, hand in hand, toward the base of the elm tree.

Once sitting inside the tiny space, Nina pulled her knees into her chest and heaved a sigh that shook her entire being.

"Is this because of college day?" Brett asked.

They locked eyes, and again, her lip began to tremble as she nodded just once. It was all she needed to do before he wrapped her up in him again, rocking her, their respective university apparel mocking Nina and her utter despair.

"It's almost June!" she said, growing hysterical. "We've been having so much fun, and soon, it's all going to be over." She hiccupped a sob. "We have never been apart. For all the years that we have been best friends, and now, in this new territory we found ourselves in last year, we have always been like this," she said, intertwining her middle and index finger. "Physically and in here," she added, tapping on her heart.

Brett's face fell into a sadness that matched Nina's. A look that didn't do much to soothe her. "I'm sorry," he whispered, and Nina knew he meant it. She knew he was sorry that he was leaving her. She knew he would pack her in his luggage if he could. "You know I have to get far away from here." He said this as if it was his first time saying it. As if they hadn't already had these conversations before. But those times were before. When August seemed like a lifetime away; now, it was knocking on their door, urging them out into the real world.

"I know, B," she whimpered. "I know." She turned around, leaning against Brett's chest, her favorite spot. And she was being honest; she *did* know. She knew that Brett could be on the other side of the planet, and it still wouldn't be far enough away from Danny Warner. But knowing that didn't make it any easier for her. And they both knew that Nina couldn't afford out-of-state tuition. The loans she had already secured for UMass Amherst were already causing her to lose sleep, even though she didn't really understand any of it. The paperwork she had done over the last year had reminded her that growing up was for the birds. She wasn't ready to be an adult, especially without Brett.

"We will just fly away for a little bit," Brett said. "And then we will come back. We will figure it out." He kissed the top of her head. "I promise."

Nina's eyes darted around the interior of the treehouse, her heart melting to a puddle of memories at her feet. She scanned for the scissors, her eyes catching the toolbox still up there from when they tried to make amateur repairs. "Initial time," she said softly, trying to smile.

Brett beamed at her, getting up from the floor.

And so they did it. They carved their initials into the cedar planks of the wall, *N & B,* not knowing that it would be the last time they would ever do it.

——————

After graduation, during the last week of May, Brett and Nina made a pact that the summer was to be savored and cherished. They vowed not to let the shadow of what was coming darken the time they had right in front of them, tight in their grasp. They promised to save their tears for their departures and not a day before.

But their plans, their promises, would be difficult to abide by because Danny Warner caught on that Brett was leaving, not only for the scholarship he did, in fact, earn, even as an outfielder, but also to get far away from him.

And Danny Warner didn't lose.

——————

Nina's arms felt weightless and tingly, and not for any reason that was good. As she approached the sideyard of the Warner's house, passing the treehouse, she heard the muffled shouts of voices that undoubtedly belonged to Brett and Danny, who she could see were in a scuffle down by the pond's edge.

Brett's texts had sent her into a tailspin as she sucked air into her lungs in a panic and jumped off her bed with lightning speed. They had come in quick succession.

Neen.

He has it in for me tonight.

I'm scared.

Can I come over?

Scared? Brett was never scared. But the escalation of Danny's violence couldn't be ignored. She didn't even bother responding. It would have taken too much time. Time she needed to get to him. Quickly.

She made it to the backyard in what felt like only a few steps. She wasn't breathing correctly; she felt dizzy and unwell.

And there they were, right at the edge of the water, and none of it felt right. It was all wrong. She knew, even before she approached them, that their lives were about to change. Because that was Nina, intuitive and all.

Looking back now, she still cringes, practically suffocates, when she relives the minutes that followed Brett's pleading texts to her. The minutes that ruined both of them.

As she got closer, she heard Brett yell the final blow to Danny Warner's ego, the words sputtering out of his mouth while Danny's hands grasped his neck. "I wish you never missed your flight that day!"

Nina's eyes widened while Brett's darted to her, bloodshot and watery. He tried to shake his head at her and opened his mouth to say something, but he was unable. Nina pressed on closer, not knowing what the hell she was going to do. She wanted to yell something. To make Danny stop. But she was mute. Deep in her gut, she knew it would waste too much time to leave and get help.

And then time seemed to stop as Danny shoved Brett's head under the water and held him down as Brett thrashed his arms and legs. His head lifted above the water, and he gasped for air so loudly that Nina thought she was going to vomit at the sheer panic in the sound. She looked around helplessly for anything she could use to help Brett.

In a moment of clarity, Nina remembered the toolbox in the treehouse. She ran across the yard and up the rickety steps and found the box right inside the doorway. Pulling out the hammer in one swift movement, she was back on the steps, shimmying down. Running as fast as she could, she reached the edge of the pond in seconds, Brett and Danny still struggling. Brett was big, and strong, too—his size and strength almost identical to his father's. As he fought to live, to keep his head above water, he didn't have the strength to do anything more than cling to survival. But he was losing; Nina could see that as she approached.

"Stop! Danny, stop!" she screamed at the top of her lungs. She looked around, her eyes darting to the houses on the street. The Coopers and the Bakers, further down the pond. The lights were all off. Where was Laura? Frantic, Nina brought her eyes back to the struggle in front of her. Brett had gotten to his feet and found the energy to punch his dad in the stomach, causing Danny to fall into the water, moaning.

Nina sighed with relief. Brett could get away now. But as soon as she settled into a moment of security, which was only mere seconds, Danny had Brett's shirt, pulling him back to the water's edge. And before she knew it, Danny was holding Brett underneath the water once again. Nina sobbed, frantically approaching the father and son. Her best friend. The love of her entire life.

She yanked her arms up behind her head, the hammer in her palms gripped with all her might. She aimed for his back, to surprise him and hopefully get him to let go. But he didn't even flinch. She hauled up again, but this time, she was stronger, and instead of his back, she hit Danny Warner's skull. The sound made Nina sick as a befuddled Danny loosened his grip on Brett and slumped into the water beside the dinghy that rested along the shore.

The sound of her own ragged breaths was the only thing Nina could hear. Well, her gasps and the ringing in her ears that dizzied her. She looked around, fighting for equilibrium, as she stumbled on the grass, her sandaled feet wet with salty pond water. She saw Brett lying in the grass, his chest rising and falling in dramatic bursts.

"Brett!" Nina screamed as she approached him, bending down to check on him. Nervously, she looked over her shoulder, fearing that Danny was going to get up and come toward them. She worried because she had hit him.

With a hammer.

Nina's insides were reeling as tears began sliding down her face, her hands on Brett's chest. "Brett. Are you ok?" She shook him gently. "Brett!"

He began to stir, moaning, bringing his hands up to his neck. "Where is he?" he asked, breathless.

"He's over by the water," Nina replied. She had trouble forming the words. "I hit him, Brett. With a hammer. He's not getting up. Do you think he's dead?" She was panicking now.

Brett sat up, and Nina helped him to his feet as they both inched closer to the water quietly. At the edge of the pond, where the water lapped in tiny, gentle waves, there was Danny, face down in the shallowness of the shore.

"Brett," Nina whimpered.

Brett ran his hands through his hair before limping, obviously in pain, toward his father. He turned him over, pulling his arm out of the water, feeling for a pulse. Brett turned his head toward Nina, pursing his lips as a grave expression spread over his tired and bruised face. "He's dead," he said, choking back a sob.

Nina began crying and shaking uncontrollably, falling to the ground on her hands and knees. She looked up to see Brett stepping out of the water and approaching her. He knelt beside her, taking her face in his hands. "Look at me, Neen," he said gently. Her eyes, wide and scared, met his. "You did this to protect me. You didn't have a choice."

Nina could tell he wasn't just trying to convince her of a truth. It *was* the truth. Drunken Danny Warner was going to kill Brett, and Nina couldn't live with herself if she had allowed that to happen. She hadn't meant to kill him.

But she had.

What's going to happen to me?

"Listen to me, Nina." Her real name on his tongue sounded foreign and strange to her ears. The seriousness settled deep into her heart. "We will call the police and tell them what happened. Look at me," he said, gesturing to his own mangled body. "The evidence is all right here."

Nina shook her head. "No. They will arrest me. I killed him, B. I killed him."

"Shh," Brett said, pulling her into his chest as he winced in pain. "We have to call the police, Nina. We have to. We don't have a choice." His voice was still calm, but it did little to settle her.

"No, he just fell and hit his head on the boat, Brett," she said frantically, trying to make up a story that was believable. "You always say that no one knows the truth about him. No one knows how he is because you all keep it locked up. You. Your mom. Seamus. No one will believe this. No one!"

"Nina!" There it was. Her name again. In its entirety. Her name coming out tangled in his frustration. "Don't make me do this."

"What if they arrest me? Or what if they arrest us both?" Her crying was out of control. "It's our word against a dead person. A murdered person!" She began to sound hysterical, and Brett tried to quiet her.

"You have to stop raising your voice. We will wake up the whole street," he said, annoyed now.

Nina put her hand over her mouth to suffocate the emotions, but it didn't quiet her much. "Brett, we can turn his body face up, right there, near the boat." She pointed in the direction of the crime. "We can get rid of the hammer…whatever we need to do." Nina whipped her nose with her forearm. "Please, Brett." He took her face in his hands and looked at her, really looked at her. "I love you, B. Everything I have ever done in my life has been with you in mind. My feelings. My heart. My soul. All of it is better because I love you with all of my heart. I couldn't let you die. I don't want to get in trouble. I can't have people knowing that I *killed* someone." She also knew that her conscience couldn't handle another death on her shoulders, either. Her sobbing continued. "What will happen to me? To us?"

Brett kept her face in his hands as his eyes darted nervously to every inch of it. "Ok," he whispered. "He was drunk and hit his head on the boat." He pulled her into him again, and she cried silently into his chest, her body shaking uncontrollably.

"Thank you, B."

The pair did what they could to erase any evidence that they were at the pond. The hammer went into a trash bag, Nina cringing as she placed it in, seeing the blood and knowing her fingerprints were all over it.

Brett took the bag from her hands. "I'll get rid of this somewhere," he said, his voice sounding far away and dulled.

Nina nodded. "Ok." She couldn't help but feel like something had already changed inside of her, and in Brett. The air around them felt tainted and thick. She looked around. "Do I go home now? What if my parents hear me? I'm a mess."

"You have to go home, Nina. You have to be in your bed as soon as possible. Like you weren't even here."

Nina couldn't help but notice that he sounded mad…or a bit agitated, at least. And his tone only made the sinking feeling inside her feel a bit worse. And sinking was the only way to describe it, really. Sinking slow and deep, like a ship lost at sea. But tonight? That was just the beginning. From this point on, feeling lost would become the only sensation that Nina would be able to personally identify with.

She looked at Brett with longing. In no way did she want to walk away from him and back to her house. How was she going to sleep after what had just happened? She wouldn't, of course. She would be up until sunrise. In roughly four hours, she was sure she'd still be lying there, staring up at the fluorescent stars on her ceiling. The ones that had been there since she was nine, a harsh reminder after this night that she was no longer a little girl.

No. She was a murderer.

She pulled Brett into her in a restless, desperate sort of embrace and then pulled away before scurrying off along the side of his house.

She passed the treehouse without even looking at it. She couldn't. It was a beacon mocking her and the fact that everything she had tried so desperately to hang onto since she was a child was seemingly slipping out of reach…and into the water with the Ghost of the Pond.

With Danny Warner.

Chapter 25

Brett 2004

Drip, drip, drip.

The sound of the leaking kitchen faucet was nagging at Brett's nerves as he sat at the table, taking in shallow breaths. The slow sounds of his mother's footsteps on the stairs caused his spine to straighten, his senses on high alert. For the last two days—since Nina had killed Danny—that is how Brett had been…in a constant state of fight or flight, and his bones, his muscles, his heart, they were suffering the effects.

Laura walked into the kitchen, and if she noticed Brett sitting there, she didn't let on at first.

"Hi, Mom," Brett rasped.

Laura glanced over at him, a glazed expression on her tired face. "Hi, hunny," she whispered, as if it was all she could muster.

Brett watched her fill a mug so close to the top with the coffee that he had brewed that it slopped over the edge of the mug as she carried it to the table. "Shit," she muttered under her breath.

Brett got up and grabbed a paper towel, wiping the spilled coffee off the counter. He looked over his shoulder at his mother, noting how lost she looked, knowing it was his fault. Well, his and Nina's. He had been watching her and attempting to help with the tasks that needed to get done to lay Danny to rest. He had been watching while his Aunt Ann helped Laura remain upright and put one foot in front of the other. He couldn't help but wonder if there was anything inside his mother that mirrored relief. But he never dared voice these thoughts, keeping them hidden inside behind the shadows that were growing darker each day.

Brett leaned against the kitchen counter and glanced around at the layout of the house. He had been so close to leaving all of this in the rearview mirror and exchanging it for a sense of freedom, but now?

Well, now, everything felt tainted, like he was running to hide, manacles on his wrists. He wasn't flying away anymore. He was running, afraid that the horrible truth would catch up to him.

Brett knew that, for as long as he could remember, he had looked at the bright side of his life, always. He was trying to remain positive and hopeful, but it didn't feel like he was able to do that now. He was broken, or so it seemed.

Brett's phone began to buzz on the table, the noise causing Laura to jump, shaking her mug. He picked it up, and seeing *Neen* across the screen caused him to roll his eyes as he turned the phone off, silencing the buzzing vibration. He couldn't even count how many times Nina had called and texted him in the last two days, most of them he'd ignored. He couldn't bring himself to talk to her, let alone be face-to-face with her. He knew he wasn't being fair, but he still couldn't bring himself to be reasonable.

Everything was too fucked up for that. At the moment, he blamed Nina for it; the jumbled mess of his brain blamed her for everything; whether that was right or not, it was what it was. He actually couldn't even bring himself to care.

The afternoon of the funeral was a sweltering day; the humidity and the reality of the situation made it entirely too difficult to breathe. The town rallied around the Warners, offering their condolences and bringing casseroles a plenty to the house.

"Do you want me to sit with you?" Nina asked outside the little Episcopalian church located on the banks of the harbor. Brett noted how small her voice sounded, and it angered him. He wanted her to be fierce; instead, her weakness that was shining through annoyed him. He needed the old Nina, but as he noticed with himself, she was also gone.

Brett eyed her, emotion flaring in his eyes as he waited a beat before responding. "I should probably sit with my mom and Seamus." Regretting the words as soon as they came out, Brett watched Nina's face fall. "But I'll find you after, ok?"

Nina nodded. "Ok," she said. "Of course." Then she turned on her heel, and Brett watched her walk toward her parents. His shoulders slumped, hating himself for the confusion he was wrestling with and, subsequently, how it was impacting Nina. His Neen. But for the time being, he knew no other way to deal with it than to avoid her.

Brett sat through the ceremony, feeling as if he was floating above, looking down on it all. From the corner of his eye, he watched Seamus's jaw twitch every so often. His brother never shed a single tear during the two days he was home for emergency leave from the Army, which was no surprise to Brett.

Is this really the family I came from? Brett found himself wondering during it all. From a family that was frightened of the father figure. Where the father figure tormented the family, tried to kill his own son, and ended up being killed by the neighbor. And the remaining members of the family were relieved but never would admit it out loud. Two brothers who should share a deep bond, yet the closeness would never come to be. A mother who wasn't strong enough to save them. Was this truly his family's story?

Brett looked over at the Jacksons one row back, Nina's pale face frightening him a bit. He looked at her, the one who *had* saved him. A lump formed in his throat, the conflicting emotions bubbling so fiercely, he didn't know what to do about them. The love he had for Nina, his Neen, was something he would never be able to deny. But things were ruined now. Broken beyond repair. And the sadness of that reality was his undoing.

Chapter 26

Nina 2004

THE REST OF THE summer played out like a living nightmare for Nina Jackson. Brett and Nina's promises they had made to each other at the end of May mocked them all summer long following the night by the pond's edge.

The shadows were no longer waiting for them in August; they were swarming around them here and now, pushing them into despair and unease at every turn. It was true that they had both suffered, but they each dealt with it in their own way, causing a rift to grow between them.

Nina was always jittery and on edge. She couldn't sleep, and the dark circles under her eyes alarmed her when she looked at her own reflection.

Now that Danny was gone, Brett had become angry as he began to process all the terrible things that had happened to him.

But Nina took his anger personally because it always seemed to be pointed right at her. She would lie awake in her bed, going over and over that dreadful night in her head, convincing herself that she hadn't meant to kill him. She knew that to be true.

And yet, Brett's anger toward her made her question every little thing.

Their friends, too, sensed that something was amiss. Nina caught Johnny's eyebrow raises aimed toward the two of them. It was expected, of course, for Brett to be off, his father having passed from an untimely and tragic death. But everyone seemed to notice the weirdness between him and Nina, too.

The death was considered an accident, as Nina and Brett had hoped. The police had asked a shaking Laura an array of standard questions that morning, and she ended up admitting that Danny was not only vile and abusive at times, but his drinking was more than just a small problem. His blood alcohol was .22 and the toxicology report even found cocaine in his system.

Though the blood found on the boat very well could have been Brett's, it was never even tested, thankfully, since it had been labeled a tragic accident.

By the end of July, the stress had caused Nina to drop a significant amount of weight, which led Emma to ask her if she was on drugs.

Drugs? No, Emma. Actually, I have barely eaten or slept in almost two months because I killed Danny Warner. And then staged it to look like a drunken accident. That's all.

Nina had smirked, thinking in her head that she *wished* that was the problem. "No, Em," she said quietly as they sat on Stoney Beach, watching the waves crash against the edges of Woods Hole jutting into the sea. "I'm not on drugs." She squinted into the sun, her words barely a whisper.

"Then why are you acting all weird? Is it because of college? And everyone is leaving in a few weeks?"

Nina turned her gaze to her friend, contemplating what to say next, a pensive expression on her haggard face.

Emma was looking at her, worried, waiting for a response. "Yeah, that's it," Nina said, forcing a smile. "College nerves."

It was the first Saturday of August, and the summer clock was ticking by, slowly now. Back when the summer had started, Nina wanted to stop time, make it last forever. But after the incident, her restlessness had become unbearable. And the tension between her and Brett was eating away at her, piece by piece. Time seemed to be dragging on, and not in a good way.

Alone in her house, Nina sat on the couch, her back rail straight, her eyes red and wide. It was so eerily quiet; she swore the settling bones of the house were talking to her—sending her a message she couldn't decipher. Nothing made sense anymore and the unrest was rattling her deeply. With shaking hands, she texted Brett.

My parents are at a wedding. I don't want to be here alone. Can you come over?

Nina waited, staring at her phone for thirteen whole minutes before Brett replied.

I'm at Johnny's playing Madden. I'll come by later.

Nina wondered, sadly, why they hadn't texted her and told her to come down to the basement. Why was she being left in the dust when all she had done was protect her best friend? Why was he punishing her?

She couldn't fathom it.

Nina had pulled the curtain to the side and peered out the front window. For what seemed like hours, she repeated this gesture over and over every few minutes until, finally, she spotted Brett with his head down and his hands in his pockets.

Relief flooded her.

Hearing his dulled footsteps on the stoop, she hurried to open the screen door.

"Hi," she said, aware that she sounded desperate for him to let her back into the space she had always occupied.

"Hi," he replied, offering her a smile. "Where's the wedding?"

"Plymouth," she said. "They're staying overnight." Her eyes darted to his eyes and his mouth and back again. "I don't want to be here alone, B. All night? I can't do it." She knew she sounded hysterical, and she hated it. But she couldn't help feeling that the darkness had begun to feel like a punishment for what she had done. When she crawled into her bed each night, it felt as if there was a rock sitting on her chest, making it too difficult to breathe.

The shadows on the walls.

The sounds from the night…from the pond.

A warped and mutilated vision of Danny Warner rising from the shallow water and leaving the pond, dripping with salt water…coming for her.

She was sure of it.

Reality had become too muddled to make sense of anymore.

Brett sat down on the couch and invited her to sit next to him. She did, stiffly. She faced him, her eyes burning.

"Neen, you need to relax." He sounded worried.

"Relax?" Nina said, her voice raising an octave.

"People are talking. They've been noticing that you're a bit…unhinged." Was he really saying this to her? Her Brett? The compassionate, caring, and utterly selfless human that she had loved with all her heart for years and years. Was he berating her?

Nina glared at him, her eyes narrowed to angry slits. "People are talking?" she spat. "How can you care about what people are saying when I'm here alone, struggling with what happened? You are just abandoning me, Brett!"

He shook his head, annoyed. "You're struggling because of what YOU did!"

Nina got up. "It was an accident. I did it for you! To save you. You would be dead if I didn't do it, Brett." She was sobbing then. "You know that's true!"

"But now it's weighing on you, and you can't deal with it…you should have just let me call the police, Nina," he said through gritted teeth. "Then we could move on knowing it was all out in the open, and there wouldn't be any secrets." Nina couldn't formulate any words for a response; she could barely breathe. "And now I have this weight on me, too. A burden that I never asked to carry," he said with anger and frustration in his voice.

His words sounded so final, making the air between them turn stale.

He was blaming her for his pain, and she couldn't deny it; she didn't blame him for that. The words he had spat at her were not words that she could argue. She had forced him to make a life-altering decision that they could never take back.

Nina had killed Brett's dad, and when he wanted to do the right thing, she hadn't let him.

She felt as if there would never come a time when she could forgive herself, not when she believed that Brett Warner could never forgive her. How could he? She was the reason that he felt this unimaginable guilt. A guilt that felt like it would never fade.

And how daunting a realization it was.

"I'm sorry," she muttered finally. "I don't know how to fix it."

"We can't!" The volume of his voice shocked her, and he began pacing the room. "We can't fix it," he said again, softer. Nina approached him, but to her utter horror, he backed away. "I can't even look at you right now, Nina." And then he began to cry, an image that made Nina want to throw up all the bile in her stomach.

She had broken Brett. Her strong, resilient friend was crumbling to pieces because of her. Nina fell to the ground sobbing, gasping for air, a shred of hope dangling in front of her. Hope that he would come to her and pull her into his arms. But through her sobs, she heard the screen door slam, and his hurried footsteps descend the stairs and head across the street.

Hope flickered out like a flame.

The early morning of August 16 started off a bit chilly, and Nina stood with her arms crossed over her chest at Brett's car as he shut the trunk. The summer humidity was already beginning to dissipate, and that meant summer was over, and the kids of Carver Road were catapulting into their new lives. They had all been getting ready to leave, Brett being the first to head out, having the furthest distance to go. He was driving alone to Texas, an act that Nina couldn't fathom. Driving down unfamiliar roads, sleeping in desolate towns at motels with vacancy signs…it seemed like a scene from a nightmare.

"You'll call me, right?" Her voice was weak and squeaky. She hated knowing that he probably wouldn't call her. They had barely spoken in the two weeks since he had left her broken on her living room floor, their sins spoiling everything that was real between them.

With lips tightly pursed, he looked her over, Nina seeing only pity in his eyes. "Yes, Nina." Not Neen. Nina. "I want you to make friends. Meet people. Live your life." He took a deep breath in, and she watched his expression falter, sadness taking over. "Try and forget," he whispered.

A sob slipped out, though she tried to reign it in. She knew she couldn't do that. Trying to forget didn't even seem like a possibility. She nodded, though, not knowing what else she should do. And what part had he meant? Did he want her to forget him…them? Or the terrible, horrible thing that had happened?

Tears slid down her cheeks in two continuous streams. "But B," she choked out. "I love you too much. This can't be how we are saying goodbye. It feels like a forever thing." Her panic was rising.

Brett took her cheeks in his hands. "I love you. You know that I do." His words sounded like they were physically hurting him. He took his hands from her face and ran them through his hair, looking up at the sky. "I hate this, Nina. I fucking hate it so much. But I don't know what to do about it."

Anger bubbled inside Nina's chest. Anger and other emotions she'd rather not face. Feelings that would soon change the very makeup of her soul…of who she was at her core. There was no way to stop it. "You can forgive me," she uttered softly—desperately.

He pursed his lips. "I do."

But Nina knew that even if that was true, he would never forget, so what was the point in forgiveness anyway?

As other kids from Carver Road began walking down the street to say their goodbyes, Laura came out the front door looking like she might not survive Brett's departure.

Minutes later, Nina watched Brett's car drive off down Carver Road, the image pixelated through the steady stream of tears that felt like it would never turn off. She stayed there until Brett was long gone. Even after Johnny had tried to soothe her. It was as if some part of her already knew that Brett was flying away, and he wouldn't be returning to her.

As Nina drove away toward Western Massachusetts a few weeks later, she didn't feel the way the other kids had felt. She felt the scariest feeling of all: nothingness.

And as she got to the end of Carver Road, she was unaware of the spark of a fire igniting high above her in the nest on the pole where two birds resided. As she turned off the street, the birds, too, flew off, away from their home that was burning.

Chapter 27

Nina 2016

"Nina." Brett's voice slid from his mouth, the sound of it sending her reeling, slipping back into that tiny sliver of time where she had been content with her life.

Hearing his voice after all these years was as close to unbelievable as she could fathom. Though it still sounded so familiar to her, despite all the time that had passed, she also couldn't help but feel that his presence was heartbreakingly foreign as well.

She stepped closer to him, one foot in front of the other, and Brett did the same, until they were inches apart. Nina looked up at him as he gazed down at her. She noted how he had grown slightly, but not much from when they were in high school, just under six feet back then. His face had aged a bit, a line on his forehead most certainly etched from worry—as was the identical one she had on her forehead.

A track left behind from sorrow.

Like a magnet to iron, and with an audible breath from both of them, seemingly out of necessity, they embraced, Nina fitting into his chest and Brett's arms wrapping around her with the ease and satisfaction of fitting a final piece into a puzzle.

Nina couldn't help but think that all this time apart had been an utter and miserable waste. Why had they let it happen? Why had they denied one another this peace?

Because peace is what she felt.

On the edges of her nerves.

In the muscles around her jaw.

In the part of her heart where the canyon-sized hole had been for over a decade.

Time wasn't a measurement calculated out there on the end of Carver Road that afternoon. Their embrace could have been a minute, an hour. Or it could have been infinite. Nina didn't know. And she certainly didn't care. Eventually, they pulled away but not too far from each other. Brett lifted his hands to cup her cheeks, and she listened to the sounds escape his lips. A whimper almost, his lip shaking, his eyes wet.

And then his hands were wet with the tears that fell from Nina's eyes. The tears that were cleansing her entirely.

"I'm sorry," they both said in unison, each of them sounding desperate for the other to accept their apology.

Brett shook his head. "Why are you saying sorry?" He asked, his voice husky. "It's all my fault. You did nothing wrong."

I killed your dad and made you keep it a secret, Nina thought to herself. *It's a lot to be sorry for.* "Umm," she started, but Brett cut her off.

"You did nothing," he said. "Or it's more like you did everything. You saved me, Neen, and I couldn't deal with any of it back then. The guilt ruined me, and I'm sorry. I was wrong for leaving without looking back. I *did* abandon you back then. I'm sorry...so sorry." He was actively crying now, and so was Nina.

Nina couldn't find words, so instead, she buried herself back into his chest. And even though she couldn't formulate them yet, the words she needed to say were somewhere buried inside. The anger was buried under the love and needed to come out. But she couldn't. Not yet.

"Want to go somewhere and talk?" Brett asked softly. Nina nodded. More than anything, that's what she wanted. "We can go sit on the deck," he said, nodding his head toward his house.

Nina's eyes widened at the thought—the horror of going back there for the first time in years terrified her. She didn't want to have to face her demons. But she nodded. What was done was done. She had always known that. Going back there to sit and talk to Brett wasn't going to change anything. It wouldn't give her an opportunity to alter the past.

Brett took Nina's hand in his as if not a second of time had passed, as if it was 2004. And she accepted the gesture, of course she did, and she walked alongside him, passed the treehouse on their right, around the house to the back where a dizzying effect took hold of Nina.

She stared out at the water, the horror of that night flashing through her mind, taking the breath from her chest.

"I had the same reaction when I first walked back here a few weeks ago," Brett said solemnly, validating her utter despair.

She peeled her eyes from the water and looked at Brett, scanning his face. "I heard your mom's car pull in the night you first got back," she said. "I want to ask you why you haven't come over to see me. But at the same time, I didn't come over here, so that probably isn't a fair question."

"I know, Nina," Brett started. "We have avoided each other for years. We've been living separate lives. It wasn't just going to go back to normal just because we were both here. I think we both needed to come to terms with it in our own time." They were quiet for a heartbeat. "I guess I never imagined we would both come to terms at the same moment. But maybe that shouldn't surprise me that much."

Nina agreed with him, but she couldn't shake the thought that they had both waited so long to make the walk to one another...that it felt unsettling. It wasn't the time to analyze that, though. She knew that. They walked up the few steps to the deck, and it piqued Nina's memories but looked just different enough that she was able to sit down without completely losing it. They settled into the deck chairs at the table, sitting at either head.

"So, is it as weird for you as it is for me to be back here in town?" she asked as she watched Brett squinting out into the sun that hovered over the pond. Nina chuckled in spite of herself. "I thought I was out there in the world, finally getting over…all this," she said, gesturing to the water's edge. "And getting over you," she whispered. Brett turned to her, his face pained. "But coming back here just proved to me that I wasn't actually over any of it at all."

Brett shifted in his chair. "Ever since I have been home, all I have wanted to do is go back to Texas," he said solemnly. Nina pursed her lips, letting his truthful words marinate, knowing she felt the same way about New York. "Until now."

She smiled at him, realizing that for the first time since that awful night in June 2004, she felt a tad less alone. "I missed you, B," she said quietly, squinting into the sun. "I can't believe I have missed so much of your life. It feels so wrong."

"I wish I could take it all back, Neen. I wish I could give us the time back; I do."

"Me, too."

"Am I right to assume that you didn't become a gymnast like you originally dreamed of back when we were kids?" His half smile, the one with the dimple, turned Nina's insides to a puddle of mush.

She smiled, too, looking down at her hands on the table. "To be fair, after those 1996 Olympics, all the girls wanted to be like Kerri Strug." Brett laughed loudly. "She was a hero!" Nina joked, laughing, too. "And, not for anything, B, but when we were eight, you were convinced you were going to be a Mighty Duck, so…"

"As did you," he countered, beaming.

And the memories swarmed Nina's mind, warming the darkest parts of her. Memories of a childhood painted by street hockey, fireflies and smores, flashlight tag and ice cream trucks, bonfires and bliss that she was having a difficult time fathoming now. Or it had been difficult for quite some time. But now, looking across the table at her Brett, a flicker of hope was reigniting.

"So, what did you grow up to be, Nina?" Brett asked curiously.

It was a loaded question, but Nina settled into what Brett was asking her. And so they began the arduous process of filling each other in on all the parts of their lives that they had missed.

Chapter 28

Nina - The time in between

IT WAS DIFFICULT FOR Nina Jackson to recall the minute details of what had happened during her years at college. She had shuffled through her days, trekking through campus to get to all her classes, missing many of them due to the deepening depression that was swallowing her whole. Of course, she couldn't identify the word *depressed* as being the thing that was happening to her. All she knew was that she was empty inside. Nothing mattered, and that emptiness was a dangerous place to linger.

She did make friends, though they weren't bonds that withstood the test of time. She never opened up, nor was she welcoming, struggling to let anyone else open up to her.

Nina determined what role would be the most beneficial in her survival, the act she needed to play to help her forget all that was in her past.

She did the keg stands.

She followed through with the dares from her dormmates.

And she made promiscuous decisions with guys whose faces were just blurred carbon copies of each other.

Blurred faces that triggered Nina—clouded with booze—to come close on many occasions to calling Brett's cell phone.

Just do it, she would say to herself, ready to press the send button. But each time, she failed to follow through. Until eventually, she deleted his numbers—the Warner's landline and his cell, with a fleeting hope that swiping the numbers would release the urge she kept having. It was a silly gesture, though, because she could delete their numbers from her contacts but there was no erasing those digits from her memory.

The high-rise buildings of the Southwest dorms at UMass Amherst were a city in their own right—a city where Nina lost herself in the chaos and didn't care one bit if she was found. From her room on the twenty-first floor, she would look out and imagine herself jumping—not to fall…but to fly.

To fly far away and never return.

"So what brings you in today?" a therapist assigned to her in health services asked her one early morning toward the end of sophomore year.

Nina felt like there was no way to answer her seemingly simple question, at least not in the time she had allotted. So she simply stared out the window. It was all there on her mind, on the tip of her tongue, the mess that was her life. But she couldn't put it into words. Maybe it was because she didn't know where to start. What was the beginning? How had she gotten here again?

When none of her clothes fit anymore, and her gaucho pants made her look like a tiny being swimming in fabric, she looked at herself in the mirror and was alarmed. It had been enough to push her to seek help. Because it reminded her of where she had come from and what she had been through. Her demons were back—in the form of body dysmorphia—and she was at least aware enough to know that there was nothing she could do to stop it on her own.

Her thoughts scared her, too, and she found it at least a little hopeful that she was smart enough to ask for help.

It took a few months before any progress was made with her therapist. At first, she didn't feel like she was making any headway. Progress came in slow, steady steps.

And then, in the spring semester of 2006, Nina's therapist prescribed her an antidepressant. She had begun putting weight back on and began to smile a bit more. But Nina presumed that her therapist, Jasmine, could see right through the curve of her mouth, knowing it was a bit forced.

The medication helped, subtly at first, until Nina was able to wake up one morning, months after starting it, and think to herself, *It's ok. I can survive this day if I get out of bed.*

Her grades had picked up that semester, too, which was good because she had finally homed in on a major. It was two years into college, and she knew that she would have to take out more loans to finish a degree with the business major she was switching to. She eventually wanted to start her own business, and she dreamed of her business helping women feel good and strong in their own skin.

She had been taking restorative yoga for the last year, and feeling her body stretch and strengthen in her classes gave her a new appreciation for the vessel that housed her soul.

Yoga gave her a new focus, a new group of friends, and a new lease on life. As the semester was wrapping up, Nina applied for a job as a receptionist at the yoga studio she had been going to in North Hampton, down the road a bit from campus. She couldn't go home to Harborview, not after the summer following her freshman year when she had returned home. The Carver Road kids were eager to share their experiences and how much cooler they tried to come off as. And all Nina had to show for herself was that she lost fifteen pounds (rather than gained it, like the others) and memories clouded by Rubinoff watermelon vodka.

And there was no Brett that summer. He had stayed in Texas, making the Cape Cod summer complete and utter agony.

No, Nina was not going to go home.

In fact, it would be eleven years before Nina Jackson would spend any significant amount of time in Harborview. A holiday overnight here and there, but nothing more.

Nina graduated from UMass with a dual major in business and sociology in 2009 after an extra year.

At graduation, she felt such pride in her accomplishments. For so long, this day just hadn't seemed possible, and maybe she wasn't forgetting—not entirely—but there was a dullness to the pain that she accepted fully.

With Paul and Jane in the audience of the massive ceremony, Nina was as present as she could be and soaked in all the sights and sounds of the day.

It had been just shy of five years since she had seen or talked to Brett, and the loss of him was still the biggest tragedy of the whole terrible and awful thing. Their love seemed like it should have been able to withstand virtually anything, or so she thought. But she had been wrong about that, it seemed. Though she hadn't seen or spoken to him in years, she thought of him often, wondering where he was, if his sandy hair had darkened, if he'd gotten any taller, and if he ever thought of her. Had being in college away from the Massachusetts coast allowed Brett to see where and who he was supposed to be? Did he discover that there was no place for him back in Harborview?

Just like she had found distractions in random guys, she tortured herself with thoughts of the girls who had warmed his bed over the years.

Had he fallen in love in college?

Why had he not even attempted to reach out to her? To check on her—to make sure she hadn't slipped off her rocker. He had always been so concerned for her, caring about her sometimes more than he cared about himself. And they had been so close and so in love that it felt strange that they just weren't anything anymore.

But then she also reasoned that maybe he hadn't reached out to her for the same reasons she had avoided him. Fear of rejection. In this place of avoidance, there was a wonderment—a whimsical dream—about what would happen when she saw him again one day. She feared that if she reached out, he would deny her and the door would close forever. So it was best to keep her distance, not knowing how he actually felt.

Regardless of any of it, she loved him, always.

She loved him when she laughed.

She loved him when she dreamed.

She loved him when she sat in her despair, longing for him.

As she packed up her life in Amherst alongside her parents, they questioned her why she wasn't taking a break first, going home to the Cape before venturing to New York.

"My job starts soon, guys," she had insisted, even though she had a month until her first day. "But you guys can come down with me, check out the place, and stay in New York for a few days." And so began their norm for the next seven years—Jane and Paul begging Nina to come home, and Nina making excuses why she just couldn't swing it. And then insisting that they come to her.

Because it wasn't them that was the problem. Missing them was just another side effect of the terrible thing she had done. The Jackson's believed wholeheartedly that they had raised their daughter to be a strong and independent woman. And so, with that, they learned to accept that their daughter was leaving the nest, and they weren't going to stop her. New York City was getting their Nina, and they were just along for the maiden voyage.

The New York noise was precisely what Nina needed to keep her mind distracted as she desperately tried to do what Brett had once begged her to do…to forget.

The tiny apartment she shared with three strangers in Astoria was most certainly a bit of a culture shock from coastal Massachusetts or the sleepy western portion of her home state. Nina minded her own business, spending all her time during the day at Stretch, the yoga studio where she had been hired. Her position was entry-level at best, but she loved it. Nina worked the desk, as she had at the studio in college, cleaned the studios, and learned much more than she had expected to, soaking in anything that would prepare her for what her dreams were spinning—owning her own studio.

For years, Nina paid her dues and experienced everything New York City had to offer her. Dancing late into the night on wobbly heels became something she was quite skilled at.

The noise.

It was good at drowning out everything, and she accepted that. In fact, she welcomed it. However, it sometimes became too much, and she would escape up forbidden staircases, past the No Trespassing signs, and lay still on roofs, high above the city smog. Laying up there with the glow of the city beneath her and the sparkle of the stars above was the only time she could hear the thoughts in her head.

It was up on those city roofs where she would allow herself to wonder what Brett was doing…where he was…if he was thinking of her, too.

She never allowed anyone to share her sanctuary, that is until she met Lucy Bates.

Lucy was the friend Nina needed, and it hadn't taken either of them long to realize that a bond was quickly forming between them. A few months after meeting, the new friends had made New Year's Eve plans. They spent the early evening eating greasy pizza from the shop under Lucy's apartment and drinking stale champagne as they got all fancy in dresses and shoes that most certainly would not fare well on that frigid December night. Lucy curled Nina's long tresses into voluminous waves, and both of them went heavy on the makeup.

"Let's pretend we're from Spain tonight!" Lucy shrieked, champagne already spinning her.

Nina laughed, hiccupping. "I don't know how to speak with a Spanish accent!"

"Who cares!" Lucy practically shouted. "Everyone will be drunk; no one will know the difference."

Lucy was insistent, and Nina loved that about her. It was like looking at herself in the mirror and seeing her younger, more confident self reflecting back at her, before the glass had shattered, of course.

And so began their silly tradition, one that Nina enjoyed so much—pretending to be someone else.

Midnight was approaching as the girls stumbled into their final stop of the evening, far from Times Square, something they both had agreed upon before the night even began. The dive bar called Drip was packed to the rafters, twinkling lights catching the fractals from the lanterns on the tables throughout the cramped space. Nina and Lucy ordered four lemon drops, each of them carrying two, and found the first pair of guys who looked single. It only took moments to succeed in their conquest, their intoxicating—yet horrible—Spanish accents luring in two young men who were intrigued by getting the attention of two young foreign ladies.

It was 11:49 when Nina and Lucy found themselves laughing in the dingy bathroom. The dull light did little to assist them in retouching their red lips.

"Which one do you want to kiss at midnight?" Lucy asked, slipping her lipstick into her clutch.

Nina smirked. "What do you mean?" she asked, tossing a paper towel into the garbage.

Lucy rolled her eyes. "You know what I mean, but if you don't have a preference, can I have the brunette?"

Nina eyed Lucy, unsure of what to say. "Uh, sure," she said. "I'll take the blonde." She contemplated it for a moment. She hadn't imagined herself kissing someone this evening, but the thought of it was intriguing.

Lucy linked her arm through Nina's. "Let's go," she said through her giggling.

Nine minutes later, everyone in the cramped space began counting down the last few seconds of 2010. From the corner of her eye, Nina could see that Lucy had already started making out with the brunette, whose name she couldn't recall. And Nina began drifting, the sounds and experience bringing her back to Carver Road. The corner of her mouth pulled into a tranquil sort of smile, her eyes lost in a daydream.

"Auld Lang Syne" filled the space, trickling into the images that flashed across her mind.

Johnny Cooper's basement. Noise makers. Solo cups of Sprite.

Nina.

The ball drop in Times Square on the television. The sound of feet parading down the Cooper's steps. Timmy Baker's crass jokes.

Nina!

That look Brett had given her on New Year's 2002. A look that had briefly stopped time, causing Nina's heart to flutter in a way she couldn't deny. His half smile melted her.

Neen!

Nina's eyes flickered, the noise of the bar swarming into her eardrums, the sound of her name, the name he had called her, bringing her back to the present. Her eyes darted around the chaos to see Lucy looking at her worried.

"Oh my God, Neen," she said breathlessly. "You were totally gone there for a minute."

"Neen?" Nina said, confused, maybe a bit intoxicated. "That's what he called me." The last part was a sad sort of whisper.

"Who, love?" Lucy asked, sounding worried, placing her hands gently on Nina's shoulders.

Nina blinked, subconsciously attempting to bring herself back. "Huh?"

"Nina, who are you talking about?"

Nina sucked in a slow breath and ran her hand through her hair. "No one," she lied, smiling.

Lucy smiled at her, glad to have her friend back in the present. "Ok, can I not call you Neen?" she laughed.

Nina laughed then, too, though she didn't find it funny. "No," she said. "You can call me that."

And she meant it. No one had ever called her that besides Brett. Her B.

But Brett was gone, and maybe she needed Lucy in the same way, to fill the hole that had formed inside of her. The one he had created when he left.

And eventually, Nina introduced Lucy to her haven in the sky, her forbidden rooftop sanctuary. And it was up there that Nina shared pieces of her heart that she never thought she would share with another person.

She didn't share the shadows, though. Or the secrets, the ones that no one but Brett knew.

But she shared all the other stuff. Even her experiences with Glen Gomes. And how she had the most un-endearing trait that caused her to feel way too much.

Lucy accepted Nina for who she was, never judging her for her shortcomings. Nina was different with Lucy. Unlike when she was in college and wouldn't let anyone in, she let Lucy in. She allowed Lucy to lean on her. She realized that this was how she made real friendships, after all those years of them coming so easily on Carver Road but having so much difficulty in college.

And it was not lost on Nina, how she had been drawn to Lucy from the get-go and maybe that had been a sign all along that Nina needed to let Lucy in. Of course, she had been right about that, too.

New York City was a time warp for Nina. Once she arrived there, time seemed to fly at a speed that didn't feel fathomable. In 2012, Nina and Lucy moved into a tiny studio apartment together in Brooklyn. Lucy had snagged the place from a family friend. It wasn't much, but with the discount they gave her, the two could afford it with their minuscule incomes. Using room dividers, they sectioned off their beds for as much privacy as they could manage. And their little kitchen had a tiny space on the counter where they kept their only two mugs.

If you ask Nina about that time, she would tell you that it was a blur. A sweet blur. She worked hard, she played hard, and she built a friendship that was real and worthy, for the first time in a long time. It was a time when eating ramen and leftovers was commonplace, a time of sharing all their clothes and everything else.

Shoes.

Food.

Shampoo and conditioner.

Heart to hearts on their couch that they found at Goodwill.

One time, late into the night and the early morning hours of a chilly fall Sunday morning, Lucy was telling Nina about how she had fallen from a tree she was climbing as a child, suffering a brain injury and a broken femur and elbow.

Lucy struggled in school for years after, never ending up in the law school her parents had chosen for her before she was even out of the womb.

"It was like the fall from the tree changed my personality or something," Lucy said, sipping her plastic tumbler of boxed wine.

Nina's brows furrowed. "Your personality?" she asked. "What do you mean?"

"I had always been a serious and cautious child," Lucy said. "I did what I was told and never stepped out of line. After my accident, my family fretted over me like I was this breakable thing. I guess it wasn't the accident that caused a change in me." Lucy chuckled in spite of herself. "I think it was a desperate need of mine to have some space and independence. I needed to make my own decisions but was never able to before. My brother went to law school, and so did my sister, just like my dad had. But I couldn't follow suit like a good little Bates." Nina put her arm around Lucy, pulling her into her. "I know it's stupid," Lucy admitted. "My problems are as first world as they come."

Nina smirked. "It's all relative, isn't it?" she offered, thinking of her own problems. She never could reason how she had ended up with such a deranged mind, even before she had a few deaths on her conscience. She reasoned now that there didn't always have to be an obvious trauma. There were times when she thought her biggest disadvantage was her empathic nature—her inability to separate her own feelings from the struggles of others.

As if her love and loyalty toward others was her undoing.

How depressing a thought.

"Sometimes I just feel guilty for where I am," Lucy said, looking around the tiny space that they called home. "I was born with a silver spoon, and I just dropped it without a care."

"But you're happy, Lucy, and that's what matters."

Lucy's eyes began to spill with fresh tears. She nodded at Nina's sentiment. "You're right," she said. "I am so happy."

They hugged, holding one another for a long time.

"I got a loan, Lucy," Nina said after a bit of comfortable silence. "For a studio."

Lucy shrieked. "What?! That's amazing, Nina! When did this happen?"

Nina smiled. "Today, actually!"

Lucy got up from the couch and jumped on the coffee table, doing a dance that made Nina break out into fits of giggles. They celebrated until the sun began coming up over the buildings that seemed to touch the sky, their wine buzz pulling at their lagging bodies, until they both fell asleep on the couch.

Nina sat in the nearly empty space that would soon be her studio, something she had been dreaming about since her early days of therapy. She had done it; she had made her dreams a reality.

But what to call it?

She pulled the pencil from her ear, looking down at her sketches of what she wanted the space to look like in the coming weeks. Lucy had told her she needed to name it and order a sign so that every time she walked into the space, she would feel even more inspired. And Nina agreed. But sitting there, she was having trouble thinking of a name.

N…she scribbled it on the paper, but nothing followed. She wrote the letter over and over, hoping something would come to her, letting her mind wander. She thought of the ritual of carving N and B into the wood of the treehouse, the smell of the rotting cedar. And Brett.

N + B.

She scribbled the letters onto her paper, a deep ache building in her chest. She looked around the space through clouded eyes, her heart heavy with nostalgia. And then her eyes stopped on the bar in the back lining the mirror. It was the first addition to the space. The first and only one so far.

N Bar.

It had lots of meanings, she reasoned. Not a bar like the others in Manhattan, but a play on words. A different sort of bar. A bar to transform your body and mind. The N for Nina, and the B for bar.

And Brett.

Nina picked up her phone, wondering if his number was still the same as it had been when they left Harborview. Hers wasn't, and even though she had wiped her phone clean of his contact info, she still knew the number by heart. His cell and the Warner's landline, too. Those numbers would never leave her mind; she knew that for certain.

508…she typed the area code into her phone and stopped before putting the device face down. She thought of him often, and she was doing right for herself…picking herself up from the ashes and trying to heal. But she couldn't call him, and there wasn't a logical reason why. She knew that. She knew it was stupid, but she also knew that he wasn't calling her either, and maybe that's what was best for him. She had to accept that. What they had was dead and gone; it was just something she had to get over.

And opening her own business, being happy, having a best friend—were all the things she could think of to make the world right again. She was getting there. Brett was her past, and his part in her present and future wasn't lost. He was the reason why she had become a better person. He was part of her, always, no matter what.

Nina took a breath and smiled down at her sketches and notes. She held up the name sketch with the bar and mirror in the background and texted it to Lucy.

LOVE IT, Lucy responded.

And so, N Bar was born—a thought, a dream, and finally, a reality. The space transformed over the following months into a paradise for Nina—a sanctuary for all who entered. And Nina thrived there, right up until it crumbled. She had appreciated the studio every single day that it was hers, feeling blessed for being able to crawl out of the darkness and turn on her own lights.

When N Bar began to sink—when Nina began to struggle to keep it afloat—it would take a long time for her to admit defeat. Had she failed again? What did that say about her? It was too hard a question to answer. And for the first time since she left Harborview, she was pulled back so strongly, with a force she couldn't deny.

Chapter 29

Brett - The time in between

Texas was Brett Warner's saving grace. He knew it immediately, stepping out of his car after parking outside his college dorm, right where the Garmin and the MapQuest directions had led him. The drive took three days total, having stopped for two nights—one night in Knoxville and the other in Little Rock.

Laura had begged him to fly, telling him that she would pay for his car to be sent down, but Brett refused. He needed the serenity of being alone for a while, with only the open road ahead of him and the thoughts in his head. However, by the time he reached Maryland, he was already feeling quite fidgety, and that led to a panicked feeling as he thought about all that he had done wrong in the last few months. The guilt felt much heavier in the silence.

And so, he turned the radio up louder than necessary. But he had finally made it there, to his new home, with relative ease. No hiccups aside from a nearly empty gas tank. He was saved in the nick of time by a worn-down sign pointing off the freeway in Tennessee, letting him know there was fuel nearby.

Brett got out of his car and stretched his arms up, allowing his body to become acclimated to solid, unmoving ground. He stared at the building that would be his new home, and he felt it, instantly—there was no going back.

Because that's where his mind had been back then. Everything from the past was neatly packed away and behind a closed door he didn't care to open. One that had been padlocked, just in case. He had tricked himself into believing that with this new start. And Nina Jackson must also stay hidden away. It broke his heart, but it was too soon for him to realize the severity of this loss, especially when he still felt mad about the whole tragedy.

So, he filled the emptiness with new soil and new seeds that would hopefully grow into something he could hang on to.

Brett shined on the baseball field his freshman year. In his second game of the season, he made a diving catch in the outfield to end the game, and he stared at the ball in his glove for just a moment, hearing his breath in his ears. He smiled to himself before looking up at the sky, thanking God for what he was given, a second chance at life. And with that thanks, he also begged for forgiveness, as he tended to do frequently. Forgiveness for his sins, the mistakes he'd made. Jaunting off the field, he thought, *Do you see me, Danny? I did this without you. Outfielders can get scholarships, too, you know.*

With the skills he had learned on Carver Road, Brett made friends easily, Dean Jefferson being the first bond he made. A bond that would last, too. The girls on campus flirted with him relentlessly, but it would take Brett a year to give in to those urges.

He missed Nina too much, and even though he didn't allow himself to be sad over it, his mind and heart longed for her always, a constant nagging that never fully dissipated. Because how could it, really? It was Nina after all.

———

"Yo, Brett, what the hell are we doing tonight for your twenty-first, dude?" Dean said, coming into their off-campus apartment where Brett was playing Madden with some of the guys.

Brett laughed, not taking his eyes from the screen. "Let's go to Maxine's, they barely check IDs. We all could get in."

"Maxine's!" Dean yelled, drawing out the word dramatically, causing the rest of the guys to holler, too.

Brett rolled his eyes with a laugh.

The night began as they all did back then: droves of people entering their apartment, carrying mismatched boxes of cheap beer and boxes of rose-colored wine. The folding table they kept in the supply closet had been pulled out for Beirut and they were already three rounds deep by the time eight o'clock rolled around. Brett and Dean, always leading the wins, tapped out for a round, and Brett worked the room to say hi to all the people wishing him happy birthday.

"It's the birthday boy," he heard a sultry but drunk voice behind him say.

Brett turned to see Jenny beaming at him. "Hi, Jenny," he said, flashing his smile that melted all the girls on campus.

"Oh, look at those cowboy eyes," Jenny winked, ruffling his hair.

Definitely wasted, Brett thought. *I'll need to keep an eye on her.*

Because that was Brett.

Jenny had complained during a tailgate last year, while drinking heavily, that her boyfriend had been treating her badly. Dean had said to Brett that he thought she might just be looking for attention, but Brett knew not to assume such things. He had seen too many people he loved, himself included, be torn apart without another person knowing. So, he always kept tabs on Jenny.

Even while celebrating his twenty-first birthday with all his friends.

Because…again…that was Brett.

———

Behind the smile that he used as a mask, Brett longed for Nina in secret, practically even hiding it from himself. And he eventually realized that there really wasn't any use in trying to find someone he could love. There wasn't any more space for that inside of him. And there wasn't sadness in this realization because the sadness had already been there, in the fact that he missed her beyond what seemed reasonable.

Eventually, he pretended for long enough that nothing was wrong, and he became numb (as did Nina). If he thought he heard her laugh or if the person walking ahead of him had hair the same hue as hers, a spark would ignite in his heart, if only for a moment. Until the truth revealed itself that she was still, in fact, gone.

In between taking part in the stereotypical southern experiences like line dancing and bull riding, Brett found a groove that he was able to settle in quite nicely. By the time he graduated from college, Texas was, undoubtedly, Brett's home. And when scenes of the moment out by the pond would flash in his mind, it would cause him to physically shake his head—shaking the images away. And he would quickly bring himself back to what was right there in front of him…and far from Harborview.

Where Harborview was pain and horror and death, Texas was river walks, country bars, and cowboy boots. New faces. Nothing at all familiar.

After graduation, Brett moved to Austin and, eventually, into his high-rise apartment in late 2012. The first weekend after he was settled, he started the tradition of rowdy parties in the bachelor pad.

"Four to the floor!" Dean yelled, being the first to touch the ground beside Brett's coffee table. Everyone around the table scrambled not to be the last one to touch the floor and have to drink from their cups. The deck of cards was sprawled in a circle around a glass cup, a second round of kings being played.

"Are you really playing that?" Lila asked, plopping herself down on the couch behind Brett. "I haven't played that since college."

"You graduated two years ago, Lila," Jenny said, rolling her eyes. "You're not that sophisticated," she added, laughing and gently tossing a throw pillow in Lila's direction.

Lila rolled her eyes back before adjusting her tank top, sending her eyes toward Brett. Watching Lila, Brett took a gigantic gulp from his beer can. That is until Jenny got wind of it and scooted to a chair closer to Brett.

Brett was well aware that Jenny was into him, and although he didn't care to put effort into dating her, he didn't mind the attention.

The group around the table quickly dispersed away from the game, caught up in refills and saying hi to the people coming into the apartment, to gawk (in jest), and congratulate Brett.

"Bit Tech is paying you nice, huh, Brett?" Dean said loudly in the kitchen, where a few of the guests had gathered to lean on the counters, their conversation carrying loudly throughout the space.

Brett shook his head while passing out beers to those who were empty-handed. "Not like I have any responsibilities—no one to worry about but myself," he said, holding up his own beer. "To new bachelor pads and no strings!"

Dean slapped him on the back, and the group yelled in cheers and celebration.

Jenny inched her way into the kitchen and saddled up next to Brett, putting her arm around him, an act that wasn't entirely welcomed on his part, though he wasn't sure why. Jenny was beautiful, funny, kind…a girl's girl, though, and she had trouble meshing with the guys. At that moment, he thought of Nina…longed for her even. Missing the way she fit in with the boys on the street, playing games or lounging on Johnny's couch.

"There are those cowboy eyes," Jenny's voice, thick with alcohol, pricked Brett's senses, confusing him.

Lust. Indifference. And back again.

His eyes scanned her face, her cheeks flushed. "I've been here all night, Jenny," Brett responded, a reply that offended her a bit; he could see it in her expression.

Brett felt bad for upsetting her, so he offered a smile as a peace offering. A smile that melted her, as it did all the women he smiled at. Jenny tucked her hair behind her ear, the red in her cheeks darkening. Brett wondered if Jenny would end up staying the night again, and it phased him that he didn't really care either way. Maybe a distraction would be good, he reasoned. Or falling asleep and waking up alone also sounded tempting.

"I'll be right back," Brett said, moseying around her into the living room, walking out onto the small balcony that overlooked Brattle Street. The hustle and bustle below comforted Brett as he looked down, smiling.

Looking over his shoulder back into his new apartment, Brett watched his friends laughing, and a sense of contentment settled over him. That is, until something caught his eye in the sky. It was then that he thought of Nina. Where was she? What was she doing? The inky blackness up above the tops of the buildings, speckled with a few diamonds, brought a recollection to the surface. Back in Harborview, East Beach was notorious for stargazing. Brett and Nina would go on warm nights in the summer in between junior and senior year. They would walk down the dirt path at the end of Carver Road with fresh sunburns, their hoodies covering their heads.

Nighttime at the beach was breathtaking. The waves somehow sounded different under the moonlight, more of a deep, rumbling echo—a sound that had etched itself into Brett's subconscious. The feeling of the cool sand against their burned skin was another sensation he had carried with him.

Their senses had all been activated, lying there on a threadbare beach blanket as they pointed at each shooting star that scraped across the sky.

Wishing for things that wouldn't come to pass.

And after that, the balcony would become the only place where Brett would allow himself to wallow in sadness of what was behind him. Out there, he could be alone, without distractions, without the pressure to wear his smile like a mask. The rest of the time, it was *Operation: Move Along.*

Brett became a pro at moving forward. He made his money, saved a bunch, and spent a lot, too. Went to Vegas, where he spent forty-eight hours that he didn't remember much of but knew he had had fun. He flew to California for a work conference and stayed a few days, traveling up and down the 101 by himself with the windows down and the Pacific Ocean out in front of him.

Without really noticing it, Brett took finding himself seriously. And right when things were starting to feel permanent and settled, he got the call from his mother that would bring everything crashing down.

"What do you want?" Dean asked Brett and their two buddies, Robbie and Chris. They were sitting at a high-top mahogany table near the stage at Sullivan's Piano Bar.

"Whiskey, neat," Chris said. "Thanks, dude. I'll get the next round."

"Jack and Coke," Brett said.

"Same," Robbie piped in.

Tuesday nights had become a tradition for the guys—to come to Sullivan's for dinner and whiskey after work. The owner, Maverick, had come to know them by name, and the welcoming aspect of the space made them feel like they were sitting in their own living room.

"I'm gonna go help Dean bring the drinks over," Robbie said, getting down from his chair.

When the drinks arrived, they all took a sip, and Dean sighed dramatically, leaning back in his chair. "This is the life," he said, beaming his mile-wide smile.

The others smiled, agreeing. And Brett felt the same, but he also knew that this life—as he knew it—was coming to an end. He glanced down at this phone to see a text from his mother.

Have you got your plane tickets yet?

Pursing his lips, Brett looked around the table, jumping back into the conversation, forcing a smile to match the guys' laughter.

No, he hadn't bought the tickets. He had been putting that off for weeks.

Tomorrow. He would do it tomorrow, he decided. Tonight, he would enjoy time with his friends, who had become family over the last few years. He couldn't bear to leave them and this place.

And then the guys were interrupted by Maverick's voice on the stage. "Hey, everyone," he bellowed into the microphone. "I hope you are all having a great evening. I just wanted to come up here to introduce our newest talent here at Sullivan's. I know you are going to love them, and I hope we can get them to be a couple of regulars," he said, laughing as he looked back over his shoulder at the pianists taking their seats, one of them putting his long hair into a bun. "Ladies and gentlemen, please welcome Kash Holden and Silas Dade."

The patrons in the restaurant turned their seats toward the stage and listened as the musicians began dueling "Sweet Caroline," and Brett wasn't sure how he felt about a song that reminded him of Red Sox games in high school as if the song was calling him home—whether he liked it or not.

Chapter 30

Brett 2016

BRETT TRIED WRAPPING HIS mind around the reality that was sitting across him on the deck of the house he grew up in. The house where he had grown up alongside Nina Jackson.

Nina, who had been lost to him for so long, was now within arm's reach. Seeing her sitting there, beautiful yet pained, reminded Brett of what he already knew—that the years apart had been an utter waste. The person he had always tried to protect, and who had always protected him, went out into the world without him. And he could see it written on her face that she hadn't fared well. The world, he knew, had not been kind to Nina.

"That's amazing that you were able to build a business, Nina," he said, truly meaning it, certainly proud of her. Nina squinted into the sun, narrowing her eyes in his direction. "I mean, I'm sure you'll be able to do it again, no?" he added. "Maybe here in Harborview?" She continued staring at him, or more like glaring is what it was.

Brett sighed. What was he doing? He knew she no longer wanted to talk about the time in between. It was written all over her face. They'd already done that, and that wasn't the important part anyway. Now, what she needed was clarification, as did he, of why they had avoided each other for all those years.

Who was to blame? Or was it both of them?

Nina got up from the table and leaned her hands on top of the deck gate, looking out onto the pond. Brett watched her while she moved, and then he got up, meeting her at the edge of the deck, standing close beside her.

"Nina, I—"

"Stop, Brett," she said, cutting him off. Her voice was gentle, soft. Brett's expression twisted into anguish, not knowing what to do. Pulling air into his cheeks, he held it there a moment, attempting to settle the unease. "Enough with the small talk, B," she said, sounding defeated.

Brett slowly let the air out of his lungs, the closeness to her undoing him. Taking a step toward her, he closed the tiny gap that had been there between them. He reached up, placing his hand gently on her cheek, their eyes locking on one another—the moment seeming to set the earth back on its axis, Nina and Brett's world colliding, then slipping back into place.

Brett's other hand reached up for her other cheek, and Nina brought her hands to his wrists. Brett thought she might push him away, but to his pleasant surprise, she grabbed his hands with a desperate sort of grip. And then she made the saddest sound—a sound stemming from grief, a feeling Brett was most certain he was responsible for.

He had punished himself all this time, punished himself for the shit he had allowed to fester, ignored for years. But this was the worst torture of all, worse than being without her all this time. Seeing Nina like this was the universe's punishment.

He had been a coward—it was time to face that.

"I don't know what to say," Nina said softly. "I have gone back and forth in my head all these years…from missing you to being so fucking mad, to feeling so much nothingness." She reached to swipe her tear, but Brett's thumb caught it first. Nina looked up at Brett, eyes big as saucers, moist with emotion.

And Brett knew Nina's feelings ran deep in her soul, and her heart was sewn into her sleeve. "I'm sorry," he whispered. Shallow, tired words, yes, but he truly meant them. She rested her head on his chest, and he wrapped his arms around her, pulling her into him. "I know those words don't do anything to fix what I did," Brett added.

"It's not all your fault," Nina said. "I didn't do anything to fix it either. I didn't reach out to you." She pulled away from Brett and turned to look out over the pond again, the scene of the crime. "And I know you were mad at me when you left." She kept her gaze out on the water.

"I wasn't mad at you," he said, and Nina gave him an *oh, please* type of look, causing Brett to smile just a little. "I mean, I guess I was mad, but it wasn't you I was mad at. And the guilt was pretty heavy, too. It was like a storm, all hitting at once. Back then, I had no idea how to deal with any of it, Neen." He ran a hand through his hair, glancing back out at the water. "I was scared. So scared about what would happen to us if anyone knew our secret."

He watched her, waiting.

"But why…*how* did we let this happen, B? It's me and you. We have been together from the time we were in kindergarten. It was always me and you against the world."

She paused then as Brett's heart ached. "And then the world won," he said, trying to find some reasoning behind the madness. "It's like we fought too many battles, and then we were defeated or something." It was a cop-out, he knew. But here they were, trying to make sense of it, and he was desperately trying to put a pin on the blame so they could move on. "I was too scared, Nina. I know that sounds selfish, but it's just the truth."

"Then what does that say about us, Brett?" Nina asked, sounding annoyed now. "The going gets tough, and we just disappear from each other's lives for *twelve* years?"

"The going didn't just get tough, Nina, and you know that." She narrowed her eyes at him, Brett noting that she looked as if she was searching his face for an answer. "We killed my dad. And it's a secret we've carried. And yes, I did blame you for that burden for a while. I did. And

I'm sorry about that—I was wrong to do that because…" his voice trailed off as he ran his hands through his hair, shaking his head. "I don't know. None of it makes sense. But I want it to. I want to fix it."

Nina was quiet again; it felt like eons before she said anything. "What if your mom didn't force you to come home?" Her voice was hollow. When Brett didn't answer right away, she continued. "Because I can't help but feel that if you didn't come home for Laura…and Seamus, twelve more years could have passed and we wouldn't have—"

"But we did, Nina!" Brett's forceful words cut her off. "We *both* did. We are both here." Brett sat back down in one of the chairs. And Nina sat down beside him. "We both came back. At the same time, Neen." He looked at her longingly. "Can you say that if your business was thriving, you would have come back here?" When she didn't respond, he continued. "Because I think that you would still be there if you hadn't been forced back here, too."

"I was pulled." Her voice carried out with the breeze that also tugged at her hair.

"What does that mean?"

"I am no stranger to failure, Brett. I have fallen over and over again since we left this place. And I have always saved myself. But this time, when I fell, I was pulled back here. Something made me come back. I didn't understand it at first, but now I do. I was being pulled back…to you."

Brett reached for her hands. "It's fate, Nina."

"No, Brett! *I* was pulled here. You were *forced*. I saved your life that night. I killed for you. And I would do it again…do you know that? As much as I have been broken by you…by us…I would do it again if I had to. But now I'm realizing that it's not the same with us. It's not equal."

"Not equal? What does that even mean?"

"I feel like I'm here to save you again. The insatiable need I have to protect you called to me without me even knowing it."

"Saving me now? From what, Nina?" He was getting annoyed.

"From whatever guilt you carried for abandoning me. Because even though we are both to blame for our separation, I know you hated yourself for what happened between us. But I'm here now, and I can see it in your eyes that you feel peace just knowing I'm here." Nina ran her hand through her hair, taking a breath.

"But don't you feel that too?!" He hadn't meant to raise his voice, but he did. "Do you not feel better seeing me? That we have this chance to make it right?"

"You know what, Brett?" Nina said, and he could feel the conversation coming to an end. "I have worried about you all this time. While I was in my darkest of places, subconsciously and consciously, I was worried about how you were doing through all of it. But what about me? Who was saving me?"

———

Brett sat at the kitchen table, two fingers worth of whiskey in a glass tumbler, a scowl on his face. Nina had been gone for ten minutes, and already his insides were in turmoil. He guessed that it had always been a wreck in there, his heart a broken thing that he had feebly attempted to mend with smiles and laughter. *Fake it til you make it*, and all of that.

Nina had been honest with him, it seemed. As she told him about the time in between, she had smiled some, but the truth of her pain was interwoven into the story, too.

But Brett? He had made light of it all, making his life in Texas seem like some sort of colorful dream. He made it sound like he was living his best down south. And to be fair, he had enjoyed his time there, but that was only because he had become quite good at burying the things that scared him—a habit he had learned when he was just a little boy. He was so skilled at avoidance now that filling Nina in on the twelve years had slipped off his tongue so easily, just like the lies he had convinced himself of.

"Am I really seeing this?" Seamus's voice came in through the garage and cut through Brett's thoughts, shaking him from his misery. "Brett with a glass of liquor, and it's not even five o'clock?" A rare smile tugged on Seamus's mouth.

Brett's jaw twitched, clenching. He couldn't find the desire to even respond. He watched his brother get his own glass and pour himself more than necessary before sitting down at the table opposite Brett.

Seamus leaned back in the chair. "What's got you all—" he made a circular motion toward Brett. "Like this?" Brett pursed his lips; talking with his brother wasn't at the top of his priority list at the moment. "I was sitting in my truck for a bit before I came in. Does this have anything to do with Nina? I saw her walk past my passenger's side pretty quickly." Brett studied Seamus's face, taken aback by the sincerity he thought he sensed in his tone. "The past coming back to bite ya?"

Brett sniffed a laugh. "Something like that."

"I always thought the two of you were strange."

Brett cocked an eyebrow. "Strange?"

Seamus eyed him over his tumbler, taking a heavy sip. "Yeah, wicked," he said. "You were like two people in one, moving and talking like you shared one mind or something."

"Yeah, we did do that, huh?" Brett muttered softly.

Seamus chuckled. "I thought you two were going to graduate high school and move into the treehouse."

Brett barked out a laugh, appreciating his brother's company all of a sudden.

"So what's with the trouble in paradise then?" Seamus asked, actually seeming like he cared.

Brett knew he couldn't be entirely truthful with Seamus, that was a given, but he was relishing in bonding with him. "We haven't spoken in years, and I guess you could say it got a little heated out there," he said, motioning out to the back deck and the pond. "Just blaming each other for the past and shit, I guess." He shrugged his shoulders and gulped his whiskey.

Seamus looked confused. "Still hung up on shit from the past? Seems like two people on the same wavelength, like you and Nina, would be able to let shit go. No?"

"Yeah, well, right now, it's all fucked up," Brett admitted. "And I wasn't entirely honest with her just now."

"Can't you just apologize and make it right?" Seamus asked. "It's not like you killed someone or anything." His Cheshire cat smile made the hairs on Brett's neck stand up. That look on his face…was it a knowing expression?

Brett swallowed hard and adjusted himself in his chair, clearing his throat. "Uh, yeah, of course not."

"And besides," Seamus interjected. "I'm sure if you did, it would have been called for." He got up from the table and slapped Brett playfully on the back before going back to the bottle for a refill.

Brett was frozen. Was he breathing fast or not at all? He wasn't quite sure. Did Seamus know their secret? Why was he acting like this? Brett listened to the whiskey glugging from the handle and landing in Seamus's glass. And he wanted—so desperately—in that moment to save his brother.

From the bottle.

From the past.

From a dreadful future ahead of him.

"Yeah, um, we'll figure it out," Brett said, anxious. "But Seamus, I reached out to a company that trains service dogs for vets." He paused, checking the temperature of the room. There was an expression on Seamus's face, but Brett couldn't read it. "Don't be mad. There's no commitment. I just wanted to get some information. I thought it could be good for you."

Seamus crossed his arms over his chest, staring at Brett. "Ok." That's all he said.

One word.

But it was the way he said it that gave Brett a bit of hope.

"Ok? You would consider it?" Brett asked.

"Yes," Seamus said. "Thank you, Brett."

Brett gave him a thin-lip smile and nodded his head. "No need." He got up from his seat as Seamus was making his way to him. For the first time that he could remember, his brother pulled him into a hug. And they stayed like that long enough for Brett to feel a shift in the world that was their brotherhood. A shift toward something more, and he welcomed that.

"Be honest with Nina," Seamus said. "Make it right." Brett could only smile. "I have seen a lot of unbelievable shit in my life, man." Seamus shook his head. "But nothing as wild as whatever chemistry there was between the two of you." He said the last part while walking toward the stairs. Like it was nothing more than a *tell the Jacksons I said hello* type of sentiment.

Seamus didn't know that the entire exchange between him and his brother meant everything to Brett.

***

Johnny: You still down to sell some ice cream from Ginny's truck downtown on the 4th of July?

Brett: Def.

Johnny: Nice. I'm gonna see if any of the other kids are around from the street. I'll ask Nina too!

Brett: I'll ask her.

Johnny: Cool, talk soon.

It had been forty-five minutes since Nina had left the Warner's backyard, and Brett, suffice it to say, thought it had been long enough. Before he could talk himself into giving her a little more time to cool off, he stormed across the street as if his life depended on it.

He rapped on the door, swift and firm. Three meaningful knocks.

Pacing there on the front stoop of the Jackson's house, Brett felt like he was twelve again.

A few moments passed before a surprised Nina opened the door. "Hi," Brett said, breathless.

Nina just looked him over. "Hi," she replied before opening the screen door and stepping out on the stoop. Brett noted how she hadn't invited him inside, as if the last time he had been in there still had an impact on her.

"Nina, I don't know the answer. I'm not like you. I can't read and analyze a situation like you can. If I did, I would be sad…always." Nina tossed him an offended look, and Brett shook his head. "That came out wrong," he offered to try and erase what he said. "I don't mean that you're sad all the time. Well, maybe you are. I guess I don't know because I haven't seen you in so long." He was rambling now, certainly not making any sense. He sighed, trying to pull himself together. "What I'm trying to say is…yes, maybe it doesn't seem *even* from what I told you about my life in Texas. But it's not real, Neen. Not even a little. I never dealt with any of this. Never faced it…not like you did. You sat in your emotions, and you tried to figure out what to do about it. You didn't just paint a smile like I did, pretending everything was ok. You're so brave for that, by the way." Brett paused there, stepping closer to her. He reached up, as he had done on the deck, and placed his hands on her cheeks. "You have always been so brave, Nina." Brett watched her lip tremble. "I know you don't feel brave, and I hate that so much. You have always put yourself in everyone else's shoes, and because of that, you physically feel the pain of everyone you love. Even people you didn't know, if I'm being honest. And it tore you apart; I see it in your eyes, and I'm sorry." He brushed his nose against hers, closing his eyes as she did. "I'm so sorry, Nina," he whispered, his lips so close to hers that it caused the ache in his chest to throb to life.

And so he gave in and placed his lips on hers. It was gentle at first, until it wasn't. As they once had always done, Nina and Brett fell into one another, Nina slipping between the arches of his elbows and Brett's arms molding around her body…their heartbeats syncing together. The kiss breathed life into their souls, shadows lifting like morning fog off the pond.

Pulling away was excruciating, like pulling limbs from the joints, unnatural and unfair. But they stayed close together, their foreheads touching.

"Seeing you today after all this time fixed something inside of me that's been broken for years," Brett said, placing gentle kisses on her nose and the apples of her cheeks. Nina squeezed her arms around Brett's waist, pulling him tight. "I think I broke you, too, and I want to fix it…make it right."

Nina pulled away and looked up at Brett. He looked down into her eyes, the eyes of the one person he loved beyond measure, beyond his own understanding.

"I don't know what to say," Nina said.

"You don't have to say anything," Brett tried to assure her. "Can we just start by exchanging phone numbers?" His smile pulled on one side of his face, his dimple on full display. The blushing in Nina's cheeks was a sign to him that, just maybe, she still felt something, too.

"Yeah, let's do that," Nina smiled. "Did you change yours? I'm positive I still have it memorized."

"Yeah," he replied. "I got a new one."

"Same," Nina said softly.

"And maybe, can we make plans to just sit together and catch up some more?" Brett asked. He couldn't control his hopeful feeling.

Nina let out a soft laugh, typing her contact information into his phone and calling herself so that she had his. "I'll meet you in the treehouse at eight-thirty tomorrow night." She beamed at Brett and winked, causing him to laugh.

"Yeah? Back to our roots?" he asked.

Nina nodded once before placing her hand on the doorknob. She looked over her shoulder at him, and Brett waited on the porch, smiling at her until she went into the house and closed the door. It wasn't until she was out of sight that he turned around, jogging back across the street.

Chapter 31

Nina 2016

Nina looked out the dormer window from her bedroom, gazing over to the Warner's yard—and the treehouse—a smile pulling at her lips. A giddiness she recognized from when she was a kid spread through her body. She hurried down the stairs and out the door, slowing her pace as she crossed Carver Road and walked onto their lawn, approaching the treehouse, her heart a fluttering mess. She felt tears at the corner of her eyes, her emotions entirely too powerful to control. After all, this structure had once been their sanctuary. The only place where things made sense. As she stood at the bottom, looking up at the landing, she could already smell the cedarwood and feel it under the pads of her fingers.

"Looks a lot smaller now, doesn't it?" Brett's voice comforted Nina as he approached her, coming from the house.

Turning her head toward him, she offered him a small smile. "Yeah," she whispered. "My legs feel like Jello."

Brett smiled at her. "You ready?"

Nina nodded, and Brett gestured for her to grab the ladder, which she did, looking up the rickety steps. "Are we sure these are going to hold us?" she asked.

Brett chuckled. "Yeah, I've already been up there, actually."

Nina studied his face, unsure of what she was looking for there but aware of the ache in her chest from looking at him. She took hold of the spindly ropes and began the process of climbing up the ladder. Crawling through the doorway, Nina wasn't surprised to find it was exactly as she remembered it, if not a bit more worn down. Of course it was, though, for there had been no one to shovel the snow over the last decade. No one to nail supportive planks to the waterlogged pieces.

But the air smelled the same.

Their initials were still there of course.

And the wood felt the same under the palms of her hands.

Nina got up from the floor and walked, hunched over, toward the wall where their carvings were, along with the dates. She bent back down and leaned onto her heels, staring, as the emotions bubbled right there under the surface. She felt Brett settle in right beside her, and she watched him from her peripheral as he didn't look at the wall but at her.

"It's wild, isn't it?" Brett said, his voice hushed.

A sound came from Nina that caused Brett to pull her into his embrace, and then she allowed herself to melt into him, feeling the pressure on her heart dissipate.

Before long, they were lying on their backs, shoulders touching, looking up at the familiar ceiling, and Nina felt herself slipping into the past a bit, hearing and smelling the sounds from before. It was entirely overwhelming, and she didn't know what to make of it.

"I missed you, Neen." Brett's voice was so familiar that Nina wanted to crawl into his arms and stay there forever. "I missed you so much."

Nina moved her pinky closer to Brett's and intertwined it with his; the notion was used to say *me too* when she felt she could hardly breathe, let alone utter a word. She trusted that Brett knew what she was trying to say, for they had always been able to communicate with simply a look, or a feeling.

"I don't know what to think about it, B," she began, desperate for her voice not to break. She sensed his head lift and lower as he turned to face her. "About how we—me and you—two people who once fit together in a way that doesn't seem possible…US…we just turned our backs on each other when we fell into the darkness. I know you said it wasn't just a rough patch, that it was much more than that, and it was, I know that but—"

She was interrupted by Brett abruptly sitting up and taking her hands in his. "Can we stop saying that?" he begged, his eyes filled with sorrow. "We were kids, Neen. We went through something horrible, something no one can relate to—"

"Exactly!" Nina cut in. "We were in it together, and then we were alone, and it ruined me, Brett. I lost the only person that mattered. I blamed myself, too. It took me years to put myself back together…if I'm being honest, I'm still doing it. And yeah, I could have reached out to you, and I bet, if I did, you would have been there for me. Because it's you and me. But we didn't, neither one of us."

Brett's shoulders slumped, and he ran a hand through his hair. "Can we just put it behind us? We are here together now, and we have a second chance at our friendship."

"I don't just want your friendship," Nina said, desperately. "All this time, I have wanted our *love* back."

"My friendship with you *is* my love for you, Neen. It always has been, before I even knew what love was." Nina choked on a sob. "All the versions of you," Brett said, placing his hand on her cheek. "The feral child with sticks in her hair, who showed me what it meant to be headstrong and fierce." Nina let out a teary laugh. "The twelve-year-old who taught me that holding on to our childhoods, even a little bit, was important…so important. The adult who is sitting in front of me right now, teaching me that hiding behind our traumas is cowardly. Forced smiles aren't real, but facing our demons head-on is the only way to move on…to live." Brett used his finger to lift her chin, forcing her eyes to meet his. "I'm not sure

I'll ever forgive myself for the mess I left when I drove off to college. And I know you think that I was fine all this time because I made you feel like that the other day. Because I only told you the good stuff. I loved Texas; I can't lie about that. I've become so good at faking my feelings that I only shared the positive things. But you were never far from my thoughts. Ever. No matter how much I tried to drown you out with whiskey and noise, it never worked. Not really. When it was quiet, I swore I could hear your voice. I chased down women I thought looked like you, only to be reminded that the possibility was nearly zero. I'm sorry, Neen. I'm so sorry."

Nina inhaled and let it out slowly, attempting to slow the erratic beats of her heart and get her bearings. She scanned Brett's face, thinking of the men she had used to distract herself throughout the years, hoping that one of them would replace the feelings she had for Brett and make her forget. But she couldn't fool herself; it seemed that it was Brett or no one.

Brett raised up on his knees and pulled Nina up into his chest. "Please, Neen. Please just try to let me back in. We can make it make sense again."

Nina slumped a bit, her shoulders sagging. It was entirely too difficult for her to compartmentalize her thoughts, the things she needed to say. Brett didn't give her much time to linger in the chaos of her thoughts, though.

"I know an apology doesn't come close to doing enough for this whole mess," he said. "There has been zero action for me to back up the apology. I know that." He huffed. "I thought about it last night, about the summer we left for school, after my dad died." Brett swallowed, and Nina watched his Adam's apple bob, a sick feeling rolling in her stomach. "All this time, I assumed that I had hurt you too much for you to forgive me. And so, I sentenced myself to a life without you." He shifted his body, attempting to get closer to Nina. "I was mad, but it wasn't you I was angry at. I was gutted that everything had been ruined…by Danny. Again." Brett wrapped his arms around his legs and let his head hang a moment before eventually meeting her gaze again. "He always ruined everything for me. My childhood, my relationship with my brother, my mom's life. And that night he died, he ruined *us*." There was an emptiness in his voice at the end, a sadness that was palpable. "At least that's how it felt." He gave Nina a sad expression that made her desperate to crawl into his arms. "I don't know if I'll ever forgive myself for what you went through after that. But I won't ever stop trying to help you see that I never stopped loving you."

And Nina couldn't fight it anymore. Though there was doubt there, for sure, she wanted to trust in what Brett was offering her, a desperate apology, as if his own life depended on her forgiving him. She pulled away, wiping her tears before sending him a smile and a nod of her head. "Wanna take a walk?"

For the next few weeks, Nina and Brett spent time relearning one another, the pieces that had changed while they were apart. They walked along the edges of the salt-water pond, sitting on rickety, overturned boats, sometimes talking non-stop, other times resting in the silence and treasuring the peace. One night, once the sun had begun to set, they enjoyed cups of ice cream on the docks behind Blue, their legs swinging over the lapping water that bumped against the boats in the harbor, Nina studying the changes in Brett's face. She appreciated the way he had aged—the wisdom she could see in his eyes. But it also made her quite sad that she hadn't been there to watch the changes happen slowly over time.

She had missed so much.

But she promised him she would begin to let that go. And with Brett's help, she was beginning to believe she might be able to do that.

Their hands had slowly found their way to each other again, intertwining as they once had, as if no time had passed at all.

Nina smiled at Brett, who was looking at her carefully and studying her face. "What?" she asked through a mouthful of mocha chip ice cream. He looked like he had something he needed to tell her.

Brett's eyes darted all over her face until he broke the spell and shook his head, looking down at his own ice cream. "Nothing," he said.

But Nina knew it was, in fact, *something*, and she couldn't bring herself to harp on it now. She was too busy putting her life back together.

Independence Day in Harborview was virtually unchanged from their childhood, Nina noted as she and Brett entered the center of town, heading toward the commons where the food trucks were stationed.

The flags that billowed from the street poles, the scents of fried dough and popcorn, the hum of "Yankee Doodle." A time machine is what it was, and Nina's cheeks ached from the soft smile that was permanently displayed on her lips.

"You look like you took a drug or something," Brett joked as they strolled through the crowds.

Nina laughed. "I didn't realize how nostalgic this holiday would be." She shook her head in disbelief. "I almost feel like I should be pushing my bike toward the decorating contest to win another medal."

"Maybe next year we should start one of those for adults," Brett laughed.

Next year. The two words surprised Nina a bit. A few months ago, she had no idea where she would be by the end of this summer, let alone next year. Was she actually going to be in Harborview still? Had she flown back to the nest for good? Maybe she had. And she was ok with it. More than ok, actually.

As they rounded the corner toward the grassy common out in front of the rec center, Nina heard a voice she easily recognized. Timmy Baker. "Is this real? A blast from the past right in front of my face? Nina and Brett?!"

"Timmy Baker? Is that you? Can't be!" Nina screeched. "The Timmy I knew was shorter and had a nose that was just a bit crooked from some girl who punched him when they were kids."

Tim Baker hollered a laugh that made her eyes grow wide as saucers. The same laugh that she remembered from twelve years ago briefly stopped her in her tracks. When memories of Timmy Baker had flooded her over the years, it was usually brought on by the smell of nicotine in the city. Plumes of cigarette smoke reminded her of being seventeen and watching Timmy take a drag, trying to be cool.

Looking at him now, Nina felt none of the hostility she had often felt around him as a kid. She knew that she had always loved him. The way that childhood friends love one another even if time and distance become immeasurable, too wide an area to even comprehend. Tim had been like an annoying sibling, something Nina never got to experience for real. He had taught her lessons that she hadn't realized she had even learned until right in that moment, as she stood looking at her friend who had aged a few years, too.

Timmy Baker had taught Nina to speak her mind and fight for what she believed in. To never waiver from her personal beliefs...to not be influenced by the wayward ideas of others. He taught her to laugh at herself, to laugh at life, really. To not take any of it too seriously.

He taught her that disagreeing with someone didn't mean you hated them. It was quite the opposite.

She opened her arms to Tim, an authentic smile reaching her ears. "I missed you, Timmy."

Tim embraced her and pulled her into his chest, lifting her off the ground. "I missed you too, Nina."

"Hi, Nina!" Amber said, approaching them from the ice cream truck. "So good to see you again."

Nina gave Amber a hug. "You, too!" She smiled at her new friend, coming to the realization that they all had grown and changed over the last twelve years while she was away and missed the comings and goings of her crew from Carver Road. But for the first time, there wasn't any regret beneath the surface.

It was gratitude. A thankfulness that she had made it back, no matter how long she had been keeping herself away…too afraid to face all she left behind.

She was still afraid; that was true. But being around the people who made her who she was made the clouds lighten, if only slightly.

As they approached the ice cream truck, Nina saw Johnny Cooper beaming from ear to ear, arms outstretched and ready to pull her into him. "Johnny!" Nina exclaimed. "It's so good to see you!" Her voice was muffled into his shoulder as they embraced.

"Kinda feels like it's been five minutes." Johnny's sentiment caused Nina's lip to quiver.

Hold it together, she said to herself, unable to handle the serenity settling behind her ribs…all because she was reuniting with the people who had made her.

People she had avoided for all those years that were the most important—the years when she had needed them the most.

Nina pulled away and placed her hands on Johnny's cheeks, her eyes glistening. "Thirty looks good on you, Johnny," she said softly, and he smiled endearingly at her.

"I missed you," he said.

His voice. Under the grown-up sound, it was smothered with the same cadence as when he was a teenager. And suddenly, Nina was sucked into her thoughts so quickly it startled her.

The Cooper's basement. The beach. Bike rides down the dirt road heading toward the beach where Johnny would sing Nickelback at the top of his lungs. Walks down the hallways at school, where Johnny would talk Nina off any and every ledge imaginable. Racing down Carver Road on their rollerblades. His acceptance. His camaraderie.

Johnny Cooper had been such a gift to all of them, truly.

"Nina, is it?" An unfamiliar voice pulled Nina from her thoughts. "Hi," the woman said, smiling, putting a hand out to shake Nina's. "I'm Erica."

Nina beamed. "Erica," she breathed. "It's so nice to meet the woman who nabbed Johnny." She winked at her old friend. "He's certainly one of the good ones."

"Aww, thanks, Nina," Johnny said. "How have ya been?"

Nina relaxed her shoulders, reminding herself that the question wasn't one to fear. They sat down on a bench beside the ice cream truck and filled each other in on the last decade.

"And so, you and Brett?" Johnny pondered. "Is something rekindling there?"

With the question, a chill ran down Nina's spine as she turned her head toward Brett and his smiling face. In an instant, it all flashed through her mind, the truth of what they were—what they had always been—tethered to each other in every way.

"Yeah," she said, her cheeks aching through her smile. "That's what we'll call it."

And then the crew emerged as one, arms around shoulders, lips pulled into beaming smiles, hearts thumping in rhythm together. The way it once was when they were small. When they were children. When they were kids. And then teenagers on the precipice of their lives.

A crew.

A family.

Misfitted and jagged, yet, at the same time, perfect and unwavering.

The friends who had made Nina who she was.

Empathetic. Strong-willed. Honest and loyal.

And there, beside the ice cream truck that carried their memories, the kids of Carver Road learned that their bond hadn't faded much at all despite all the time spent away. In fact, a reinvigorated love and appreciation for one another was blossoming. An unabashed appreciation for the rare and undeniably bonds they shared.

Lucy: ya know…I fear you actually aren't going to come back to NYC.

Lucy: I was holding out hope that you would recuperate and come back to me to gut it out.

Lucy: but Brett is way too hot for you to ever leave there…huh????

A million crying emojis.

Nina smiled at her friend's humor. But a text wouldn't do, so she Facetimed with her and wasn't at all surprised when Lucy barely let it ring before answering. As the call connected, Nina saw her best friend's face filling the screen. She wasn't actually crying, of course, but she could see the longing on her face, and it saddened her a bit.

"Hi, Luce," Nina said. "I miss your face."

"Ugh, same to you," said Lucy, adjusting herself on the couch where Nina could see her old kitchen counter in the background. "The crew isn't cutting it without you."

Of her group of friends in New York, Nina always considered them more like glorified acquaintances. She and Lucy were the real deal, but the rest of them? They were fun but there was nothing deep, nothing strong that bonded her to them. She imagined the loneliness she would have felt had she stayed in New York and Lucy had left.

"I can only imagine," Nina sighed, laying back on her pillows. "Do you want to come visit?" She beamed a smile, hoping Lucy would agree.

Lucy smiled. "I think it's time that I do that."

"Yay!" Nina said, feeling excited that she was ready to share her hometown with her best friend, something she was a bit frightened of before. Hope bloomed inside her chest. Hope that her healing was real. And she had a wishful feeling that her friend would come to visit and never leave.

But a visit would suffice, she guessed.

They caught one another up on their lives—Lucy on her plans for expanding her online store and her complete annoyance with the new neighbors that had moved in upstairs who seemed to never sleep. And Nina told Lucy about reuniting with her childhood friends, her increase in classes at the rec center, and the work she was doing with Mary and the Osprey Foundation.

"I can say I never really pictured you as a bird volunteer," Lucy said, not unkindly.

Nina smiled, looking out the window, thinking how the term *bird volunteer* didn't nearly explain how important the work felt to her. "No, I know," she laughed. "It's become really important to me."

"I'm proud of you," Lucy said. "You seem so happy. I can hear it in your voice."

Nina's stomach did a flip. *Happy.*

It had been a long stretch of time since she could describe herself as that. But being home and healing, facing her past, Nina had begun to realize that happiness was part of who she was.

Wild. Carefree. Loving.

And happy.

That was who she had been before life had sunk its teeth into her, making her forget who she truly was.

But she was coming back to herself. She knew that now.

Chapter 32

Brett 2016

Brett and Nina had spent the hot summer days letting each other into the spaces that had been closed off for far too long. And they visited the memories that made them smile, the ones that they cherished. The ones that neither of them let themselves think about during their time away. And they also were discovering new things about each other—that had been hidden behind the curtain all those years. Brett noted that Nina's laugh was identical to how it sounded back then. It made him more emotional than he expected when he heard it, but he couldn't help it—because she was back.

His Nina was back by his side, and the reality was a bit unbelievable.

He noted that, for the most part, she looked as if the time and space away had healed her in ways he didn't think was really possible after all she had been through. After the way she was when he left. He cringed at the thought—that, back then, he knew she was hurting, and he had walked away anyway…without ever looking back.

It sickened him, but he knew he had to start to try and let it go, to work on making it right again, while also forgiving himself—and her—for all that went down when they were still just kids.

The air whipped her hair into her face, and Brett watched her move it from her nose and mouth. His heart ached a bit, watching her when she thought no one was looking. The thoughtful expression she often had on her face had a tendency to also hold a sadness that only Brett could identify. Yes, she looked so much more alive than she did back then. But something was still amiss, and he knew what he had to do to fix it.

Time wasn't really on his side anymore; he felt it in his soul. The thought of helping her in any way that he could was filled with more urgency than he knew how to deal with.

"Is this your idea of a good date?" Brett asked, pulling Nina back against his chest.

She relaxed into him, her arm pushed against the ruddy ropes of the sailboat.

The Luna took people out in Vineyard Sound for hours multiple times a week. Since it was mostly a tourist attraction, Nina and Brett had met a couple from Savannah while they waited in line. Delilah and Felix, with their thick Southern accents, told them about their first trip to the Northeast. It was obvious that Nina and Brett were the only people from Massachusetts, let alone the Cape, on the sailboat. But it was a much-needed time away from anyone they knew, out on the sea.

The captain of the boat, a sun-loving man named Jett, who had a stark sunglasses tan line told the passengers stories of the Cape and the Islands that Brett and Nina knew all too well—the history and stories that had been embedded in their subconscious since they were little. Stories about Native Americans and European explorers, the history of Nantucket, and the oceanic science research being conducted right at Woods Hole.

Brett found himself drifting in and out of the history lesson, listening to the boat cut through the dark ocean water that he could almost reach out and touch. He was more interested in simply being with Nina without an agenda. Without the baggage of Carver Road.

There was no history for them on *The Luna*, and Brett was finding that to be quite refreshing.

"Best date ever," Nina said, turning her gaze to the sun that was beginning to shift toward setting.

Brett kissed the top of her head. Though it was a relief being back together, they couldn't (and didn't) deny the awkwardness that sometimes lingered between them. Brett knew that being with Nina was what he needed—what they both needed—but there was work they had to do to mend what was broken. He wasn't naive to that.

"Enough from me!" Jett bellowed into the ocean air. "My mates will be coming around to see if you would like anything to drink—beer and wine is six dollars, and all mixed drinks are seven. Be respectful of the other guests on the boat, and enjoy the light snacks that will be passed around. Don't throw trash over the edge, or I'll toss you right over to get it." Jett laughed so heartily that Brett swore he could see all the way down his mouth. The guests also chuckled, but with less enthusiasm.

Nina sat up straight and stretched her arms up into the air, moving her body. "Rock, paper, scissors?" she asked, smiling.

Brett's eyes smiled back at her, and they shifted their bodies to play.

"This game reminds me of you," Nina said lightly.

"Yeah?" Brett replied.

Nina nodded. "Remember? We always used to play this."

"Yeah, I know." He laughed. "But we all did. Why does it remind you of just me?"

Nina's eyes met his, and she just looked thoughtfully at him for a moment. "There was a day back then where we were playing on the bus ride home, and I remember it so clearly. Me, you, Johnny, and Addison." She shook her head as if she was trying to push it away. As Brett scanned his brain for the memory she was talking about, he landed on it rather quickly. "We were playing, and then, all of a sudden, I was more embarrassed than I had ever been."

Brett remembered. Addison called her pudgy. "I remember that," he muttered, taking her hand in his.

"When we got off the bus, you made me feel human. Like nothing could hurt me. It's when I knew that I loved you in ways I couldn't comprehend at the time. You hugged me, right there on the street, and for a second, I felt content and distracted from the mess my mind felt like at the time." Nina sighed deeply. "You had always been my peace." Brett watched her swallow her emotion before she softly spoke again. "So, when you were gone, I was ruined."

Brett reached his hand up to her cheek and moved his body closer to her before taking her face in his hands and placing his forehead against hers. Nina had always been *his* peace—since the first time they played together at the end of Carver Road.

Her fight. Her compassion. Her inability to let anything go that meant something to her. The way she always made him feel like he was worthy. How she always had his back. And this had been their agenda over the last month and a half: smiling about their memories and crying about the end when they broke into pieces.

"Neen," he started. "You know that you were always that for me, too, right?" She reached up and put her hands on his wrists, squeezing them. She nodded, but Brett felt the questions radiating off her. "I know," he said. "I know it's hard to trust it, huh? It's hard to trust that because I left and didn't find you, I—"

"B," Nina interrupted him. "I told you; I don't blame you for that. Because I did it, too. It's just…" Her voice trailed off with the wind.

"What?"

Nina smiled at him, wiping a tear and shaking her head. "Let's not harp on the past right now," she said, looking out at the stretch of land that was Martha's Vineyard in front of them. Brett's face twisted in confusion. "Right now, I want to enjoy this moment right here with you. Try and build a future, right?"

Brett smiled, but he felt her hesitation that didn't exactly match the words that she was saying. Something was holding her back.

Dusk had blanketed the harbor when Jett anchored his beloved sailboat in his spot along the docks outside Reggie's Clam Shack. The sky had turned a deep purple and was just beginning to show specks of stars. The air, letting go of the day's humidity, was comfortable, and in the gentle gusts of wind came the smell of brine and fried seafood.

"Watch your steps, there," Jett bellowed for all the guests to hear as they shuffled off, single file, onto the weathered planks of the docks.

"Thanks, Jett," Brett said, shaking the captain's hand. "Nice for some locals to get out and do something touristy sometimes." He winked, and Jett smiled at him, lines forming in the corners of his eyes.

"Ain't that the truth!" Jett replied. "You two have a good night, now."

"Thanks," Nina said, waving with a smile. "It was amazing."

As they walked down the dock toward the sandy lot, Brett took Nina's hand in his, and Nina rested her head on his arm as their sandaled feet crunched on the sand that littered the pavement. When they reached the car, Brett pulled Nina into him, leaning his body against the hood of his truck. He tipped her chin up so that their eyes met, the dim lights along the dock brightening her dark eyes. He kissed her with intention—the gesture saying things without words. *I'm here. This is right. I love you.*

Nina let out a noise that sounded like a whimper, and Brett pulled away just enough to look at her. "You ok?" he whispered.

"Mmhmm," she uttered euphorically, her eyes closed, a goofy smile on her lips. She wrapped her arms around his waist, and they swayed there, to the beat of a song they both knew by heart even though no music was playing.

Maybe it was a minute, maybe an hour, Brett wasn't sure, but when Nina spoke, it was music to his ears. "Remember those ospreys that you showed me all those years ago? The ones that lived by the pond?" she asked.

"Yeah?" he said, wondering where the topic was coming from.

"Well, they mate for life," she informed him. "Did you know that?"

Brett scrunched his eyebrows. "No, I didn't," he said, sniffing a laugh and shaking his head.

"Yeah, my mom told me. It's part of the reason I started volunteering with Mary and the cause. It felt kind of monumental before I really understood it. But now, being here with you like this, it makes more sense."

"Yeah?"

"Yeah," Nina said softly but confidently. "They leave each other each year for the fall and winter, flying to different places, but they always make it back to each other in the summer."

Brett studied her face. "Are you serious?"

Nina nodded. "Yeah. And maybe we spent a little more time apart than we would have liked, but we made it back to each other. And it feels like a forever thing."

"Then why does your face look like you're leaving something out?" Brett asked this with a playful look, though he truly wanted to know what she was holding back.

Nina sighed. "I'm still working on myself, B. I need you to be patient."

"I will never stop being patient with you," he said, rubbing his thumb gently on her cheek and his dimple showing.

Nina went up on her tippy toes and kissed his forehead, then his nose and cheek before lingering on his lips.

Brett pulled her into his body. "N plus B," he whispered into her hair.

Chapter 33

Nina 2016

May 7, 1944

My dearest Mary,

I hope this correspondence finds you well. I can tell you that I am, in the physical way, quite well. I am strong, Mary, and I'm fighting to get home to you. It's thoughts of our reunification that truly are the only things that keep me well and strong in my mind.

I watch the sun rise and fall, and that is the proof I need to remember that somewhere, the world will right itself from the destruction I see here. Because destruction is the only way for me to describe it. I don't wish to worry you. I don't dare give you reasons for new kinds of nightmares. But because of what I see here, know that I fight for you, always. I fight for my Mary. I imagine it is you and only you who needs freedom and liberation.

I feel like my life has turned into a never-ending sin, but when I think that I am only fighting for you, it makes it worth it. It makes it okay. I will make it back to you, where I dream we will have that farm you said you wanted, with misfit animals that you will nurse back to health with your heart of pure gold. I see it, Mary. The future. I promise it all to you.

Until we meet again.

With all my love,
George

Nina hadn't meant to drip a tear onto the dusty, old, brittle letter. But the sentiment was too strong, seemingly sent directly to her. This message she was deciphering—it was a lesson to learn: since the dawn of time, people have fought for the ones they love for more than one singular reason. And the dreams of the young can—and often do—come into realities sweeter than she could comprehend.

It gave Nina pause, thinking of senior year and how she and Brett had planned out their lives in a silly and juvenile way. That they would return to Harborview eventually, after they had flown and blossomed. They would come back, and Nina would own a bookstore in town, and they would have a simple, little home on some body of water that would have an epic fireplace where they would show their kids the Christmas movies they had loved while drinking hot cocoa with candy canes sticking out. It was a dream she hadn't recalled in years. Had forgotten about it, really.

Mary had handed the letter to Nina as she was leaving the farm earlier in the day, telling her that she wanted it back of course. But Mary had said that she felt it would be helpful for her.

Nina carefully tucked the dusty letter back into the yellowed envelope, running her fingertips over the address that had been written over seventy years prior. She tucked the letter into the bedside table drawer for safekeeping until she could get it back to Mary.

And then Nina remembered what lovely Mary Harlow had told her about the ospreys near her farm. How Bonnie and Clyde had killed to protect one another. And it felt like there was a gap between her and Brett. She didn't mean it like it was some sort of competition, but she wasn't blind to the faults she brought to their relationship. She had done this big and horrible thing and made Brett hold it on his shoulders for her. Nina couldn't help but feel like they would never be on even playing fields. Yes, everything she did that fateful night was to protect him, but the decision to keep it hidden was selfish, and she knew that now. It would always be a cloud hanging over her.

He had told her not to think about it like that, not to worry. And she was trying not to, for him. But it all felt entirely too raw. Too heavy a burden. A darkness that overshadowed her heart.

She couldn't help but wonder if Brett had it in him to protect her in the same way if he had to. Of course, she wouldn't wish it on anyone, but because she had killed for him, because of her love, was it possible for them to ever be even? She knew most people didn't have to contemplate things like this, but then again, most people hadn't killed to protect the person they loved.

She was startled by her phone vibrating on the table. It was an incoming message from Brett.

I'm out getting stuff for my mom. Want to meet me at East Beach in like 30? I have to talk to you about something.

Nina sighed, placing the phone in her back pocket and heading toward the door.

Nina, I realized I can't do it. I can't live with the fact that you killed my dad. Even the tone in Nina's head had a mocking twang to it. Brett had given her nothing but love and respect since they had reunited, and she knew she had to work harder to simmer the negative self-talk.

Chapter 34

Brett 2016

THE BREATH BRETT PULLED in was shaky at best. He turned his body toward Nina, taking her hands in his. Part of his own healing, he knew, was admitting to Nina a truth he hadn't told another soul about until now. And she needed to know. Her guilt was his guilt, and he saw it constantly, pulling at her mouth, taking the smile he loved and turning it into an almost constant frown—at least when she thought no one was looking. She needed to know that they shared this same weight. It wasn't fair for him to keep it to himself anymore.

"What is it?" she asked softly.

"I hadn't meant to kill him."

Nina's face twisted into confusion. "What? You didn't," she said. "I did." Her voice trailed off a bit at the end, and Brett watched her try to figure out what he was talking about. He imagined she was thinking of that night at the pond's edge—combing through her memories as if she had missed something or forgotten some crucial detail.

But she hadn't forgotten. Of course not. He shook his head. "Not him," he said. "Not Danny."

And so, he told Nina about his own desperate need to save her once before. About how he had, when they were teenagers, watched her slip into a darkness that he couldn't save her from, no matter how hard he had tried. He had watched her body change and shrink, her eyes sink and darken. He had watched the marks she made on her arms with something sharp grow further and further up her arm as if she was desperate to detach her heart from her sleeve so she couldn't feel anything anymore. Though she covered them with rubber bracelets, he still saw them. But he didn't know how to reach her. Or what to say. He was ashamed of that now.

He had watched the bruises appear on her arms. The damage to her spirit that had wrecked him the most. His Nina was flying away…or more like sinking, and he hadn't known how to catch her. How to pull her back to the earth.

Brett told her about the day he had been alone at the mechanics with Mr. Gomes's car. Nina wouldn't let Brett report him. She had worried about her own reputation because her teacher had threatened her if she did. Brett hadn't wanted anything to upset Nina anymore. But Mr. Gomes had to be punished for what he was doing to her.

Brett knew how to tinker with brakes. He knew what to do to make it so that the brakes would be faulty. He hadn't expected to kill him; he hadn't really even thought it through at the time. He was driven by the undeniable pull to protect Nina. His heart, his soul. He ached because she ached, and he didn't know any other way to protect her.

Strong, kind, salt of the earth Brett had done the unthinkable.

Glen Gomes wasn't the first person to fly their car into the ocean at the end of Pontiac Street, and he wouldn't be the last, either. And he *was* under the influence, it was true—like all of the others. But also, his brakes were faulty, and Brett was the only one who knew that was the reason he had floated through the air into the ocean.

When Brett was done telling Nina, he studied her face. Her eyes were wide, unblinking, her chest barely moving with her shallow breaths. "I blamed myself for his death, too," she said, more for her ears than his. She turned to meet his gaze. "But all this time, it was you."

"Neen, please don't—"

Nina put her hand up, stopping him. "All this time," she said softly, "Our loyalty…our love…" She paused, pulling her hand to cover her mouth, suffocating the emotions. "It *was* equal."

Brett's brows furrowed. He had assumed she would be angry that he had kept this from her all this time, but that wasn't what seemed to be happening as he watched her come to terms with this new knowledge that Brett had killed to protect her, too.

"I'm sorry I didn't tell you back then, Neen," he said, meaning it with all of his heart. "I thought it would be better for you to not know what really happened. To just go on believing what we were all told. I thought it would be easier for you to move on if you believed it was an accident."

"I get it," she replied. "Truly, I do."

At that moment, Nina thought of the ospreys and what Mary had told her, and it all seemed to make sense now. Why she had been drawn to those birds…drawn back to Harborview.

Back to the nest.

"Really?" he asked, surprised. He was taken aback by her reaction, the ease at which she was accepting his truth.

Brett opened his arms, inviting her into his embrace, and she didn't waste a moment shuffling inside the safety of his wing.

They embraced in silence for a few moments, only the sounds of the gulls and the ospreys overhead and the lapping of waves out in front of them as the sun descended at their backs.

"Hey, B?" Nina said, not taking her eyes off the ocean.

"Yeah?" he said, his voice husky.

"Knock, knock…"

Epilogue

Harborview - 7 Years Later

F ROM THE SEAGULLS' VIEW in the nest on the pole at the end of the main street, the lights from the little businesses shone out on the street, welcoming in its guests all day. The people below bustled under the setting sun, smiling and embracing—wearing scarves to keep the early December chill away. The seagull, who occupied the temporarily abandoned osprey nest on the pole that was constructed by the Osprey Foundation, watched the lights from the two stores at the end of the street turn off and the owners exit. Nina Warner locked the door to N Bar Squared, and Lucy Bates locked the door to You. They walked, with linked elbows, toward their cars in the parking lot, away from the businesses that they had built together. Right alongside one another in New York and then right here in Harborview. Two stores that were welcomed with open arms by the town; two stores that promoted and represented acceptance, forgiveness, and new beginnings.

Six years prior, the ospreys, new to the town, had sat and looked down from their nest on a pole one summer afternoon, as the crowd had gathered for the ribbon cutting—Nina and Lucy holding the scissors, beaming from deep inside their hearts. Brett had stood to the side, a proud smile on his lips. One hand held his phone to record the moment; the other gently rocked the stroller that held sweet Olive Warner. The pride Brett had for his wife couldn't be measured.

Seamus stood by his brother, wearing a smile that had become easier for him to have in recent months, with his service dog, Axel, sitting at attention right by his side. And Laura, on the other side, had fresh tears glistening her proud face.

Nina's parents beamed, Paul finding himself utterly speechless and Jane hanging on his arm for strength. Their daughter had always made them proud, but it was different because now she was home, and she was staying.

And so, they thrived. The merging of the Jackson and Warner families settled the equilibrium. The balancing of their worlds was felt on a physical level—what was supposed to be all along finally coming together.

The years ticked by, seasons coming and going, measured by the flights of ospreys coming and going from their nests on the poles. Olive grew "like a weed" Brett always joked, friendships were strengthened, and hearts were mended and healed.

Mary passed in 2019, leaving her homestead to the town to be kept as an animal sanctuary, which Nina keeps an eye on, owing Mary more than she was ever able to give her while she was living.

Nina and Lucy relished in the relative closeness they had again and made their group of friends use different accents when they went out. All in memory of their time in New York when they were young and broke.

And now they are all settled into what their years of hard work and healing had offered them: peace.

Nina hugged Lucy goodbye in the parking lot. "Are you sure you don't want to join us tonight?" she asked her friend.

"No, the bath, a glass of red, and my book…it's what's calling my name," Lucy replied with a smile.

"Suit yourself," Nina said as she climbed into her car.

It was Saturday night, and Nina was more than looking forward to the big night in they had planned.

She turned the car left onto Maple Street and drove with Granite Pond out her passenger side window, past Johnny and Erica's condo, and into the driveway of her and Brett's gray shingled house. She shut the car door and inhaled the smell of hickory smoke that billowed out from her chimney. Inside, the lights were aglow, and she could see that Johnny, Erica, and their six-year-old son, Grant, had already walked down from their place.

Nina's heart warmed, seeing her friends and family smiling through the glass panes.

"I'm home!" she announced as she opened the side door and hung her coat and scarf on the hook in the kitchen—Nat King Cole's voice singing "The Christmas Song."

"Mommy!" Olive yelled, her feet thumping loudly on the tiled kitchen floor.

"Hi, my love!" Nina said, scooping her daughter into her arms. "Are you ready to watch *The Santa Clause* for the first time?"

"Yes, yes, yes!" Olive squealed, her breath smelling of candy canes that Nina knew Brett had snuck her from the tree. "Grant hasn't seen it either, Mommy."

Nina put her daughter down and hugged Brett, who was standing patiently, waiting for Olive to be released from Nina's embrace.

"How was work?" he asked.

"So good," Nina sighed happily. "The new Pilates class started, and it was a big hit!"

Brett kissed the top of her head, and hand in hand, they walked into the living room.

"Hey, guys!" Nina greeted Johnny, Erica, and Grant.

"Hi!" Erica said. "Sorry we are a little early. Grant was a little too excited." She rolled her eyes playfully.

"Oh, you know I don't care about coming home to you all here," Nina assured her.

"The chili's ready," Brett said to the group. And seeing the kids' hopeful expressions, he addressed them too. "And the hot cocoa is ready, too." He winked at them as they squealed and jumped up and down.

They all settled around the living room, eating their food and sipping their drinks, the kids getting chocolate mustaches, which caused fits of laughter.

The Maple Street crew was forming right there on the street. Their new crew. Bonds built over decades, and new ones forming between the beautiful children that the Carver Road kids had brought into the world. And their traditions held fast.

Olive and Grant's names carved in messy scrawl in the tree in the backyard.

The grownups teaching the children about the pictures the clouds formed.

Breaking in their new rollerblades for games of two-on-two street hockey: Brett and Olive against Johnny and Grant.

Spooky stories told while sitting around smokey fires out by the pond.

The beautiful moments of Brett and Nina's childhood repeating themselves.

Brett got the TV ready to stream the movie while nostalgia scaled Nina's spine, a happiness that nearly made her cry.

The feeling of contentment.

The feeling that she was loved.

Her life now was what she had always dreamed of.

The giggles of her daughter brought her back to the present, and she took her gaze to the kids sitting on a pile of pillows and blankets in front of the TV.

"Hey, G," Olive said. "My dad told me a new knock, knock joke today. Wanna hear it?"

Acknowledgements

Thank you to my readers for picking this book up. TBR shelves can be daunting and I'm honored you gave this one a chance.

Christy, the covers of my books bring me so much joy thanks to you! I honestly didn't think I could love a cover more than No Such Thing but this one?! You captured the feel of this story perfectly. I can't thank you enough.

Erin, I'm forever grateful for your expertise, attention to detail, and your ability to push me out of my comfort zone in the editing process. What would I do without you? :) Thanks so much.

To my beta and ARC readers, it still amazes that there are so many of you willing to take your precious time and allocate it to my stories. Your encouragement and excitement is top notch. Thank you.

To my Murk Book Club, I'm so thankful to you and your encouragement during this three year process—always checking in for updates when we meet and being the best cheerleaders!

To my family—near and far—I can always feel your support in my journey as a writer and I appreciate the love more than I can say.

And to my Fab 5, my team. <3 We have been through the ringer this year and I'm luckiest to live under a roof with the best support system. M, Y, M and L. You are my loves, my heart and soul. It's all for you.

About the author

Krissy Lanier lives in Massachusetts with her family. She has been writing for as long as she can remember and though she teachers kindergarten, she dreams of a time when she can write all day, every day! She is passionate about foster care and Type 1 Diabetes awareness and hopes to one day write a children's book about type 1 to raise money for research. You can follow her along her writing journey on Instagram @krissylanier_writes

Also by Krissy Lanier

<u>The When Pigs Fly Duet</u>
When Pigs Fly (Book 1)
No Such Thing (Book 2)